Ghalib stepped back from me,

cocking his head as if he was making a decision about me. "Do you know how to dance?" he asked.

"A little," I answered.

A mischievous gleam came into his eyes. "Good," he said. "Take off your gloves." I could imagine how intense the sensation of our hands clasped would be without anything protecting me. His eyes shone, as if he sensed my dilemma. "Of course, you are always free to decline...."

"No," I replied quickly. I drew off first my left glove, then my right. It felt like I was undressing.

Ghalib took the gloves out of my hands; he seemed to vibrate with pleasure. "Shall we?" he asked, tucking my gloves into one of his inside pockets. I nodded.

He clasped my bare hand in his and laid his other hand on my waist. Electric current flashed between us, as if we completed a circuit. The pulses jumped through the silk of my dress, the fabric of his jacket, racing though me, then him, and back to me again. I couldn't help it; I imagined being pressed skin to skin with this man, nothing but heat and electricity and friction between us. The blood rushed to my face.

Also recommended...

You may also enjoy these other ForbiddenFiction works:

Blindsided by Ann Ruby
It begins as a case of mistaken identity. Brenda is escaping into the mountains of Montana for a week of relaxation. Instead, she finds herself naked and pressed against a hard, aroused man, intent on a weekend of sexual domination. When the real submissive walks in on them, he realizes the mistake made at the front desk and is horrified, willing to do whatever he can to make things right. Brenda is intrigued. When she asks him to take her on as a substitute, he is blindsided! Can a weekend that satisfies their deepest desires, both sexually and emotionally, turn into more? (F/M)

Wicked Fairy Tales, a ForbiddenFiction Special Collection
An anthology of bedtime stories for adults!

Just what kind of happy goes into "happily ever after?" As children, it was enough that Pinocchio got to be a real boy and that Red wasn't eaten by the wolf. As adults, we have a slightly different perspective. Being a real boy means having boy parts, and being eaten by someone big and bad doesn't mean quite the same thing it once did.

Ever wonder what mermaids do with the swimmers they seduce? Or why a dragon might prefer a castle-guarded princess to a nice, easy field of sheep? What if your fairy godmother wasn't circumspect in what wishes could be granted, or if that dainty little fairy had a much bigger appetite than one might guess?

Held in Dreams

Ava Burquette

ForbiddenFiction
www.forbiddenfiction.com

an imprint of

Fantastic Fiction Publishing
www.fantasticfictionpublishing.com

HELD IN DREAMS
A Forbidden Fiction book

Fantastic Fiction Publishing
Hayward, California

© Ava Burquette, 2013

CREDITS
Editor: D.M. Atkins and Kel Draves
Cover Design: Siolnatine
Cover Art: Angela Taratuta
Production Editor: Erika L Firanc
Proofreading: Jae Knight

SKU: AB1-000093-02 FFP
ISBN: 978-1-62234-102-3

Published in the United States of America

DISCLAIMER

This book is a work of fiction which contains explicit erotic content; it is intended for mature readers. Do not read this if it's not legal for you.

All the characters, locations and events herein are fictional. While elements of existing locations or historical characters or events may be used fictitiously, any resemblance to actual people, places or events is coincidental.

This story depicts fictional BDSM; it is not intended to be used as an instruction manual. It contains descriptions of erotic acts that may be immoral, illegal, or unsafe. The characters are not models for the Safe, Sane and Consensual forms embraced by most current practitioners of BDSM. The author takes license with the use of BDSM for dramatic effect. Do not take the events in this story as proof of the plausibility or safety of any particular practice.

Contents

Chapter 1

Kidnapped

I got on the bus that morning and didn't meet anyone's eyes. It was an unspoken rule among the regulars who used public transport and I was as regular as it came. Don't encourage conversation. Don't look at your fellow riders. Put your nose in a book. Plug in your MP3 player. Shut out the world. If you don't, you don't know who might sit next to you.

I picked a seat and pulled out my magazine so I didn't notice when the men boarded the bus. Heavy footsteps weren't uncommon on the way into town. When the other riders gasped, I looked up in time to see the last of the six gunmen board the bus. The driver froze in his seat. I froze in mine.

The gunmen made no attempt to conceal their weapons. One put his handgun to the bus driver's temple and said, "Go. No stops. Stay off the main roads."

That was when I noticed the seventh man. He was tall and unarmed, moving down the aisle with an easy grace. It struck me that none of the gunmen, nor the seventh man, had taken any pains to conceal their faces. These men were beautiful. Not one of them had a face that anyone could easily forget, particularly the unarmed man. His hair was long, thick and white; his eyes so bright green, I could see them from the back of the bus. I couldn't make out his age; he could have been anything from thirty to fifty. I was fairly sure I could give an accurate description to the police if I got out of this. For that reason, I believed they intended to kill every one of us. My fear intensified.

The green-eyed man moved lazily down the aisle, two gunmen following him. The rest of the armed men positioned themselves around the bus, one with his gun trained on the driver. The seventh man inspected each rider. What was he looking for? I turned to the window as he approached, trying to hide my face. Maybe if he thought that I hadn't seen him, he'd let me live.

"Move," he commanded. The man sitting next to me, an Asian guy in a polo shirt, jumped to obey and I jumped to follow. "Not you," he said to me. I couldn't help it. I looked up.

When my eyes met his, he smiled. My face became very cold. I had never been more frightened. Nonetheless, despite myself, I struggled with an odd fascination. These men were so oddly attractive, they were surreal. In particular, the green-eyed man had features that were delicate and vaguely feline. His eyes were fringed with thick, improbably dark lashes. Once I looked him directly in the face, I couldn't look away. I eased myself back into my seat against the window and the man slid in beside me.

"It's a pleasure to meet you, Elaine," he said. His voice was velvety—musical, even. He offered me his hand, slim and white with long, tapered fingers.

Politeness ruled me and fear subdued me. I accepted his grasp, my cold hand in his warm one. When our fingers touched, I jolted. It was like I had gripped a live wire. Current coursed up my arm and into my body. A flash of bright light blinded me for a moment. Heat flooded my face. I thought that the green-eyed man had done something to me—electrocuted me, perhaps—but when his face came back into focus, his expression was shock. He kept looking at my hand like he didn't know what it was. Then he smiled. It was a beautiful, intense, hungry smile and it was directed at me. I pulled my hand away and scooted closer to the bus window.

"I'm sorry," I said. "Should I know you?"

"Do you think if we had met before, you could have forgotten me?" he asked gently.

"No," I couldn't look away from his eyes. "It's just that you know my name," I managed to add.

"Ah, yes. I do, indeed." The words lingered in the air for a few moments but he didn't offer me any explanation. "Actually," he continued, "I know many things about you. You're a history buff. You work as a secretary but you sing as a hobby. You collect unusual pens." My heart raced.

How could he know these things? I lived alone. I did just about everything alone. My life was hardly an open book. He put his long fingers under my chin, bringing heat to my cold cheeks, and turned my face gently, as if to view it from every angle. "I know all about you," he whispered.

"How could you—"

"Because I've been watching you."

He had been watching me? I couldn't imagine why. It must have been the dullest surveillance anyone ever did. I turned my head so that my skin lost contact with his fingers. His touch sent electricity all over me and I could hardly think while he was so close. "I don't understand," I said. "Do you want something from me or—"

I looked up and his smile, his *predatory* smile, stopped me mid-sentence. When he spoke, his voice almost purred. "I do want something from you—several things, in fact."

"Like what?"

"Well, for starters, when I walk off of this bus, I would like for you to come with me." He didn't blink.

My words were gone. My breath became shallow. He came with armed men. Could I decline? I had to try. Heaven only knew what he would do to me when he got me away from other people. Then, there was my sister Rachel, newly married and pregnant. She would go nuts if I went missing. Fear clawed at me and I barely whispered the only word I wanted to say. "No."

"No?" he asked. His face was polite, but his jaw was set. He lifted an arched eyebrow, looked at one of his gunmen, and gave a slow nod.

The gunman grabbed a passenger—a woman that I recognized from months of riding the same morning bus. She usually wore a turquoise hat and a matching turquoise raincoat in the Spring and Fall. Those were the kind of details you noticed about people when you saw them every day, but didn't really know them.

When he lifted her by a mix of collar and hair, she shrieked and tried to pull herself free. He wrenched her into a standing position and held a gun to her head.

"Put your hands at your side," the gunman told her. She obeyed with a muted sob and looked around for anyone who could help her. "Sir?" he said, looking at the man next to me.

"Don't." The choked word escaped me. I hadn't intended to speak. For a moment, I didn't even know the word had come from me. I was standing but I didn't remember getting to my feet.

The green-eyed man held up an impossibly long finger at the gunman and gracefully rose, like he was unfolding himself. "I beg your pardon, Elaine? What did you say?"

"Don't do this," I said, not looking at him. "If you have to hurt someone, hurt me."

"That's very lovely," he said, sounding amused, "but I don't care what happens to these people. The only way that they will be spared is if I leave this bus. And the only way I'll leave is if you come with me." There were more than thirty people, looking at me, and terror warped each face. The green-eyed man gave me a sly look. "Surely, you don't want me to execute them."

At that exact instant, the man across the aisle grabbed the green-eyed man from behind. Even though the passenger was larger, and even though he had the element of surprise, the man next to me didn't budge. I flinched at his flash of rage. With a quick, nearly imperceptible movement, the green-eyed man dislodged the passenger's grip and twisted his arm behind his back. The green-eyed man hadn't even stood; nonetheless, the passenger writhed on his knees in the aisle. "That was stupid," the unarmed man hissed. "Nobody had caused any problems. We were getting on so well."

"That girl doesn't want to go with you," spluttered the passenger.

The green-eyed man shoved the passenger at one of the gunmen. "Yes," he said. "That's why I'm making threats."

The man next to me nodded at the gunman and I saw him lift his weapon. I had only one thought. *They're going to kill that man because he tried to defend me.* "No!" I yelled, trying to push past the green-eyed man, trying to get to the gunman before he could pull the trigger. But the man next to me wouldn't allow it. He caught me in his arms and held me, my back pressed against his chest, the hot current of electricity flowing through me when I contacted him. I struggled, wanting him to let go of me, trying to regain my own senses, not wanting to feel... what? Electrified, stimulated by his touch. He wouldn't let me go. I couldn't break through his restraining arms. "Stop this! Just stop!" My voice quavered with tears.

"Shh, Elaine," he soothed in my ear.

"No," I said. I struggled again but there wasn't any point. I had never been so manhandled. My eyes were on the two gunmen, like angels of death, holding their weapons in a fatal way, waiting for a command. I had hoped that I could negotiate for the woman's safety, but I knew with a sickening certainty that the man who tried to help me would be dead in seconds if I didn't do something. I wrenched against the green-eyed man and he loosened his grip enough that I could turn to face him. I looked at his face and waves of heat flowed over me. "Please don't hurt these people," I said.

His expression was gentle. "You know what I want. Come with me and I won't even punish the hero." He cast an amused look over my shoulder. "Walk off this bus with me now, Elaine. All of these people will just go back to their lives. Deny me and those two will just be the first."

Anger replaced fear. I spoke through gritted teeth. "You're a bastard. I hardly know you and I hate you."

He tilted his silvery head. "Is that a 'yes?'"

I thought of Rachel again but then I heard the woman in the turquoise coat sob. I couldn't let this happen. "Take your hands off of me and it will be."

He let me go. My knees were weak, but I wouldn't give him an excuse to touch me again. The electrical pulses had ebbed when we broke contact. The man looked at his gunmen. "You can release them," he said, nodding at the two passengers. "I don't think we'll need them further." The gunmen shoved the man and the woman back into their seats. Once they were reseated, the green-eyed man urged me into the aisle. "Give us a head start," he told his men, "then go on ahead." He turned to me. "Elaine, after you."

The gunman by the driver said, "Stop the bus." It rolled to a stop and the driver cast one more frightened look.

"These people won't be harmed after I get off?" I asked, hesitating at the door.

"You have my word."

I glared at him. "Is your word worth anything?"

"Why, Elaine, I'm almost hurt." His expression was innocent—angelic, even. "And, yes. I keep my promises." I looked back at the passengers. Every frightened eye was on me. Gently, the hand on my back urged me forward and I stepped onto the sidewalk.

We were in a quiet neighborhood. There wasn't a soul in sight. I had hoped for more people. The man was so conspicuous that I didn't see how he could avoid attracting attention to us. Maybe if I screamed....

"I wouldn't do that," he said. "In fact, why don't I just remove the temptation?" He placed a finger against my lips and I started to gag. Something was caught in my throat. I doubled over, coughing, and dislodged it, spitting it on to the sidewalk. It looked like a large, gold bead and it rolled until it hit the man's polished shoe. "You want to be more careful with that," he said, picking it up and putting it into his pocket.

"What is it?" I tried to ask, but there wasn't any sound. Only my breath. A cold chill passed over me. He didn't need to tell me what had happened. Somehow, that bead was my voice. He had my voice in his pocket. Who was this man?

This was a nightmare. I stared at him, my mouth open. If I hadn't been so stunned and he hadn't been so close, I might have run.

He smiled at me. "There, now. That's better. And here's our transportation." A black limousine pulled up to the curb and the back door opened on its own. "After you," he said, taking my arm with a firm grip. I didn't have any choice; I climbed inside.

Leather seats. Soft classical music. A drink bar. Windows so dark, I couldn't even see out. The man settled back against the seat, sighing like the bus had been a trial for him. I perched at the edge of my seat, turning my face away from him, looking at the blank, black window.

"A drink?" he offered me. "Water?"

I didn't answer or make any motion. There wasn't much I could do about my situation, but I wasn't going to let him act like I was a guest. My whole body shook with fear and anger and exhaustion. I was in his car headed God-knows-where and I had no idea what he wanted with me.

"Look at me, Elaine," he commanded in a low voice. I ignored him. I felt his fingers on my hair and that strange feeling, that pulsing current of energy, ran through me. Then, I did turn. I glared at him, pointed to my throat, and held out my hand. But, instead of ignoring my pointed demand or acquiescing to it, he took my palm in his hand and traced the lines with his fingers. Shivers shot through me. Tingles pulsed up my arm and brought the blood to my cheeks. I tried to withdraw my hand but, again, he wouldn't release me. Instead, he looked at my face, seemed to notice my flush, and smiled.

"Your fate line is in tatters," he commented, looking back down. "You've been a bit directionless, I would say. A woman of your musical talents doesn't belong in a secretarial pool. I suppose you decided to go the practical path. Pay the bills." One of his long fingers traced my ring finger from its base to its tip, sending more flush to my face. "That's not your style at all, Elaine. You're far too whimsical for that. Look at the length of your ring finger."

I pulled on my hand again, and again he ignored me. "This is a good hand," he said. "There's passion and creativity... intelligence." His eyebrows drew together with a delicate wrinkle. "Sensuality." He traced a very deep line slowly. Then, he stroked it again. His touch was urging something within me. The pulses of wild current seemed less haphazard now. They flowed through me, warming me, urging me. I finally yanked my hand free and the pulses stopped.

I indicated towards my throat again, hating the sensation of being muzzled. "Not yet," he said softly. "I want you to know that you made the right decision on the bus. You don't need to doubt yourself. I would have killed those people. I would have killed everyone on board and taken you anyway. It would have been disappointing for me and harder for you, but I wasn't leaving without you. Do you understand?"

I shook my head.

"No?" He asked. "That's rather charming." He turned his head and seemed to listen. "Finally. We're here."

Where? Where were we? We couldn't have been in the car longer than a half hour. I hadn't even felt the motion of the vehicle until now; it rocked like the road was uneven. The movement slowed, then stopped, and the limousine door popped open. "Please," he indicated with a graceful gesture, "after you."

I stepped out of the car and blinked twice. I didn't know where to look first. We were in an impossible place. An island. Crazier still, we were on a flat plateau on top of a mountain. In the distance, in every direction, a mist of blue water surrounded the land. The land we stood on was at least fifty feet above the water; the sheer cliffs behind me were a dizzying drop to the rocks below. How could we have driven here? It wasn't possible and my mind tried to reject it.

But what was equally impossible was that I saw people falling out of the sky beyond the edge of the cliff. They were pale and indistinct but it was undeniable. Their arms pinwheeled; their legs kicked. I watched them without blinking until I thought my sanity might snap.

I turned away and focused on the only structure on the island: a stone mansion. It was gray and grand, surrounded by trees that whipped in the stiff wind. It had towers, almost like a castle, and lights shining through stained glass windows. It wasn't a home you lived in; it was a place you toured. Nothing made logical sense. Tall trees shouldn't thrive in this salty, windy environment. Cars shouldn't be able to drive to islands. I should be able to speak.

"I know," he said with a contented tone, completely misreading my awe. "It is magnificent. I wanted you to see it. That's why we didn't drive into the garage."

"Jason," he said to the limousine driver, "see Elaine to her suite."

My suite?!? My puzzlement turned to alarm. He had made living arrangements for me. How long did he intend to keep me here? This couldn't possibly be a permanent arrangement, could it?

Jason took my arm. He looked older than the green-eyed man—distinguished, dignified, and handsome in his own way, but lacking his beauty. Jason was also strong. He propelled me several paces before I managed to twist around and look back.

The green-eyed man watched me go, his lips parted, his head lowered, like a hunter. The bodies falling from the sky formed his backdrop. My heart lurched. I wanted to ask where I was going. Was I ever going to get my voice back? The man must have seen the panic on my face but it didn't alter his expression. He swept his gaze over me, his hunger edged with satisfaction.

I looked around wildly, first at the car, then at the cliffs, then at Jason. A sound echoed over the wind. It was the roar of an animal. A lion? A tiger? What could animals like that be doing here? It didn't make any sense. Any more than the people falling from nowhere made any sense. The servant gripped my arm a little harder. I didn't have any choice but to let Jason lead me inside. Between these men, the impossible cliffs, and the promise of wild things on the island, escape was impossible.

Chapter 2
Curiouser and Curiouser

Jason propelled me into the mansion but I yanked my arm away before he could drag me any further. He seemed to get the message; he lead me, rather than pulled me, over marble floors, up grand staircases, through wide hallways and narrow ones, under chandeliers of silver and crystal, until we finally stopped at a door. I'm sure that Jason's intension was to confuse my sense of direction. It worked. I had no idea how to get back to the front door.

"Your rooms, Miss." Jason opened the door and gave me a little push when I didn't step inside right away. "The Master wishes to dine with you this evening. There are fresh clothes laid out for you. Get some rest and I will come for you in a couple of hours." He exited in one smooth motion. I opened the door to watch him go and he didn't even turn back. Obviously nobody was all that concerned that I might escape. I closed the door and let myself take a couple of slow breaths. Aside from the kidnapping, nothing bad had happened to me yet; I tried to take courage in that.

I decided to have a look at my suite. The first room, the room I stood in, was an ornate sitting room meant for entertaining. A small couch. A couple of embroidered chairs. Some thin-legged tables. I passed through quickly. Who, exactly, did he imagine I was going to be hosting?

I entered the next room. A study. The walls were lined with books and there was a squishy, comfortable couch. I turned my attention to the books on the shelves and I got a little chill. Clearly, the books had been purchased with my tastes in mind: poetry, classics, books on my wish list that I hadn't gotten around to buying, and every title that was stacked by my bed. How could he know so much about me?

I moved into the third room—an enormous bedroom. A large window took up one whole wall with a stunning view of the outside. Unfortunately, it was a view of the cliffs with the falling bodies. I put the window to my back. There was a huge four-poster bed with a shimmering golden gown laid on it. Jason told me that there were fresh clothes laid out for me for dinner. Surely he didn't mean this formal, fussy costume. We'll see about that. I had on black slacks and a high-necked blouse, one of my favorite office outfits. It was far more modest than the strapless gown with its yards of fabric but none in the right places. Besides, why should I do anything to please my captor?

Two doors lead off of the bedroom. One was a walk-in closet, filled with more dresses. Gowns, cocktail dresses, skirts and blouses, racks and racks of shoes and delicate, slender drawers filled with gloves of various lengths. The other door led to a bathroom with a huge tub. There were soaps and oils under the sink and a vanity stocked with every type of cosmetic.

I covered the entirety of my confinement in less than twenty minutes and didn't want to see any more. It was so planned—so permanent. I didn't know how long the green-eyed man had been watching me, but it must have been for quite a while. You couldn't just put something like this together in a couple of days. As lovely, as attuned to my tastes, as it was, I knew it was nothing more than a fancy prison cell.

I went into the sitting room and paced back and forth for a couple of minutes. I didn't want to just sit and wait in this suite. Part of me wished that I dared try to escape, despite the fearsome falling bodies outside, despite the unmistakable animal roars that I heard before we entered the mansion. Even if I found the front door, I didn't know if I could find the courage to step through it. The outside scared me as much as the green-eyed man.

Nothing said I had to just wait for my captor to call me, though. It was like a form of torture, waiting for the call to come, for the guillotine to fall. My door was unlocked. Why just sit here? So, without caring what it might cost me, I left the room and entered the hallway.

The labyrinthine corridors somehow seemed more complicated than they had when I was with Jason. It was as if the mansion itself conspired to keep me in my room. I was certain that I hadn't come down the serpentine stretch of hallway before and, yet, I found it again and again and it repeatedly dumped me back in front of my room. After what must have been forty-five minutes of wandering in a loop, I turned on to a dark hallway with only one door. It stood ajar and golden light spilled onto the floor. I hadn't found anything else, so I moved closer.

I peeked through the cracked door and scanned what looked like a workshop. Half-carved sculptures of huge, monstrously muscled men, an equally intimidating Minotaur with an intricately carved phallus, and one evil-looking satyr stood proudly on one end of the room. There was a hulking sculpture of a man with bulging muscles and enormous wings, like Michael the archangel. They were all twice the size of an average human with twisted, lustful expressions. It was hard to believe that they had come from a block of stone.

I scanned the area and listened carefully. I didn't hear anyone. There wasn't any reason not to take a closer look. I squeezed through the door without moving it and stepped inside.

The magnificent, horrifying sculptures were only half of the room. The other side was a potter's bench. There was a nearly-finished per-fectly formed clay cat on the bench. It looked almost like my sister's cat, Oscar. It sat directly next to a clay severed human head. A tall curtain was drawn across one corner of the room. It was like some-thing you would see at an art gallery to shield a magnum opus until the moment was perfect to reveal it.

I crept closer. If the green-eyed man had made these sculptures, he wasn't just a sociopath; he was also a brilliant artist. Which, on reflection wouldn't make him the first of his kind.

Curiosity had brought me this far so I stepped towards the black curtain. I was close enough to touch it when I heard voices. A female alto, throaty and sensual said, "It was good of you to see me."

"I believe that I mentioned that I wouldn't be available for a few days." The answering tone was cold but the voice was unmistakable. It was my captor. Without thinking, I slipped between the part in the curtains and turned to spy through the crack.

"Yet, here you are, fully available," the woman said with a cul-tured little laugh.

The green-eyed man entered the studio. I held my breath. I wished that I could stop my heart. I was certain that he could sense me, smell me even. But I couldn't bring myself to stop watching.

A woman entered the room behind him. She had a long fall of curly dark hair and the most perfect dusky skin that I had ever seen. Like the green-eyed man, she was too vivid to be real. Every curl of her hair, the curve of her figure, the delicacy of her features was like the ideal of a woman, rather than a real person.

"Why are you here, Alexis?" the man asked.

"I missed you," she replied. She eyed the huge sculptures. "Have you abandoned your monsters? I was hoping that you might let me play with the Minotaur when he was done."

"He isn't going to be done for some time," the man said tersely.

"Pity. Monsters are your forte," she said, crossing the room to the potter's bench. She ignored the severed head and touched the cat. "Kittens? What's next? Bluebirds?"

"I'm in the midst of a project, Alexis. It's a private matter."

She stroked the kitten with a long fingernail. I swear, for the briefest instant the cat sculpture seemed to stretch to meet her, like a real cat would. I blinked. I must have been more tired than I thought.

She turned to him. "Even the busiest of men must have a tension release." Her hand went to his crotch and she massaged up and down slowly.

Heat flew to my face, I knew that I should stop watching, try not to listen, and give them some privacy. But I didn't. The green-eyed man looked neither embarrassed nor aroused. His perfect posture didn't budge. He turned a cool eye on the woman and said, "I have a dinner engagement soon. I don't have time."

"Then we'll be fast," she replied.

He pushed her hand away. "I said no."

"No you didn't," she replied. "You said that you have projects and dinner plans. But this tension of yours, we can take care of that in a matter of moments. You'll feel so much better. Like a new man." Her hand returned to his crotch. She used her spare hand to pluck the buttons of her blouse open. Her breasts were as perfect as the rest of her.

"You're embarrassing yourself," he said, stepping away from her. "If this is all you wanted, feel free to see yourself out."

She hesitated for a moment. Then, her voice came out softly entreating. "Please."

The syllable seemed to have a magical effect on him. He turned back towards the woman. His face wasn't kind; his teeth were slightly bared and his eyes narrowed to dangerous slits. "What did you say?" he asked.

Her voice became much less certain. "Please."

His demeanor completely changed. It gave me a chill to see it. Instead of coolness, he exuded heat. He became predatory, like a large cat. "Please what?"

She lowered her eyes. "Please, Master."

He slipped right up next to her, seeming to relish the inches of height he had on her. He put a hand on her shoulder and without saying anything, forced her to her knees. He towered over her for a moment. I imagined myself there, kneeling where this woman knelt, being dominated by this man, and the sensation was so overwhelming that I swayed.

"Go on," he told her in a low voice. She reached for him and he grabbed her wrists. "No hands," he said.

She nipped at his pants, struggling to get them open. He didn't help her. In fact, he actively hindered, jerking her by the wrists whenever she had an effective grip on his pants. She broke a sweat, and his expression grew more and more satisfied. He was enjoying her humiliation and my resentment against him grew as I watched them.

Finally, she freed his penis and without any preamble he jammed it into her mouth. I heard her gag. He released her wrists and took two handfuls of her hair, pumping into her hard. Her eyes teared but she didn't struggle. She dug her fingernails into his backside, moaning, and set up a driving rhythm. Finally, when I thought this whole scene would be over in no more than a few minutes, he pulled out of her.

Roughly, he yanked her to her feet and smashed her face-first against the closest wall, holding her with a flat hand in the middle of her back. He entered her roughly without even removing her skirt. She cried out, seemingly half in pain and half in pleasure. "You relish this abuse," he said in a low, accusing voice. "If I whipped you, you would moan like a whore."

"Yes, please. Anytime you want me."

He slammed into her harder. "It's Victor you need. You belong with him."

"I want *you*."

He ground her into the wall, lifting her with each thrust, punishing her for wanting him. "Don't come back unless you want me to really hurt you."

She moaned like the idea had more pleasure associated with it than anything else. Her fingers pressed into the wall. He went rougher and harder and her cries grew louder. Finally, without a sound, he shuddered. Then, he withdrew without letting her finish.

He pulled up his pants and said, "Now go, Alexis."

"No cigarette?" she asked, putting her blouse back on. He leveled a look at her. "At least see me out," she said, buttoning her shirt.

"Very well," he sighed. "But no shenanigans. I actually *do* have an engagement."

She took his arm. "Shenanigans? Me?"

They left the room and I allowed myself a long exhale. I throbbed with want and questioned myself as to how I could allow such a depraved show of lust to affect me so. My hands shook. I forced myself to wait until I couldn't hear footfalls or voices any longer before I moved.

I almost forgot what brought me to the curtain in the first place. I glanced behind me and froze. My barely calmed nerves fired anew. It was a life-sized sculpture of me sitting in a chair—a near perfect rendering. I was nude, my head thrown back, my long hair dangling with the illusion of softness. My knees were parted just the slightest bit and my hands were poised to touch something, as if there was a companion sculpture that had been removed.

I turned my back on the lusty carving. I crept out the door and back into the hallway. Before long, I found the door to my room. I wished again that I dared run. Even if it was just to the cliffs to fling myself off. Anything to end this nightmarish waiting and this aching need. But I couldn't bring myself to do it. I saw the falling, ghostly people like a traumatic flashback. I remembered the animal sounds that warned me that I may not even make it to the cliffs and that my death may not be that peaceful.

So, I huddled in one of the embroidered chairs in the front room and waited to see what my captor's next move would be.

Chapter 3
The Failure of Defiance

"Miss? Miss." A voice. Near my head. Did I fall asleep on the bus? "I'm awake. I'm sorry," I tried to say, but no sound came out. My own silence gave me such a jolt that I snapped awake. Jason stood over me. "You were asleep," he said. "It's time for dinner. You should dress. I'll wait."

I stood and stretched. Then I indicated to my rumpled slacks and blouse. I was dressed. I wasn't going to put on a costume for that man's pleasure. "Oh, Miss, the Master will not be pleased," Jason said. He sounded frightened but I would have none of it. I nodded at the door. Without any other choice, he led me out.

We passed through another maze of hallways until we reached a wooden door. Jason knocked and opened it for me. The room was set up for formal dining. A small table set for two with heavy silver, eggshell china, and crystal goblets. Candles blazed everywhere. The green-eyed man was there, wearing a tuxedo, looking curiously at me as I entered the room. Again, I was struck by the unnatural beauty of the man. In formal clothes, he looked even more surreal. He cocked his head and glanced at my clothes.

"I was thinking of something a little more formal, Elaine." He crossed the room with the delicate grace of a dancer and stood in front of me, close enough to touch me. I lifted my chin and practically dared him to send me away. The tinge of aggravation on his face was worth it. "No matter," he finally said. "As this is your first night, I'll accommodate you."

The room started to spin slowly, giving me a rolling vertigo. At the same time, the décor seemed fluid. The dark wood transformed

16

into lighter, homier shades. Crystal became China. Candles disappeared. It resembled a family dining room: comfortable and casual. The green-eyed man's clothes had changed, too. Instead of a tux, he wore soft brown leather pants and a cream tunic. I looked around, panic overwhelming sense. How did he do that? How did the room change? Was he a hypnotist? I blinked a couple of times, hoping my vision would clear and the formal dining room would return. It didn't. An amused smile played on his lips as he watched me.

"Shall we?" He indicated to the dinner table. In my shock, I didn't protest or resist. I just sat down and he sat across from me. His eyes were always on me, like a spotlight; it embarrassed me how his presence affected me. I was a prisoner and this man had threatened murder to bring me here. He had stolen my voice. He was an evil bastard with impeccable manners and pretty eyes, I reminded myself.

Jason placed our food in front of us and the man started to eat. I hadn't eaten all day, but I didn't touch my plate. I leaned back in my chair and folded my arms over my chest. Passive resistance. I would be Gandhi.

He glanced at me, noticed, and returned to his food. My stomach gave a loud rumble. He looked up again. "You are behaving foolishly, Elaine. This won't win you your freedom." I met his eyes and gestured towards my throat. I was sick of being silent. He gave his half-eaten plate of food a rough shove and glared at me.

"If you are finished with your dinner, there is something that I would like to show you." His voice was stern.

He reached over, gripped one of my hands, and yanked me to my feet, sending electric jolts shooting through me. "Come," he ordered, dragging me after him. I tried to pull my hand out of his but he wouldn't let me. He pulled me out the door, down a hall, and to a seemingly bottomless stairwell. Torches were fixed to the wall casting deep shadows on the stone.

We descended. It was as if we were headed to the center of the Earth. He didn't speak to me. Only our footfalls echoed in the stone corridor. When we reached the bottom, a pair of guards stood in front of another door: a man and a woman. They were large and coarse. Both of the pair had wild, coppery hair and stocky, large bodies. The woman flushed when she saw the green-eyed man. "Hey there," she said awkwardly. "Didn't tell anyone you were coming. We could have had something ready."

"I'm not here for pleasure, Joan," my captor said, holding on to my hand even tighter. "This is Elaine and she needs to see your little playground. We're having difficulty communicating, she and I."

"Stubborn little nugget, is she?" Joan said.

"You could leave her with us," the man said, sweeping me with a lascivious look. "Is she as tender as she looks?" I know I must have looked outraged.

The green-eyed man had an expression edged with humor. "I'll let you know when I find out." He nodded at the door. "May we go in?"

"Be my guest," said the male guard, chuckling at his own joke and standing to heft the door.

"Thank you, Carl," my captor said.

The door creaked; it seemed to me like the hinges got little use. We stepped into a long straight hall. He pulled me a few paces inside before the smell hit me: human waste and filth. There were people down here. My eyes slowly adjusted to the darkness. I was in a prison. With a leap of panic, I tried to pull my hand out of his.

"No, Elaine," he said, his voice gentle, firm, melodic. The anger that had flared around the two guards melted and left me only with the skeleton of fear... that and the pulsing want that had never really disappeared. I didn't know if the green-eyed man felt it or not. I saw no evidence of it as he practically dragged me down an endless hallway.

Someone passed me on the left. Something transparent and colorless and moving in slow motion. I gasped and stared. It was a person who seemed to be trying to run. His knees were high and his arms pumped. He passed us and I peered after him. He ran with all of his might, but still wasn't moving much faster than we were. His eyes were fixed on something far ahead but I couldn't see anything but the endless darkness. My captor didn't seem the least bit concerned. He just dragged me on.

More ghostly figures inhabited the cells. A young man sat inside one cell playing a piano. He muttered to himself, "I can never remember that part. Never remember. It's gone." The music he played from was blank. Another cell held a woman who cradled a bundle of blankets. She dug into the fabric with her fingers. "She's missing! My Lilly, she's gone!" Her despair was chilling.

He dragged me onward.

As we progressed down the hall, the scenes grew more sordid. A woman bent over a table being forcefully taken by a man double her size. Another woman crying as a man held her against a wall and fondled under her skirt. A young man, surrounded by other men as they pissed on him. I wanted to stop my captor, ask him why he would let this happen in his house, why he wasn't freeing these people. But I couldn't break away from him and I couldn't ask any questions. I was as helpless to end the prisoner's misery as I was to end my own.

We continued down the hallway, past dozens of scenes. Finally we came to an empty cell with the door open and he led me inside. I stiffened. Instinctively, I tried not to pass through the doorway, but he pulled me inside the cell.

"This, Elaine, this," he gestured to the twelve by twelve room without dropping my hand, "is your cell. This is the place where you will end up if you displease me. Not free — not back in the drudgery of your past life — but here. More of a prisoner than you could ever imagine. You have a choice: your rooms upstairs or your room down here."

I looked around the small cell. Something about it looked sickly familiar. A voice whispered to me that I'd been here before. My captor wouldn't release my hand; the pulses of heat wouldn't stop. Loud moans came from all around me. Somewhere a whip cracked. I jumped and my heart jumped too.

The green-eyed man closed the distance between us and I tried to back away a step. I felt like prey; queer warning prickles running down my back. My retreat didn't matter. He closed the distance once more and his fingers found my face. He brushed the hair from my forehead and placed his fingertips under my chin. When his eyes met mine, fear and pulsing heat exploded in me. "Understand," he continued, "I don't wish to punish you. Your very presence pleases me. You will have to strive to displease me. Since that seemed to be the path you had chosen, I felt you deserved fair warning about what the outcome would be." He drew a thumb across my eyebrow and I swear his hand trembled.

"Have you had enough of this place?" he asked. I nodded, wishing that I could look away from him. Lack of food and those relentless shocks of electricity left me dizzy and fuzzy-headed. I could tell that he wanted to say something more but he stopped himself. He took a deep breath. "Jason will be at the entrance. Go there and he will see you to your rooms. I have business to attend to."

I backed out of the cell, turned for the entrance, and speed-walked back down the hall. I saw the running shades coming from the other direction. I questioned my sanity. Were they ghosts? Was I hallucinating? Was I mad? The exit door was locked and I pounded on it. Tears threatened but I forced them down. The doors shook. They opened. I raced through. The first face I saw was Jason's and I headed straight for him. He looked as relieved as I felt. For the life of me, I didn't know why.

"Good to meet you, Elaine," Carl, the male guard said. "Hope you visit us again soon." I shot him a tearful look. I didn't have the strength for anything harsher.

"Let's get you back to your rooms," Jason said to me, his tone gentle. We climbed all of those innumerable steps until my muscles were shaking and I was sweating. He led me through hallways and corridors. It looked like we were taking a different route. There was at least one painting that I had not seen before.

"Here we are," Jason said, stopping suddenly in front of a door. "And...." He looked around nervously and thrust an apple and a piece of bread into my hands. "I wish it could be more, but you must really be hungry at dinner tomorrow night or he will know."

I was touched. 'Thank you,' I mouthed. He gave me a creaky smile, as if he had forgotten how. Then he shooed me inside the suite and he locked the door behind me. I knew that he risked that horrible prison by defying the green-eyed man and I wondered why he did it.

I was dead tired. My mind kept flashing with images from the prison: the ghostly spirits running in slow motion, the woman being forcefully taken over a table, and my familiar cell. The déjà vu was unnerving. How on Earth could I have ever been in this mansion and not remember the event?

I chewed the crusty bread slowly. It wasn't much but at least it gave my stomach something to work on. I set the apple aside for later. As tired as I was, I didn't want to sleep.

I tried the door to my suite and, again, it was unlocked. I slipped into the empty hallway. This time it didn't take long to find the workshop. Light still spilled into the darkened hallway and I heard voices within. Two male voices. Every instinct told me to flee but then, I heard my name. I edged as close to the door as I dared.

"...Elaine will adapt," I heard the green-eyed man say. "She hasn't even been here for one full sleep and wake cycle."

"Or, you'll break her, Sir," another voice answered. It was Jason. I was sure of it. I peeked around the door and saw Jason lay a glass of wine on the sculpting bench while my captor, facing away from the door, worked in clay.

"I'm *not* going to break her."

"She isn't even accepting food."

"Unless you offer it."

There was an awkward silence. Heat came into my chest and face. Nobody was safe in this house.

My captor continued to speak. "*I* offer her a feast and she refuses. But a crust of bread and an apple from *you* and it's like you're her lifeline."

"Sir, I meant no disrespect—"

"Is that what you want to be? Her lifeline? The one she turns to when my behavior just proves too harsh?"

"I would *never*—"

"But that's what you've done. Elaine and you against me." He held the sculpture of the severed head to where I could see most of it. The eyes blinked. The mouth worked. I pinched my lips together to keep from making a sound until I remembered that I was still mute. Who was this man? How did he animate the inanimate? How did he steal my voice? My mind flashed to the sculpture of me behind the curtain and my face grew even hotter.

"I'm the villain," he continued. "I'm the one who kidnaps and imprisons. You're the servant who passes her food on the sly."

He paused, clearly waiting for Jason to answer. The servant stayed silent.

Finally, the green-eyed man continued. "Get out of my sight. Don't let me see you until tomorrow night." I heard Jason take a step closer and I tensed to move. Then, my captor spoke again. "And Jason, if Elaine refuses to dress for dinner, refuses food, or is in any other way defiant, I'll consider you her accomplice."

"Sir!"

"Get out."

"But, Sir—"

I dashed away from the door and scampered to the closest cross hallway, ducking around the corner. I got as low to the ground as I could, hoping the shadows would hide me. Then, I peeked just in time to see Jason exit the room and slump with his back against the opposite wall. The light from the workshop fell across his face. For the first time, he looked old. Haggard. Worn and frightened.

I drew back into hiding. After he walked by, I wandered until I found my room. I didn't want to be compliant with the kidnapper. I didn't want to give him any satisfaction. But I also knew that if I could keep him from harming Jason, I had to try.

I finally fell asleep on the couch in the study. When I woke up, I wondered how long it would be before Jason arrived. I looked at the gold gown that had never been removed from my bed. I couldn't—I just couldn't wear that thing. I couldn't let someone dress me. Some other dress—any other dress. I strode to the wardrobe and riffled through the rows of gowns. I found another that suited me. It was just as formal and just as beautiful but more conservative. Wine colored and long sleeved, tight through the bodice and slightly off the shoulder, it didn't expose as much skin as the gold gown. I gathered the undergarments and shoes and laid the whole array on my bed. It would do.

I sat down in front of the vanity and looked at my face in the mirror. Mousy. I had always thought I looked mousy. Long dark hair, a thin face with a pointed chin, and big gray eyes. I had to do something about that. I twisted my long hair up on my head. Then, I put on make-up. Finally, I put on the evening gown and inspected myself in the mirror. I couldn't remember the last time I took so much care with my appearance.

I grabbed a book off of the shelf and took it to the sitting room. Maybe I could focus on that. But I couldn't. My hunger would interrupt my reading and I would remember my fear. I was almost grateful to hear the door handle turn.

Jason entered and looked around fearfully. When he saw me, his face relaxed. "You're ready for dinner, Miss?" I nodded and laid my book aside. "If I may...." His voice trailed off. "Never mind."

I stopped him and gave him a questioning look.

"I was just going to say that you look... beautiful." I smiled at him. He led me through the mansion and this time I watched the paintings. Turn left at the portrait of the woman sewing, left at the snowy landscape, right at the pen and ink of a horse, and up the short stairs... I couldn't remember it all. Once again, I was horribly muddled when we arrived at the door. Once again, he knocked and opened the door.

It looked the same as it had the previous evening: the delicate china, the glowing candles, and the heavy silver. The green-eyed man had his back to the door but turned quickly as I entered.

In that moment, I realized how tightly he had always controlled his facial expression. I saw surprise and pleasure—and something more primal. The hunger that radiated from him, the danger that edged him—it was desire. It was so different from how he looked with Alexis in his workshop. The way he looked now, I knew he would never push my hand away. I swayed where I stood. If it hadn't been for my gown, I might have tried to back away.

"Good lord," I thought I heard him breathe. But I wasn't sure. Immediately, his polite expression covered any show of emotion he might have had. Only his eyes continued to glow. He didn't look away from me when he said, "Jason, you may go. Wait for me in your chamber." Clearly the night wasn't over for Jason. I hoped that I could do something to make it better for him.

Chapter 4
Doing the Right Thing

The green-eyed man approached me quickly. He was sleek and tall in the tuxedo — stark black and white that looked like moving shadows over light. His hair was like silver on the cloth. He took my hands in his, sending heat to my face and looked me up and down. "You're breathtaking," he said. I lowered my eyes, wishing I could hide my face entirely. It was ridiculous being called breathtaking by this man.

"Just one thing would complete you," he commented, lifting my chin. His eyes swept over me. He reached into his coat pocket and retrieved something that glittered in the candle light. A necklace. It was diamonds and garnets as deep as my gown. He stepped behind me and I held my breath as he fastened it — a choker — at the base of my neck. "Come see," he said, guiding me to a gilded mirror on the wall. My own frightened eyes looked back at me. "Do you wish to thank me for the gift?" he asked. I shot him a look of disbelief. Thank him? Was he kidding?

"No?" he asked, a note of cruelty entering his voice. "An apple and a crust of bread win your gratitude, but jewels leave you cold?" My heart sped. At least I didn't have to pretend I didn't know about his anger with Jason. I know my face must have been pale. "I find insubordinate servants tiresome," he continued, as if to himself. "Perhaps Jason has grown too comfortable in his place here. Of late, he's only witnessed punishment and not experienced it." His eyes focused on mine in the mirror, a challenge in them. "Are you too full of stolen food to dine with me tonight?" I remembered this man's words to Jason. *If Elaine refuses to dress for dinner, refuses food, or is in any other way defiant, I'll consider you her accomplice.* I shook my head and his expression softened. "Come, then."

We sat down and two servants entered with platters, dishing food onto our plates, filling our goblets with wine. He wasn't touching his food — his eyes were on me. I couldn't eat while he watched me. I sat, my back straight, my eyes fixed on the table cloth, and waited. Adrenaline sizzled through me.

The servants disappeared. "A toast?" he suggested, lifting his glass. He waited for me to join him. "To you, Elaine. To the challenge." He clicked my glass while I sat there puzzled. Is that what I was to him? Some sort of challenge? Certainly I had failed. Here I sat, dressed as he wished, sharing dinner with him as he wished. Some challenge. What was I doing here?

A glow came into his eyes. "You're positively bursting with questions, aren't you?" A smile played on his lips. "I could get you paper and pen."

I shook my head and lifted my chin firmly. If he wanted to hear my thoughts, he could return my voice. I wouldn't communicate any other way. And I wasn't going to ask for it again, either. He would either give it back or he wouldn't. He either wanted to speak with me or he didn't.

"As you wish," he said, picking up his fork. I followed his example, remembering how hungry I was. I tried to eat slowly, cutting my food into small pieces. The man seemed lost in thought. His sooty lashes lifted every once in a while so he could look at me, but he didn't speak. When we finished our plates, the two young servants reappeared like magic.

"Dessert, sir?" asked the beautiful young man. He looked like a poet from a Shakespearian play.

The green-eyed man cast me another look. His eyes lingered on my face. "Not yet, Matthew. Bring me the black box."

The servant seemed to know exactly what he was talking about. "Yes, Sir." He was gone and back before the other servant, a young woman, had refilled the wine goblets. He laid a fuzzy black jewel box before the green-eyed man.

"I will call you for dessert when we are ready," the man told the servants. The boy jumped to obey. He was out the door in moments but the girl paused to cast a surreptitious glace at me. She had delicate, fragile features with smooth, pearly skin and a long sheet of silky black hair. She looked like a China doll. The green-eyed man cleared his throat and gave her a pointed look. She started and practically ran for the door.

When they were gone, he stroked the top of the box and watched me. It was like he was trying to decide something and, for once, his face was drained of all amusement. Finally, after a long minute, he lifted the box and placed it in front of me. He nodded to it to indicate that I should open it.

I did. On the silken pad inside was the golden bead that held my voice. My brow furrowed. Could it be that easy? He would just give it to me? No quid-pro-quo? No games? Maybe he would release me the same way. Some day when I pleased him with my behavior or dress, he would just put me in his flying limo and whisk me back to my home. I lifted the bead between my fingers and looked at him.

"Go ahead," he said. He moved the goblet of water closer to me. "Drink plenty with it so it doesn't get stuck." I put the bead in my mouth and chased it with the rest of the water in the goblet. It tasted sweet, like honey. When the over-sized lump hit my throat, it dissolved away.

"You had questions for me?" he asked softly.

I had a million questions. They swirled in my head, not making much sense. I wasn't even sure if I wanted to know the answer to some of them. I met his eyes and took a sip of my wine, trying to calm myself. Finally, I tried my voice. It was smooth. It didn't sound cracked or gruff, like I hadn't used it in over a day. I asked, "Do you want me to call you 'Sir?'"

Then, he laughed. I had watched emotions playing over his features since he kidnapped me, but nothing like this. His laughter was beautiful and musical, like strings. And it was infectious. I caught myself smiling in response, quite against my will. "No," he replied, still chuckling. "Please don't. My name is Ghalib."

"Ghalib." It suited him in a strange way. "Why did you kidnap me?" There it was, out in the open. He didn't even flinch at the word 'kidnap'.

"Because I couldn't think of any other way to get you to come with me," he said, as if it was the simplest thing in the world. "Would you have accepted a less forceful invitation?"

I didn't break his gaze, though it left me a little muddled. "No. But, I wasn't asking about your methods. Why me?"

He toyed with his goblet. "Unfortunately, you aren't ready to hear the answer, yet. Another night, perhaps."

Another night? How many nights? I pushed the question away. He probably wouldn't answer that one either. Instead, I asked, "Are you going to hurt me?"

His eyes probed my face—serious again. I didn't look away. I willed him to answer me. "If I hurt you, trust me when I tell you you'll enjoy it," he said in a low voice. I shivered with chill and thought of his conversation during sex with Alexis. *If I whipped you, you would moan like a whore.* I lowered my eyes and my hands trembled. This man was dangerous.

He reached across the table and lifted my chin. Heat flooded my cheeks. "Don't look away, Elaine," he commanded. "Hurting people is something I'm very good at. What you mean to ask me is if I intend to *punish* you. If you should take defiance to an unattractive extreme or if you go out of your way to displease me, as you did last night, you will be punished. It probably won't be in any way that you imagine now, but I assure you that you won't enjoy it."

His fingertips traced my jaw line, sending shivers over me. I didn't look down. I couldn't look away. "Just as I can hurt you, just as I can strip you of everything and leave you to rot in my prison, I can also give you more than you would ever imagine. If I wish, I can make your very dreams come true."

"All I want is my freedom," I said. "I know you can give me that. Please, Ghalib, tell me you're going to let me go."

When I said the word 'please' fire flashed behind his eyes. His breath quickened. His fingers left my face. I felt a little more clear-headed. "Were you ever free?" he asked. "Maybe this is your free-dom."

"No," I said. "I can't leave if I want to. I can't talk to my sister. Somebody is choosing my clothes. This isn't freedom."

He tented his fingers, like he was thinking. "In a sense, it's no dif-ferent from how you have been living. Not a narrow choice of evening dresses, but a narrow choice of business suits. Not restricted inside my home, but restricted by circumstances into a dismal little apartment. Once you are over the initial shock of being here, you may find these limited choices preferable to the ones you had to make before."

"You're holding me against my will."

He drew his chair around the table, closer to me, and smiled a little. "I'm aware of that."

"Please let me go."

Again, he seemed to quicken at the word 'please'. "I won't," he answered, his voice husky.

My voice trembled. "Why not?"

"Enough questions for one night," he said. When I opened my lips to protest, he laid a long finger over them. "No, Elaine," he said. His touch stopped me cold.

I put my hand over his and his eyes widened. I pulled his finger from my lips, feeling the iron strength under his skin. I had surprised him. That's the only way I was getting away with pushing his hand away. Before he could get angry at my defiance, I spoke.

"One more thing," I said. "Not a question. A request."

His eyebrows lifted. "Go ahead."

I took a deep breath. I couldn't believe what I was about to say. "Please don't do anything to Jason. I know that you didn't intend for me to eat last night, and that he disregarded your wishes, but he didn't do any harm. And he was kind to me."

"He was kind to you?" Ghalib said, a dangerous edge to his voice. "Unlike how I was?"

My anger rose. "One could say that."

"Would *you* say that?"

"I wasn't the one who did," I said pointedly. "That was you. And if your conscience hurts you, that's your affair."

He gave me a long look and flipped my hand over on the table. He ran a finger over the web between my pointer finger and my thumb. "There it is," he said, smiling at me.

"What?" I asked shortly.

"Your temper," he replied. "The good news is that you cool off quickly."

I pulled my hand back. "Forget I even mentioned Jason."

The hungry intensity returned to his face. "If you're serious about me not punishing Jason, perhaps we could trade favors," he said smoothly. His eyes grew intense and calculating. "No need to look so frightened," he told me. His voice was low, like a purr. "I have a desire to hear you sing. That's all. If you would indulge me, I would only reprimand Jason and not punish him."

I was surprised. I don't know what I expected. Not this. I couldn't deny that there was a proud part of me that wanted to show off. Especially for this man who left me so befuddled every time I was near him. I also wanted to stay strong and stubborn. I didn't want to do anything that would bring the bastard pleasure. "I—I don't know. It's been a long time."

"It's your choice."

I thought of Jason's face when he handed me the apple. He had been frightened. "I'll try. I can't promise anything."

A smile of unrestrained pleasure lit up his face. I hadn't thought that it was possible for him to look more beautiful, more exotic, or more magnetic. A wave of fear crashed over me. What was I thinking? Magnetic? Beautiful? Get your head on straight, Ellie.

"Dessert?" he asked crisply. "Then music?"

The servants filed back in, setting small, opaque dessert plates in front of us. The girl that I had noticed before placed the open black box on her tray and cast me another look. I wondered about her. How much did she know about me? Did she know why Ghalib had taken me? I wanted to talk to her but I tried to ignore her. I didn't need any more trouble right now.

When dessert was finished, Ghalib pushed his chair away. "Do you need to wait thirty minutes after you eat, or is that just for swimming?"

"No," I said, ignoring his joke. "Any time is fine. Do you want me to just sing here or—"

"In this room? With the acoustics and no accompaniment?" he asked me, standing. "Of course not."

"The acoustics...?"

"Bring your water," he said, pulling out my chair. He guided me, with a hand on my back out of the dining room. We followed a hallway to a staircase and climbed it until I was breathless. He measured his pace so that my hem wouldn't trip me and soon we arrived at a door.

We entered a room with a shining, black piano at its center. Chairs and small round tables were placed all around, like a piano bar. A woman in a black dress sat on the piano bench, waiting for us. Had he planned this ahead of time, knowing what he was going to ask of me? Our footsteps echoed. In this room, you could hear a whisper from fifty feet away. I took a swallow of water and put my glass on one of the tables. My stomach churned. It had been years since I sang for an audience.

"What am I singing?" I asked without looking at him.

"The music is ready for you," he said. I approached the piano and glanced at the sheet music. It came flooding back to me—my years of choir and vocal lessons; standing beside a piano, nowhere near as fine as this one, singing for an audience; testing the limits of my own voice. I had loved to sing and I had been good at it. But that was a long time ago.

I skimmed the music and recognized an aria from an opera that I had once loved. "This is very advanced," I said, turning to face Ghalib, who was already sitting in a chair, gracefully reclined. I had only sung this particular song a couple of times and never for an audience.

"Try," he told me.

I took a very deep breath and nodded at the girl at the piano. She played the introduction and I felt reality slip away from me. My eyes closed. When I opened my mouth, the notes flowed out of me. It was high for me—a soprano part. Without warming up, I should have had more trouble. But, the singing was so effortless that I could concentrate on the emotion behind the piece: innocence and delight. The pianist altered her style to follow me and I forgot that Ghalib was even there. When the music ended, I came back to myself with a flush.

When I saw Ghalib's face, I was startled. His expression was one of pure delight, like I had infused him with the mood of the aria. As I stood there, waiting to see if I had fulfilled my part of the deal, his eyes turned hot and hungry. He leaned forward and I got this disconcerted impression that he might lunge for me. "Another," he said. It was a command in a low growl.

A chill went over me with a surge of adrenaline. I felt like prey being stalked. His gaze was unabashed and unblinking. I heard the frightened pianist shuffling music and I knew I should go look at the sheet music but I was frozen to the spot. The only thing that gave me any calm was that he maintained his seat.

The introduction started and jolted me from looking at Ghalib. Thankfully, again, it was from music I knew. An English carol that was lilting and fun. I came in naturally at my entrance, closing my eyes and breathing deeply, paying attention to the dynamics and my tone. I controlled the pace, slowing down the tempo of the nervous pianist, trying to make it as beautiful as I could. As I came to the last repetition of the chorus, my fear retuned. I didn't want to look at Ghalib.

I didn't have a choice. He sprung from his seat, like a dancer, and approached me with a goblet of water. The accompanist jumped to leave and Ghalib held up his hand. "Stay," he told her. "We're not done yet." My back was against the piano and Ghalib was standing too close. I accepted the water goblet without looking away from his face. Slowly, I eased myself away from him, into the curve of the piano.

"Do I make you nervous, Elaine?" he asked in a low voice.

Truth sprung to my lips. "Yes," I breathed. "Very."

I flushed at my own words and he chuckled, but his intensity didn't recede. I had never wanted to run from anyone like this but when I had edged into the curve of the piano, I had eliminated my own chance for escape. He put one hand on the piano to one side of me, as if it was a casual move. Then, he brought his other hand to my hair. My heart stuttered. "Why do you wear your hair like this?" he asked.

"Like what?" I breathed.

"Tight. Severe." He loosened the pins and my hair tumbled over my shoulders. He combed it with his fingers. "I thought you'd be soft," he told me. "And I was right."

"Please don't," I breathed, lowering my eyes.

"Don't do what?" he asked in a low, gentle voice. "Touch you? Compliment you?" He held the length of my hair to his nose and inhaled. "Enjoy being near you?"

My whole body trembled. "This is making me very uncomfortable," I said.

He placed his fingers under my chin, forcing me to look at him.

"I don't want to make you uncomfortable. You have nothing to fear from me, tonight." He took his hand away and backed off a step. Then, he tapped the side of the water glass in my hand. The liquid inside turned red. I stared at it. The tang of wine reached my nose. "We must see what we can do to calm those nerves," he said, nodding at the glass.

"How did you do that?"

He smirked. "Magic." His intensity was muted slightly by his humor.

I sipped the wine. It was fruity and it warmed me."Thank you," I said. "This does help." The fact that he had backed away helped more.

"Yes?" He hadn't broken his gaze. "Do you have the energy for one more song?"

I took another breath, steadier this time, and nodded. I expected him to go back to his seat but he didn't. He stood right in front of me, as if he intended for me to sing to him. The pianist started and I recognized the piece. The Habanera from *Carmen*. I had never sung that aria and my French was abysmal. I swallowed two more quick gulps of the wine and started.

It was a sensual song and I did my best to give it that flavor. The wine loosened me. I wasn't quite as terrified as I should have been. I could hold his glowing gaze.

On the final note, my voice cracked. "Oh, I'm sorry," I said automatically, flushing.

"No," he said. "It reminds me that the hour is late and not all of my pleasures can be sated in one night." Again, I felt that chill. How many nights? I knew it was fruitless to ask but questions swirled just under the surface.

He looked at me and I expected him to say something else. But he didn't. His eyes traveled from my face, down my body, and back up. The electric chills that I usually felt when he touched me surged over me just from his nearness and his intensity. "Have I completed my side of this deal?" I asked. "Jason won't be punished?"

"Yes," he said. "He already knows of the service you've done him."

"Then, may I go? I'm very tired."

He stood straighter, more formally. "Of course, Elaine." His civility didn't diminish the heat of his gaze. "Until tomorrow night, then." He stepped aside to let me pass.

I moved to the door as quickly as I could. I needed to get away and clear my head. I needed to think. I couldn't do that with Ghalib in the same room, it seemed. Jason was on the other side of the door, waiting. "Come with me, Miss. I'll take you back to your room."

I gave up trying to pay attention to the path we took. It didn't make any sense anyway. We climbed another set of stairs and I was sure that my room was at least two floors down.

When I reached for the doorknob, he put a tentative hand on my arm. "Thank you, Miss," he said gruffly. "I know what you did for me tonight. The Master's punishments are inspired. I appreciate what you did to spare me."

"You were kind to me," I replied. "I'm just glad Ghalib let me help you."

He smiled his creaky smile and opened my door for me. "I'm happy to see that you can speak again," he commented as he closed the door behind me.

"Me too," I breathed to the empty room. I couldn't give it too much thought, or my sanity would crack. He turned my water to wine. He turned my voice into a gold bead. If I dwelt on it I would be up all night. So I pushed the confusion from my mind and dressed for sleep.

Chapter 5
Truth is Stranger Than Fiction

When I woke up. I knew that someone had been in my rooms while I slept. I still couldn't bring myself to sleep in that enormous bed, buried in the innermost room of the suite, next to the window with the perfect view of the falling people. I sat up on the couch in the study, clutching a blanket to my chest, and peered into the sitting room. A huge, steaming thermos, a croissant, and a bowl of fruit had been placed on one of the tables. I peeked into the bedroom and saw that someone had put away the wine-colored dress. I had an icky, creepy-crawly feeling.

"Hello," I called. No answer and no sound. Whoever it was had left.

I went to the front room and sniffed the thermos. Tea. The croissant was still warm. Without being told, I knew it was a reward for the night before. I ate slowly and tried to think about what I was going to do. What could I do? When I was done with all of the food, I still didn't have any answers.

I had come to one perplexing point: nothing particularly bad had happened the night before. Ghalib hadn't brutalized me. He hadn't violated me. He didn't seem to want to traumatize me; when I asked him to back off, he did. Yet, he insisted that he wouldn't let me go. What was he holding me for? To sing to him? To have dinner with him? It made so sense whatsoever.

I leaned back in the embroidered chair and closed my eyes, but when I did, I saw Ghalib's green eyes looking back at me. Instead, I tried to imagine Rachel and her gray eyes that were so much like mine. I missed her. We had never gone this long without talking.

A knock came from the hallway door. My eyes flew open at the same time the door did. A pale, wide-eyed Jason stood in the doorway. "Miss," he said in a breathless voice, "the Master is calling for you. Would you be so good as to get dressed?" I blinked at him. "Quickly," he added.

"What's going on?"

"*Please*, Miss." His voice had a panicky note to it.

Something told me that I could undo all of the good I'd done the night before with a wrong move now. "Come in and sit. I'll be a minute."

I closed the door to the bedroom and went to the perplexing array of clothes in the walk-in closet. I grabbed the first simple dress I found. It was yellow and like a sun dress. I threw on a white sweater with it and braided my hair back. In five minutes, I had splashed water on my face, put on a pair of shoes, and headed back out to Jason.

He barely looked at me; he just held the door and waited for me to walk through it. Then, he led me through the maze of hallways and stopped in front of a familiar door that stood ajar. The workshop. My cheeks went cold and my heart seized, He knew. He knew I'd been snooping and eavesdropping. I was about to be punished. I bit my lip and stepped inside.

Ghalib stood in the middle of the workshop with another one of those creatures of stunning perfection. A brightly colored scarf covered her hair. Her features were all angled and sharp. Ghalib's face was twisted in annoyance. He made a gesture towards me. "There she is. Unharmed, just as I said."

The woman stepped forward. She cocked her head at me. "I come as a proxy to my mistress, Lady Nyx."

"Who is Nyx?" I asked.

The woman shot Ghalib a reproachful look. "She's the overseer of this world. She's its mistress and its servant. She sees to the welfare of humans brought to this place and has sent me to inquire as to your well-being."

"She looks after humans and oversees this world? What world? Well, please tell her that my well-being is pretty poor, given that I was kidnapped and brought here against my will." I glared at Ghalib.

"It is too early to be discussing this," he said in irritation. "She's been here less than two dream cycles."

"She is un-collared, unclaimed, and here in the flesh. And you clearly brought her here under duress. She is a human adrift. You should have told her of these things before you brought her here. You *must* inform her now or Nyx will return her to the human realm."

"She has *no* right—"

"She has every right to restore the equilibrium where you have unbalanced it, Ghalib."

"Fine," he said tightly. "I'll tell her later tonight."

"Now," the woman corrected. "Nyx instructed me to bear witness."

Ghalib's jaw set. "Fine," Ghalib bit out. He walked over to me. "I'm going to ask you to keep an open mind, Elaine."

A shiver went through me. But I lifted my chin and looked at Ghalib directly. "I'll do my best."

"Close your eyes," he said. I shot him a stubborn look. "Trust me."

"I *don't* trust you," I said. The woman smiled. Ghalib and I locked eyes for a moment. He was clearly reaching the end of his patience. I sighed and closed my eyes.

"I want you to think about all of the odd things you've seen since you've been here," he whispered. His lips brushed my ear and a tiny charge went through me. "The way I stole your voice, the humans falling over the cliff outside, the way I changed an entire room before your eyes that very first night." His hands took mine and he led me across the room with my eyes still closed. "Open your eyes," he said.

I was standing in front of the sculpture of the angel. It towered over me. Then, as I watched, it knelt. My jaw dropped. I could hardly think. It reached out a huge, hard hand to me and I reached to touch it. It was nothing but cold, unyielding stone but the fingers curled around mine. It lifted my hand to its lips. "How...?" I breathed.

"Enough tricks, Ghalib," the woman said in a bored voice. "I don't wish to be here any longer than necessary."

"How did you do that?" I asked. The sculpture froze when I took my hand away.

He wore the most serious expression I'd ever seen on anyone. "I'm not human, Elaine. I'm a Dream Architect."

I'd never heard of such a thing. "A what?"

"I'm called a Dream Architect. My race creates dreams for your race."

"Is this a joke?"

"I'm very serious. You're in a realm called the In-Between, where the human spirit goes when the body sleeps." He spoke slowly, like it was very important that I understand this. "Think again about the strange things you've experienced since you've been here. Imagine that what I say is true, and you'll see that the strangeness will make much more sense."

I blinked at him. His serious expression didn't fade. I thought of the falling people outside and the shades running in the prison downstairs. The scenes I had witnessed in the prison cells had seemed so improbable. My own familiarity with my prison cell returned to me and something clicked in my mind. Heat flooded my cheeks. I took a step away from Ghalib.

"Oh my God," I whispered. "The prison."

My cell had looked familiar because I had dreamed of being there. More specifically, I had dreamed of being prisoner to a man who used me. He had pinned me to a thin cot and ridden me until the orgasm woke me. I remember being so glad that other people couldn't see the things I dreamed.

I crossed the room to find a chair and sank into it and I struggled to hold back tears. "Have you seen every dream I've ever had?" I asked, my voice choked. What embarrassment had I been a party to that I didn't even remember now?

Ghalib knelt in front of me, like the angel had. "Not *every* dream," he said. It wasn't comforting.

I didn't dare ask him what he's seen. I wasn't even sure I wanted to know. "Am I dreaming now?"

"No. I was dissatisfied with having access only to your spirit. I brought all of you here. You should know this is a place that very few humans get to experience in the flesh."

"Please don't suggest that this is some sort of privilege," I snapped. "I would rather you send me home and spend your privileges on someone else."

His face set in a stern expression. "That isn't going to happen. You need to stop asking."

"Ghalib," the woman reprimanded. "Nyx would not approve."

I glanced over to the woman. "I don't want to be here. This Nyx. Will *she* send me home if I ask her?"

"She has the ability," the woman replied, crossing the room to me.

"She should stay out of this," Ghalib growled at the woman. "The way she stays out of most everything that is supposed to be her responsibility."

The woman glared at him. Then she turned back to me. "Poor child. What Ghalib has done is unfair. I shall speak to her on your be—" She laid a hand on the top of my head and cut off her own sentence. The sizzle of electricity shot through me, almost supplanting my anger and embarrassment.

She looked at Ghalib. His frustration melted into satisfaction. "Well, this *does* change things," she said.

"What does?" I asked, looking back and forth between them.

"She'll have to be shared," she said, an expression of pure sympathy in her eyes when she looked my way again. "You know the law."

Ghalib rose. "Not yet. Such abuse would ruin her."

My heart started to pound. I stood, too. "*I* don't know the law," I said. "What does she mean, 'shared?'"

They both ignored me. For a moment, they regarded each other in silence. Then, the woman sighed. "Three cycles. That's the time you have."

"Thank you," Ghalib replied.

"I don't do it for you," the woman said. She touched the top of my head lightly, with just her fingertips. The current of warmth was so pleasing that I wanted to kiss them. She watched me as my breath picked up. "Poor child," she repeated.

Then, before my eyes, she dissolved away. There wasn't a puff of smoke or a sprinkle of glitter. It was as if she had never been here.

I barely had time to recover from the cryptic conversation when Ghalib stepped up close to me. His eyes were intense, like he was memorizing the lines of my face. "We should talk."

"Yes, we should."

"Come." I followed him through the hallways, into his magnificent tiled foyer, and out the front door. The wind caught my dress the second we stepped outside. Animal sounds traveled on the gusts. The trees bent and I pulled my thin sweater around me. I followed him down the path to the cliffs, to where ghostly humans fell like shooting stars from nowhere.

I stopped suddenly and stared at the falling figures. Ghalib stopped, too, and looked where I did. "They're people who are dreaming that they're falling," I said.

"That's correct," Ghalib said. I realized that this was another place in his world that I had most certainly been before.

"Do I look like that when I dream?" I asked. "All colorless and transparent and barely here?"

Ghalib's serious expression softened. "You are actually unusually vivid." He pulled the braid over my shoulder and ran it through his hands. "I guessed the richness of your hair before I ever touched it because of how vividly you dream."

I looked away. "You have to stop this."

His hand in my hair urged my face back towards his. "I don't think I *can* stop. Nor would I choose to if I could. There is nothing casual about what I feel for you, Elaine."

Heat flooded my cheeks. "This is all very unfair," I told him.

"I can see how you would feel that way."

"And selfish of you," I added.

He flinched like my criticism stung him. His expression turned resolute. "Name a place you've always wanted to see."

"What?"

"One place. I know that there are many for you; name just one. We'll dine there and talk."

"Is this a trick?" I asked.

"I promise you, no tricks tonight. Only answers."

I hesitated, thought a moment, and said, "Italy. I've always wanted to see Italy."

He nodded once and took my hand. "Done."

Chapter 6
Careful What You Wish For

He didn't make a gesture or perform some over-the-top magical flailing. It was just suddenly as if someone had poured concentrated acid over everything: the mansion, the trees, even the ground itself. The substance of the world around me melted away and all that remained was terrifying void.

Without earth to stand on or anything to orient me, I swayed and nearly fell. Ghalib caught my arm. He was the only real thing. The pulsing current between us was the only thing that could assure me that my body hadn't melted away, too.

There was a strange sound all around us, as if we were inside of an egg that was being slowly pulled open. A cracking, splintering sound. Then, like a strange special effect, the landscape sprung up around me. We were in a narrow alley at dusk. The streets were stone and the houses were multi-layered with flowers spilling over terraces. Street lamps mounted on the sides of buildings aided the fading glow in the sky.

I was still disoriented and I stumbled. Ghalib caught my arm. "Feeling all right?"

"Give me a minute." I took deep breaths until my dizziness passed. People walked past on the main street, speaking in rolling, soft vowels.

"Are we really in Italy?" I asked.

"Yes," Ghalib replied. "I brought you back to your world so that we could speak completely privately."

I lifted my chin. "What if I make a scene?" I asked. "I could make a dash for the American Embassy."

"We're nowhere near an embassy. And if you made a scene, I should be very cross with you. Besides, it wouldn't help your situation in the slightest." He didn't seem particularly concerned about my threat. "Hungry?" he asked.

"Yes."

He led me to a small bistro at the end of the alley. It was dim inside and lit with candles. We were given a table in a corner, far from the door. I noticed the people in the establishment turning to look at Ghalib. Women. Men. Servers. Patrons. The heat and desire were written across some of the faces like a banner. Others seemed more confused by their reaction. I was glad that I wasn't the only person that he affected this way.

We sat and Ghalib spoke in rapid, fluent Italian to the host. The man nodded once and left. I couldn't hold back. "You're a Dream Architect?"

"That's correct."

"You make dreams?"

"It's a little more complicated than that, but yes. Nightmares, actually."

"And since you kidnapped me, I've been living in your dream world?"

"Again, correct. The In-Between." He looked relieved, as if I'd handled this much better than he thought I would.

I couldn't keep the anger out of my voice. "Tell me now why you did this."

"Because I wanted you."

I just looked at him for a moment in angry disbelief. "Did it ever occur to you that I may not want *you*?" I snapped. "That maybe there were other ways to go about this? That taking me forcibly from a bus on my way into work might have been the teensiest bit traumatic?" My voice raised and other patrons turned to look at us.

A waiter hurried over. Ghalib soothed him in Italian and the waiter gave me a wary look. I couldn't have possibly cared less.

"Yes," Ghalib said when the waiter left. "I did think of those things."

"I have a sister. She's four months pregnant. She probably worried sick."

"Rachel. Yes."

"But because you wanted me, none of that mattered."

"Perhaps 'want' wasn't a strong enough word."

The waiter came back and filled our wine glasses. Ghalib spoke to him again. He nodded and left.

"Send me home," I said.

Ghalib's jaw set; his lips pursed. "No."

We just looked at each other — me glaring and he determined. He wasn't even touching me. We weren't in his strange dream world. But still, the pulsing current throbbed around me, like the air was charged. He reached across the table and I moved my hands away. A flash of annoyance flickered over his features.

I ignored it. "That woman. Nyx's proxy or whatever. What did she mean when she said that I would have to be shared?"

He hesitated. When he spoke, I could tell he was choosing his words carefully. "I've been keeping you at my home, not telling other Architects about you. In this specific case, that is not allowed. Soon, I'll have to give other Architects the chance to get to know you."

My heart sped up. Adrenaline tingled to the tips of my fingers. Although Ghalib had taken me and held me against my will, he hadn't forced me to do anything else, aside from wearing a dress. These other Architects? Would they be so respectful? I remembered how Nyx's proxy had called me a poor child.

"You look frightened," he said.

"Should I be?"

He considered for a moment. "Yes, Elaine. I think you should."

The waiter interrupted, laying plates of steaming food in front of us. I had been hungry but I wasn't anymore. Instead, I reached for my wineglass and gulped half of it.

"There is an alternative to being shared," Ghalib said once the waiter had left. "You could allow me to claim you."

I waited. He knew perfectly well that I wouldn't know what that meant.

"You would become mine," he continued. "No one would be able to touch you without my permission."

"No," I said automatically.

He flinched but then his face resumed its impassive, unemotional veneer. "As you like. In three cycles, you'll pass to another Architect, stay in their home, and live on their hospitality."

He started to eat and I forced myself to as well. My stomach was in knots. Before long, I was hardly doing more than pushing food around my plate.

"Tell me your thoughts," he said.

I looked up. His face was soft with concern. Emotion welled and threatened to make me cry. I forced it back down. "I was wondering what it would be like to be claimed." The words came out in a rush. "Like slavery? Like being a prostitute?"

"We call claimed humans 'pets'," he said. My stomach twisted and I gave up on food altogether, reaching for my wine again. "Would you like a chance to see how it is for other humans?" he asked.

His eyes were intense. I couldn't hold them. "What do you mean?"

"There's a gala tomorrow night. Architects attend with their humans. We could go." His tone was deceptively light. I could tell from the way he was leaning forward, that he wanted me to say yes.

"I don't want to go to a gala. I want to go home." The minute the words were out of my mouth, I was ashamed of them. I sounded like a child.

"I'm sorry, Elaine. That isn't going to happen. The sooner you accept that, the easier things are going to go for you."

"Why? It's not as if I could call the police on you. It's not as if I could do anything to you. I couldn't even stop you from coming to see me, if you insisted."

He pulled his chair around the small, round table and lifted his hand to touch me. I shied away but he would have none of it this time. He slipped his fingers into the hair at the base of my braid. The electricity pulsed around me; heat flew to my cheeks. My stomach stopped churning and a pulse between my legs kept rhythm with my accelerating heart. He tilted my face until we were eye-to-eye.

"Do you feel that?"

"Yes," I breathed. "What is it?"

His thumb stroked down my neck and I couldn't hold back a tiny whimper. "It's the reason why you can't go home, Elaine. It's the reason why you must be shared." He drew his fingers down the back of my neck and up again. I had the terrifying impulse to lean into his hand, increase his contact. I couldn't pull away, the best I could manage was staying as still as a rabbit. He brushed his thumb across my lips. I made another small sound and a faint, intense smile played on his lips. He leaned into me, his breath against my ear even as his fingers continued to stroke my neck. "You're a very gifted human." His lips brushed my cheek and I shivered.

A quick burst of Italian to our left made me jump. I pulled away from his hand, from the warm flood of sensation infusing me. We both looked up. It was a woman in a tight black dress with a low neckline. Her olive skin was velvet and flawless, and her bold, handsome face was framed by a bob of silken, black hair. Her eyes were black as ink and directed only at Ghalib. She spoke again, smiling, revealing a bewitching dimple.

He responded to her in Italian, looking amused as she leaned over the table to whisper something in his ear. His amusement twisted into something no less amused but much more malicious. He spoke more Italian, his low soft voice making the language sound like a song to me. Her dimple disappeared but his expression didn't change. She stood upright and he elevated an eyebrow at her, speaking briefly once more. She paled and backed away. When she turned and walked away, she threw him a fearful look over her shoulder.

"What was that all about?" I asked.

He paused for a moment, considering me. Then he grinned. "She said that I was wasting my time on an Ingénue, like you. She thought you looked a little innocent."

"Innocent?" I said, surprised. A woman in her thirties didn't get tagged with the term 'innocent' all that often.

His eyes burnt. "Is she wrong?" he asked, his voice delicately sly. "You're not innocent?"

"I thought you knew all about me," I replied, meeting his gaze with a challenge of my own.

"I might have exaggerated a little about the extent of my knowledge." He tilted his head. "I still have things to learn."

I lifted my chin. "I'll answer your questions when you answer mine."

He chuckled. "Fair enough. She said that if I was willing, she would give me a night to remember. She wanted me to go home with her. She said that I should be with someone that I don't have to woo. Of course, I'm omitting some of the more explicit description of what she wanted to do."

"Is that what you're doing? Wooing me?" I asked.

His gaze lingered on my face and, for the first time, a flush came into his cheeks. "I'm not sure that's the word I would have used."

"What word would you use?"

He grinned and ignored my question. "So, would you describe yourself as innocent?"

How do I answer something like that? It wasn't as if I was a virgin. It was true, though, that my experience was very, very limited. I lost my virginity in high school. But that was before my parents died, before Rachel became my responsibility, before dating became something low on my list of priorities. After Rachel went to college, I tried a couple of relationships. Of course sex was involved. And, in retrospect, it was probably the best part. But, all in all, I could count my sexual partners on one hand.

I struggled to come up with acceptable answer. "No," I finally said. "Not innocent. Inexperienced."

Ghalib cocked his head. "Intriguing."

The waiter saved me from further conversation, which had taken a turn that I wasn't sure I liked. He brought more wine and cheese which I picked at as I pondered the woman—her darkness, Ghalib's lightness, her forcefulness with him. Here was a woman who would have gone willingly with him if he had hijacked her bus. Not knowing who or what he was, she would have gone.

"You're lost in thought," he broke in, the teasing note back in his voice. I looked up, startled. "You're thinking of that woman," he said with uncanny accuracy.

My flush returned. "I was wondering why you told her no."

"How do you know that I did?"

It was my turn to smile. "Please, Ghalib. I may not speak Italian but I can read body language. Women don't look like that when they get a... favorable reply."

His expression transitioned into something chilling. I was almost sorry that I had asked. "You're right. I wasn't feeling as vindictive as

I sometimes do. She had no idea what she was offering me or what I do to women like her."

A chill of fear and an unexpected surge of arousal struggled for mastery within me, leaving me a little breathless. "Tell me," I said.

He glanced to the side, as if he was considering his words. He also seemed to relish this topic. "She enjoys conquest. But a woman like her could never conquer a creature like me." His intensity increased, like he enjoyed thinking of the possibilities. "Still, it can be amusing to play." He looked at me directly. "Amusing for me, you understand. Not for her."

I met his eyes. "If that's what you do to women like her, what do you do to women like me?"

I had hoped that his smile would wane, but if anything, it widened. "That's hardly a question that I can answer in a single evening, Elaine." His voice lilted with a taunt. "That's a question that could take years for me to answer."

His eyes darkened with meaning. I caught my breath and felt a tremor run through me that wouldn't stop. Instinctively, I reached for my wine glass, ignoring my shaking hands, and forced down the liquid, willing myself to calm down.

"Something wrong?" he asked with a smooth tone.

"You would have hurt that woman," I said, the warmth from the wine giving me strength. "Why would I ever allow myself to be claimed by you?"

"Because I want to do very different things to you," he said, his voice gentler. "Things you'll enjoy. Things you'll beg me to do again."

A flush stung my cheeks. "Stop," I said, looking away.

"Do you think I can't?" he pushed. "Or are you afraid that I can?"

"Please, just stop."

He tilted his head and studied me. Then, he scooted his chair back. "We should return home before you're completely exhausted." When he said it, I noticed that he was right. My body was tired and my brain didn't want to work anymore.

He led me out of the restaurant and around to the back, where there was an alley. I heard the cracking, peeling sound again and the city melted around me. In another moment, his mansion appeared in the distance, surrounded by his bending trees. He took my arm and steered me back to the entryway where Jason stood waiting. Idly, I wondered if he had just stood there all night.

"See her to her room," Ghalib commanded.

I let Jason lead me and before I knew it I was standing in front of my door. "Good night, Miss," Jason said.

"Good night, Jason."

I changed my clothes and paced the front room. My situation had gone from bad to terrifying. More Architects? Being shared? Living in a dimension outside of the normal world? Being propositioned by this strange, beautiful creature. My heart thundered on and I knew there was no way that I was going to really sleep.

I couldn't stay still for long. I let myself out of my room again to wander the halls. I wasn't shocked when the hallway dropped me into the darkened hallway where the workshop was located. I was wondering if this mansion would always take me to the workshop when I left my room. Or would it take me to where Ghalib was? Or was it like lucid dreaming—you just had to learn how to control it?

I crept up to the door and peeked through the crack. For a moment I wasn't sure what I was seeing. Then, my mind sorted the lines and angles, the stone and flesh. Ghalib was naked, pressed to the statue of me, holding her in the middle of the room. Her stone arms were around him; his hands traced the curves of her flesh-less body. Her hands played over him, too.

I didn't know whether to be horrified or to acknowledge the throbbing insistence at the sight. It was twisted. It was odd. And somehow, it was erotic. He was gentler with the facsimile of me than he had been with the very real Alexis. I could imagine his hands tracing my body this way and the sizzling electricity it would cause. I tried to push the arousal away, but it wouldn't go.

Finally, I backed away and wandered the hallways for a bit longer. I walked past my room. I walked past the darkened hallway. I didn't go anywhere new. When I was too tired to walk another step, I let myself into my suite, settled myself on the couch in the study, and tried to imagine myself in my small apartment at home. Eventually, I fell asleep.

Chapter 7

A Dangerous Game

I couldn't have been asleep for more than a couple of hours when a sound brought me straight up off of the couch. At first, I thought I must have been dreaming but I couldn't remember a single dream I'd had since the kidnapping. Which, actually, was a blessed relief since there was a fair chance that I could run into the players at any time.

No, it was a woman's voice that woke me. It was growing fainter, but I could still hear it. "No! Please! I didn't mean any harm!"

The desperation in that voice spurred me to my feet. I hurried into slippers and a robe. Then, I entered the hallway and listened. I thought I heard voices to my right, so I followed that hall. It wound and turned. There were steps and more steps. And finally, I came to a stairwell that seemed to go straight down. I recognized them; the steps that went to the center of the earth. The prison. The very last place I wanted to go in this house. But then I heard the woman cry out again and I hurried forward.

At the bottom of the steps, the ginger guard named Carl stood in front of the door. Joan was nowhere in sight. "You need some help?" he asked.

"What's happening in there?" I asked. A woman yelled and I jumped. "It woke me up," I added.

"Ghalib's dealing with a servant. You shouldn't worry yourself about it." He looked me up and down and offered me a lecherous smile. "You want to keep me company?" he asked.

Another cry sounded from within the prison. "What did she do?" I asked.

He shrugged as if it hardly mattered.

"Can I go in?" I asked. I wasn't sure why I wanted to. Morbid curiosity? More incentive to hate Ghalib?

"I don't know if that's the best plan, Sweet—"

The heavy door opened and Jason poked his head through. "*Who* are you talking to?" He spotted me and his eyes widened. "Miss?"

"I heard yelling," I said.

"And I'll talk to whoever I please. Tell Ghalib I'm not one of his servant lackeys. I may work here but I don't work *for* him. Understand?"

Jason hadn't heard a word of Carl's speech. He looked at me and I could see the gears in his head turning. Finally Jason pushed the door a bit wider. "Come in, Miss," he said. "Hurry."

Carl protested but I slipped through the door and closed it behind me. A woman cried out; it sent shivers over me. Jason walked faster and I trotted in my slippers to keep up. The smells were just as terrible as I remembered. The sounds were worse. I took care not to look to the right, where dreamers gasped and moaned and begged in their cells. Nor did I look to the left where spirits did their slow motion sprint, their eyes fixed on the endless hallway.

A light shone ahead of us. We headed straight for it. When we reached the illuminated cell, I blinked twice. A naked woman hung from the ceiling, her wrists bound in shackles. She was familiar and beautiful: Asian and young with a long heavy sheet of black hair. She stood on tip-toe to relieve the tension on her wrists. Her pearly skin was coated in sweat. Her nipples were clamped and a chain ran between the clamps. Joan was in the cell with the girl. The guard hung a weight on the chain and the girl cried out.

Ghalib leaned against the wall on the inside of the cell and watched. "Did you find out who Carl was talking to?" Ghalib asked without looking over.

"He was talking to me," I said, wrapping my fingers around the bars, looking at the way the girl's small breasts were painfully stretched. "

"Elaine?" Ghalib said, finally turning to us.

The poor tortured girl looked at me, too, and it finally struck me how I knew her. She had been one of the servants on the night Ghalib gave me my voice back. "Why are you hurting her?" I asked, finding the door to the cell and opening it. I went to the girl and lifted the weights from her breasts. She moaned.

"Hey, Ghalib," Joan protested. "Do you want me to teach this little snoop a lesson, or not?"

"Hold on," Ghalib said, standing and moving towards me. He looked at the girl. "Lisa, my dear, would you like to tell Elaine why you're here?"

The girl, Lisa, looked over my shoulder to Jason then back to me. "Just because I wanted to meet you," she said with a hitch.

"Me?"

"I was curious. I knew it was forbidden but I n-never met an Om—"

"That's enough," Ghalib interrupted softly, but with stern command. "It wasn't quite that innocent, was it? Shall I show her? Look up," he commanded Lisa, a harsh quality to his beautiful voice. When she looked up, he laid his palm on her head, his thumb on her temple. "Elaine, close your eyes and try to relax," he said to me, repeating the gesture on my head.

A flash of light blinded my eyes. Electric current ran through my body, making my fingers tingle. Suddenly, my vision left me. I saw only blackness and I jumped back with a jolt of panic. "Relax," Ghalib said. It was like his lips were right next to my ear. I took a deep breath and waited.

The darkness lifted like someone had turned up the brightness on a television. I was in the room where Ghalib and I had eaten dinner on the night Lisa had served us. Two people came into focus. Lisa and—oh good lord—me. Me in the wine colored gown and she in Ghalib's tux. She kissed me and I responded, sliding my hands under her jacket, slipping it off of her shoulders. She let it fall to the floor and pushed me backwards, still kissing me, urging me to sit on the table. Her hands went behind me, releasing the zipper, helping the bodice away from my torso. She slipped her hands under the top of the dress, pulling it down, her fingers teasing over my exposed nipples, her kisses smothering my moans. My heart started to race and my breath grew ragged. The electricity I felt whenever Ghalib touched me turned into a throbbing, aching need.

What was I seeing? Her plans for me? Her fantasy? Her desire?

The vision wasn't finished. She pushed my gown up over my knees, over my thighs, nudging my legs apart. Her kisses didn't stop and neither did her hands as they caressed the inside of my legs, slipping up under my gown. My back arched and I drew my knees up. She gave me one last kiss and fell on her knees.

"Please stop this," I managed to whisper. Instantly the image was withdrawn, but not before I saw Lisa's head disappear under my gown. Ghalib took his hand from my head and the blood rushed to my face. I stumbled to my feet and staggered to the prison bars, forcing myself to breathe in the foul air. The throbbing hadn't stopped when I moved away from Lisa and Ghalib. Suddenly, I had the inexplicable urge to offer myself to Ghalib. If he would take me against the wall, right here, right now and rid me of this growing need. I pressed my cold fingers to my hot face and tried to calm down.

I turned to Ghalib, letting anger substitute for lust. "You're deplorable. She's just a child and you're going to torture her in this awful place for what? Having thoughts about me?"

"Not for her thoughts," Ghalib said. "But for her actions. She was trying to find your room." An amused tone crept into his voice. "I care only about your virtue, Elaine."

"What nonsense," I said, carefully unclamping the clips on Lisa's nipples. Though I tried to be gentle, she whimpered.

"Don't let him leave me here, Miss," Lisa whispered. "I wouldn't have taken liberties. I swear."

I looked over to Ghalib who had clearly heard the full exchange. He lifted an eyebrow, as if to ask what I intended to do. I looked back to Lisa. "I can't do anything," I said. "I can't even free myself."

"Ask him," she begged, looking at Ghalib. "Please. You saved Jason." Her voice lowered until I could barely hear it. "They haven't even started with what they intend to do to me. Please."

I turned to Ghalib. "If I ask nicely, will you spare her?"

"You don't want her to be punished?" Ghalib asked quietly, his voice tinged with cunning. He was finally showing some emotion, watching me with an intense expression like my answer was critical.

I faced him, meeting those eyes that seemed to emit their own light. "She didn't do anything."

He cocked his head. A smile played on his lips for the first time since I entered the prison. It was like Lisa had disappeared and the prison had faded. There was only the interaction between us. A chill of fear flashed over me but I held eye contact.

"I do have a weakness for your charity," he said, walking at a stroll towards me. His predatory tone was turned on me — and something more. Something my mind kept struggling to understand. He stopped before me. "Perhaps we could come to an agreement."

"You already have something in mind," I said in a low voice, never looking away. His smile deepened.

"Many things, actually." There was something different about him. A reserve, a restraint that I had only vaguely recognized had been lifted. What remained was even more raw, more intense, more magnetic than before. He was teasing me, testing me. It was like he was inviting me to play a game with him.

"Tell me," I replied.

"Tonight, when we go to the gala, I want a companion. Not a prisoner. Not an unwilling, frightened victim who demurs as much as she dare — " He paused for a moment to let his meaning be clear. "I want you, Elaine, to make me believe that you are willing to be my escort tonight. Dress to please me, do as I ask and I'll be lenient with Lisa." He was so close that I had to look up to see into his face. He was daring me. He wanted, very badly, for me to accept. I knew it. I knew it as surely as I knew Lisa begged me with her eyes where she hung and that Jason had edged a step closer. Ghalib looked me up and down in my robe and slippers, sending heat through me. The throbbing hadn't really stopped after the vision and, now, it was growing even more distracting. "Such a difficult decision," he commented with a teasing tone.

"If I agree, and you ask something of me that I can't or won't do, what happens?" I asked.

His expression was already triumphant, like I had already agreed. "You can always refuse me. The evening will be over and Lisa will remain here." He could hardly have moved closer, yet somehow, his influence seemed to grow stronger. The pull towards him was impossible to ignore and, given my current heightened state, nearly impossible to resist. "Do we have a deal, Elaine?"

"No," I replied, taking my turn at the game. He drew back a fraction and looked slightly surprised. I couldn't help but feel some pleasure at his reaction. "It occurs to me that in this deal, I am the only person making a sacrifice and I am the only person getting no reward."

He cocked his head, as if he was, once again, amused. "I see that now *you* have something in mind."

"I want Lisa," I said, seeing the jealousy spark on his face. "I want her to bring me food and keep me company." The truth was that I missed my sister and this young serving girl reminded me of her a little. Not that I would have admitted that to anyone. "Understand," I continued, turning to Lisa, relieved at the excuse to break eye contact with Ghalib. "I'm not interested in your fantasies about me and if you behave in any way inappropriately, I'll see you back in the cell myself." I returned to Ghalib. "I would like a companion."

His predatory smile returned and he looked more stimulated than I had ever seen him. "You are a surprise every day, Elaine. Very well. I think that can be arranged." I noticed that he didn't bother to ask Lisa. Neither did I. It was a bit of a comfort to know that someone had less control over their own fate than I did. "Do we have a deal, now?"

"We do."

Lisa' whispered, "Thank you, Miss."

"Don't thank me yet," I replied. "I'm hardly the obedient type. There's every possibility that I could fail miserably." I saw her stricken face. I sighed. "I will try."

"Tonight, when the evening is over, we will come down together and give the news to Lisa." Ghalib turned to Joan. "Nobody touches this one until tomorrow at light, or they will answer to me." Joan didn't look very pleased at the command, but she nodded.

He led me out of the cell and the door closed with a clang. I heard Lisa's muted sob behind me from where she still hung from the shackles. "Could you at least let her down?" I asked.

"Shall I have her brought caviar, too," Ghalib taunted.

"Let's just go, Miss," Jason said, offering his arm. It was as if he wanted to get me away from Ghalib before I asked for too much.

Ghalib delayed me with his electric touch on my robe. "I'll see you tonight," he said. There was something intense about his tone, something more than the usual, that made my breath stop. I didn't answer. I just let Jason lead me away.

As we walked back to my rooms, Jason ventured in a low voice, "What you are doing for Lisa is very kind."

"What I am doing for Lisa is very foolish," I retorted. "What on Earth am I thinking, making deals with Ghalib?" I turned to give Jason a stern look. "You really must stop telling people about what I did for you. He isn't going to let me get out of this by serenading him, like last time."

Jason's face gained some color, despite his apparent age. "I'm afraid that word has gotten around. You must understand, Miss, the Master's punishments are, well, you've seen the prison. And that isn't the end of it. Sometimes he sees to you himself." He looked around nervously, like he knew he had already said too much. "Until now, nobody has ever been spared once he has made the decision to discipline."

"Until I bargained for you?"

He lowered his head. "Yes. That was the first time."

"I can't save everyone. I'm nothing more than a prisoner here, myself."

We arrived at my door. "I think we both know that's not true, Miss. And not everyone deserves your help. Lisa does."

I sighed. "I guess we're going to see what I can do." I went inside. Already there were changes. The clutter had been cleared. And, more disturbingly, clothes had been laid out on my bed. A golden gown, more elaborate than the one I had rejected the first night with a boned hoop slip, to make getting through doorways utterly impossible. Oh goodie. And it wasn't just the dress, strapless and embroidered with glittering gems. There were white gloves with a golden shimmer, gold shoes, and an ornament for my hair.

I went into the sitting room and lay on the couch there, more tired than I had been before. But I couldn't nap. I couldn't stop thinking. Would I be able to do as he asked? To pretend that I wanted to be his companion, to be the type of company he craved? I hardly even knew what that meant. Last night, when we had been in the restaurant, talking about the Italian woman, he had seemed to enjoy the repartee. In the prison when I had engaged in his little games, he had practically glowed.

Perhaps he just liked the challenge. If I could accept the throbbing heat every time he touched me, somehow be a tantalizing companion and yet parry his advances, he might be content with that. He might even enjoy the sport. Something was whispering that I was on the right track and I took a deep breath.

I had never even tried to do anything like this before. I wasn't a tease. I wasn't a social butterfly. Often, I had trouble keeping up my end of a fairly mundane conversation. But I would make an effort.

I got up and went into the bathroom, trying not to look at the gold dress. I was starting to get used to this routine: curl my hair, pin it up on my head, apply my makeup, put on my undergarments, and, finally, the gown and gloves, adding the hair ornament as an after-thought. When I looked at myself in the mirror, I shook my head. It was like I was going to some elaborate prom. The gown even had a short train. Ugh.

I went into the sitting room, but I didn't sit. I was too nervous and it felt like the gown was too big for the tiny chairs. I just paced and waited, walking into the study, fingering the books, and back out to the sitting room where there was less to look at. Keep your chin up. Keep your back straight. Treat him like any other date. Play hard-to-get where you can and maybe try some humor. Easy.

Not easy.

My stomach rolled under the gold silk. I couldn't relax. I don't know if I was relieved or not when I heard the rap at my door.

Jason was speechless at the sight of me. I could almost have laughed if it hadn't been so serious. I gave him a tight smile and moved towards him, but my train got caught on one of the chairs. "Here, Miss," he said, hurrying forward, "let me help you."

The train had a gold loop that I hadn't noticed before that he slid over my gloved wrist. It made moving easier but the skirt was still a challenge.

"I'm going to break my neck," I said, taking Jason's arm.

"Just go slowly," Jason advised. "The Master will certainly ac-commodate you tonight."

He took measured steps and I tried not to stumble. The path to the tiled foyer seemed shorter than I remembered. Or, maybe it was because I was in the elaborate dress and the mansion was giving me a break. Who knew? I could make out a form standing in the window, even from a distance. It had to be Ghalib. I could see his silver hair. And his figure was unmistakable—powerful, languid, and impossibly graceful. "Is it too late to change my mind?" I whispered, only half in jest.

"I think he's seen you," Jason whispered back. And he had. Where he had been leaning against the wall, he was now standing expectantly. I took a deep breath and squared my shoulders.

Chapter 8
Festival of Pets: Useful Talents

"Good evening," I said. Ghalib stepped forward. I hoped to disarm some of that hungry intensity that radiated off of him. It didn't work.

He inclined his head politely but his eyes were anything but polite. They swept over me in a slow, deliberate way, not bothering to shield his desire. This might be a little more challenging than I thought.

"Good evening, Elaine," he said, striding over to me. He took both of my gloved hands in his, still managing to send a muted throb through me, and looked me over again. "Turn around for me," he commanded, his voice musical and assured.

I flushed but obeyed as gracefully as I could, holding up my head. After one slow turn, I faced Ghalib again and held his gaze. "Have I forgotten anything?" I asked, letting a teasing note come into my voice.

His lips curled into a smile. "Not a thing. Except...." He held his hand out and on it was a necklace. Well, something like a necklace. It was supple gold, studded with gems that matched my dress, filigree, and more than two inches tall. It looked to be half choker and half....

"Is that a collar?" I asked.

Ghalib didn't blink and he had a determined set to his jaw. "Yes. It is necessary for the gala." He waited for me to take it, almost daring me to decline.

I lifted it out of his hand, looked at it, and glanced back up at him. I didn't want to put it on, but I could tell I was going to have to unless I planned to give up on Lisa. Tease him, I reminded myself. Play the game. "Lovely," I said. It wasn't as convincing as I would have liked, but Ghalib looked amused. The collar parted like a bangle bracelet at the back and I bent the gold so that I could slip my neck into it. The metal warmed against my skin and seemed to shrink to fit me. He took a step closer to me and ran his finger over the filigree, making me hold my breath against the sensation.

"Your first time in a collar, I assume?" he whispered.

I didn't see a point in lying to him. "Yes. You introduce me to yet another first." His face shone with wild delight. I wasn't even playing his game very well and already he seemed pleased.

But too much contact, too much time in his proximity was going to leave my head swimming. I struggled to think of something to say. "So, we're going to a gala where Architects and pets go together?"

"Yes. It's a ball, of sorts, called the Festival of Pets."

I went cold and struggled not to lower my eyes. "Catchy name," I managed.

He chuckled. "Don't be frightened. You are wearing my collar, which will tell everyone there that, for tonight at least, you belong to an Architect. Pets also have leashes, which will distinguish you from them. For your own protection, I would suggest that you not wander off."

"Of course not," I said. Was he kidding? I was going to be glued to his side.

"This would be a very bad place to campaign for your freedom, misbehave, or embarrass me. I'm not just talking about Lisa's future, Elaine." His voice was edged with warning.

"I understand."

"Under no circumstances are you to remove your gloves unless I tell you to."

That surprised me a little. "I won't," I said.

"Shall we go?" he said.

"Wait," I said in a low voice. I decided to take another shot at playing this game he seemed to enjoy so much. The collar of his tux was turned up in the back and I smoothed it with my gloved fingers. I brushed a silvery strand of hair off of his shoulder. "There."

I withdrew my hand but he captured it with his own. "I could grow accustomed to this level of attentiveness."

"I wouldn't advise that," I answered without thinking, flashing an amused smile of my own. Where was this coming from? It felt like if I didn't fight the throbbing current when I was near him, it would guide me. It would tell me what he wanted and how best to deal with him. But it was a double-edged sword. It also left me breathlessly aroused.

"Are we ready now?" he asked, taking my other hand. I nodded and before I realized what was happening, the entrance hall melted around me. A new scene sprung up around me, leaving my head swimming for a moment. We were outside of another mansion, this one shorter and built with heavier material than Ghalib's; it almost looked like a fort. The bitter wind tore against my gown and stung my skin, snow swirled in the air. Light shone through the windows of the mansion and couples entered through the open front doors up on a sprawling veranda.

"Ready?" he asked.

"As much as I'll ever be."

He smirked. "Let's go inside."

Ghalib led me up the wide stairs, a hand on my back, and into the entry hall. It was easily as large as Ghalib's and blessedly warm. A fireplace, large enough to stand up inside, blazed with a huge fire that warmed the whole area.

A tall, dark-haired gentleman with silver at his temples walked over to us. His face was obscured, shadowed no matter how the light hit him. I couldn't make out expressions or features. It was the strangest thing that I had ever seen. "Ghalib. What a surprise. I can't remember the last time you came to my little affair. Introduce me to your companion."

Ghalib inclined his head and accepted his hand, a small, amused smile on his lips. "Victor, this is Elaine. Elaine," he said, turning to me, "this is our host, Lord Victor." I knew the name Victor. I couldn't place it but I remembered hearing it before.

He offered his hand and I shook it. To my surprise, I felt a weak current of electricity pass between us, through my glove.

Victor froze but Ghalib didn't give him long to analyze the sensation. "Where is your lovely Selma?" Ghalib asked.

"She misbehaved today," Victor said. His words were steeped in annoyance. "It was as if she knew it was the worst possible time to distract me and conspired to do precisely that. She's in the tower, awaiting her punishment." He still hadn't let go of my hand.

"How frustrating," Ghalib said with gentle emphasis; his amused smile was touched with a hint of cruelty. He leaned closer to Victor. "Do you need help with her discipline? I could return later tonight, if you like...."

Victor's breath quickened. "Certainly. It would be an honor." I suddenly remembered where I had heard Victor's name. Ghalib had suggested him to Alexis when they were having sex.

I flushed. Victor still held my gloved hand. The muted energy pulsed between us. He didn't seem to be conscious of it, but our contact affected him: his breathing hadn't slowed and his hand tightened on mine.

"I think we'll move along into the dining hall," Ghalib said. "That is, if you'll release Elaine."

Victor let go of my hand like it was hot. "My apologies," he said. "Until later."

Ghalib grinned and laid his hand on my back. He cast one look back at Victor as he led me down a corridor to a huge set of double doors. He rapped twice with his knuckles and the door swung open.

Dozens of Architects accompanied mortals in collars and leashes. The Architects—men and women—all inexplicably beautiful, held slim chains that hung slack between them and their pets. Every Architect wore formal dress, in gowns or tuxedos. The pets ran the entire spectrum, however. Some wore tuxedos and gowns; others were less dressed. Most glittered with gems. I saw creamy, pale skin, and golden tans; shoulders as dark as polished mahogany and beautiful, smoky complexions. Most of the pets were skillfully manicured, their skin and hair glistening under the candle light.

Ghalib moved forward but my legs wouldn't respond. He turned with an annoyed expression, saw my face and his annoyance faded. "Quite a sight, isn't it?" he asked, sliding his hand up from the small of my back, which was covered by the gown, to my bare shoulder. The jolt of throbbing energy almost made me jump. My lips parted and my breath came faster. His fingers stroked my skin and the sensation magnified. "Shall we go in?"

The sizzling need coursed through me, making my skin tingle. My guard was down. I didn't know, until then, that I had been resisting this strange, urging sensation. The second I let go, the second I didn't try to fend off the feeling, it turned into a warm current. It coursed through me, whispering to me about the people in the room. The very tall brunette liked to wear a strap-on, a large one, and penetrate her pet while she stroked his penis. The man in the corner fellated his pet so often that the poor boy was having trouble keeping up. And the woman standing next to the redhead....

"Yes," I said, standing up very straight and surveying the Architects. He led me into the room and off to one side, a little apart from the other couples. Sexual desire seemed to swirl in the air. Their eyes were hungry and they coveted each other's pets. The secret knowledge of their desire gave me a voyeuristic pleasure.

Ghalib slid his hand down to the small of my back again. "Your face is positively glowing," he commented.

"Would you —" I flushed but decided to push ahead. "Would you touch my skin again?" I asked. He narrowed his eyes at me, looking intrigued. "Please," I added. A predatory look came to his face, but he controlled it.

He placed his fingertips lightly on my shoulder and warmth flooded through me. "That one there," I said, nodding at a male Architect with his male pet. "His pet likes to be the one in charge. He doesn't really prefer it but he allows it."

Ghalib stared at me. "How do you know that?"

I shook my head. "And that one," I said, nodding at a brunette Architect with her Asian girl, "she chose that girl because she can put her legs behind her head. Just that one skill was all she was looking for."

His fingers traced soft lines over my shoulder. "You are the most intriguing mortal I've ever met," he said. "What an enlightening talent." His eyes burnt into me and his magnetism tugged on me.

A deep voice rumbled next to Ghalib. "I don't believe it." The Architect who stood over us was a bald man, his head like polished onyx. He smelled like cut grass and autumn air. "I couldn't be more surprised to see anyone at this affair than you," he said to Ghalib. "And I couldn't be more pleased, my friend. Introduce me to the girl who makes you think long-term." His smile was so infectious, I couldn't help but smile back.

"This is Elaine," Ghalib said.

"Elaine," the man said, lifting my gloved hand in his massive one and kissing it. The shiver of electricity pulsed through my glove but it almost immediately turned warm and pleasing. It was so calm and so lovely, I hated to let go of his hand. "Congratulations on pinning down this serial philanderer."

It was my turn to look amused. I turned to Ghalib. "You're a philanderer?"

His cheeks flushed just a hint. "Recovering."

"I'm Markus," the huge bald Architect said. "This is my Tobias."

"My pleasure," I said.

Markus lifted a huge iron chain with links the size of my fist. A large blond man stepped forward. The chain attached to an iron collar that ringed his neck like a shackle. But, clearly, he was strong enough to wear it well. Broad-chested, and heavily muscled, he offered me a full-lipped smile.

Markus stepped closer to Ghalib. "Every year this affair grows larger. I wonder if keeping pets has become a fad."

"If so, I pity the mortals," Ghalib replied.

I glanced at Tobias who was watching me. I wondered where he was from; the pet looked like some sort of sun god, his skin bronze, his hair golden. 'New?' he mouthed to me. I quickly nodded. His smile was slow—almost lazy.

Ghalib watched Tobias smiling at me. "We should greet some of the other guests," Ghalib said with a hint of jealousy. He turned to Markus. "You and I should get together soon."

"Agreed, my friend."

Ghalib touched my shoulder again and the heat flooded through me. "Come, my dear, let's take a seat before they serve dinner."

Through the crowd, I had hardly noticed the U-shaped table covered in a pale yellow tablecloth and set with gold-edged china. He guided me to the top of the U, but before we could sit, a stately, blond Architect, a woman who held the leash to her red-headed pet, lightly approached us.

The Architect was like a carving of Aphrodite and her pet could have been a titian model. A triple layer of pearls encircled her neck, a pearl leash attached her to her Architect, and she wore the costume with a proud mien. Adoring glances passed between the two women and the red-head seemed to bask in her confinement.

"Anna," Ghalib said, delight entering his voice. He leaned over to kiss her. "I'm so glad to see you. I've been meaning to have you over for dinner. You and your charming Julia." He nodded to the pet, who flushed and curtsied.

"I had no idea that you had taken a companion," Anna said, looking at me with curiosity. "What a pleasant surprise."

"Elaine," Ghalib said, "this is an old friend. Anna and her pet, Julia. You must kiss them hello to please me."

I blushed, more attracted to both of the women than I wanted to admit. Ghalib's fingers were still against my skin and I knew that these two delighted in the pleasure of sex. Nightly, they basked in the joy of each other's ecstasy. The energy around them was so pleasing I gave Julia an impulsive little squeeze when she leaned in to kiss my lips.

When Anna bent to kiss me, when her lips touched mine, color exploded behind my eyes. Heat suffused me. Even though we were only in contact for a second, my mind flashed with images. Julia tied to a bed, teased with feathers. Anna straddling her face, her fine, slender legs trembling. Anna pulled away from me, her lips open, her blue eyes wide.

"Who is this girl?" Anna breathed.

Ghalib had a sly, secretive smile. He brought his fingers to his own lips and winked at her.

"Are you mad? Bringing her here without a leash?" she whispered.

"It's not by my choice that she isn't leashed."

Anna's eyes widened. She turned to me. "You haven't refused him, have you?"

I flushed hotly and Julia giggled. I saw both Anna and Ghalib shoot her a stern look, but she didn't notice. "I have two cycles left to change her mind," Ghalib offered. "I thought maybe you and Julia would come over, help me convince her."

I felt ambushed. "Ghalib—"

"Hush," he said.

"Of course we will," Anna said. "Julia and I will be delighted." She gave Ghalib a conspirators smile. "May I...."

Ghalib's smile widened. "You wish to touch her?"

Anna's eyes were drawn to me, though I could see that she was trying to be polite. "If you wouldn't mind."

Ghalib's fingers played on my back. "Would you remove a glove for Anna, my dear?" Ghalib asked.

I felt a little like I was being whored out but I drew off my right glove and held out my hand. Anna stepped forward, her eyes glowing, and pressed it to her cheek. Heat flowed up and down my arm and her face flushed a beautiful pink. "Thank you," she said, her eyes flickering between Ghalib and me. Even though I wasn't sure what was going on, I smiled at her.

"You're very welcome," Ghalib said. "I will contact you soon about a more private get-together. But for now, we must take our seats. I'm afraid that all of the excitement will wear out Elaine and our evening is barely half over."

He pulled out my chair and I sank into it, unaware of how much the evening had drained me already. With his fingers removed from my back, I could relax a little more. I looked at the beautiful China and admired the chandelier over our heads. I enjoyed the surrounding so well, it was several minutes before I noticed that Ghalib had been silent. I turned and saw him surveying me with interest.

"Why is it that you never seem so impressed with the décor at my home?" he asked.

"Because I'm deceitful," I replied honestly.

He chuckled. "Are you? Well, I would like it very much if you would speak candidly with me now." I nodded slowly, feeling a chill creep over me but making sure my face remained unchanged. He leaned closer. "You know of my preferences for toying with aggressive women. I would like to hear about what tempts you. Beautiful women? Powerful men? Ropes and chains? Moonlight and rose petals?"

"That's hardly fair," I responded, my tone much lighter than how I was feeling. "You haven't told me what tempts you. Only what amuses you."

He smiled darkly. "I would think that my temptations would be perfectly obvious." He let his eyes slide over me until the heat came to my face.

I lowered my face but his fingers immediately went under my chin, lifting it again.

"I haven't really explored my..." I struggled to find the right word. My face stung like it was sunburned. "Options."

"Men?" he pressed.

"A few."

"Women?"

"No, never."

"Games? Costumes? Positions?"

I lowered my eyes again and this time he let me. "No games. No costumes. Mostly, just—you know—regular positions."

"Oh, Elaine," he said, tracing a finger around the curve of my ear. Shivers and shocks raced through me. "What a shame."

"Why a shame?" I asked. "It's not like sex was ever bad."

"No?" he asked. "Just normal, average—"

"Normal doesn't have to mean average." He just looked at me as if I was speaking another language. "You look confused. Shall I describe my last sexual experience to you?"

He entwined his fingers and rested his chin on them. "No. I prefer to look to the future."

"Do you want me to describe my *next* sexual experience to you, then?" I joked.

"What if I describe it to you?" he asked, his voice a velvety purr.

I didn't know what to say. Suddenly the teasing had outreached me. I was uncomfortably hot.

"No?" he asked, clearly sensing he had the advantage, putting his hand back on my shoulder. Heat, like electric fire, vibrated through me. My lips parted and he leaned in to whisper in my ear. "You're red as an apple. It's adorable."

He traced his fingers over my shoulder to my neck, and toyed with the edge of the collar again. I could barely catch my breath. He leaned close, so his lips were right next to my ear and whispered, "It's a delicious sensation, isn't it?" His breath made me shiver. "Very few beings experience it, human or Architect. Eventually, you'll beg me to do this to you."

Something in me broke. A wall of restraint crumbled. Repressed desire boiled to the surface. I didn't want to be a good girl right now and the sizzling heat was urging me to follow my instinct. My right glove was still draped across my lap and Ghalib was so close. I slipped my bare hand between the buttons on his shirt and, for the first time, voluntarily grazed his skin with my fingers. Electricity seemed to jump from me to him. I heard his breath catch. "Who's going to be begging who?" I whispered back.

Shock registered on his face. It gave me almost sexual satisfaction to have surprised him so. "Do you think you can make me plead with you, Elaine?" he whispered. "Nobody ever has before." His hand traced the curve of my shoulder.

Of course I didn't. I was a rather normal girl who didn't know a single sexual trick. How was I going to make this creature do anything? I was now quite sure that when this evening was over, I would look back on my behavior and cringe. What would possess me to toss out sexual challenges to a creature who only controlled himself around me through force of will? But even as I questioned my actions, I heard myself say, "Hypothetically, what if I promised to be your pet, agree to be claimed, but only if you beg me."

He laughed a loud, joyous, unrestrained laugh. People turned to look at me. "Touché, Elaine," he said, still chuckling. I drew my glove back on.

I tried not to be too smug. It was just one verbal win. I still had a long evening ahead of me.

Chapter 9
Festival of Pets: Earning Lisa

By now, most of the Architects and pets were seated. Victor, still standing, clapped his hands. The chandelier darkened and torches on the walls ignited. With the fireplaces, the whole room was filled with moving light. "Entertainment!" Victor called. The huge doors to the room swung open and a dozen girls, dressed like genies, raced to the polished floor inside the U of the table.

Music floated on the air with undulating tones and rhythm. The girls began to dance. Was it the dance of the Seven Veils or something more primal, more basic? I knew only that everyone seated around the table was leaning into them, swaying to the motion of the music.

It was beautiful. They draped silken scarves over one another, their glittering fingers tapping to the rhythm. I was as transfixed as anyone there. And my applause was as loud as anyone's when the music ended.

Victor accepted the applause graciously and clapped his hands again. A harpist began playing in the corner, even as a dozen servants filed into the room. One placed a plate in front of me but I wasn't hungry. I picked up my fork anyway, determined not to give Ghalib anything to complain about.

"You're shaking," Ghalib commented.

"Am I?"

He nodded at my hand and my fork was vibrating. "Have some wine," he suggested, moving a glass closer to me. I sipped at it and the alcohol went straight to my head. But it did help; in a few minutes the vibrations stopped running through me.

Delicately, I picked at my food. Anna and Julia were halfway down one of the arms of the U. Julia noticed me looking at her and winked at me, blowing me a kiss.

"It seems you've made a friend," Ghalib commented. I flushed and he smiled. Julia mirrored my blush and looked away when she noticed that Ghalib was watching us.

I managed dinner better than I thought I could. At first I just pushed food around my plate but the dishes were so rich and delicious that I managed to finish more than half of it. It helped that Ghalib chatted with the Architect on his left. Without his constant influence, my nerves were much more manageable.

As the meal drew to a close, Lord Victor stood. The refined conversation faded to silence. "There are several choices for your post-dinner entertainment," he said. "If you are interested in pet swapping, please retire to the Sitting room. I think most of you know where that is?" Beautiful heads nodded and over half of the guests rose, leading their pets out of the room. "If you would like to be part of the Claiming, I ask that you retire to the lounge. I've procured some lovely specimens this year. I think you'll be pleased." About half of the remaining guests left the room. "And finally," he said glancing around at the thirty or so couples that remained, "there will be dancing in the ballroom for anyone who is interested."

Ghalib turned to me and offered his hand. "Come, Elaine," he said. He led me out of the banquet hall, back into the entryway, and into an even larger room with magnificent mosaic of a wolf as the floor. An orchestra played in the corner and a crystal chandelier, lit with actual candles, illuminated the room. Couples were already entwined on the dance floor.

Ghalib stepped back from me, cocking his head as if he was making a decision about me. "Do you know how to dance?" he asked.

"A little," I answered.

A mischievous gleam came into his eyes. "Good," he said. "Take off your gloves." I could imagine how intense the sensation of our hands clasped would be without anything protecting me. His eyes shone, as if he sensed my dilemma. "Of course, you are always free to decline...."

"No," I replied quickly. I drew off first my left glove, then my right. It felt like I was undressing.

Ghalib took the gloves out of my hands; he seemed to vibrate with pleasure. "Shall we?" he asked, tucking my gloves into one of his inside pockets. I nodded.

He clasped my bare hand in his and laid his other hand on my waist. Electric current flashed between us, as if we completed a circuit. The pulses jumped through the silk of my dress, the fabric of his jacket, racing though me, then him, and back to me again. I couldn't help it; I imagined being pressed skin to skin with this man, nothing but heat and electricity and friction between us. The blood rushed to my face.

Thankfully, Ghalib was flushed, too. It seemed that our contact affected him as well. "This sensation, this magnetism you feel has a name," he told me. "It's called 'Drawing'." His voice was husky. "As I said before, it's very rare."

I struggled to maintain something of a dancing posture. "Yes?" I asked, proud of how steady my voice sounded. "How rare?"

"It happens from time to time between Architects. I've personally known three couples who experienced it, out of the thousands of Architects. I have experienced it once myself. Very weakly, of course. Nothing like what I feel between us." Our dancing became more graceful; the talking helped. "I'm speaking of reciprocated Drawing, you understand. Unrequited Drawing—where one Architect experiences the Draw but the other does not—is a bit more common."

"How often is someone like me, a human, involved?" I asked, doing my part to keep the conversation going.

His eyes darkened. "Mortals like you are even rarer and more pleasurable. You come from a purely physical realm and bring purely physical pleasure to the Drawing. We Architects can't duplicate that sensation."

The music changed and our dance changed with it. "Now," he said, "I would like for you to answer one of *my* questions."

"Go on," I said.

"How can I tempt you to stay here with me voluntarily and be this intriguing every night?"

I was so taken off-guard, I stumbled a little.

"Because," he continued, righting my stumble, "now that you know what I am, you know there is literally nothing that I can't do

for you. There is no dream I can't fulfill, no longing I can't dispel."
He pulled me a little closer and spoke more quietly. "I can grant anything, Elaine. Even desires you don't yet know you have."

I hid my nervousness. "Bribes?" I asked pertly. "Are you doubt-
ing your irresistibility?"

"I'm resistible?" he asked, sounding amused.

The Drawing coursed through me, urging me. I ignored my fear
and concentrated on that. "So far," I said.

He laughed again. "Obviously, I haven't been trying hard
enough."

"Well, perhaps you're not used to trying at all," I said, only half
joking. "Too many gorgeous Italian strumpets vying for your attention. God only knows why you would decide on someone like me,
who would make you work."

I expected him to be angry, but his eyes sparkled. "That's an easy
question to answer. I never wanted them as I want you."

Again, I had the urge to tease him. I traced the curve of his ear with
my finger tip, as he had earlier that night. His breath grew ragged. I
smiled, withdrew my hand to his shoulder, and gave him a prim look.
"I suppose, then, your strategy should be trying to get me to want you
as much as you want me."

He started laughing. "You are an unspeakable tease," he told me.
"I think you've nearly turned it into an art form."

I smiled, ready to reply when over his shoulder, I noticed Victor
dancing behind Ghalib with a blonde. "Victor's behind you," I said.

Victor's head lifted at his name. "Ghalib. Elaine. Care to swap
dance partners?" he asked.

Ghalib and I stopped dancing but his hand tightened around
mine. "I'm being unspeakably rude," he said, "but I must decline. I've
only had Elaine for a couple of days and I'm afraid I'm still rather
protective. Besides, we're about to leave."

"No, surely not," Victor said, stopping his waltz. "It's still early."

"I'm afraid we must. Elaine is easily over-stimulated. I must get
her home."

Victor inclined his head, the shadows on his face still hiding his
expression. He reached for my ungloved hand, grasping it before I
could do anything to stop him. The current of electricity that jolted

71

between Victor and I was impossible to ignore. He held my hand so tightly that it hurt. But the Drawing swelled and sexual pleasure took the edge off of the pain.

"Good God," Victor said. "Where did you find this girl?"

"Release her," Ghalib said with a note of menace. Victor was slow to comply. "As I said," Ghalib said, putting his hand over Victor's, "Elaine is easily over-stimulated. Let her go." Reluctantly, Victor dropped my fingers. "I will return later tonight. As I promised. We can talk then," Ghalib added.

"I shall look forward to it," Victor replied, his eyes still lingering on me. "In the meantime," Victor said, satisfaction tingeing his tone, "since Elaine is without a leash and without a Master, I would like to make this my formal invitation to Elaine."

"Noted," Ghalib said tightly.

He led me out the front door into the swirling snow. Before I knew it, Victor's castle melted away and Ghalib's home sprung up to replace it. The snow ebbed but the wind grew fiercer. Ghalib led me back into his castle.

"What was that all about?" I asked once we were in the foyer.

Ghalib's jaw was still clenched. "Recall when you learned that you were to be shared?"

"Yes," I said, feeling dread creeping up on me.

"Victor has just claimed your first visit." I froze, staring at Ghalib. "A nightcap?" he offered.

"Please," I breathed.

He led me down a corridor and into a room that must have been his library. Books lined the walls. A sturdy desk stood in the corner and a fire crackled in a normal-sized fireplace on one wall. Leather couches and chairs were arranged around the room.

"Sit," he said. I settled into a leather chair, my dress billowing around me. Honestly, it was ridiculous. I couldn't believe that people really used to dress this way.

The collar around my neck suddenly loosened. During the Festival it had fitted my neck perfectly, moving with flawless flexibility against my skin. Now, it fitted more like a bangle. Then, the back opened and it fell into my lap. I picked it up and looked at it. "Powerful little trinket," I commented.

"You have no idea," Ghalib replied.

Jason came into the room with a bottle of wine and two glasses. Ghalib didn't say anything while Jason worked the cork and poured the wine. He just watched me.

Keep it light, I reminded myself. "So, how did I do?" I asked, handing him back his collar as Jason placed our glasses of wine and retreated from the room.

"Anna and Julia could hardly stop watching you. Victor has already invited you to his home."

My hand trembled and the wine in my glass rippled. "Tell me about him," I said.

"I would prefer that you form your own opinion," he said cryptically.

I decided that I didn't want to think about what would happen when Victor came for me. I reached for any other topic. "What about Lisa?" I asked.

"Ah, Lisa," he said, like he had been waiting for me to bring her up. "I must admit, I'm very satisfied with your performance this evening thus far," he said, but his face took on a sly look. "There is only one, final element to our evening that I would request," he continued. "Then we can go to the prison and reveal your success to Lisa."

"And what is that?" I asked, keeping my voice light, but taking a large gulp of wine.

He cocked his head and smiled. "It would please me if you would kiss me good-night."

I got a chill. This Drawing thing was almost intolerably intense with just casual touch. What would kissing him do to me? Would I be able to control myself? But I couldn't quit now. After all that I had done this evening, losing Lisa at this point, over a stupid kiss, was unthinkable. And he knew it.

I lifted my chin and took a deep breath. "A kiss? Simple enough."

He didn't answer; he simply stood, rising elegantly, patiently in front of me. I tried to ignore the part of me that was titillated. I'd kissed people before—a few people I'd hardly liked. Of course, that wasn't exactly the problem here.

I tried to ignore all of the doubt and guilt. I was only a few steps away from him. I stood and closed the distance between us before I could change my mind. The Drawing current crackled through me and over my skin. It urged me to tease him. I lowered my eyes and drew my finger across his chest through his silken shirt. His breath caught. I felt unlike myself: powerful, sensual, playful.

He lifted my face, bending to kiss me but I drew back. "I thought you wanted me to kiss you," I chided gently.

"I do," he said. I stood on tip-toe and pressed my lips against his. And in that instant, I lost every element of control I had over the situation. I lost the teasing and pretense. All that was left was Drawing—intense, raw, compelling desire—more than I believed a mortal body could hold. And I throbbed with it.

His arms were around me, his hands caressing my back, but I felt trailing fingers all over my body. His lips were on mine but I could hear his whispered voice in my ear. "Yes," he urged me. "More." When my eyes were closed, I saw images, flashes really, of he and I, our bodies entangled. I saw his hands on me, him painstakingly peeling my clothing away. I saw him bringing this intense sensation to a heart stopping peak after hours, days perhaps, of taunting artistry. Suddenly, with a throb, I understood what he meant when he said that it would take years to show me what he wanted to do with me. His desire was almost insatiable and directed exclusively towards me.

His lips slipped from mine and trailed soft kisses to my ear. "You said I wasn't irresistible," he whispered. "What do you think now?"

The Drawing still shivered through me. It urged me to tease him. "I thought you didn't want me to resist tonight," I said sweetly. "If you'd like more of a challenge, I can oblige."

I drew away from him. Or I tried to.

His arms tightened around me. "No," he said. His eyes were as dark as emeralds. One of his hands slid up my back and his fingers wove into my hair, tilting my face to be even with his. It didn't even occur to me to resist. When his lips touched mine, they were more demanding. The Drawing urged me and I couldn't help but respond.

The flashes came faster, like a movie. The two of us, naked, entwined, and glistening with sweat. Me, supple in his hands. I could hear my own moans.

This kiss had to stop. I had to stop it. I had no intension of being taken right here on the library floor. But stopping was much harder than I thought it would be. Finally, I managed to draw back, pushing on his chest, backing away so that he couldn't capture me in his arms again. I was shaking and out of breath and there wasn't any way to hide it from Ghalib.

Triumph crowned his features. "Need a moment?" he teased.

"I was feeling a little claustrophobic," I said. My legs shook but I refused to sit down.

"You're far too tense, Elaine," he said, smiling. "I could help you relieve some of that tension."

A current of Drawing ran through me, giving me strength. My heart slowed. My legs grew solid again. I shook my head. "No more sweet Italian bistros for me," I said, letting myself pout a little. "Just thinly-veiled sexual offers. The seduction must be over."

He smoothed back my hair. "You don't find yourself sufficiently seduced?"

"No. Not for everything you want from me."

He laid his hand on my shoulder and the Drawing pulsed between us. His thumb caressed my skin in slow circles. It was a delicious sensation that I did my best to ignore. "What is it that you think I want from you?" he asked.

I offered him my own slow smile. "That isn't a question I could answer in an evening, Ghalib. That's a question that I could take years to answer." I raised my eyebrows at him.

He threw back his head and laughed, a wonderful sound, a joyous sound that even made me happy. "All right," he finally said, still chuckling. "You win. Shall we retrieve Lisa?"

"Yes," I agreed. "Let's."

Lisa was like a delighted puppy. Ghalib led me down to her cell, opened her prison door and her shackles, and nodded towards me. "Meet your new mistress, Lisa." She rushed to me naked, hugging me until my face was burning. She thanked us both.

Jason waited at the entrance of the prison. With one lingering look, Ghalib passed Lisa and me to him. "I have work to attend to," he explained. I breathed a sigh and my shoulders physically relaxed. I needed time away from him; he was just so exhausting.

Jason walked between us and looked at Lisa. "Your duties have been explained to you?" he asked her.

"Yes."

His expression turned severe. "Absolutely no indiscretions, Lisa. Nobody will be able to rescue you if you misbehave again."

"I won't." I couldn't help but notice her adorable pout.

I caught Jason's eye. "She won't," I said. Lisa's pout deepened.

Jason stopped at a door. "Your new quarters, Lisa," he said. "Your mistress must be awakened by mid-morning. She and the Master are entertaining a guest tomorrow night." Lisa nodded and slipped into her room.

"Victor, I hear," I said.

"Yes." Jason looked around, as if spies followed us. "I must not say anything more except—be careful. Even though you will find it distasteful, you must be charming."

"Why would I find being charming distasteful?"

"I'm sorry, Miss," he said softly. "I can't."

It never ends.

Chapter 10

Rock and a Hard Place

I awoke with a start, immediately aware that I wasn't alone. Lisa sat on the other end of the couch, watching me. My heart already hammered and I hadn't even been awake thirty seconds. "Jesus, Lisa. Don't do that!"

She blinked. "Do what?"

"How long have you been there?"

"Less than an hour. Why do you sleep on the couch?"

I sat up and thanked the-powers-that-be that I had on a long night shirt. "I can't sleep in that bed. It's too big and half the walls are windows. What if someone watches me?" I said.

It wasn't meant to be a pointed comment, but she still took my meaning. She flushed. "I'm sorry, Miss," she said, standing quickly. She looked scared.

"I'm glad you're here," I said gently. "I've been lonely. Can't you just act normal around me? Ghalib already watches me like he's studying me."

She seemed to relax a little. "I understand. I'm sorry, Miss. I should have thought." She turned to get my robe and I climbed off the couch. "I brought you something to eat and I'm going to draw you a—"

Her hand brushed my arm as she helped me on with my robe. I must have been getting used to the sensation because the crackle of heat barely made me pause. But, Lisa's eyes widened even as her sentence stopped.

"It's OK," I told her. "I'm finding that I have that effect on just about everyone around here."

She bit her lip but quickly regained control of her expression. "I'll have to be more careful," she said.

I ate the fruit and bread she brought me while she drew me a hot bath. I had never bothered with the bath oils and gels that were stocked in the cabinets before but Lisa added something to the water that turned it lavender and smelled like lilac. It was heavenly.

"Could you help me pick an outfit?" I called from the bathroom. "I'm dining with Ghalib and Victor tonight."

"Oh, yes!" She sounded delighted. "I would love to."

Lord Victor. Ghalib wanted me to make up my own mind about him, but I couldn't help but dig for information. "Do you know Victor?" I asked. She came to the bathroom door with a towel and helped me out of the bath. "Oh, yes. A little better than I'd like."

"What do you think of him?" I asked.

"He's no gentleman," she said. "Not like Master Ghalib."

"Ghalib just had you shackled to the ceiling in his prison with weights hanging from your breasts," I pointed out.

"It's still better than the things that Lord Victor does," she said dismissively. I had my first chill of fear for the evening.

"Come, Miss," she told me. "I'll do your hair."

She indicated towards a chair and I sat. "The Master and Lord Victor are in a perpetual rivalry," she said, manipulating my long hair with deft ability. "Their mansions, their dream creations, their mortals. The Master had the coup de grace last night when he brought you to the Festival. I've already heard that Lord Victor covets you terribly." Heat came into my face. Obviously, it wasn't common knowledge that I had already been claimed. "He's rather forceful, but I can't imagine the Master will let him have any time alone with you tonight."

I forced down my rising panic and kept my face calm. "All of the Architects here seem forceful to me. Look at Ghalib. My kidnapping, the constant threat of punishment...."

"True," she agreed. "The Master can be very resolved when he sees something he wants. And he's certainly not above a strict, memorable punishment." She wound long sections of my hair around her brush, leaving a tumble of dark curls. "But Lord Victor is something else entirely. He is amused by pain and fear. Pleasure for him must mingle with pain to be completely satisfying." She brushed my curls back and twisted my hair on to my head. "Many of the other Archi-

tects find him rather base." She added. With a couple of clips she secured my hair into place. "All done," she said.

She held up a mirror. It was perfect. She found a new way of doing my hair that accentuated my heart-shaped face. It was sleek and
sophisticated.

"It's lovely," I said. But I was distracted. Not only was I thinking
of my upcoming time alone with Victor, I remembered Ghalib's eagerness to return to his mansion to help him punish some poor creature
named Selma. In fact, Victor seemed eager to have Ghalib take part
in the punishment, too. Perhaps the two Architects bonded over the
mortals they tormented. And I would stand between them tonight.
Not just one impossible companion, but two.

I drew on my dress, a black, strapless, floor-length creation paired
with delicate heels.

"He specifically said no gloves," Lisa added as she zipped my
slim dress. "But he sent these." Diamonds. A choker, bracelet, and
earrings. My heart hammered. "Perfect," Lisa declared after I put
them on. I sat down to put on my make-up and but the stones around
my neck caught my eye. It wasn't a collar, but it was close. I tried not
to think about it. I just concentrated on my lipstick.

Lisa waited for me in the study with a wine glass. It had a couple of
swallows of wine in it. "To relax," she told me. "You look nervous."

"I am. And you should join me," I said. She smiled and a second glass materialized in her hand. But we barely sat before a knock
sounded at the door.

"Is he early?" Lisa snapped in irritation. "Probably came here
twenty minutes ahead of time just to make sure that we're not—" She
cut herself off as Jason entered.

He glanced from me to her, me seated on an armchair and her
seated across the room on an ottoman. Lisa crossed her legs. "I've
been a very good girl," she told him.

He looked at me. "She has," I confirmed. "The hair is her creation."

"And the wine, too, I imagine," he remarked dryly. "She's done a
lovely job, though," he added grudgingly. "Come, Miss. They wait."

My stomach clenched but I nodded. He led me through the winding corridors quietly, as if he was deep in thought. When we arrived

at a door, he paused. "Remember what I told you last night about being charming?" he asked.

"I remember."

He nodded once at me and opened the door. This was a room I hadn't seen before. Or maybe it was all the same room, transformed into new manifestations. Either way, it was another dining room, darkly paneled and darkly lit. Ghalib and Victor turned towards me, Ghalib looking like a Greek god and Victor shadowy and mysterious.

I squared my shoulders and managed a smile. "Good evening," I said, my voice low and steady. I crossed the room to them.

"Good evening, Elaine," Ghalib said with a practiced courtesy. "You remember Victor from last night?"

"Of course," I replied. He offered his hand, like a dare, and I took it, ready for the electric jolt that coursed through me.

"Mmm, Ghalib, you are a lucky creature," Victor said. He turned my hand palm-side up and pressed his lips to the inside of my wrist. I didn't pull away but my body stiffened. It was strange, not seeing the lips that touched me. The Drawing with Victor had a sharper, more biting edge. "She's not as well-trained as I would have expected," Victor commented airily, still holding my hand. "I'll have to work on that." I swallowed.

Ghalib only smiled. "Nonsense. This is the height of delectability. How she wanted, so badly, to withdraw. I think I can even define the instant she mastered her impulse to flee." Ghalib took my wrist, sending heat up my arm, and pulled it out of Victor's grasp. "You would see her broken," Ghalib added. "I would only see her tamed."

"It's like poetry," Victor said dryly.

Ghalib touched my necklace lightly. "How is Lisa working out?" he asked me.

"Very well," I answered. "The clothes, the hair, all her doing."

"Lisa?" Victor asked. "Not the same servant girl you acquired from me? I had thought you intended to use her for your personal amusement."

Ghalib gave him a cool look. "You misunderstood me. And, incidentally, she is one who could have used more stringent training. She considers instruction mere suggestion."

Victor snickered. "You can't blame me for that. Spare the rod... Isn't that how it goes?"

The doors to the room opened and three servants entered with platters. "Ahh, dinner," Victor said, gripping my upper arm, the Drawing urging me to stand up straighter. "Come, my dear," he said, steering me towards the table. I glanced over my shoulder at Ghalib who looked bemused and a little irritated.

Victor didn't release me when we reached the table. He clenched his hand on my arm, his finger nails biting into my skin. I gasped and heard his low chuckle. When he loosened his grip, he left behind moon-shaped bruises on my skin.

The Drawing increased, making the pain manageable. I hated this Lord Victor. Jason had warned me that I mustn't let anyone see my distaste. I must be charming. But, I detested the idea of being at his mercy. I hated the idea of living in his house. He wouldn't give me the same courtesies Ghalib did, and I hated him for making Ghalib look kind.

"What delicate skin you have," Victor exclaimed with false concern. "You must tell me if I injure you. Sometimes I don't know my own strength." He lifted my arm to display the marks and Ghalib's expression darkened.

The Drawing coursed through me. I cocked my head at Victor; I didn't hesitate to look at him directly. "I think you know your strengths," I said. "Just as I know mine."

He still held my arm and I laid my hand over his. Current jumped from me to him. This time he was the one to gasp.

"Shall we eat?" Ghalib asked, an amused smile playing on his lips.

We sat at the triangular table and servants placed our dinners in front of us. A smooth-faced boy, the same boy who was there with Lisa on the night I got my voice back, filled my glass with water and I noticed Victor's face turned towards him. The boy noticed it, too, though I could only tell by the flush on his ears. When the rest of the servants moved to retreat, Victor caught his wrist in that bruising grip.

"What's your name, boy," he asked.

The boy's color deepened. "Matthew, Sir."

"Matthew." Victor said the name like was tasting it. "Have you noticed your Master's guest here?" He indicated towards me with a nod of his head. The boy's eyes automatically found me. Brown eyes. A poet's eyes.

"I... yes. Of course," Matthew stammered.

Victor's grip tightened around Matthew's wrist. "If you were the Master here, what would you do to her?"

Matthew's whole face was flushed. Arousal and pain gave him a heightened appearance. He looked at Ghalib who nodded slowly, as if to permit his honesty.

"If... if she were willing, neither of us would see the outside of my bedchambers for some time."

He was so sweet and earnest; I felt bad for him.

Victor's other hand went to Matthew's crotch, where a noticeable bulge had formed. "I see," Victor replied. "You seem equal to the task. So what would you do to her?"

The boy looked confused, as if he had already answered the question. His eyes sought out Ghalib who offered no help. Then he looked at me. The Drawing urged me to help him. It told me that if I didn't, nobody else would. Victor squeezed Matthew's arousal; the boy flinched.

"What Victor would like to know," I heard myself say, "are the details of how you would take me." Ghalib turned to me, his green eyes aglow. I met his gaze. "Would you play with me and tease me until I begged for release?" I turned to Victor. "Or maybe you don't need the game of seduction. Maybe you would just have me stripped and bound so that I was always at the ready for you." Victor's shadowed face didn't belie any emotion, but his grip loosened on the boy. I looked up at Matthew. I didn't need the Drawing to tell me what his choice would be. "Or maybe you're a romantic. Rose petals on satin sheets. Whispered nothings by candlelight."

"Yes," Matthew said breathlessly.

Ghalib laughed and Victor soon joined him, releasing his grip on the boy. Matthew's face was almost purple. "Poor boy," Ghalib laughed.

"He's no sport at all," Victor muttered. "Fetch me more ice," he ordered, slapping Matthew's buttocks.

Ghalib picked up his knife and fork. "Are you so stringent with your own servants, Victor?"

"After last night, I should think you would know the answer to that question." I hoped that neither of them noticed my shiver.

We ate in silence for a while, until Matthew trotted back to the table with the ice, left it, and practically ran out. Victor, who had finished one glass of wine and all of his meat, turned his attention back to me.

"So, tell me Elaine, have you become acclimated to our little corner of the universe, yet?"

"Not yet, I'm afraid."

"I would think that it would be easier for you than most mortals, with you being an Omnilight."

Ghalib's head snapped up. "I haven't told her everything, yet," he said. "I was trying to ease her into the situation."

"What haven't you told me?" I asked, looking at Ghalib.

He sighed. "I was going to speak to you about this later tonight, anyway."

"She's coming to my house in less than one cycle," Victor said. "I insist that she be informed."

Ghalib's eyes met mine. "Do you recall when I said that you were a very gifted human?" I nodded once, not sure I wanted to hear what was coming. "You're what Architects call an Omnilight, a magnet for the Drawing. It is the rarest phenomenon known to us."

"The Drawing I feel when I touch an Architect? That isn't normal?" I asked.

"Humans almost never feel the Drawing. Omnilights are very rare," Ghalib said. "You are very valuable to us. It's why Nyx won't send you home."

My breathing came faster and I could feel the panic rising. "And it's also why I have to be shared," I said in a dead voice, already knowing the answer.

"That's right," he confirmed. "Architects will line up to touch you. You will be used for the sensuous experience you produce. Unless you give yourself to one of us, you must be shared among all of us."

"The last two Omnilights were never pets," Victor said dismissively. "It's not commonly done."

"But it can be," Ghalib insisted.

Victor turned slowly to Ghalib. I sensed his smile behind the obscuring shadows. "You want to keep our little Omnilight here to yourself, don't you?" Victor taunted. "Are you smitten?"

Ghalib shrugged. "Could you blame me? Look at her."

"Have you even tasted her, yet?"

Ghalib looked up from his meal. "Let's say I've sampled her." I thought of our kiss from the night before and my face burned. Ghalib grinned at me.

"And?" Victor asked.

Ghalib smiled and thought for a moment. "Apricots," he finally answered. "She tastes like apricots and cream."

Victor lifted an eyebrow. "Really?"

Quicker than I could see, faster than I could react, he grabbed the back of my head and pulled me into a very awkward kiss. I couldn't see his features, even from close up. But I felt his lips on mine, forcing my mouth open and his tongue tasting the inside of my mouth. The kiss was so forceful that my teeth cut my lip, making me taste blood.

Which only intensified the vision. Me in a dungeon, in a place I knew must really exist in that arctic castle of Victor's. I was bound and naked with a bar between my feet to spread them wide. I was bent over something, leaving my backside and my back completely vulnerable. Sweat soaked my body and rosy welts crossed my skin.

I didn't want to see any more. I tried to break the kiss, but Victor's hand was like a vice on my head. His other hand fumbled for the hem of my gown, lifting it to my knee, sliding his fingers under it. I finally managed to brace against his chest and wrench myself away.

"Honestly, Victor," Ghalib said, sounding bored. "Were you kissing her or trying to swallow her whole?"

Victor sounded amused. "I just wanted to taste these apricots you speak of. All I noticed was blood and wine."

"Perhaps it was your technique," I suggested coolly, blotting blood from my lips on a white napkin. "A bruised fruit often has a very different taste than one that is ripe."

Ghalib's eyes glowed and Victor made a sound of irritation.

I was in a desperately precarious position. Anything that dampened their mood could be punished. Anything that heightened their sport was dangerous to me. Not just one predator but two. Not just an unspeakable tease but a resistant captive was required. And all the while, the throbbing, urging Drawing guided my words and attuned my instincts. I couldn't forget that tomorrow I would go with Victor. Anything I did to make him angry would be revisited on me then.

As the meal drew to a close, a light tap sounded at the door. "Master," Jason said quietly, "Madam Alexis asks for a brief audience."

"Alexis?" Victor said. "She never visits me anymore."

"That's because she detests you," Ghalib said, laying his napkin aside. "Excuse me. I won't be a moment." He closed the door softly behind him.

Victor hardly missed a beat. "Tell me, my dear," he said, sliding his chair closer to mine, "What is your tolerance for pain?"

"Excuse me?" I asked, turning towards him.

"Are you pierced, tattooed, branded?"

"None of that," I said with a shaky voice. "Except for my pierced ears."

"Excellent," he said. "I like making my own holes."

"What if I don't want there to be any piercing?" I asked.

He put a dry finger to my lips. The jolt of Drawing was jagged and rough. "Then, I'll just have to make sure you change your mind."

Several of Ghalib's servants entered the room, removing dishes and refilling goblets. Matthew was among them and came over to Victor and me. "The Master asked me to bring you to the observatory. He said that he would meet you there." Matthew turned to lead us but Victor seized his wrist again.

"Help the lady out of her chair," he growled. Matthew flushed and offered his hand, flushing harder when I took it. Victor handed me my wine and offered his arm, which I reluctantly accepted.

On the way to the observatory, Victor amused himself by taunting Matthew. "What fine, supple cheeks you have," he commented, pinching the boy's buttocks hard. Matthew didn't respond. "I must speak to Ghalib about his intension with you. I could use a new steward. You might be just the fellow."

Matthew stiffened and a faint grin played on Victor's lips. The boy seemed relieved when he finally showed us into the observatory. He bowed at the door and closed it behind us. A great, glass dome curved overhead and the stars blazed through it. A few tall tables, perfect for standing next to, were arranged around the room. Victor led me to a table but I couldn't keep my eyes off the ceiling.

"It's so beautiful," I said.

"It's just stars," Victor replied. "I prefer my pleasures to be a bit more in reach. Don't you?"

"I don't know," I said. "There's something to be said for the un-available."

Victor chuckled. The door to the observatory opened and Ghalib entered, carrying his refilled glass of wine. "Good," he said. "I was concerned that you had Matthew so befuddled that he wouldn't be able to carry out my instructions."

"He did tolerably well," Victor said. "And Elaine and I had the most interesting conversation while you were gone."

"Really?" Ghalib said, his eyes cutting sharply to me. My stomach clenched. "What did you talk about?"

"She said that she has no piercings, no brandings, hardly any marks at all."

Ghalib looked wary. "I imagine you object and seek to rectify that."

"I thought you might have put your mark on her," Victor said. Ghalib didn't answer. "But, you didn't want to hurt her, did you?" Victor's voice was like silk. "Tell me, Ghalib, why have you only sampled Elaine when I know you crave her? You are not a patient creature."

Ghalib cocked his head to one side. "I've been rather enjoying the teasing."

A harsh laugh escaped Victor. "Bullshit. We're the same, you and I. We enjoy the having, not the wanting." Victor closed the distance to me. He took the wine glass out of my hands and laid it aside. Ghalib watched but didn't protest. "You've been protecting her. That is so sweet." Victor's words were mocking.

I froze stock still, like a rabbit. "Easy, my love," Victor whispered to me. "We're not going to hurt you... much."

Chapter 11

Walking a Fine Line

I held my breath. "Don't move," Victor told me, crossing behind me. He removed my necklace, laying it next to my wine. He raked his fingernails across my back and down the back of my arms to my elbows.

His hands tightened on my elbows and he forced them together behind my back. Something soft—a strip of silk or a velvet rope—looped my elbows. Victor made the knots tight, so tight that I gasped.

"You make sweet music," he whispered. I turned towards the sound of his voice but a soft finger on my cheek stopped me. "No, my dear," he said. "You must face your Master."

Without thinking, I faced Ghalib.

My heart thundered. Drawing washed through me, making every touch throb. I couldn't blink; I didn't move. I only saw Ghalib; I only felt Victor.

Victor's hands went into my hair and the hair clips loosened. Dark curls tumbled over my shoulder. "Something to hold on to," Victor whispered.

There was nothing that I could do. A struggle was what they wanted. Victor pushed my hair over my shoulder and his lips found my neck. A shiver of Drawing made my lips part; Ghalib's intensity deepened.

"You want her. Why not take her?" Victor said over my shoulder. "Does she usually push you away? She won't push you away now."

Ghalib laid his glass aside and closed the short distance to me. He placed his hands lightly on my shoulders, releasing another wash of sensation. His hands slid slowly down my restrained arms, over Victor's caressing hands, to the tie at my elbows. He seemed undecided: wild with desire, heavy with want, but painfully restraining himself. This wasn't how he wanted me. This was Victor's fantasy, not his. I'm sure he saw the fear in my face but then, Victor put his hands in my hair, pulling my head back.

The quake of Drawing from Ghalib's lips on my neck was shattering. Victor's teeth scraped at my shoulder as Ghalib's lips and tongue traced a line from my neck to my collarbone. I trembled and the shiver only encouraged them. Victor pulled my head even further back.

One of Ghalib's hands traveled back up my body, over my waist, brushing the side of my breast, skimming my bare shoulder, and went into my hair. His fingers found Victor's and Victor released his grasp. When I lowered my head, Ghalib's face was right next to mine. His eyes were so green, they didn't look real.

He didn't ask. He didn't tease. He just kissed me, tasting my mouth, gently biting my lips, his kiss grew deeper and more intense; the images he sent me did the same. Flashes of rough sex. Him wrestling me to his bed, spreading my legs with his thighs, and thrusting. Him bending me, fully clothed, over a billiards table, not even bothering to remove my undergarments all the way, pounding against me. The Drawing was relentless. I didn't want to want him, but I did.

Drawing flashed like a warning through me. This had to stop. It couldn't continue. Victor tightened my binds and his fingers teased down the zipper of my dress. The bodice fell away, just leaving me covered by a strapless black bra. It wouldn't be long before this whole situation was out of control. My mind fought the Drawing, raced for a solution.

The only thing I could think of were Lisa's words: Ghalib and Victor were in a perpetual rivalry. I was the prize of the moment. Perhaps I could do something to spark Ghalib's jealousy. It was a long-shot but it was worth a try. If I could just get rid of one of them.

Ghalib's hand's went to my ribs; he stopped kissing me just long enough to pull my dress into a puddle on the floor. Victor scraped his nails all the way down my back. Now was as good of a time as any. "Please, Ghalib," I whispered breathlessly. "Please stop this." This protest was his particular brand of fantasy. Me, begging him to stop. Me, powerless and aroused.

At the same time, I struggled a little against Victor, pulling away slightly, straining against the bondage. It was the very type of resistance that I knew would madden him. It was what I would do if I was trying to bring him pleasure.

It worked better than I had hoped.

Ghalib drew back to look at me, it seemed. His expression heightened. At that moment, Victor squeezed my arms together painfully and bit my shoulder. His teeth cut into my skin. Drawing swelled to match the pain and I cried out.

Ghalib's face flashed with jealousy. I didn't even try to hide my arousal. I let him see that Victor affected me too.

Victor looked up at Ghalib and loosened his grip on my arms. "Oh, dear," he said.

Ghalib didn't look away from me. "It's been a very entertaining evening, Victor, but now I'm going to have to ask you to leave. Elaine and I have a few matters to discuss."

Victor raked his fingernails over my shoulders. "If you wish," he said to Ghalib. "It's only one more night for me to wait."

Ghalib looked over my shoulder at him.

"I can see myself out." He gave my arms one more fierce squeeze, but he didn't untie them. He left and let the door slam behind him.

I was left tied, alone with Ghalib in the observatory.

He still stood in front of me, watching me. I prayed that I had made the right decision by trying to get rid of Victor. My situation hardly seemed improved. My arms were still tied behind my back. I wore only the strapless bra, panties, and my high heels. Victor may have left but the danger wasn't gone.

Ghalib didn't move to touch me, but his voice was caressing. "Now, what were you saying?"

"What?"

"While Victor was here. You whispered something to me."

Adrenaline made my fingers tingle. I had given him a taste of his fantasy and he wanted more. How dangerous would it be to disappoint him now? "I asked you to stop," I managed.

"You begged me to stop."

"Yes, I did," I said.

"But, as you once confessed to me, you're deceitful." A slow smile shaped his lips. "Oh, I suppose you probably did want us to stop – but more than that, you wanted me to get rid of Victor."

Oh, God. How transparent was I? "Yes," I said.

"And now you have your wish," he said, stepping towards me, his hands brushing my shoulders, stroking my arms to where my elbows were bound. I held my breath against the surge of electricity.

He leaned forward, his lips pressed to the hollow of my throat and I exhaled in a ragged rush of breath. I swayed away from him but he held me in place. His long, white hair tickled my shoulders. It just made the sensation all the more maddening. I couldn't help but be aware that I was practically naked.

"Ghalib..." I said, the protest coming involuntarily.

"Shh," he hushed against my skin. His lips found the top of my cleavage, which peeked out from the slipping strapless bra. His tongue dipped into it and I made a little noise in my throat. He kissed back up to my ear and bit the diamond earring playfully. "It's no secret that I want you," he whispered. "It's the last night you'll be here. Say yes."

I wanted him too. He was my captor, my kidnapper, my tormentor and I wanted him. "No," I whispered but my voice was weak. I knew he could hear that I didn't mean it.

"Say yes," he teased.

"N –" He stopped me with a kiss. The visions were almost too much. They were so real, so corporeal I actually felt his lips on my nipples and his urgency nudging me between my legs. It was as if we were already there. I moaned involuntarily.

Ghalib steadied me with his hands and used his body to force me backwards, laying me down on something soft. Lying on my bound arms hurt a little and arched my back. I opened my eyes. The observatory was gone. The stars still blazed overhead but now we were outside – on a bed. Fear and arousal shot through me.

Ghalib untangled his arms from around me and lay next to me on the bed. "Ghalib, stop this," I said, trying to roll off the bed to get on my feet. He restrained me with a hand on my chest.

"Stay put," he commanded. "We have a few things to discuss."

It was painful, but I laid still. "Do you see how easy this was for me, Elaine?" he asked. "How very simple it would be for me to restrain you and take you anywhere I want? And from there, do anything I want to you?"

I wished I could tease him. Deflect him somehow. But I was too shaken. "I do."

"Good," he said, smoothing my curls. "Imagine yourself here with Victor," he instructed. I shuddered. "What do you suppose he would do to you?"

"I know what he would do," I whispered, looking up at the stars. "He would hurt me, then he would rape me. When he touches me, I can see how cruel he is."

"Good," he said. "I wouldn't want you to be shocked tomorrow night when he comes for you." He ran his fingers lightly over my stomach. "You can avoid this. Be my pet. Say yes, Elaine."

"No," I said.

"He won't care if you like what he does to you," Ghalib urged.

"Neither do you."

"I suppose you think that Victor and I are just the same," he said. "One of us is as good as any other."

"No. That's not true."

"Really."

"I prefer your company to Victor's. I could imagine this evening being very enjoyable if he hadn't been here."

"Oh, I see," he replied, his eyes darkening. "Then tonight might have been my lucky night, but for Victor?"

A sudden jolt of warning flashed through me. "That isn't what I—"

"Shh, Elaine," he cooed, his fingers on my lips. "You don't need to explain. The situation is rectified. Victor is gone and the whole evening lies before us." His finger slipped from my lips to the top of my bra, tracing the swells of my breasts.

Maddening tingles and shocks played over my skin. I started to sweat. I wanted to touch him back—to strip his suit jacket away and tease a flush from his cheeks.

I tried to stop my thoughts. They were dangerous. If he kissed me right now he might see them. Did I want to be taken right here? Still, my self-control was slipping.

"I don't know why you deny yourself this pleasure," he said, his hands finding the tie at my elbows and releasing it. But I wasn't free.

He captured my wrists in one of his hands and held them behind me. It was almost worse than being tied because his touch brought the Drawing. His free hand brushed the side of my breast on the way to my waist.

"Ghalib, please." This time I wasn't teasing. There was tension in my voice. The fire in his eyes flared when I begged.

He pulled me close. "I can't believe I ever took your voice away," he said between kisses. "The way you beg is perfect." The visions mingled with reality and my restraint melted further. The pressure of his lips grew more insistent. His free hand stroked my body, not favoring any one spot, just teasing the flesh, making me wild with need. The visions from our kiss aligned with what was happening now. He was getting his every wish. I kissed him back; I couldn't stop myself.

Ghalib moved my restrained hands up my back to the clasps on my bra. "Take off your bra," he ordered. His lips returned to mine and my fingers moved to obey. At the last minute, I stopped.

"No. I don't want this," I whispered.

"Nonsense," he said impatiently. "You do want this." He released my wrists, unclasping it himself. It fell away and his hands went to my breasts. Then his lips found my nipples. I couldn't stop my response; my hands went into his hair. I moaned with the feel of his tongue against my sensitive skin.

My resistance, which had been barely hanging on, broke. Without it, desire washed over me in crushing waves. He was right; I did want this. I pulled his face to mine, kissing him, an explosion of color bursting behind my eyes. He didn't resist me, even though I sensed his surprise. He was too far away from me. I slid my arms around him, pressing my bare chest to his silky dress shirt. I kissed him again and heard him moan.

Another wave of desire took me and I let it guide me, licking his lips, kissing down his neck to where his collar began. It wasn't enough. I needed more. I pulled at his buttons, kissing and biting at his chest, until I found his nipples.

"God, Elaine," he gasped as my fingers pinched and tugged the gasping breath out of him. I unfastened the rest of his buttons.

"Quiet," I told him, kissing him to silence him, climbing up on his lap to straddle him. I put my hands into his hair. It was full and lush.

I loved it.

I didn't know what was happening to me and I didn't care. The fear was gone. Tension had melted away. The only thing in the universe that I wanted was already between my legs. Drawing urged me to keep going and I didn't see any reason not to.

I stroked his chest, going lower and lower, until I found the thick bulge that even his loose pants couldn't conceal. I traced my fingers over it lightly. His shuddery moan began to resemble a whimper; it excited me even more.

"I think I found something you like," I whispered, my fingers still caressing him. I kissed him, forcing him to lay back.

If nothing had interrupted us that night, I would have taken Ghalib. But, as I straddled him, enjoying the power of my sexuality and the pleasure on Ghalib's face, a knock sounded.

Immediately, my senses returned. What was I doing? What on earth was I doing? I leapt off of him and scrambled to find my dress. I zippered myself into it in one, fluid movement.

"Damn," Ghalib said, sitting up. We were still outside but I heard the distinct knock again. I backed away from the bed, trying to catch my breath and calm my heart. I couldn't trust myself. "Yes," he barked. A door opened, seemingly, in thin air. Around it, the observatory formed again. When Ghalib stood, shirtless, the bed disappeared.

Jason pushed the door open. His eyes widened when he saw Ghalib and he looked like he wanted to retreat. "Yes," Ghalib prompted impatiently.

"Lord Victor... he thought he left something... a lighter, Sir. He asked me to fin—"

"It will wait until morning. Tell him that. And no further interruption."

Jason cast a look at me, then looked back to Ghalib. "Very good, Sir." Jason made a hasty retreat.

The door closed and I turned around. Ghalib didn't bother replacing his shirt. He just swallowed a whole glass of wine in three gulps. "Would you like some?" he asked, refilling his glass. I didn't move. "Relax," he said, sighing. "Persistent as I am, even I can't hope to capture that spark again tonight."

I crossed the room and accepted the wine. "What happened to

me?" I asked, trembling.

He smiled. "I misjudged you. I thought your passions were un-awakened. Now, I see that they are very much awake. You just happen to have a wall of self-restraint around you. When the Drawing broke through your restraint, well, you saw the results."

"I shouldn't have done that. The way I behaved, that was a mistake, Ghalib," I said, the heat coming into my cheeks.

"The only mistake was mine. I should have told Jason not to interrupt us. I would love to know where you were headed."

"You know exactly where I was headed," I said darkly. "It may not have been your fantasy, with me coerced but—"

"No, but I would have gotten over my disappointment," he said with a smile, topping my wine again. "Because it would have confirmed to me what I already believe to be true."

"And what is that?" I asked.

"That' you're mine."

"Yours?" I asked, feeling a prickle of irritation. "I'm not yours, Ghalib."

"I see that you would prefer I be less possessive," he teased.

I backed away from him, ignoring the sensuality, ignoring his eyes. "I would prefer that you stop acting like you own me. I'm a captive, with no choice but to be here. And, tomorrow, I'll be in Victor's house and I will no more belong to him than I belong to you. No matter how many times he pierces or brands me."

He took what he had done to me so lightly. Stolen me from my world, from my sister, and brought me into his. He had turned me into a freak and paraded me around like a designer dog. He scared me and he enjoyed it.

The amusement left his face. "You're quite right," he replied soberly. "You don't belong to me. Despite being held here, you remain unclaimed."

"If you gave me a choice, I would return home," I told him.

"I know," he said. He sounded sad.

"May I return to my room, now?" I asked.

"Of course, Elaine," he said, looking at me thoughtfully again. "Get some rest."

Chapter 12

Hard Choices

When I woke up, the first thing I thought was: today is the day that I must go with Victor. I remembered all of his references to branding and piercing. I saw his plans for me when the Drawing shivered through me. My stomach wouldn't stop jumping. I had already dropped several pounds and didn't see that getting any better during my stay with Victor.

Was I really going to do this? Let Victor take possession of me? I didn't even know how long I had to stay with him. Dread gnawed like a rat in the pit of my stomach. Before the night was over, I would be alone with Victor. I told myself that I could handle this. The Drawing would help me deal with any pain. I had to believe that it was true. I had to believe it because my only other choice was to allow Ghalib to claim me.

The word 'pet', the very idea, made me want to retch. I tried to imagine myself collared and leashed, like the humans at the gala. If I allowed this to happen, I would be completely dependent on Ghalib's good will. How long would it be before he treated me like Alexis? How long before this careful interest wore off and he became harsh?

Staying with Victor would be a transient experience. Being Ghalib's pet would not. I tried to convince myself that I had already made my decision.

I rolled off of the couch and was in the bath when Lisa came in. "You're up early," she called. "The Master told me to bring you down as soon as you're ready. He has guests planned."

"I know. Victor is coming to take me."

She stepped all of the way into the bathroom. "Please reconsider the Master's offer."

"Don't make this harder," I told her. "I can survive my time with Victor. If I say yes to Ghalib now, I'll never get away from him."

She opened her mouth and closed it. Finally, she said, "Yes, Miss."

"Would you choose a dress for me?"

"Yes, Miss," she repeated in that same dead tone.

Dressing was a silent affair. She selected a beautiful rose colored gown with subtle embroidery. It was simple and when I wore it, I felt like a flower. Lisa brushed my hair until it was silk. When she was done, she said, "You look lovely. I'll take you to the Sitting room."

Jason didn't come for me. I wanted to say good-bye and didn't know if I would get the chance now. I followed Lisa through the twisting corridors, wondering if Victor's house would be a maze like this. Maybe he wouldn't even give me the chance to explore. The Drawing whispered that I was right. That I would be bound for my entire stay with him.

Lisa rapped at a door and opened it. Ghalib stood with two women. I remembered them from the Festival of Pets. The blonde, cool Architect named Anna and her redheaded pet named Julia. I broke into a wide smile. The relief of not seeing Victor was as good as a drug.

Ghalib crossed the room to me. "You remember Anna and Julia?"

"Of course," I said enthusiastically. Anna squeezed my hand and flushed at the pulsing energy. "I thought I would only see Victor tonight," I added.

"He's due shortly," Ghalib said without smiling.

"We're here to demonstrate the favorable possibilities of a Master-pet relationship," Anna said.

"I'm not interested." My voice didn't sound sure.

"Failing in that," Anna continued, "we will witness the exchange. And I've already made the next claim. After Victor, you come to my home. You only need endure three cycles with him."

The flutter in my stomach went wild again. "Three days. I can do that."

Julia took my hand. "You're ice cold!" she exclaimed. She led me to the blazing fireplace and pulled me down on the hearth. "I can't wait until you come stay with us. I've been thinking about you since the festival."

"I've thought about you, too," I said, flushing. I didn't want to be curious about her situation as a pet, but I couldn't help it. I didn't want to be tempted to accept Ghalib's collar but my dread at Victor could not be denied. "Did you really volunteer to stay here with Anna?"

"Oh, yes," Julia said enthusiastically. "I'll admit, I was a little shocked when I first saw Anna in real life. I kept dreaming about this beautiful woman. Then she showed up at the diner where I waitressed. I thought I'd gone over the edge."

"I know that feeling," I muttered.

"It was such a nasty little restaurant and she looked completely out of place. Then when I tried to take her order, she asked me to come away with her. My life kind of sucked and I didn't think I had anything to lose. Plus those dreams of Anna were so exciting. I'm so glad I said yes," she said, her face lit with a romantic glow.

"So, you agreed to be her pet right away?" I prompted.

"No, I was her companion for a few weeks, like how you are with Ghalib. Then she offered me the collar and I accepted. I never want to go back to that awful little apartment where I used to live. Julia takes care of me and I... I take care of her." She flushed pink. "What did you used to do?"

"I was a secretary." I used to say 'administrative assistant' to try to make myself feel better about my job. There was no point to that here. "It was so boring."

"It's not boring here," Julia teased.

"No. Never a dull moment."

Her voice lowered. "Are you really an Omnilight?"

"That's what they keep telling me."

"What's it like?"

I thought about how to describe it. "Whenever an Architect touches me, it's like foreplay." I could have said a million more words but they all seemed too weak. "When they kiss me, I see their fantasies. I saw you in Anna's head."

"She has a one track mind, my Anna," Julia grinned.

"What's it like, being a pet?"

"Strange," she said. "I can hear her in my head, sometimes, calling for me. And when she gives commands a certain way, I don't have any choice but to obey."

"Do you regret agreeing to it?"

"No," she said. "Not usually." She took both of my hands and squeezed them. "I'm so glad you're here."

"Look at them Ghalib," Anna said, watching us from across the room. "You'll have to come over when Elaine is with us."

"I would like that," he said.

"Consider the invitation already extended."

Jason entered the room. "Lord Victor is here," he said.

Ghalib offered me a hand and I took it as I stood. The Drawing between us was smooth, like aged whisky. I didn't have time to contemplate the feeling because Victor was there in a moment. His face was still in shadows, but his demeanor was excited glee. My stomach lurched. I wanted to cry.

Jason showed Victor into the study. Anna and Ghalib moved closer to Julia and me, as if they were trying to protect us. My heart pounded painfully.

"Ghalib, Anna, Julia... Elaine," Victor greeted us in turn. He accepted a wine glass from Jason.

Anna inclined her head coolly. "Victor. It's been ages."

"Too long. However, I don't like to interfere with mistresses who are overprotective of their pets." His eyes traveled hungrily over Julia who held him in cold contempt.

"You don't permit Victor access to Julia?" Ghalib asked.

"Of course I don't," Anna replied. "Julia comes away black and blue every time she's near him."

Ghalib nodded. "Please sit," Ghalib said to Victor, indicating towards a chair.

"No. I'm eager for Elaine and I to start our evening." He turned to me. "We should start out the right way. Put your hands behind your back."

I did as he said. I was too afraid not to. Cold metal snapped tight around my wrists. When his skin brushed mine, the Drawing whispered that the branding irons were already in the fire. I closed my eyes and tried to breathe myself to a calm place.

"Would you stay for an aperitif?" Ghalib asked.

"No."

"Then, may I have a word with you before you go?"

"Stalling?"

Ghalib grinned. "Can you blame me?"

Victor heaved a sigh. "Very well."

They stepped to the other side of the room and I edged closer to Anna and Julia. "She's trembling," Julia said, rubbing my bound arms. "Isn't there anything that you can do to stop this?" she asked Anna in a whisper.

"No. We're here to observe. Nothing more."

"But Anna. It's *Victor*."

"I'm well aware of that," she said, casting a look towards Victor and Ghalib.

Their volume climbed. "I'm asking for a favor. That's all."

"You're trying to exert control where you have no right to," Victor hissed back.

"She's been in this world for all of five cycles. You'll have the chance to claim her again," Ghalib said. "Brand her and pierce her the next time you have her."

"Just because you wasted your time with her, don't ask me to do the same."

"It was *no waste*," Ghalib said hotly.

"Unrequited devotion does not become you, Ghalib," Victor taunted, his eyes cutting to me. "You have no right to be protective. The Omnilight does not belong to you!" He spoke of me like I was an object. A jolt of anger joined the jolt of fear.

"If she belonged to me, I wouldn't have to ask," Ghalib muttered.

"I am done with this conversation," Victor said. "Elaine, Come!"

He called me like a dog. I didn't budge. Instead I turned to Ghalib. "Why do you care if he brands me or not?" I asked.

"The pain is excessive, I'm told," he said stiffly. "And he rarely stops at just one." He turned back to Victor. "I don't suppose you'd allow me to barter something in exchange for her unmarked skin."

"I can think of nothing I would accept in exchange for that experience," Victor said stubbornly.

"Nothing?" Ghalib asked. His tone changed and I recognized it.

It was sly and persuasive. "I remember an evening we spent not all that long ago that didn't turn out as you had envisioned." Victor's ears turned red. "Perhaps you would enjoy a chance to redo the night. Push for a different outcome."

Victor seemed to be thinking. "Perhaps I would. Is this a formal offer?"

"Yes. No branding, tattooing, or piercing."

"You'll willingly wear shackles?

"I will," Ghalib said, looking at me.

"Is the branding restriction only for Elaine's skin?"

Ghalib's lips set into a grim line. "It could be. If you would allow me to see her once while she's in your home."

"We have a deal. I'll restrain myself and I'll have you to dinner one night." He turned to me. "Come, Elaine."

I hesitated a moment while Victor waited. My anger rose again and I didn't even try to fight it back. I crossed the room as Victor had commanded, but I bypassed him on my way to Ghalib. "I am not OK with the fact that you kidnapped me and keep me here against my will. Do you fully understand that?"

"I believe I do," he replied, looking at me curiously.

"This place is very intimidating to me."

"I can only imagine."

I glanced at Victor, who tapped his foot impatiently. Then I met Ghalib's green eyes. "Do you still want me to be your pet?" I asked. My voice faltered on the word 'pet'.

A slow-spreading smile illuminated Ghalib's face. His voice was earnest. "More than I can say."

"It's a little late for this, don't you think?" Victor objected.

"No," Anna replied coolly, "It's not too late until you leave Ghalib's house with her. You know that, Victor. The law is very clear."

My heart pounded so fast, I was almost dizzy. Ghalib's gaze seemed to bore into me. "Is this a formal offer?" he asked, echoing Victor's words, taunting him without looking at him.

"You won't brand me?"

"I told you," he said softly, "I'll only hurt you in ways you'll like."

I shivered. "You won't share me?"

"I will eventually. I'll have to. It would be very rude to never share an Omnilight. But, I'll wait as long as I can."

I couldn't ask about the things that really scared me. Would he rape me? Would he treat me like he did Alexis? What sort of perversions did he have planned for me?"

"Elaine?" Ghalib asked.

"Show me this collar."

Chapter 13

Somebody's Pet

I could practically taste Ghalib's pleasure. Victor watched open-mouthed, as if his favorite toy had dissolved before his eyes. Ghalib held out his hand and a collar appeared on it. Not the same one that I had worn to the Festival, but similar. Gold filigree, but so thickly encrusted with gems, you almost couldn't see the fine, delicate metal-work. Ghalib opened it at a hinge. I took a shuddery breath and Ghalib smiled.

"Tell me you belong to me," he said.

"I belong to you," I whispered.

"Say that you do this of your own free will."

"I submit to you of my own free will."

"Say that you serve the pleasure of your Master."

That one nearly stuck in my throat. "I serve at the pleasure of my Master."

I closed my eyes and he slowly closed the collar around my neck. I heard it snap; I felt it shrink. Soon it became soft and flexible, moving with my skin. At the same moment, the metal shackles fell from my wrists and clanged to the floor. I opened my eyes and Ghalib was staring down at me. "Say my name," he whispered.

I felt the command. Before I could even process what he wanted, my lips formed his name. "Ghalib." It was as if the collar compelled me to act. His lips brushed mine ever so softly, then he looked over my shoulder.

"Victor, I think you should go."

I looked behind me. Victor had picked up the shackles and they sagged between his hands.

"You can't blame me," he said. "You would have done the same."

"Perhaps I would have," Ghalib agreed. "But I still would like for you to leave."

"Not even one congratulatory glass of Champagne?" Victor asked. "It's not as if I played no role in Elaine's decision to become your pet."

"That is true," Ghalib told him. "But we must celebrate together another time, when I am less angry with you. And, of course, there is no need for our agreement any longer."

"Of course," Victor said, sounding particularly grumpy. As quick as that, Victor disappeared. If everyone hadn't been so tense, and I hadn't been wearing the collar, it would have been as if he had never been there.

"Come, Pet," Ghalib said, using the word as if he liked the sound of it. He pulled an ottoman in front of his chair so that I sat below him and in front of him. Anna mirrored the action with Julia. I didn't demur. I couldn't think of anything except where I might have been sitting at this moment if Victor had taken me.

Ghalib told Jason to set up the dining room and bring champagne. His voice practically lilted.

"What a delight this is," Anna said. "I expected half of this evening to consist of consoling a morose Ghalib and going home exhausted."

"Thank you, Anna," Ghalib replied dryly.

"And though I know you probably long to be alone with each other, I'm grateful we're to share dinner," she added.

"I'm grateful you're staying, too," I said too quickly. I doubt anyone missed the fear in my voice, but I tried to lighten the tone when I said, "It's hard to enjoy anyone's company when you know Victor is lying in wait."

Anna laughed in a refined tinkle. "Perhaps I shouldn't point out that you've only traded Victor for Ghalib."

A shiver ran through me. Ghalib leaned close to my ear. "An excellent exchange, if I may say so."

I didn't know how to respond, so I didn't. Jason poked his head in and indicated that the dining room was ready. Ghalib took one of my arms and Anna the other. I felt like a live wire between them.

Julia was the one who noticed. "Is it that intense?" she asked.

I nodded, breaking contact with both of the Architects and falling into a chair. "It can take my breath away sometimes."

"That's because you're still fighting it," Ghalib said, taking his own seat.

Matthew and Jason served our food and I considered what Ghalib said. It was true that I struggled against the Drawing when Ghalib touched me. But lately, I'd been noticing the energy more and more without any touch at all. It was like an invisible miasma, swirling and whispering. That type of Drawing didn't jolt me or leave me breathless. Was it really because I wasn't fighting it?

I realized that Ghalib was talking and I tuned back in. "...suppose I'm going to have to host some sort of event to introduce her. I wonder how long I can delay that."

"If all goes well tonight, I would not count on having much time," Anna replied.

"Damn."

"Is it her comfort you're thinking of, or your own?" Anna asked.

Ghalib smirked. "Both. I can imagine the comments now."

"Something to do with the fact that you run through human partners like you're planning on experiencing each member of the race at least once?"

"Yes," Ghalib replied, looking at me. "Something like that."

I felt the Drawing urging me to tease him too. "I thought you said you were a *recovering* philanderer," I said.

"He said he was recovering?" Anna asked with raised eyebrows. "Alexis is still dying to service you. I heard that Selma had a rather rigorous night a short time ago and Victor confided in Markus that he had a human selected for you when you are ready for variety. That's not even counting whatever humans you've been dallying with and Victor's attempt to bed you tonight."

"I've had no human partners since Elaine came and Victor hardly wanted to bed me," Ghalib said. "However, the rest is true enough." Ghalib looked at me. "I have a substantial appetite. But at the moment, I have a very specific craving."

I struggled not to react.

"For her sake, I hope Elaine has matching desires," Anna said.

Ghalib smiled. "I can't wait to find out."

I shivered again and remembered the things that his mind had shown me. Only me. All of these hungers and thirsts were mine to handle.

Julia put a sympathetic hand on my arm. It was then that I realized that Ghalib scared her, too. He didn't seem to miss anything, either. His eyes skimmed over her hand and he leaned forward. "How do you like my new pet, Julia?"

She jumped and snatched her hand back, like she had been caught doing something wrong. "I like her very much."

"She's never been with a woman," he said.

My face flamed. "Ghalib!"

"Shh," he hushed and my lips pressed closed at his command.

"You haven't?" Julia asked.

I shook my head, afraid to use my voice and have it fail.

"I would like to watch you kiss her," Ghalib said, his voice as smooth as silk.

My heart pounded and pink came into Julia's cheeks. "Anna?" she asked.

"I would like to see you kiss her, too," Anna answered.

She turned her chair towards me. My heart raced more out of excitement than fear. I closed my eyes and she kissed me. I was immediately struck by her softness. Her lips were satin. Her chin and cheeks were silk. Her hands went to my waist and Anna sighed.

A light touch rested on my shoulder; Drawing vibrated through me. It was warm, arousing, urging—easy to get lost in. I deepened the kiss; her hands trailed up my ribs. She was so warm and soft. I wanted more. I wanted all of her. I slid her dress up to her thighs and caressed her legs. She whimpered and the sound of it reminded me of where I was and what I was doing. I pulled back.

Julia smiled at me. "You sure you haven't done this before?"

Ghalib traced small circles on my back. Pleasure hummed through me. Julia kissed me again. She drew my dress up until our bare knees touched. She stroked my upper legs. It was good to feel heat with another person. We broke our kiss and Julia winked at me.

"My Julia loves to put on a show," Anna said fondly.

Ghalib took his hand from my back and sat down. "Perhaps you'll have your chance sometime soon," he said in a secretive tone. Before I could question it, he turned to me. "So Elaine. Women?"

I wanted to hide my face but the Drawing gave me courage. "I would say yes."

"She's very inexperienced, " Ghalib reported to Anna. My face just kept getting hotter. "Only men. Only one at a time. Nothing more exotic."

Anna looked fascinated. "You don't say."

"I wish he wouldn't," I muttered.

"You've never been with more than one lover?" Anna asked. I shook my head. "Never performed for an audience"?"

"No," I said. I'm sure I sounded horrified.

Anna and Ghalib exchanged a significant look.

Anna watched us with a knowing smile. "I think it's time we took our leave."

"Must you?" Ghalib said politely.

"I find myself anxious. I need some time alone with my Julia and I daresay you would like some time with your new pet."

"I would," Ghalib admitted, his eyes hot on me. "But we must arrange another private meeting soon. I am eager for our girls to play more."

"As am I," Anna agreed.

Julia kissed me again. "I can't wait to see you again. I'm so glad you didn't go with Victor."

"Me too," I agreed, kissing her back.

"A pleasure, my dear," Anna said, laying her hand lightly on my shoulder.

"Even more so for me," I replied, the heat coming to my face.

They used the door to leave the room, even though I'm sure they could have transported from anywhere. I was still smiling when I turned.

Ghalib was in the middle of the room watching me. His amusement had melted away. I didn't say anything; I just waited. I was well aware of the situation: being collared and alone with a man who can command me. His face was aglow with pleasure. Apprehension battled with Drawing. Since he was the one officially in charge, I let him make the first move.

He circled me once, appraising me from every angle. "I can hardly believe that you're really wearing my collar."

I forced myself to take long, slow breaths. *Don't fight the Drawing. Don't fight the Drawing.* I repeated it like a mantra in my head.

"Come here," he ordered.

My body responded immediately. It was the strangest sensation, like my body was under the control of another mind. I smoothly crossed the room and stopped directly in front of him. "Oh," I gasped.

He smiled at me. "Oh, indeed," he teased. He looked at me for a long moment without touching me. I didn't know how utter lack of contact could be so stimulating. "Think of it, Elaine," he said, his voice still light, "you could be with Victor right now."

"Yes," I said.

"Taken," he added.

"Raped," I corrected.

"Branded, too, if I had left him to do whatever he liked."

"I know."

"I think you may owe me something for giving you an alternative to that fate."

"Something besides submitting to you, wearing your collar, and giving up my freedom? Something more than all that?"

He chuckled. "When you put it that way...."

He lifted a hand to touch me and I backed away a step. "What if I don't want to have sex with you?" I asked.

His hand lowered. He seemed to be thinking, though he didn't look angry. "I could accept that, for tonight," he finally answered.

"Not for the long-term, though?"

His expression grew very serious. "No. Not for the long term. One more night or two won't harm me though, now that you're mine."

I shocked at the possessiveness in his voice and I reminded myself that he wasn't going to force me into anything right now. I also thought of the bargain that he struck with Victor on my behalf. The Drawing hummed around us and I tried to listen to it. Then I flushed, knowing what it was telling me to do.

He stepped forward and touched my cheek. "What's this?"

I took a breath and before he could question me further, I started to sing. It was a poem from the seventeenth century set to music, one that I had never forgotten from my vocal lessons even though I was more than a decade away from the last time I sang it. It didn't require accompaniment or special acoustics. I was close enough to Ghalib that I could sing softly.

His eyes widened in rapt attention. I made it through three verses without looking away. When I drew out the last, lingering note, his eyes were bright. His breath came fast.

"Thank you for your willingness to protect me from the worst of Victor," I whispered.

I lowered my eyes but his fingertips caught my chin and tilted it back up. Then, he kissed me. It wasn't entirely unexpected but the wash of energy seemed especially strong. It didn't jolt me, though. I was finding it easier and easier to accept the sensation. It also helped that his lips were soft and teasing, even though the images he sent were anything but soft. Me, naked and chained to his bed, chained to the leg of the dinner table as he fed me bits, chained to his belt by a short leash that confined me to my knees. I couldn't think or act. I could only watch and feel. If Ghalib hadn't broken the kiss, I doubt that I would have.

"I love the things your mind shows me," he said.

The Drawing urged me to play. "What do you see?" I asked.

He drew me to the fire and we sat down on the warm hearth. "Lately, it seems like your interests are widening. Tonight, it was you bound to a bed while you were taken from behind." I grew warm and he grinned. "Sometimes I see Julia toying with you. Sometimes it's me in your head, taking you."

"Really?" I asked, trying to keep my composure. "You and Julia?"

"You're surprised?"

"Actually, yes."

He gave me a sly look. "What about you? What do you see?"

Drawing pulsated in the air. I felt strange—different, sensual, confident. "I see myself in various situations," I told him. "You seem to be distracted by the idea of chaining me to things."

He chuckled. "I confess, it's true."

The energy started to feel smooth, like warm vibrations. I decided to push my luck a little. "I have a question," I said.

Ghalib turned very serious. "Anything."

"Why do you have a life-sized nude sculpture of me?" I lifted my eyebrows at him. "You know, in your studio, behind a curtain."

Ghalib's laugh sounded embarrassed. It made me feel a little stronger. "Cold comfort, I suppose," he said. "Were you snooping, Elaine?"

"You didn't expect me to just stay in my rooms, did you?" I asked.

"I suppose I didn't."

The presence of that statue left me with such mixed feelings. It was flattering and twisted. I was aroused and sickened by it. "How long have you had that thing?"

"In your time? A few months."

I know I must have gone pale. So long? "Please tell me you haven't had sex with it."

"I didn't," he said quickly, looking horrified at the thought.

"Because that would be seriously concerning behav —"

"I didn't."

I looked at him for a long moment. It was probably the longest amount of time I'd ever let myself study the delicate features of his face. Delicate, but fierce, like a genie made entirely of fire. He wasn't human; the more I looked at him, the more sense it made. "How do you make the sculptures move?" I asked.

The firelight flickered on his pale skin. "I don't *make* them move. I *let* them move." He pinched his lips together, like he was trying to figure out the best way to explain his thoughts. "It's my talent. It's what I do to contribute to human dreams. I create the 'props', if you will, that you interact with."

"That's crazy," I said.

"Anna paints landscapes," Ghalib offered. "That's her talent. Her paintings are used to make the settings for dreams. Victor does the equivalent of metal work. He enjoys welding his creations."

"These are all used in dreams?" I asked.

"Yes. Dream Makers use the items we make to create the actual Dream for the human."

"Dream Makers?"

"Like Joan and Carl downstairs," he replied. "When we get the details correct and they use the items well, it's a very satisfying experience for the human and the Dream Maker."

"What happens when everything isn't right?"

"You get fragmented, nonsensical dreams. And, quite frankly, very grumpy Dream Makers."

I laughed and his lips twitched into a smile. "Architects like Anna and Victor and me are called the Gentry," he offered. "We interact differently with the Drawing than Dream Makers. We have a closer relationship to that energy."

He picked up my hand and stroked it in harmless ways, tracing lines over my palm, stretching my fingers, and squeezing the pads of my fingers. I didn't jolt because I didn't fight the tingling arousal. The Drawing vibrated in me, telling me that he was calm — easy — enjoying the conversation.

"You seem different," he said.

"You mean other than the collar?"

"Yes. You aren't usually so open in your curiosity."

"I'm a little more relaxed," I said honestly. "It's easier to do that when you aren't being constantly pressured for sex."

He chuckled. "It will be more relaxing for both of us when pressure isn't needed," he insinuated.

"Oh, yes," I said, rolling my eyes. "I can't imagine that situation being tense at all."

"Eventually, I envision reaching for you when I want to, taking you however I like, and leaving you completely languid." He dropped my hand and brushed a finger across my lips. "You're going to love it when we consummate this relationship. I honestly don't understand the resistance."

I could have reviewed with him all of the reasons why: the kidnapping, the separation from my sister, the way he scared me, all of the sexually laden conversations that left me feeling threatened. But I didn't. Instead, I did my best to maintain the lightness of the situation. "I'm going to *love* it? What if I don't? What it it's terrible for both of us?"

He laughed. "I have full confidence that it won't be terrible."

I rolled my eyes at him.

"Sculpture isn't my only talent. There are many things I do

well."

I lifted my eyebrows. "I have no talent whatsoever. Maybe you should get out while you still can."

He laughed again. "Then it will be my job to find your talents and exploit them for my own gain."

He leaned closer to me, like he was going to kiss me again. I decided that it was a good time to leave. I sat up. "I'm tired. May I return to my room?" He hesitated, like he wanted to demand a bit more time. "You always have the statue of me if you grow lonely," I teased.

"I may have to order you to stop bringing that up."

He didn't stop me from standing or leaving. I knew he watched me as I passed through the door. Thank goodness, the hallways were more obliging than usual. I barely walked five minutes before I came to my room.

Then, I opened the door, ready for some well-earned rest.

Chapter 14
The Ritual

Lisa sat tense and pale-faced in my sitting room, where I had left her. It looked like she was mourning someone's death.

"Oh, Miss!" she exclaimed, jumping to her feet with delight. "You didn't go with Victor. How wonderful!"

"I couldn't agree more," I said. She hurried to get me nightclothes and a robe. "And Anna and Julia were delightful," I added, following her into the bedroom. I stopped dead. "What did you do in here?"

The wall that was entirely windows was blocked with greenery. Great flowering plants that reached the high ceilings lined up in ornate pots along the window. Vines dangled, like a curtain to the floor. The room smelled like a flower garden and felt nearly private.

"I wanted to surprise you. I figured, when the Master got another chance with you, it would be ready," Lisa said, flushing. "My talent is growing things. They just grew faster than I thought they would. I didn't want you to sleep on the couch anymore."

"This is beautiful," I said. "It smells so good."

Lisa's smile got even brighter. "Would you like me to draw you a bath or—"

"Yes, and stay to talk with me."

"Very well," she said, sounding pleased.

The bath was just what I needed: warm, fragrant, and relaxing. I just reclined into it while Lisa drew a chair into the bathroom. "Your collar is so beautiful," she said.

"I just couldn't go with Victor," I said, getting a chill even in the warm water. "You used to work for him, didn't you? Was he—"

"He was cruel," she said plainly. "He liked me very much, which

112

meant he spent an unusual amount of time tormenting me. My happiest day was when Master Ghalib won me from him."

"Won you?"

"They had a wager of some sort. If those two have any weakness, it's gambling. Lord Victor lost and had to give up one of his servants. I was chosen. I knew it was because Master Ghalib knew it would deprive Victor of his favorite sport. I didn't care why he did it. I was glad to go."

The Drawing whispered to me. "But you weren't just a servant to Ghalib, were you?"

She hesitated. "The Master has intense sexual appetites. He and I... he was briefly — "

"It's all right," I soothed. "I was just curious." I thought for a moment about the turns the conversation had taken that evening.

"Do you know anything about a night Ghalib and Victor spent together?" I asked.

"Oh, yes, when Victor was first made a lord, he threw a dinner. I think it was the first time he and Ghalib ever met. He taunted Ghalib and flirted with him unspeakably. That night Ghalib stayed."

"What happened?" I asked in a low voice.

She paused. "What I know is that in the morning, when Ghalib left, he looked very amused. I saw him go. He told me, 'For all of his talk, he doesn't play very well when the tables are turned.' One of the other servants told me that he had to help Victor to his bed and that he was covered with bites and welts. They've been rivals ever since."

I got another chill. I intuitively knew about Ghalib's darkness but I had never experienced anything like that. If I had gone with Victor, it would have been worse than I could have imagined; he would have had his revenge with me. Yet, staying with Ghalib suddenly became much more intimidating. I stepped out of the tub and started getting ready for bed.

My nightgown was almost sheer white cotton and dozens of little pearl buttons fastened down the front. While I buttoned, my mind turned. What had I done by accepting the collar? I hadn't had a good option but still I doubted my decisions. I crawled under the covers and drifted off to sleep with that thought in my head.

Elaine. I opened my eyes but my room was still dark. Lisa was nowhere around and it felt like the middle of the night. Why was I awake? *Elaine.* Again, I heard it, like someone whispered my name in my ear.

I stepped out of bed and pulled on my robe. *Elaine.* I recognized that voice. It was Ghalib's and it compelled me. My mind wanted to ignore the summons but my body obediently responded. I stepped into the hallway.

Elaine. I followed my instinct and it led me to the front door. I hesitated. Was this a trap? Was I allowed to go out there?

Elaine. My body responded and I exited the front door without another thought.

The wind was harsh but warm as I walked towards the cliffs in my bare feet. The full moon was huge and golden. It lit my way. Where was I going? I still didn't know. All I knew was that I followed the voice that summoned me.

Finally, I saw ghostly figures at the edge of the cliffs. Human bodies tumbled in the background. And there was some sort of stone platform. Ghalib's white hair glinted in the moonlight and there were six other people there, all dressed in ghostly white robes. I shivered. What was this?

Ghalib saw me approach and stepped forward. "Come here," he commanded. My body obeyed. While I crossed scrubby grass, I stole looks at the others. Anna, Victor, Markus, and three others. Beautiful, magnificent creatures with hungry, eager eyes.

"Ghalib, what is this?" I asked with a trembling note of panic. I remembered the guarded conversation between Anna and Ghalib, wondering how I would deal with this evening. My terrified heart accelerated.

He smiled at me. Intense and unapologetic. His fingers went to the belt of my robe and untied it, sliding the garment off of my shoulders and letting it flutter away on the wind. "You must be quiet," he told me. His fingers moved to the buttons of my nightgown, releasing the dozens of little pearl catches with expert speed. "You must be obedi-ent, and no harm will come to you." He pulled my nightgown off and sent it off on the wind to follow my robe. I was only in my panties.

"For God's sake!" I whispered, trying to cover myself.

"Shh," he hushed. It wasn't a command so I bit my lip to quiet my fear. He pulled a knife from his robes and cut away my undergarment. "This is a ritual that must be done. It notifies everyone that an Omnilight has been found and claimed."

With gentle hands, he moved my shielding arms to my sides. It didn't matter how gentle he was, though. The Drawing flashed through me. His fingers grazed the side of my breast and my nipples stiffened. Ghalib smiled down at me.

He turned me to face the others. "This is my pet, Elaine. We are here tonight to release the Drawing and to notify the In-between that there is an Omnilight in our midst."

My heart thundered. I bit my lip harder. The Architects raked their eyes over me and I knew there was no escape. I stood up straight and lifted my chin, letting the Drawing gather around me. It hummed through me; arousal rose to meet fear.

One by one, they wordlessly approached me, kissing me, stroking my buttocks, my breasts, leaving me breathless and throbbing. The Drawing with so many Architects touching me, kissing me, was overwhelming. Each Architect had a different flavor. My heart raced and my body ached. I craved release, not just from this night but all those that preceded it.

Ghalib came around to the front of me and kissed me hard, tasting the inside of my mouth, biting at my lips. I whimpered, the coursing vibrations urging me to clasp handfuls of his hair. Then, the six other Architects were around me, licking at my breasts, kissing at my back, nipping at my buttocks, their tongues teasing my legs. Ghalib's kiss grew wild, showing me primal coupling. My arousal rose and rose. They pulled my arms behind my back. Fingers everywhere, except where I wanted them most. A loud moan escaped me and they backed away.

"Magnificent," Anna commented.

"Agreed," another replied. "She's very talented."

I thought that they must be able to feel the heat coming off of me, like I was a radiator. "To release the Drawing, to announce your presence, you must orgasm in the presence of seven," Ghalib whispered to me, coming to stand behind me. A jolt of fear shot through me followed by a wild heat. "We can touch you," he continued, "but it must not be an Architect that brings your climax. Only another mortal is permitted that honor."

Five of the Architects, sans Victor, opened their loose robes and five pets emerged. Julia, Tobias, one other beautiful blonde, and two sturdy men — all bare, all flushed, all collared, and all eager. "Choose, Elaine," Ghalib whispered in my ear.

I looked from one to the next. How could you choose a lover from people you didn't know? How was I going to be able to orgasm in the presence of seven? I had trouble orgasming if there was a mirror in the room. The Drawing jolted me. "I can't do this," I whispered to Ghalib.

"You can," Ghalib whispered. "We all want nothing more than your pleasure. Just let us give it to you."

My breathing came faster. Tobias winked at me but my eyes kept stopping on Julia. In my life, I had never had the courage to experience a woman. I glanced at the other Architects. They watched me expectantly. I couldn't escape this. I had to choose.

"Julia," I whispered. The other pets disappeared and only she, smiling and beautiful remained. She approached and pressed her body against mine, stomach to stomach, our breasts flattening each other's.

"I'm so glad you chose me," she whispered and she kissed me deeply, passionately. Even without the Drawing, I throbbed. I grasped her shoulders, pulling her closer, kissing her harder. The Architects sighed and I tasted the soft skin of her neck. I was reluctant to break our kiss.

Anna moved forward, standing in front of the other Architects. "Come," Ghalib instructed me, taking my hand. Julia took my other hand and Anna walked beside us. We made our way along the edge of the cliff to what I could only describe as a white, marble altar. It was like a tabletop. The Architects gathered around it.

He motioned for me and Julia to climb up on the altar. I looked at the falling bodies. "Here?" I whispered.

"Here," Ghalib replied. I crawled onto the marble slab that was about the size of a double bed, so the Architects gathered around could easily touch me or kiss me. Without being told, I laid back. Fear stirred my stomach, but it wasn't as strong as the arousal. I just wished that we weren't at the edge of that cliff, the falling bodies like suicides witnessing my passion.

"Stand with me, Anna," Ghalib said, summoning her with an elegant gesture to the head of the altar. "Your pet is a tribute to you."

Anna moved to his left. "As is yours," she replied.

As one, the Architects reached in to touch me. They pulled my arms away from my body and restrained them there. Others pulled my knees back so that I was vulnerably exposed. Anna put her hands under my chin and pulled my head back so that I could see only her, Ghalib, and the flying, falling humans in the sky.

"Watch me, my Dear," she said.

I felt hands exploring my body. Fingers on my breasts, light strokes along my inner thigh, lips pressed to the arch of my foot. Each touch was that of an Architect. Each touch sent currents of desire through me. Julia hadn't even touched me and already I was arching my back and moaning. I could feel the Architects' approval.

I couldn't see Julia with my head drawn back. But I knew it was her when sharp little teeth pinched at my nipples, making me gasp. Her tongue trailed over my stomach, kissing and nipping, bypassing my passion and lapping at my inner thighs. Finally, her fingers separated me and her tongue slipped into my wetness.

"Oh, God... yes," I breathed. Her playful tongue urged my hips higher. The architects stirred around me. Their lips found my skin, sucking at my fingers, abrading my nipples, kissing my ankles, intensifying the Drawing until I thought my body might explode from the heat.

I tried not to look at the sky but I saw the spirits sailing by. My passion climbed. I wished to be somewhere else. Somewhere calm. I moaned and tossed. When my eyes opened, the sky was clear and glittering with stars. I heard the pounding of waves. The Architects shifted but I couldn't question why. Julia's tongue drove me to distraction.

"Not too quickly, my Love," Anna said. Immediately, the speeding rhythm of her tongue stopped. I wanted to cry out, but I bit my lip.

"As you wish, my Mistress."

I don't know how long I lay on the altar being taunted and teased by Julia. With perfection in timing, she altered her tempo or stopped touching me altogether before I could reach my climax. Once. Twice. Three times. The Architects around us kissed me and stroked my skin, creating an impossible level of Drawing.

I couldn't control myself any more. I gasped and moaned, arching my back, gripping at anything close enough to my hands, bucking with my hips. I looked up at Ghalib's and Anna's delighted, radiant, heightened expressions.

"Oh, please..." I gasped looking from one to the other, unsure who to appeal to.

Ghalib smiled down at me. "I think she's ready."

"Yes," Anna agreed. "Go ahead my pet."

Julia's tongue settled into a relentless, rhythmic stroke. It followed my moving hips with artistic perfection. And finally, finally, I began to rise into orgasm. At that moment, Ghalib leaned over and kissed me.

It was unlike any orgasm that I had ever felt. My whole body spasmed and it almost felt like I actually emitted energy. It was as if the pent-up Drawing just exploded out of me, like a bottle rocket. I bit Ghalib's lips, even as I cried out and thrust my hips insistently at Julia. She was pleased to oblige, licking and stroking until my gasping cries abated. My orgasm seemed to last for minutes. When it was over, Ghalib leaned back and smiled at me.

My arms and legs were released. Anna let go of my chin. I looked around. We were no longer on the cliffs; we were on a beach. Everyone seemed stunned.

Anna mopped her damp forehead with a handkerchief. "She changed your landscape, Ghalib."

"I didn't do that," I said.

"Yes, you did, Pet," Ghalib said. "Though I have no idea how."

"Between that and the orgasm, we should have everyone's attention," Victor said huskily. Laughter sounded around the altar.

Julia crawled up next to me and put her arms around me. "That was extraordinary," she whispered in my ear. Someone covered us with a blanket.

"Yes," was all I could manage.

"Were any of you present for the last Omnilight ceremony?" one female Architect asked. "Poor boy. We had to hold it three times before he could perform. Then we had to send out an announcement, the affect was so weak."

Victor chuckled. "His talents were more evident one-on-one. Though, to be fair, his spark of Drawing was always very weak. Not like this one." He indicated towards me.

"Have you had her, Ghalib?" a male Architect asked. He was dark, like a Native American. I flushed.

"No. No Architect has had her, yet."

"The little tease," Anna said fondly, looking down at Julia and I wrapped around one another.

"I will admit I've been enjoying the foreplay," Ghalib said. "With the intensity of the Drawing, it's nearly satisfying."

Victor looked at me with a wistful smile. "Pity, Elaine. I have little patience for a tease."

"That's no surprise, Victor," I replied smoothly, feeling extraordinarily confident. "Unless, of course, you *are* the tease." He flushed and everyone laughed.

Ghalib looked as happy as I'd ever seen him. "Everyone must come up to the mansion for refreshments. Elaine, Julia, join us once you've dressed."

Julia and I crawled off of the altar and walked hand-in-hand back to the mansion. I know the Architects watched us go. I also knew that Julia was still excited, her nipples taut, her fingers brushing my skin more often than necessary. But we didn't dare steal even the tiniest moment to ourselves. The Architects would be waiting for us after such a display.

Chapter 15

Nyx

I led Julia through the halls, which seemed to meander more than usual, giving us more of a chance to catch our breath and clasp hands. Finally, I found my door. Lisa waited for us. "Oh, Miss!" she exclaimed. "Even I felt that! If the inquiries aren't coming in about you already, I would be shocked."

She had laid out silken robes for us: blue for Julia and green for me. "You felt what?" I asked, pulling mine on.

"The Drawing. Your culmination. It was delightful. And this is your mortal? Julia? I wish I could have seen the ritual."

"I'm sorry," Julia said sweetly. "You felt her orgasm?"

"No," Lisa replied. "I felt the Drawing. It was like I was pressed body-to-body with an Omnilight for a second. I can only imagine how strong it must have been for those of a higher station than me."

"Everyone must have felt that then," I commented.

Julia grinned. "I think you're right. I've never been part of anything like what we just did. It was wild."

I kissed her. "I'm so glad you were there."

We made our way to the library where I knew, instinctively, that the Architects were gathered. For once, the halls didn't twist me all over the mansion. "Ahh, there they are," Anna commented. "We thought maybe you had decided to enjoy one another alone."

"No," Julia said, "but perhaps one night with yours and Ghalib's permission."

Ghalib smiled at me. "Come here, Pet." I obeyed without a choice. He nodded at a low, padded stool in front of his chair and I sat. Julia mirrored me in front of Anna.

As the other Architects chatted amongst themselves, Ghalib toyed with my loose hair, running it through his hands like he was testing its weight. The Drawing current coursed through me and, like at the Festival of Pets, I sensed the Architect's preferences, fetishes, and fantasies. Even after the intensity of the ritual and the incredible release, I began to pulse with arousal.

Jason and Matthew came in with trays of wine. I'll admit that I was a little relieved to see Matthew. After that evening when Victor tormented him, I hadn't seen the servant boy. I didn't know if Ghalib might not give him to Victor to soothe hurt feelings. Clearly, Victor still had hopes for the boy. When Matthew offered his tray to Victor, the Architect took the opportunity to pinch the boy hard on his thigh.

Jason lifted his head, like he heard a doorbell, and walked out. "Don't forget Elaine," Ghalib said to Matthew. Matthew crossed the room to serve me and I couldn't help but notice his eagerness. When he passed me my glass, his fingers brushed the back of my hand. A sweet shiver of Drawing warmed my arm. I didn't acknowledge it, but I knew Ghalib's quick eyes caught the transgression. He narrowed his eyes at Matthew but didn't say anything.

"Well, Ghalib, you are now going to be forced to open your home and have a gala. Unless, of course, you prefer to receive all of the curious individuals," said the Architect with the bronze skin and long black hair of a Native American.

"What fun, Nikiti," Anna said. She turned to Ghalib. "It's been so long. You must."

"Perhaps," he said noncommittally. "Unless one of you would like to host it."

"No," Markus laughed. "You won't get out of this one. I'm eager to see what sort of affairs you hold."

Jason came back into the room and cleared his throat. "Sir, Lady Alexis is here. She demands to see you."

Polite, refined laughter filled the room. "Bring her in," Ghalib said. He stood and offered me a hand, indicating that I should stand, too.

A moment later, a beautiful woman entered. I recognized her. She had hair as black as crow feathers in a dark tumble of curls down her back. She was the woman that I had seen the first night, the woman that Ghalib had taken roughly against a wall. She looked around at all of the other Architects in irritation. "What is the meaning of this Ghalib? Did I or did I not just feel the presence of an Omnilight?"

"You did," Ghalib said in amusement.

Her beautiful face flashed in anger. "Why was I not part of the ceremony?"

"Now, Alexis. Come in. Sit. You have no pet. You know how the ceremony works." A chair appeared out of thin air and Alexis perched on the edge of it but Ghalib and I remained standing. It was as if he enjoyed towering over her.

She scanned the room again. "Victor has no pet and yet you invited him. Victor, for God's sake."

"Don't worry. I'm not offended," Victor said dryly.

"Goodness, Alexis, it wasn't personal," Ghalib said in a way that made me wonder if it was. "Victor had already met Elaine, as had Anna and Markus. If you kept a pet, you may have met her as well and been part of the ritual."

"I don't wish to have a pet," the woman hissed.

"I know what you wish for," Ghalib said with deep meaning, a hard, cruel note in his voice. The other Architects leaned forward. Ghalib and Alexis locked eyes and nobody spoke.

Ghalib still held my hand and I felt the anger radiating off of Alexis. She was... jealous? She didn't want me to know her desires but the Drawing was strong. I got glimpses of Alexis' thoughts. Her, in Ghalib's prison voluntarily. She, shackled to the stone wall in that dank dungeon being strapped with a wide piece of leather. He, taking her roughly, punishingly, while she was chained.

I turned to look at Ghalib. "Is there anyone in this place that you haven't been with?" I asked.

Ghalib chuckled. "Yes," he replied. "You."

Everyone in the room laughed, including Alexis. Even I had to smile. Ghalib resumed his seat, opened his legs, and pulled me down to sit between them. He moved the foot stool out of the way with a sweep of his leg. Alexis' laughter dried up and she glared at me.

Jason returned to the room with another glass of wine that he quickly passed to Alexis. "I'm sorry, Sir," he said. "But Lord Charles and Lady M—"

"Tell everyone that they must wait for a formal introduction," Ghalib told him, "and that I am otherwise engaged."

"I suppose I should be pleased that you let me in at all," Alexis muttered.

Ghalib looked at her with that sharp, cruel quality. "Yes, you should."

"And you aren't even going to allow me to touch your new pet?" It was as if she had trouble with the last word.

Again the room grew quiet. "Very well," Ghalib assented.

I didn't want to touch this woman. I didn't want to know what she did to the Drawing current. Her affection for Ghalib was obsessive and her hatred for me absolute. Still, I offered my hand.

When she gripped my fingers, the shock of Drawing was as strong as any I had ever felt. But it wasn't a smooth current, like Ghalib's; or a lusty one like Anna's; nor even a sharp, cold feeling, like what Victor inspired. Alexis' Drawing was ragged and frayed. Pleasurable, yes, but wild. Unpredictable. Her breath caught and for a moment, her dark eyes widened in shock.

"Kiss me," she demanded. She didn't wait for Ghalib's permission; she wasn't gentle. Her lips smashed against mine. I couldn't hold back the images. I saw her, wearing my collar. Ghalib's fingers caressed her skin as they often caressed mine. In her fantasy, I was a servant that Ghalib practiced his cruelty on: overturning my serving tray, punishing me with a cruel strapping, and spending his passion from the punishment with her. When the kiss broke, I felt raw.

"Come, Elaine," Ghalib said. "You are exhausted. Just sit with me."

He was right. I'd had nearly no sleep and the Drawing had been coursing through me all evening. I was a frayed nerve. When he indicated for me to sit between his legs again, I didn't hesitate. I didn't even mind when he pulled me back to lean against his chest. His Drawing didn't hurt me the way Alexis' had.

Jason entered the room again. "I'm sorry, Sir—"

"I said no further interruptions," Ghalib snapped.

"Yes, Sir, but Nyx's here."

"Tell the envoy that she must wait for another night."

"It's not just the envoy," Jason said softly. "*She's* here, Sir."

The fun drained away from everyone's face and everyone sat up straighter. "Stand, my pet," Ghalib commanded. I did, though I was still rather confused. I saw Anna lock eyes with Ghalib in a serious exchange. He cleared his throat. "Send Nyx in."

Nobody spoke. A few moments later, Jason opened the door and a woman entered. Or, at least she seemed like a woman. Her hair was long and straight and black. She gave off a golden glow; her long hair blew like there was a breeze, though the room was still. Slowly, she scanned the room until she found me. Gliding, possibly floating, she approached me.

"Are you the Omnilight?" she demanded in a beautiful, terrible, echoing voice.

"I am," I replied.

She looked around the room. "They are all afraid of me." She was right. I could feel it, too. "Are you afraid of me?" she asked.

I looked at her beauty, her wildness, and realized that I was actually more frightened of Victor and Alexis. "No. Not exactly."

She smiled and the beauty of it nearly broke my heart. She lifted a glowing hand to my face but she didn't touch it. She didn't need to. I could feel the Drawing, like it was a semi-solid aura around her hand. The surge of current was so intense that I swayed.

"You are strong," she commented.

"Thank you." I took deep breaths. It was as if I hadn't had the most forceful orgasm of my life less than an hour before. Again, I throbbed and pulsed and craved release.

Her hand lowered to my breast, not touching me, not even touching my robe. My nipples hardened again; I knew everyone could tell through the silky material. She reached closer, her fingertips tracing my hardened nipple. The rhythm of my heart grew uneven.

Her lovely face looked pleased. "Yes, you are strong. An Omnilight and a conduit. The current runs well through you. Would you like to come serve me?"

"Excuse me?" I asked.

"You cannot take a human pet as one of your servants," Ghalib said, a hint of steel in his voice. "The rules prohibit it."

"What if I choose to break those rules," she snapped. Her glow grew brighter. Her eyes flickered to Ghalib. "Who will you take your complaints to?"

Anna assumed a more regal demeanor than usual. "The bond between her and Ghalib won't break just because you remove her from this house," she said. "He can still call her from anywhere and command her actions."

Ghalib' wore an expression so enraged, I hardly recognized him. "You had *three days* to claim her if you were going to—"

"I was unaware of the level of talent in this Omnilight," Nyx replied coolly.

"Until the ritual?" Ghalib guessed. "I suppose you regret the choice to not check on the Omnilight yourself. Whatever occupies your hours must be simply fascinating. The problem is that it isn't doing your job." His voice was coated in sarcasm.

"Ghalib," Anna whispered in warning.

Nyx turned to me. "Would you like to leave this house? Come with me and serve me?"

Ghalib's voice made my skin prickle. "If you take her, I will order her back here every day."

I looked back and forth between the two of them. Nyx was the one who finally sighed and looked back at Ghalib. "Very well. I claim first right, then, if you ever find such a pet too challenging to maintain."

His eyes flashed with anger but his voice was even. "Of course, Nyx. If I ever do, I will contact you first."

She leaned closer to me and I think she blew on me. I smelled roses and pine. "A gift," she said.

She cupped her hand and slipped it between my legs. "Oh!" I gasped. Without preamble, without touch, I orgasmed. It was every bit as strong and intense as the one I experienced on the beach. I struggled to maintain my shaking legs. My knees wanted to buckle. I cried out and before I knew it, Ghalib was behind me, supporting my weight. Which was good, because my peripheral vision faded to black. Static in my ears drowned out any sound. Unconsciousness finally claimed me and my last thought was that at least Ghalib was there to catch me when I fell.

When I awoke, I was in my bed and Lisa sat in a chair next to me, the perpetually blooming trees her backdrop. Memories rushed me: the ritual, Alexis, and most of all Nyx. I wondered what had happened after I passed out.

"You're awake!" Lisa exclaimed. "Thank goodness. I'll be right back."

She jumped up and dashed out the door. I pulled myself into a sitting position and took an inventory of myself. Nothing hurt. I felt fairly well-rested. I barely had a chance to pull back the covers when Lisa came rushing back in. "Oh, no, Miss. I have strict orders not to let you out of bed until you've eaten."

"I'm fine," I protested. "How long was I sleeping?"

"More than a day." She arranged my pillows behind my back and pushed me back on them. Then she covered my legs again. "After the ritual and your interaction with Nyx... I'm amazed you woke so soon. Nyx could have put you in a permanent coma."

I frowned. I didn't get the sense that she wanted to hurt me. In fact, her touch left me feeling better and stronger. "Really? Honestly, I think if I hadn't been so tired, I would have been fine."

A knock sounded on the bedroom door and Jason let himself in. He carried a tray that he laid across my lap. "I'm glad you're OK, Miss. We were all very worried about you."

"I'm fine," I said a little more forcefully. "What's with all this fuss? You're acting like I'm an invalid."

Jason and Lisa exchanged looks.

"Nyx could have really harmed you, the way she touched you." Jason said. "Clearly, it was meant to be a punishment for the Master. She'll have to ask permission if she wants to see you. Nyx doesn't ask permission of anyone for anything ever."

I looked at Jason and Lisa. They were completely somber. It was almost funny to me. "Nyx is Ghalib's problem," I said. "But as for me, I'm fine." I took a bite of vegetables to prove my point and they tasted so good, I just kept eating.

Jason broke into a smile. "I'll inform the Master. He'll be glad to hear it."

When he left, Lisa pulled her chair closer to the bed and watched me while I ate. I imagine that she was supposed to make sure I finished my plate. She didn't need to worry about it; I was starving. "So, what happened after I passed out"?" I asked.

"After you fell and Nyx left with her envoy, a couple of the Architects had to call their pets to carry you to your bed. Ghalib laid you on the floor because he was afraid that any more exposure to the Drawing might harm you. Miss Julia cried." She added the bit about Julia with a romantic sigh.

"Could someone let her know I'm OK?" I asked.

"I'm sure the Master will send out a general announcement."

I finished my food without the slightest trouble. "There," I said. "I've eaten. Can I get up and have a bath now?"

"OK," Lisa said reluctantly, heading for the bathroom to get the water ready. "But then, straight back to bed with you."

I stood, expecting to stumble or feel weak-legged. I didn't; I felt great. The bath was wonderful. I lay in the warm water until Lisa's fretting started to get on my nerves. The relief on her face was visible when I stood up.

She helped me on with a fresh nightgown and her fingers brushed my shoulder. "Oh!" she exclaimed. "It's stronger! The Drawing is... more, now." I hadn't felt anything different. Just the same shiver of electricity, but Lisa was brightly flushed.

I crawled into bed believing that I wouldn't possibly sleep. But it wasn't very long before I drifted off.

Chapter 16

Firsts

I opened my eyes again and Lisa was still there. "Feeling better, Miss?"

"I told you," I said, sitting up, "I feel fine. Now I feel extremely well-rested and fine."

She smiled. "The Master would like to see you for dinner, if you're well enough."

I wished I hadn't been so quick about getting out of bed. I could have bought myself a day or two more without Ghalib. I wasn't eager to rejoin him after the display on the altar.

I got up and bathed, brushing my hair. I was flushed and healthy-looking. More healthy than I had ever looked before. When I got back to the room, Lisa had laid out a green gown. It was a loose, draping, elegant thing with a low-cut front. It was as if the thing was designed to bring attention to my collar.

Lisa swept my hair into a low chignon while I put on make-up. We finished just in time. Ghalib's smooth voice called in my mind. *Elaine.* My body complied.

I walked the hallway with perfect confidence, even though I really had no idea of where I was headed. I didn't try to fight it; I let his summons lead me. I ended up in the foyer, where he stood waiting for me in front of one of the windows. The paths from the house still led to a beach that was visible from the house.

"Are we going out?" I asked hopefully.

"No. I wanted to have you to myself," he said, without turning. "I can't believe you changed the landscape."

"I didn't."

"Yes. It was you. We all felt it."

"Why haven't you changed it back?"

"I rather like it." He turned and his eyes fell on me like spotlights. "Come here," he ordered.

I crossed the room and stopped in front of him. Uncharacteristically, he didn't touch me. "How are you feeling?" he asked.

"Very well rested."

"No dizziness?" I shook my head. He put his hand on my bare arm and gasped aloud.

"It's stronger," I said, enjoying the waves of warm vibration.

"Yes," he agreed, not removing his hand. "Still not dizzy?"

"Nope."

He touched my face and leaned in to kiss me. In less than a second, his thoughts flooded my mind. Mainly, it was images of me beneath him moaning and moving in eager time with him. It wasn't a fantasy; it was his determined plans for this night. Drawing seared through me and more details flooded my mind. In the images he sent me, we were on the foyer floor, bundled and bucking where we now stood.

I broke the kiss but Ghalib wouldn't let me pull away. "Dizzy, now?" he asked.

"A bit," I answered breathlessly.

A smile edged with hunger played on his lips. I became acutely aware of the collar and my helpless position. He could order me to fulfill any fantasy and I would have no choice but to obey. Even though the Drawing made me feel powerful, Ghalib was still my Master.

He seemed to be thinking the same thing; he touched my collar. His finger slipped along the low neckline, between my breasts. The Drawing hummed around me, making my skin warm and sensitive. "I have a flood of invitations for us but I declined them all for tonight." He looked me up and down. "I thought I would like to have you to myself."

A flash of fear seared through me; the Drawing transformed the fear into throbbing need. I didn't know what feelings were mine, what feelings were Ghalib's, and what feelings were induced by the Drawing. I lifted my chin and tried to gain some control.

"And here I am," I said lightly. My mind cast around for some sort of distraction. Anything except a conversation about an evening alone. "I love the beach," I offered. "Shall we take a walk?"

He registered surprise. Then his slow smile spread. "A short one, I suppose."

He held open the door for me and guided me along the path with his hand on the small of my back. The wind whipped at me but Lisa's Chignon held up against it. I slipped off my shoes when the hard earth turned sandy.

I had only ever been to the beach once. This shoreline was nothing like that place. The ground was hard; sharp stones, rather than shells, littered the ground. Waves beat angrily against the earth. Even the setting sun seemed cold and remote. "You're sure I created this?" I asked.

"Without a doubt," he replied.

"I've never been to a beach like this," I said, looking out at the water.

"No," Ghalib said, looking down at me. "This is the beach in your subconscious. It's flavored by you, Elaine. By your wants and worries."

We walked along the shore until we reached the altar. I flushed and tried to continue past it, but Ghalib took my hand to stop me. We stood at the head of the altar, where he had watched me orgasm under Julia's tongue. "It was difficult watching you with Julia," he said.

I prickled with embarrassment. "It was difficult being watched."

"You responded beautifully, though," he continued smoothly. "Once you accepted that the ceremony was going to happen, you were magnificent."

The steady throb between my legs intensified. During the ceremony, my desire overcame my prudish shame and inhibitions. I thought of my life before the kidnapping. I had been ruled by fear: fear of loss, fear of poverty, fear of violence, fear of not being able to take care of my sister. The beach where I vacationed had been warm and golden. My fear had made it bitter and gray.

"Are you cold?" Ghalib asked.

"Apparently," I muttered.

He looked at me quizzically, but didn't ask me to explain. He just took my hand and led me back to the house. The Drawing flashed between us, easing the hard thoughts that hurt me.

"I have plans for us tonight," he said once we were inside. He didn't let go of my hand but led me back into hallways. We walked in silence for some time. Then, he stopped at a door and pushed it open.

We stepped into a room with soft chairs and low tables, like a sitting room. It was tasteful but unremarkable in this mansion. I looked at Ghalib and he closed the door behind us. Then, he took my hand and silently led me through the sitting room and to another door. Inside was an enormous bed and a room filled with dark masculine furniture.

"This is your room," I said.

"Yes," he said, closing that door behind us, too. The Drawing was strong but not strong enough to mute my desire to flee.

He turned to me and without preamble, kissed me. His consciousness expanded into mine, but it was the same image: the two of us, nude, joined, and moving against each other. This time, we were in the center of his huge bed. Even with the Drawing showing me his every desire, I shivered. The collar I wore changed everything. He could order me to do things I found repugnant. I would have no choice. Should I have gone with Victor? Would that have been the better choice?

He broke the kiss. "You're frightened and distracted," he said, trailing kisses along my jaw line. I was also aroused and throbbing. It was a curious, contradictory feeling. "I know what will help with that." He kissed me again. His hands trailed over my arms. Something cold and hard snapped closed around my left wrist. I broke the kiss, turning my head to see. The same cold restraint closed around my right wrist.

Ghalib backed away a step, admiring his work. Silver cuffs encircled my wrists. They were attached to chains that hung from the ceiling. Had they been there when I walked in? "How is this supposed to help my nervousness, Ghalib?" I asked.

"Because while you're in my shackles I don't give you any orders; I just pleasure you."

The chains clattered and I glanced at them. The extra chain slowly receded into the ceiling until my arms were spread over my head. I physically shivered and the chains clanged in response. Ghalib strolled to his bed and sat, slowly unbuttoning his shirt. Then, he stripped the garment away. His torso was lean, pale, and muscular.

When he strolled back over to me, he reminded me of a panther. He leaned in close and inhaled next to my hair. "You have no idea how many times I've imagined you in this very situation," he purred into my ear.

My heart stuttered into a panicked pace even as my throbbing took on an urgency. I pulled on the restraints but they were solid. My breathing picked up. Ghalib watched my struggle, seeming to enjoy it. The sweat broke on my forehead and I forced myself to stop resisting. I reminded myself that he hadn't hurt me. At least not yet.

He drew a small, glittering-sharp knife out of his pocket and traced the edge of my dress' neckline with the blade. At the lowest point, he dug the blade into the fabric and sliced it to the floor. I struggled to silence a whimper. He walked behind me and caught the blade at the bottom of the low back, cutting that fabric open, as well. He slipped the sharp knives under the sleeves and the dress fell to the floor.

I stood with my legs tightly together. Only panties and a backless bra covered my nudity.

He knelt in front of me and threw the strips of dress on to the bed. He tapped my foot. "Step," he instructed, pulling the dress away from my feet. I expected him to stand, but instead, he slid his hand over my calf, down to my ankle, and lifted my foot. He pulled off my shoe. He repeated the process for other foot. Finally, he stood.

Carefully, ever so carefully, he peeled the bra away from my skin, kissing the skin that he freed. He tugged the adhesive away from my nipple, licking the tender skin. The Drawing rolled over me in an avalanche of pleasure. I arched into his lips.

He repeated the process for my other breast, soothing the skin with his tongue, watching my nipple pebble at his touch. I couldn't fight the pleasure. I didn't want to.

He kissed up my body, his fingers playing with the elastic of my panties. He kissed me gently on the lips, his hands sliding under the only fabric that covered me. It was like he was testing the texture of my skin. "You're still nervous," he said, in a teasing tone.

"This isn't... how I..."

"I remember. No games. No costumes." He kissed my neck under my ear.

"Just the usual positions," I added in a shaky voice.

He stroked my body from my hip up to my breast. The nipple was so hard that it ached. He circled it with a finger. "I can show you such things," he said. He kissed my neck, nipping with his teeth.

I felt the same strange and familiar sensation of my control breaking. It was like how I felt in the observatory on the night that Victor had left us alone and aroused. Heat flashed through me. The Drawing purred. It gave me courage. "Show me, Ghalib," I whispered.

He pulled back and looked at me, a smile spreading. "What did you say?"

I met his eyes. "Show me, please."

The silver shackles opened; I shook them off easily and rubbed my wrists. For a moment he was as still as a statue, just looking at me. Then, he kissed me again, his lips insistent. I couldn't keep my hands from his skin. The visions flashed faster and faster: his eager lips between my legs, his hands spreading me, and my writhing pleasure. I broke the kiss to catch my breath.

His expression was molten. "I think I'd like to try out your collar," he said. The Drawing grew more intense; it battled my fear. I waited, my heart alarmingly fast. He backed away and cocked his head. "Take your hair down," he instructed.

My fingers went automatically to the pins that held the low, sleek mass of hair in place. I dropped them, one by one, onto the floor, watching Ghalib's eyes the whole time. When my hair was free, it hung in a messy tumble more than halfway down my back.

"Come here," he ordered.

I obeyed automatically. His hands went into my hair, combing the length with his fingers and draping it over my breasts. "I love your hair loose," he said. "I love that it's long and wild." He caressed my nipples through my hair; my breath came in shuddery whimpers.

"Take off your panties," he ordered. I had no choice but I could choose about whether or not I met his eyes while I stripped the scrap away. A pink flush colored his cheeks. I felt the urge to lower my eyes but the Drawing gave me boldness. I held his gaze and waited for the next order.

His voice was gruff. "Take off my pants." I responded automati-

cally, falling to my knees in front of him. I reached for the fasteners, unable to push away the image of Alexis in this same position. I
remembered how he had restrained her hands while she worked to
remove his pants. In my mind's eye I saw the brutal way he had taken
her mouth. A shiver went through me.

My fingers brushed the skin of his lower stomach; he groaned.
Carefully, I stripped the pants away, letting my fingers graze his skin.
Without being told, I took off his shoes and socks, too. Then, I peeled
his undergarment away, freeing his erection.

I knelt and waited, dreading his next instruction. Ghalib didn't
move. I stole a glance upward; his fists were clenched and his eyes
fixed on me.

"Touch me," he said. It wasn't an order.

The Drawing infused me. Any shred of control I might have re-
tained melted away. I slipped my hands up his thighs to his erection.
My hands tingled with Drawing and his muscles twitched. "Yes," he
whispered. I surged with arousal.

I took him in hand, gently at first, then more firmly. His eyes closed
and his hips swayed with my pulls. I was fascinated by my affect on
him. His legs trembled and he made small sounds of pleasure.

"Stop," he finally ordered. My hands fell to my sides. "Stand."

I obeyed. He pulled me to him, pressing the length of his naked
body against mine. We both gasped at the sensation; the Drawing
sizzled at every point of contact. He backed me to the bed, his body
corralling me. His lips were everywhere, nipping my neck, finding
my mouth, and teasing my ear. His hands fumbled and groped. I fell
back on the bed and he followed me down.

He worked his hips between my thighs; his hardness pressed
against my leg. "You want me," he whispered. "Say it, Pet."

I flushed uncomfortably; yet how could I deny it? "I want you," I
whispered back.

He nudged at me and inserted just the tip of himself into me. "Yes,
you do," he teased. He rubbed his erection into my wetness. I couldn't
help but writhe beneath him. "It's lovely," he added. "I could watch
you for hours."

Without thinking, I lifted my chin and reached for his arousal.
I guided him into me, one hand on his manhood and the other on

his hip, not stopping until he was buried completely. It took him off guard. "God," he gasped, steadying himself.

"Who wants who?" I asked, clutching at him with my knees. My voice was low and sultry; I barely recognized it.

He moved in and out of me once very slowly. "I deny nothing."

He started to thrust in rhythm and it was as if the friction created Drawing. It suffused me, making me ache for more. His lips found mine. My mind must have shown him my need because he responded by doubling his pace and intensity. I tightened around him and he moaned.

Suddenly and without exiting me, he rolled me on top of him. A low moan rolled out of me as I settled into a position astride him. I rolled my pelvis. "Do you like that?" he asked.

"Yes."

"Then move," he ordered. My thighs flexed in response and he smiled.

When I found a rhythm, he sat up. "Don't stop, Pet," he purred. He grabbed one of the torn pieces of my dress. "Close your eyes," he said. Slowly, as I tried to keep moving, he wrapped the fabric over my eyes. "There," he whispered, his lips so close to mine that I could feel his warm breath. "Perfect. Now, pleasure yourself on me."

My need drove me. I worked my hips and thighs in an awkward, unfamiliar way to get the friction that I craved. Ghalib's hands went down my arms and grasped my wrists, holding both of them behind my back with just one hand. "Move, Pet," he urged, his lips brushing mine.

As I worked myself on his erection, he toyed with my nipples. A tight, deep pleasure started to expand. My panting breath was edged in a whimper. "Are you close, Pet?" he asked.

"Yes," I gasped.

"If only I would just help a little."

The Drawing whispered to me about Ghalib's pleasure. He wanted me to beg. I just couldn't bring myself to comply. "We'll both just have to be patient," I said, trying to hide the sly edge. I slowed my motion, knowing it frustrated him more than it did me.

I got the desired results. He growled and flipped me back over on my back. He forced my legs back near my ears and thrust into me again. This time he had all of the leverage. He slammed into me. I twisted two handfuls of bedcovers as the waves of ecstasy rose from somewhere deep inside.

Ghalib cried out, still slamming into me until only spasms of pleasure were left. It was only then that he released my wrists, removed the blindfold, and withdrew from me. . Still, he wouldn't let me break physical contact with him. He lay next to me on the bed, tracing patterns on my skin.

"There, now," he said. He planted a flurry of small kisses down my torso. "Are you pleased with the new things I've shown you so far?"

I flushed. "Yes," I whispered.

"And are done with all of this foolish nervousness?"

I hesitated but when I spoke, I was as truthful as I could be. "Ghalib, I'll probably always be nervous around you." He pulled back. "I wear this collar. You can force me to do anything."

His voice grew soft and gentle. "Did you object to any of the orders that I gave you tonight?"

My cheeks flamed. "No, not this time."

"This time?"

"How can you know if you've crossed a line if I can't object?" I asked.

"You're my Pet, Elaine. There are no lines." I huffed in frustration. "You're still very new to this," he said gently. "Other pets learn trust for their Masters. You will, too."

I flashed with irritation. "Until then, you'll just have to learn to accept my nervousness." I met his eyes. "May I return to my room, please?"

His expression turned very sober. "Of course. Until tomorrow."

Chapter 17
Markus' Hospitality

When I woke the next day, my stomach clenched. My face flushed at just the memory of me in silver handcuffs being teased by Ghalib's fingers. I remembered my pleading tone. I closed my eyes and hid under the covers. It was like I was in heat; it was humiliating.

I lay in bed and stretched my sore limbs. Another reminder of how inexperienced I was. Nonetheless, even though I tingled with embarrassment, I throbbed for my next meeting with Ghalib. It was all so confusing and distressing. I pulled a pillow over my head.

That was where Lisa found me some time later and she ushered me into a shower. With minimal effort on my part, I was dressed in a slim, floor-length dress in deep green. At my request, Lisa left my hair long and sleek. I chose a pair of glittering earrings and was ready by the time Ghalib's voice echoed in my mind. *Elaine.*

I followed his summons to the foyer again. He turned and openly admired me. "And I didn't think it was possible to desire you more."

I flushed. "And yet..." I said, my voice unsteady.

He looked at me for a long moment, the Drawing swirling, like convections in the air. I waited for the fear and trembling to start, but I just didn't feel that. The night before left me feeling powerful and desirable. For the first time, I thought I might be equal to Ghalib and his games.

"We have an engagement this evening," Ghalib said, lifting my hand to his lips and kissing my fingertips. "I'm tempted to cancel with Markus," he said between kisses.

I remembered Markus and that I liked him. True, he was enormous and more masculine than any being I'd ever known. But, I got no sense of cruelty from him.

The Drawing hummed with a warm vibration. He ran his tongue around the tip of my pinky finger. The warmth spread up my arm. I put my hand on his chest and smiled. "I think that would be very rude of you."

He nipped at my knuckle. "I suppose you're right." His eyes twinkled.

He stepped up very close to me and held me to him. The room melted around us. The air changed. Then, a landscape sprung up around us, including what I assumed must be Markus' home.

It was a huge, stone, square structure with a line of columns across the front. Trees in the brightest shade of autumn color, and so large in circumference that I couldn't have gotten my arms around one, forested the area around the mansion. The air was crisp and smelled like firewood.

Ghalib led me to the front door and knocked with a brass knocker. Before long, two muscled men pushed the door open. They motioned for us to come inside. We were barely two steps inside the door when Markus and a smaller man met us.

"Ghalib!" he greeted in a clear, booming voice. "You came!"

"Of course I did," Ghalib said, clasping his hand. "I promised, didn't I?"

"Thank you for this honor," Markus said, turning to me. "Elaine, welcome to my home."

"Thank you," I said. His grin was so bright and cheerful and big, it was impossible not to answer it with one of my own.

Markus put a heavy hand on the boy standing next to him and spoke to Ghalib. "This is Brandon. He requested the chance to be your service boy tonight."

Brandon flushed. Ghalib wore his amused smile. "You requested me?"

"Yes, Sir," Brandon replied.

"Isn't that charming," Ghalib said, looking the servant up and down. "Have you been here long?"

"I'm only recently promoted," he said. "I remember you from when you were a Dream Maker."

"Really."

"Your nightmares were legendary."

Ghalib chuckled. "Nightmares are rarely seen as arousing."

"But genius often is," the boy replied earnestly.

Ghalib's face flashed with pleasure. His expression took on that hungry look. He pulled Brandon in for a long, slow kiss. I watched the boy respond to him. He pressed himself to Ghalib's body and slid his hands over Ghalib's back. Heat rose in me, watching them. Ghalib's hand traveled to the bulge in Brandon's leather pants. He squeezed it and Brandon moaned against his lips. When Ghalib broke the kiss, he was looking at the boy with the heat he usually reserved for me.

"You'll do," Ghalib said in his seductive purr.

"You've made this young servant very happy," Markus said, ruffling Brandon's hair like he was a puppy. "And Elaine, my Tobias volunteered to see to your tension. He is human but very pleasing."

I had trouble pulling my eyes away from Brandon's hand stroking Ghalib's leg. "That's very kind. Thank him for me. I'm afraid that I can't think of anything that could relieve my tension without compounding it."

Markus and Ghalib exchanged a look. I wondered if they had been discussing me. "I'll see to you tonight myself," Markus said. "Nobody leaves my house tense or unfed."

I had to laugh. He was a pleasure to be around — his easy charm, his happy, beautiful face, his booming, joyful voice. He laid his huge hand on my back; warmth and joy washed over me. My smile widened until it hurt my face. "That is the loveliest feeling," I said. "The Drawing with you is so friendly."

"It's because I don't have sexual feelings for you, I expect," he said.

I smirked at him. "I guess we'll just have to be good friends," I said. Markus' smile was blinding. He guided me with a hand on my back out of the foyer and into a huge hall that looked like it belonged in a medieval castle. Men, clad in leather pants and heavy metal cuffs, milled around. Some were kissing.

"Are these all pets?" I asked.

'Markus' laugh boomed. "No. Mostly servants. A few human guests. Only Tobias is a pet."

We stopped at a long table at the front of the room. Markus sat in a wooden chair that was so large that it must have been designed specifically for him. I sat on a tall chair next to him with his hand casually over mine. It was just enough contact to keep the warm, comfortable joy flowing through me.

Brandon pulled out Ghalib's chair. "An appetizer, Sir?"

Ghalib sat. "Yes."

Brandon pulled Ghalib, in his chair, a little out from the table and knelt in front of him. Ghalib undid his pants and lowered them to his thighs; his erect penis seemed very large to me. Brandon licked the length in long, luxurious strokes before he took the whole shaft into his mouth. Ghalib looked up and met my eyes.

"This is all a show for you," Markus muttered so that Ghalib couldn't hear him. "He's doing everything he can to get your attention."

Brandon sucked and drew on Ghalib in earnest. The magnitude of my arousal at seeing him pleasured surprised me. "He has it," I replied.

Ghalib had two handfuls of the boy's long hair. His eyes didn't leave mine. His thrusting rhythm grew faster. His lips parted. My heart sped.

"Truth be told," Markus said in that same low voice, "I'm supposed to help Ghalib get you calm enough to have sex with him on a regular basis."

Ghalib's hips lifted out of the chair. He thrust hard into Brandon's mouth. Brandon took the whole length without struggle. "The honesty is refreshing, Markus" I said. "Thank you." Ghalib tightened his grip on the boy's hair. He shuddered and moaned. When his tremors subsided, he looked at me again and seemed pleased that I was still watching.

The Drawing was mostly warm and friendly, with Markus touching me. Still, a hit of Ghalib's erotic flavor found its way in. "Bravo," I said.

Ghalib laughed and looked a little surprised as he drew his pants back up. "Thank you, Elaine."

"Food!" Markus called. Servants trotted to the table with huge platters of roasted meat. An enormous bird of some sort rested on a steel platter. There were piles of shaved beef, and a pig with an apple in his mouth. It tasted even better than it smelled. Brandon sat at Ghalib's feet and Markus regaled us with stories of his last project for the Dream Makers.

"...all they tell me is that they need a life-sized, working carousel. So I go all out. It can run really slowly, or fast, like for a nightmare. And I made all kinds of crazy things to ride. Dragons. Harpies. A pony-boy." He made a sheepish face. "They failed to tell me that the dream was for a four-year-old. Scared the sense out of her."

"I approve," Ghalib said as he slipped meat to Brandon.

"I imagine you would. The Dream Makers didn't find it so amusing."

Ghalib's expression of enjoyment melted away and he zeroed in on something over my shoulder. I glanced back and noticed that a serving boy had approached me. I turned, well aware of Ghalib's gaze on us both.

The boy looked at me with frightened, earnest eyes. "Excuse me, Miss. I wondered if you had a chance to try the quail eggs. They're very good."

I glanced over my shoulder. Markus was snickering into his big hand and Ghalib seemed as bewildered as I was.

I turned back to him; his cheeks were as pale as death. "I raise the quails," he added faintly.

I glanced behind him at the five servants standing in a group, watching expectantly. The Drawing told me that he had been goaded into this situation. They all wanted to know what it felt like to touch an Omnilight, but they all feared Ghalib. This boy was the newest to Markus' home. He knew the least. And he really did raise quails.

Confidence infused me, "You're very brave," I told him, nodding towards Ghalib. "He's rather protective of who I talk to. Those must be some amazing quail eggs."

"They're... they're very good," he repeated, stammering.

I stood. "Do you know what else is very good? The touch of an Omnilight."

He didn't answer right away and he still couldn't look at me. Finally, he whispered, "I've heard that."

"Your friends put you up to this, didn't they?"

His cheeks turned red. I put my hand over his and the energy flowed easily from me to him. His body tensed. He closed his eyes and I squeezed his hand. He made a low moan. I leaned across the table, lifting his chin as Ghalib had done to me so many times, and brushed his lips once with mine. Just long enough to see him taking a human man who was wearing a collar. His own pet.

I broke all contact. His eyes flew open.

I leaned in close. "If I were you, I wouldn't tell them a thing."

He smiled and looked over his shoulder. Then he backed away a step, bowed, and exited out the side of the room. The five boys broke into a run to catch up with him.

Markus shook in unrestrained laughter once they were all gone. "Quail eggs?" he laughed.

"Stop it," I said, smacking him. "He was sweet."

"You toyed with him and you know it," Markus said.

"No, I didn't."

"Yes, she did," Ghalib answered for me. "I wish I could have recorded it." He smoothed Brandon's hair and stood, crossing to me in two, quick strides. He leaned over me and whispered in my ear, "I cannot wait for you any longer."

I looked around pointedly. "Do you intend to take me right here?" I asked.

Ghalib pressed his lips to my neck where my pulse throbbed. He worked his way to my lips. I saw us naked, entwined, rolling and moaning, stopping to thrust and kiss, then wrestling for top position again. All on the banquet table."Yes, I do," he said.

I drew back as much as I could. "No," I whispered. "So they can all watch us? I won't, Ghalib."

He brushed his lips against mine without really kissing me. "Yes, you will," he murmured.

Markus must have laid a hand on my shoulder because the current of friendly Drawing tempered Ghalib's lusty energy. I heard Markus' voice. "You can do anything you want here, Elaine. The only thing we don't allow is shame."

Ghalib kissed me again, this time harder and with more insistence. But there was something else, too. A delicious sensation between my legs. The feel of lips and tongue. Soft and warm and wet and consuming. I broke the kiss and looked down.

Brandon knelt between his legs and pleasured him for the second time that night. I knew beyond a shadow of a doubt that I was feeling Brandon's mouth when Ghalib kissed me. I shuddered with desire that I couldn't deny — or, more importantly, that I didn't want to deny anymore. I didn't wait for Ghalib to kiss me again; I pressed my lips against his and the sensation hit me like a battering ram. My kisses became a frantic, primal demand for more. I drew my nails down his shirt to Brandon's head. I put a hand in his hair and a new flavor of Drawing joined the current. Brandon moaned with Ghalib inside his mouth. Ghalib and I moaned in unison at the vibration.

Ghalib broke the kiss and we were both breathless. Heated. "There she is," he said. Brandon returned to his place next to Ghalib's chair and Ghalib lifted me onto the banquet table. The servant scrambled to move the platters out of the way.

"Take off your undergarments," he ordered.

I had no choice but to obey. I had on only panties. In seconds, they were on the floor. I sat on the edge of the table.

He slid the green silk of my dress to my thighs and stepped between my legs. The room was silent. Drawing swirled like magic. He put his hands behind my knees and spread my legs, stepping in closer. His erection brushed the inside of my leg. His hands slid up the inside of my thighs, his thumbs making slow circles as his hands went deeper. He parted me and stroked my wetness. I couldn't stop the moan.

His strokes came faster and he leaned in to kiss me quickly. He showed me a flash of the mirror image of what we were doing right then: his hands working between my legs, his erection brushing my skin, my legs trembling.

His breath was against my ear. "Don't come without telling me."

The Drawing urged me and I didn't want to fight it. I dragged his face back to mine, kissing his surprised lips with bruising force. I knew he could feel every stroke his fingers made as we kissed. Instantly, he found a perfect rhythm. His fingers flew. The deep glow of orgasm started in my stomach. I knew he could feel it. I kissed him harder.

His erection nudged me from a perfect angle. One thrust and Ghalib would be inside me. I couldn't have stopped now if I wanted to. My hips twisted against him; I drove myself as much as he drove me. I had never anticipated a release this much. My pleasure leapt and leapt again, until my climax broke over me like a wave. Ghalib made a noise against my lips and took his thrust, inserting himself in one smooth motion.

My orgasm throbbed around him. He let it ebb before he withdrew and pounded into me again. The pleasure of peaking washed over me again. The Drawing brought the sensation to a new height. I cried out but he captured my lips, pounding me in a rhythm that renewed my orgasm with each stroke. He bit at me and I bit back. His pace sped up and my hips swayed to meet him.

I cried out with every stroke, my nails digging into Ghalib's back. I was unable to care that we were being watched from every side or that we weren't the only pair coupling. I didn't care that we were primal and base and that there wasn't a bit a charisma about this sex. We raced together towards the release we needed. He rode me hard but with precision. I felt the build again. My body trembled. I closed my eyes and the ballooning pleasure filled me. I couldn't help but cry out. It seemed like my orgasm was making every muscle in my body vibrate. When I was done, he kissed me again; I felt him rise into his own orgasm. He didn't close his eyes; he watched me with every stroke.

I fell back on the table when we were done. The men around the room lifted their glasses to us. Heat flooded into my cheeks. If avoiding a spectacle was my goal, I had certainly failed miserably. Now, post-orgasm, my greatest instinct was to flee. But, from the look on his face, Ghalib had no plans to let me go anywhere.

He grinned at me. Clearly he wasn't embarrassed in the least. "We seem to have made a bit of a scene," he said.

I flushed hotter. "A scene, Ghalib? We just had sex on a dinner table in front of forty men."

"Do you object to the audience or the furniture?" he teased, clearly in a good mood.

"Both. All of it. I hope this is out of your system, now." I was well aware that I was blaming him for my desire, too. In my moment of embarrassment, I didn't care.

He looked surprised. "What do you mean? You can't be talking about my desire for you."

"Yes," I replied. He lifted his eyebrows at me. "Didn't it at least take the edge off?" I asked.

He extended a hand and helped me sit up. Drawing rose again when his hand touched mine. "I could take you again this instant," he whispered.

"Try to control yourself," I said.

"I have been controlling myself for a rather long time now," he said, slipping his hand up my leg again. "I'd like to be out of control for a while."

I didn't want to admit it, but I wanted him again, too. The fear was gone; the Drawing had replaced it. I couldn't ignore it, no matter how I tried, and my sexual appetite had never been so healthy.

"Perhaps I'm a little late in asking," Markus said with a dry tone, "but would you two like a room?" Markus hadn't moved a bit since we started coupling. He lifted a glass to his lips, as if this sort of thing happened on his banquet table all of the time.

"I'm so sorry, Markus. I don't know what's gotten into me." I answered quickly. "We shouldn't need a room."

"All evidence to the contrary," Markus said, looking at me still sprawled on the table. "Although if you would like to have another round on the table, I would hardly object." He looked out at the men around the room that were on their knees in front of other men. The one bent over a table, being sucked and taken at the same time. "You add spice to my home, Ghalib, as always."

"I'm pleased if you're pleased," Ghalib said. "And not to be contradictory but a room would be welcome. I'm not sure I'm done with my pet for the evening."

"Ghalib," I protested.

"Quiet," he said in a gentle command. I was forced into silence.

Markus smiled at me. "Elaine, if I don't see you again tonight, it was a real pleasure. I feel like I've made a friend, so make sure that the two of you aren't strangers." He turned back to Ghalib and smiled one of his brilliant, friendly smiles. "As for that room, it's the second door on the right on the third floor."

"Thank you," Ghalib said to Markus. The room spun and my head spun with it. When the motion stopped, we were in a stone chamber with a blazing fireplace and a huge, white bed.

I bit my lips together.

"You can talk now," Ghalib said.

"You aren't even a little bit satisfied?" I asked again. "After all that?"

"All what?" he asked. "Months of waiting and you think just this could be enough?" His smile turned sly and knowing. "It didn't take the edge off of your need, either, did it?"

"I'm very tired," I lied.

"No you aren't."

His hands went behind me and he unfastened the back of my dress, letting it fall to the floor. Aside from the shoes, I was fully naked. My hair was long and sleek. His eyes lingered approvingly on the long, dark lock that fell over my shoulder.

I should have been overwhelmed. The show in the dining room should have satisfied me but it didn't. He was right; I wanted more. As the desire grew, the shame ebbed. I only twinged with a slight regret that I was giving Ghalib his every fantasy. But, even that wasn't as strong as the Drawing that compelled me.

He looked me up and down twice. Me, in heels, wearing his collar. I lifted my chin so he could see it a little better. That little motion was all it took. He pushed me to the bed and on my back. He pulled his shirt off without undoing the buttons and pressed his bare chest to mine. The vibrations made my heart stronger. It beat in time with his.

He nibbled my skin until I didn't think I was capable of withstanding any more pleasure. Then, he lifted himself off of me to remove his pants and positioned himself between my legs again.

He captured my two wrists in his hand and held them over my head. "Hold onto the headboard," he commanded, taking his hands off of my wrists. I reached automatically, without a choice, gripping the bars there. "Yes," Ghalib whispered. "He thrust into me slowly, with no intention of really making either of us orgasm. It was a lazy pace with maddening build. I was too wet and too aroused to get the friction I needed. I moaned and tried to urge him to take me harder.

He brushed his lips against mine gently. "You could probably convince me to move faster," he purred.

I knew I could but I was afraid to do it. I remembered what had happened when Alexis had pleaded with him. Too well, in fact.

"No," I said in a shaky voice. "You get scary when people beg."

"I do? Too bad," Ghalib said, making his strokes shallower, pinching at my nipples. He kissed my face, bringing the Drawing heat to every part of me. He licked my neck and made a pleased sound.

The orgasm just wouldn't rise. His teasing was perfection. He withdrew out of me and I whimpered. He made a path of licking and kissing down my torso. Between my breasts, over my stomach, to between my legs. His tongue explored me, found its spot, and massaged. I still couldn't release the headboard; my hips tilted despite me.

His tongue slowed and only the tip offered a faint pressure. I groaned.

"I can make you come," he teased, his breath warm against my most sensitive places. "You know what I want to hear." His tongue took a couple of teasing swipes.

My body trembled. I was undecided.

"I'll do my best not to be scary," he said with a little taunt in his voice.

My hesitation was arousing to him. He kissed my inner thigh. "Don't stop," I said softly. "Please."

His eyes glowed. "What do you want, Pet?" he asked.

"Please make me come," I whispered.

"So shy," he said caressingly. "Ask me louder."

His tongue stroked me again I couldn't hold back. "Please," I begged. "Please, don't stop."

His stroke became long. His tongue was devastatingly soft. I moaned as I rose, my body twisting on the bed as pleasure made movement instinctual. I cried out as the orgasm shook through me; I was sure they heard me downstairs.

He kissed back up to my face. "You can let go of the headboard," he told me, pulling my freed arms around him. He lay on top of me, his hips wedged between my thighs, the Drawing like a warm current between us, around us, through us. He smirked at me. "Is sex between us as terrible as you feared?" he teased.

My cheeks got hot. "No. But I can't imagine it's as satisfying as you expected, either."

"Incorrect," he said, kissing my lips again. His passion hadn't faded in the least. Experience hadn't slaked desire; it had only added details. As he kissed me, he guided himself into me, as if he moved on pure instinct. The Drawing gave me no choice as to how I would respond; I arched into him and he sucked a quick breath. "It's better than I envisioned," he said breathlessly. "I'm disappointed in myself that my imagination was so lacking."

Before long, we were moving together, my hands pressing into his back, my hips twitching to meet his thrusts. Now that I had orgasmed twice, I could pay more attention to the details of our coupling. The way he was almost too large for me. How athletic his body was. And when his shaft hardened, I knew he was about to climax again. He became rougher but still not cruelly so. He ground into me, his rhythm disintegrating, his breath ragged. When he was done, he just lay on top of me. "Finally," he whispered.

His touch was lazy on my skin. Soft kisses made me warm. His skin pressed to mine and my body rushed with excitement again. I ached like I hadn't been taken three times already. A soft wave of doubt shook me. I was acting like I imagined the Italian strumpet would have. I was giving him his fantasy. I turned my head away, wishing that I could will the arousal away. He lifted himself up on one arm and looked at me. "Answer me honestly," he commanded. "What are you feeling?"

My response was automatic. "Arousal. Regret. Defeat."

"Regret? Defeat?" he asked in a soft voice. "Now, why is that?"

"Regret that you had me so easily."

"So easily?" he said in wonder.

"Defeat that I couldn't resist this, even after all you did to me."

"Ahh," he said, tracing patterns on my skin with his finger. "Taking you away from your life."

"And my sister."

He continued his soft touch on my skin. "You feel arousal too, though."

"Yes."

"Still?"

"Yes."

"So you were deceitful when you said you were tired?" he

teased.

"Yes."

He looked at me directly. "Could you resist me if I wanted you again?"

"I don't know," I said honestly. "The Drawing is very strong."

He kissed my neck and my passion sparked again. "I could take you all night," he whispered. "And all day. I could give up my sculpting and do nothing else."

"Until you grew tired of me."

He lifted his head. "Excuse me."

"Isn't that why you take so many lovers?" I asked. "Because nobody can keep your interest for very long."

"It's more complicated than that," he answered, looking very serious.

"Really?"

"Yes. And with you it grows more complicated, still." He touched my collar. "Fortunately, you're mine and not even Nyx can change that. There are years before us."

"I don't know what you're talking about."

"I know," he said. "I'll just say this. Nothing about having you has been easy." I flushed. He gave me a long, lingering kiss. His mind flickered through dozens of settings, him taking me in each one.

I broke the kiss. "What? No fantasies of chaining me to things tonight?"

He chuckled as his hands did quick work of dissolving my regret. "No? I must be slipping."

When Ghalib finally returned me to my room, I was shaky, breathless, and exhausted. The Drawing was relentless. Every time he touched me, it swelled. Every time it swelled, I responded. We never did return to Markus' hall. We didn't leave the third floor room. My lips felt bruised. My thighs were sore. And my passion hadn't abated in the least.

Ghalib treated me as if he thought I might disappear. He walked me to my suite himself. "Would you like to invite me in?" he asked.

"The evening doesn't have to end here."

"No, Ghalib. I need to rest and think."

"No?" he asked gently, sliding a finger over my lips, knowing that the Drawing sparked anew every time he touched me. "Are you refusing me?"

"I suppose so," I said, "though it seems silly to call it that after all we did tonight."

"It's only a fraction of what I've planned," he said.

"We don't have to achieve all of your plans in one evening," I said.

"True," he agreed. "Nor would it be possible. Still...." He looked at my door wistfully and kissed me again, as if he hoped that alone would change my mind. Even without my invitation, he lingered at the door until I physically disengaged myself from him and went inside.

I could still sense him even as the distance between us increased. He was aroused. He wanted me more. He was fighting the urge to pull me out of my room. I couldn't shut it off.

I showered as quickly as I could and fell exhausted into my bed. Only sleep could give me the freedom I needed. I barely remembered climbing into bed. I fell asleep to his lusty thoughts.

Chapter 18
Coming Out of My Shell

"Miss?" Lisa whispered.

I opened one bleary eye.

"Miss?" she whispered again. "I know you had a long night, but the Master called for me to wake you up and get you ready."

"The throbbing heat started. And with it I could feel Ghalib's impatience. He didn't need to sleep. Sculpting was nowhere near as satisfying as sex with an Omnilight. And why was I taking so long? Had he hurt me? Was I ill?

"Is it just Ghalib and me for dinner tonight?" I asked, sitting up.

"I think so."

I went to the closet. "Then I think I'm going to pick something a little more casual than usual to wear." We dug through the wardrobe until I found what I was looking for: a fitted, velvet jacket, a crisp white shirt, tight dress pants, and high-heeled boots. It looked almost like a horseback riding outfit and it was much more my style.

"Do you think this will be OK?" I asked.

Lisa's face glowed. "It's sexier than a gown. I love it." I hadn't been shooting for sexier but I had no intention of changing my clothes now. I just finished pulling my hair back and putting on my make-up when I heard my name echoing in my head.

Elaine.

"He calls," I said dryly as my body rose on its own. Lisa just looked at me. "Ghalib's calling. I have to go."

I left the room and let the call lead me through the morphing hallways. Through a low-ceilinged corridor and down a short flight of steps. Then down a longer flight of steps. I came upon Ghalib, standing in the hallway above steps that seemed to go down forever. I recognized it as the way to the prison and shivered a little.

Ghalib smiled at me and the Drawing surged, muting the fear. "There you are," he said, his green eyes sliding down my body and back up again. "How are you feeling?"

"Sore," I answered. "Tired."

"Satisfied?" he said, his unblinking gaze never faltering, never leaving me.

"Not in the least," I answered.

His smile widened. "Good. Come here."

I moved towards him without a choice. The Drawing swirled around me, urging me to flirt, to play. I didn't know if I could. When I stood directly before him, I said, "You're a little free with those commands."

He chuckled. "I'm sure the novelty will wear off in time." His hands went to the buttons of my crisp, white shirt and he unbuttoned the top two buttons. "I want to see my collar on my pet." My heart sped up and I looked away from him. "Still reconsidering your decisions?" he teased.

"I'm reconsidering every decision I've made since I met you," I said truthfully.

He touched my cheek. "I have something to show you," he said. "Come with me." He led me down the steps. Only Joan waited at the enormous entrance door. "Carl's inside," she said. "Seeing to things."

"Am I in trouble?" I asked.

"Not at all," Ghalib said. His voice had a secretive quality, though. Joan opened the heavy door for us.

The smells were just as bad as I remembered, though the noises were substantially less. The transparent people running in slow motion passed us on the left. Up ahead, I noticed a glow coming out of one of the cells. "What is that?" I asked.

"You'll see," he replied. The secretive quality increased.

As we approached the glowing cell, the smells changed. It was powder and Lysol rather than human waste. I glanced at Ghalib. He had a tiny, satisfied smirk.

I stepped in front of the cell and everything stopped. My heart. My breath. It was a perfect nursery in pink and white, the window open with a fresh breeze blowing through. My sister stood there, holding a baby wrapped in a pink blanket. Someone who deeply resembled me stood in the room with her.

"She was only four months pregnant when I left," I breathed.

"She's not much beyond that now," Ghalib whispered. "She dreams about her baby frequently. She keeps dreaming that it's a girl, but she's actually having a boy."

"How do you know that," I asked, unable to look away from Rachel. She was the perfect mother as I knew she would be.

"The unborn have dreams, too," he explained. Sometime in the next five months I would become aunt to a nephew that I would probably never meet.

"Can I talk to her?" I asked.

Ghalib shook his head. "Technically, she shouldn't be dreaming here. This isn't where expectant mothers go when they're asleep. I made a deal with another Architect so that you could see her. But we can't have interaction with her."

"She dreams of me."

"All the time."

My eyes wanted to fill with tears and I blinked them away. "God, I miss you, Rach," I whispered.

She looked at the look-alike of me in the room. "I miss you too," she said in an airy, echo-y voice.

I wanted to tell her everything: that I was OK; I hadn't been harmed; that she could stop looking for me. I wanted to tell her how much I loved her and her baby. While I watched, she faded. Then she came back. Then she faded again.

"What's happening?" I asked Ghalib.

"She's waking," he said.

"Bye, Rach," I whispered.

Then she was gone.

I touched the bars of the cell she didn't even know that she was in. It took a moment to control my emotion. "Can I see her again, sometime?" I asked Ghalib without looking at him.

"I will try." He put a hand on my arm and arousal mixed with loss in my mind. The Drawing was too strong. Arousal won. "Are you ready to leave here?" he asked. "I have something else to show you."

I backed away from the cell. It was empty now, anyway.

Ghalib led me out of the prison, up the steps, to the foyer, and out the front door. The wind whipped at my hair. I noticed that it was still a beach that edged Ghalib's landscape. He hadn't repaired my alterations of this world.

Ghalib guided me with a hand on my back. As we walked, he spoke. The image of my sister faded as the Drawing reasserted its influence. "I nearly didn't let you sleep," Ghalib told me. "I nearly called you to me a dozen times."

"Are you always this insatiable?" I asked.

"Oh yes," he replied. "I just don't usually have a partner that can match me."

"I don't know whether to be insulted or flattered," I said." "Now, I can imagine what that poor Italian woman was in for if she managed to capture your attention."

There was a building in front of us. Something roughly the size and shape of a barn. I was sure I had never seen it before. "I wouldn't have been that harsh on the strumpet," Ghalib said thoughtfully. "She wouldn't have been able to handle that much and I don't really enjoy it unless the victim is feisty."

"Like Victor?" I teased.

He stopped walking and looked at me. "No. Like you."

My breath caught and he smiled. Damn him.

He turned to the building. "You inspired me to create this."

"A barn?"

"No. What's inside."

My heart took off again. This couldn't be good. Ghalib looked like someone about to enjoy a morsel of particularly delicious food. He put his hand on the barn door and opened it.

I looked inside and froze. What was I looking at? "Come along, Elaine," he commanded. My legs unfroze, I stepped across the threshold, and the door closed behind me.

It was a single, huge room. The walls were hung with black and red silk, run through with gold thread. Hundreds of candles illuminated the room. A huge bed, bigger than any bed I had ever seen, was equipped with handcuffs and shackles. Padded shackles hung from the walls. Various devices, resembling gym equipment were placed around the room. Immediately I saw the potential. If used with the attached restraints, anyone's body could be bound in awkward or alluring positions. Blindfolds, silken and beautiful, hung from one wall; springy crops and stiff paddling implements hung from another. A slender armoire stood in one corner. I opened a drawer. Costumes. Gloves. Stockings. Another drawer. Feathers. A third drawer. Gags and what I could only assume were nipple clamps. The last drawer was entirely dildos and vibrators.

Ghalib's stone statues stood in every corner of the room. Reproductions of huge, muscled men, like had been at Markus' house; delicate women like Anna; and mythical creatures of both genders, lined the walls, as if they were ready to serve. I had no doubt that they could move. I shivered to think of what else they could do.

"*I* inspired this?" I asked.

"Oh, yes," he said in a low voice.

I went over to the shackles that hung from chains attached to the wall. The smooth metal was heavy in my hands. "These shackles have no lock," I noticed. "If you're put into them, how are they opened?"

His eyes grew even hotter. "They open when you orgasm."

A delicious tremor of fear and arousal vibrated through me. I inspected each odd piece of equipment, both out of curiosity and to keep from looking at Ghalib. As I surmised the intent of each piece, I flushed more hotly. Slowly, I made my way around the room until I was back next to the wall restraints.

The Drawing grew before Ghalib even approached me. The current started to wash away my fear. By the time he stood next to me, the arousal was overwhelming.

"What do you think?" he purred.

I faced him squarely. "I think you've put a lot of thought into this place."

He smiled. "Kiss me," he commanded. It didn't need to be a command. The Drawing was relentless. I met his lips with force of my own. Perhaps it was the increase in Drawing or maybe it was the enthusiastic response, but he backed up a couple of steps until his back was against the wall.

I don't know why I did what I did next. Except that the Drawing suggested it to me and I didn't fight the instinct.

As we kissed, my hands traveled up his chest, to his shoulders, and down his arms. He made a low noise in the back of his throat and I kissed him harder. My fingers slipped down to his wrists and before either of us realized what I was doing, I snapped the shackles closed around both of his wrists. He was bound to the wall.

He broke the kiss and looked at me in disbelief. I backed away a couple of steps and surveyed my work. He pulled on the chains but they wouldn't budge. He smacked the cuffs against the wall but they were too sturdy. He narrowed his eyes at me and tried to slip his hands out of the restraints. Amusement drained from his face and his jaw clenched. I was feeling something like glee.

I sauntered to the bed and sat on it. "You look angry," I commented.

"You once asked me what sorts of things I might do to punish you," he said in a tight voice. "When I'm free, I think I might have to acquaint you with some of my favorite techniques."

"Now, Ghalib," I said, pulling my legs up on the bed, "that's hardly any way to convince me to help you out of this little predicament." I thrilled with the wild delight of being in charge. It was twice as pleasing knowing that Ghalib was powerful and yet still perfectly helpless. A side of me that I didn't even know existed wanted to take my time teasing him.

"You want something, then?" he asked in an irritated tone.

I shrugged. "Not really. If you can't send me back to my mortal life, I'd say you, helpless, shackled to a wall pretty much covers what I want." I watched the angry color flood into his face. "Of course you could command me—"

"No," he interrupted, "I can't. I can't command you while I'm bound. I designed this room so that Anna and Julia or Markus and Tobias could play if they liked."

I stood and walked over to him. "Oh, dear. Then, you really are stuck." I unbuttoned one of his shirt buttons. I watched arousal overcome his irritation; it was a powerful discovery. "You said that you were the only creature to have mastered Victor. Tell me, has anyone ever mastered you?"

"No," was his curt reply, but his voice was husky.

I unbuttoned another button and brought my lips close to his skin. "Maybe I should go and tell Victor where to find you. Perhaps he would like another chance to play with you." I was careful not to really touch him but I knew he could feel my breath.

I waited for him to answer but he just stood perfectly still with his jaw clenched. "No?" I asked.

He still didn't answer.

"If you don't say something, I might think you like my idea."

He took a sharp, little breath. "I would prefer you not hand me over to Victor," he said tightly.

"I suppose that's only fair," I replied. "You did spare me. Maybe Alexis...."

"I certainly would prefer Alexis."

I narrowed my eyes at him. I pressed my finger against his skin and let the Drawing whisper to me. "Ahh, I see," I said. "Alexis would rather be the one in shackles. And you're pretty sure that you could convince her to release you." Ghalib's jaw tightened.

His eyes, intense and vivid, raked me. I took off my velvet jacket and laid it on the bed. "What do you intend to do?" he asked. "You can't go anywhere in this world and you can't return to your own."

I walked slowly back over to him, opened the rest of his shirt buttons, and pulled his shirt out of his slacks. I drew a finger down the middle of his chest to his belt and listened to his sharp intake of breath.

"Do you think that Nyx made the Drawing stronger in me when she touched me?" I asked.

"I think you're going to regret th—"

I covered his mouth with my hand. "Just nod or shake your head, then. Like I had to do when you took my voice away." I waited a beat and he blinked. "Do you think that Nyx made the Drawing stronger when she touched me?" I repeated. He nodded. "Good," I praised. "You're suspicious of her for doing it, aren't you?" He nodded again. "Very good." I removed my hand.

Ghalib yanked at the shackles again. "You're enjoying this," he accused in a low voice.

I pulled a chair from the side of the room, turning it so the high back faced Ghalib, and straddled it. I rested my chin on the top of the back rest. "Tell me what you did to Victor."

"When?" he asked.

"The night that things didn't go the way he wanted them to. The night you offered to do over with him on the condition that he not mark my skin."

"Do you really want to hear this?" he asked.

"I want to hear it so badly, that I might find a way to release you, if you tell me."

He looked at me hard for a moment, like he was trying to figure out if I was telling the truth. "We retired to his suite," Ghalib said slowly. "It was a crude place. The Marquis de Sade couldn't have been any baser. We drank wine and he made terrible passes at me. But, I was amused. He was the most amusing thing I'd seen in years. Most of my partners lacked his sheer appetite. Of course, he likes sex in a very specific way —"

"With his partners begging for mercy," I suggested.

The first smile I'd seen since the shackles closed around his wrists spread across his face. "Yes. But he does bring enormous zeal to sex. Victor could never have what he wanted from me but I knew I could take what I wanted from him. I convinced him to let me bind his arms and hang him from the ceiling with the understanding that I would submit to the same treatment."

I stood and slid his shirt over his shoulders, getting a full look at his lean, muscular chest. I ran my hands to his nipples just to remind him of the Drawing. His breath came faster. "What a liar you are," I whispered, sitting back down.

"And what a tease you are," he replied.

"Go on."

"Victor didn't want to enjoy being mastered. He had just been made a lord and was feeling very powerful. Yet, despite that, each time I took him, he begged me to stroke him. The slower I pounded him, the more I hurt him, the larger his erection and the louder he called out when he climaxed. He was completely seduced within the first hour and has been ashamed of it ever since. I left him there, dangling from the ceiling after our night. He's never approached me sexually again. I think I scare him."

"I think you scare a lot of people."

His eyes were hot on me, almost burning my skin. "The only person who has cause to fear me right now is you."

"And yet, I find myself oddly calm." I smiled. "I want your servant, Matthew to come here," I said. "How do I do that?"

"Just call him," he replied, a curious note in his voice.

"Matthew?" I called.

He appeared instantly before me and his eyes widened in alarm. "Miss?" he said with a tremble. "Are you all right? Is he harming you?" I wanted to laugh because the scene in front of him demonstrated that quite the opposite was happening.

"I'm quite all right," I purred to him. "I just need your help."

"Anything I can do," he said breathlessly.

I walked to Ghalib and looked at him squarely. "There is something I want from you before I release you."

"And that is?"

"You have to promise me that Matthew won't be punished for anything that happens. From this point forward, he is only doing as I say."

"Are you being protective of him?" His voice rang with jealousy but I ignored it.

"What if I am?"

"I don't know if I like it."

I shrugged. "I could leave you here. Matthew and I could go and have dinner. Maybe even a little post-dinner fun in his room. You'd be able to feel it, wouldn't you? Every stroke, every climax, every time he drove —"

"Stop," he said, like the very thought pained him. "Very well. Matthew is an innocent."

I got that heady feeling of power again. I knew it wouldn't be long-lasting, but I wouldn't waste it. I walked over to Matthew and kissed him, mostly because I knew it would irritate Ghalib. Matthew held me gently, encircling me with the sweetest vibration of Drawing imaginable. His lips were eager. I had to break the kiss and Ghalib was glaring at both of us when I looked over at him from the circle of Matthew's arms. "Mmm," I murmured, untangling myself from the servant. "Delicious Matthew. I need for you to perform fellatio on Ghalib. He needs an orgasm very, very badly."

159

He looked surprised, then frightened. "I'm... I never... he doesn't..."

"We've never been lovers, Elaine," Ghalib supplied. "I think he may be a little nervous."

"Relax, Matthew," I said, looking only at Ghalib, "I'm going to help you."

I walked to the wall of blindfolds and retrieved a green silk scarf. When I approached Ghalib he flinched away. "Come on," I cooed. "Don't be such a poor sport." He glared at me but finally submitted.

I unfastened his slacks, lowering them slightly and nodded to Matthew to release his penis. Ghalib was entirely erect, entirely engorged, despite his anger, completely aroused. Matthew knelt in front of him but I put a hand on his shoulder to slow him down.

I kissed Ghalib, running my fingers down his back, over his buttocks, spreading his cheeks until he moaned softly. Then I stepped back and nodded to Matthew.

While he took the length of Ghalib into his mouth, I guided his hands, letting my fingers brush Ghalib's skin, hearing him respond to torrents of Drawing released with every stroke. I knelt beside Matthew, kissing his cheeks, even as I laid my hand on Ghalib's lower stomach, knowing the Drawing was so strong that it would ignite his whole lower body. Before long, Ghalib was thrusting haphazardly. Finally, I could feel the rhythm he needed and I guided Matthew's willing lips. Ghalib's whole body shuddered. He groaned and the shackles fell from his wrists.

"Go, Matthew," I whispered to him. He kissed me once quickly on the lips; he was gone as quickly as he had arrived. As fast as I could, I got to my feet and backed away a few paces.

Ghalib pulled the blindfold from his eyes and blinked twice before he found me. His face was flushed with anger and exhilaration. He drew up his pants but didn't bother with his shirt. "Don't move," he ordered me and I was rooted to the spot.

He walked close to me, then walked around me like he was surveying one of his sculptures. "You're quite the surprise," he commented. "What shall I do with you?"

Chapter 19

Performances

I shivered, standing there, frozen to the spot. I couldn't move. Ghalib's command bound me as completely as handcuffs and ropes could. He circled around me once and stopped in front of me, a cruel twist to his amused smile.

"I believed that you would be the first being bound in this room. I intended to show you how pleasing hours of foreplay could be." He cocked his head and smiled at me. "But now I think you need a lesson in who is the Master here."

He ran his hands over the material of my shirt. Then, with a harsh jerk, he ripped open the buttons, fasteners flying everywhere, bouncing off the floor. Until now, I hadn't really considered how strong he was. But the shirt barely offered any resistance. My heart pounded hard.

"You must know that it wasn't Matthew's lips I craved around me," he said, his voice harshly beautiful.

He placed a finger on my lips, tracing the crease between them, slowly forcing the tip of his finger inside my mouth. For a moment, I resisted, clenching my teeth but then the Drawing flowed around me. I felt myself smile and slowly, I unclenched my teeth and drew his finger in, my tongue tracing the underside all the way to the joint and back to the tip.

I had his attention. His eyes were hot with hunger and his face was flushed. I bit down on his finger until he took a sharp breath. I think he got my meaning. Anything he put in my mouth would go there at his peril.

His smile grew wider. He withdrew his finger and grabbed handfuls of my open shirt, dragging me to his lips, his teeth biting at my skin, his lips finally finding mine. He kissed me harshly, punishingly, bruisingly. I flashed with images. Me, on all fours, with him behind me. I was fitted with a bit, like a horse would wear, and he drew my head back even as he thrust into me. I heard my own stifled cries.

Something about Ghalib was almost feral. He still didn't behave cruelly; instead, he seemed wild. I struggled against his grip. He broke the kiss and shoved me onto the bed. Before I could even sit up, he was on me, his lips back on mine, his hands ripping my shirt away, his hard chest rubbing into me. The heat between us was blistering. I tried to scramble away. It was fruitless. He dragged me back.

"Stop," I gasped.

"I will never stop," he growled. His lips went to my neck. The elastic on my bra snapped and he tore it away so that his lips could find my nipples. He bit at them roughly until I cried out, my hands in his hair, not sure if I was going to push him away or urge him on. His fingernails raked my side, leaving tingling trails on my torso.

He captured both of my wrists in one of his hands and forced me into a sitting position. If his hands had been iron cuffs, I couldn't have been any more restrained. The harder I fought, the gentler his touch—on my face, my breasts, my back. I broke out in a sweat from the effort and his eyes glowed. He kissed me as I fought, his tongue playing with my earlobe.

"You're mine, Elaine," he whispered in my ear. "I don't want you to have any illusion that you could possibly escape." He forced my wrists towards the bedposts and I saw what he intended to do. The padded shackles. He was going to bind me to the bed and have both hands free to work me. Sudden claustrophobia shook me. I bucked underneath him like a wild thing but it didn't matter. He was so much stronger than me.

The shackles closed around my wrists with a snap. I was on my knees, my legs clenched together, facing the head of the bed with Ghalib behind me. I couldn't see what he was doing but I felt his hand slide around me and tease my pants zipper down.

"No!" I insisted, giving a mighty wrench. The restraints were solid. I couldn't get away. An arm went around my waist; I tried to twist away from him only to feel his grip tighten around my waist and his other hand slide inside of my pants. He felt for my wettest spot while his tongue left a cool line down my spine. Involuntarily, I moaned and my clenched knees relaxed. "That's right," he whispered.

The Drawing current rose to a new peak. "Oh!" I gasped.

"I want to take off your pants," he said, his hand still working me. The heat between my legs seemed to radiate all the way to my knees. "But I'm not going to do it unless you ask me."

I had a choice. It wasn't an order. I wanted to be strong.

But, I wasn't. The Drawing didn't help, either. It ramped up my arousal; it made me want to please Ghalib. I didn't even sound like myself when I spoke. My voice was breathy; he couldn't have missed my arousal if I had been giving him driving directions. "Please take off my pants, Ghalib," I said, looking over my shoulder at him.

He flushed in satisfaction and stopped stroking me. I nearly groaned at the loss of sensation. He slid my slacks down and over my boots. Then he repeated the process with my panties. He left my boots in place and admired his handiwork for a moment.

His voice was no less husky than mine. "Kneel, Kitten," he said. I knelt and he forced my knees wide apart. Then he dragged me backwards on the bed so that my arms were stretched by the restraints. One of his hands went around me, between my legs, stroking. The other went to my back, then my buttocks, then probed at my anus. His fingers were maddening.

One hand continued to stroke in an irregular rhythm, stoking my pleasure. The other probed and massaged and worked. Finally, he penetrated me. "Oh!" I exclaimed.

"Shh," he hushed, "show me you want it."

I did want it. And since I had gone this far into my humiliation, why not go a bit further? My hips twitched and thrust, impaling his finger deeper and deeper into me. It was the only way to get his stroking fingers into the right rhythm. He added a second finger; then a third. It was pain and pleasure holding hands; the Drawing pushed me on. Finally, I felt my peak. I rode both hands fervently. I was moments away.

His voice was in my ear and his stroking slowed. "You must do something for me."

"What?" I gasped.

He positioned himself behind me; his erect penis pushed against me. I knew what he had planned. "Say yes," he whispered.

For once I didn't hesitate. I was riding a wave of Drawing. "Yes," I said. His penis opened my anus, spreading me much more than his fingers had. The Drawing vibrated, humming as he eased himself into me an inch at a time. One of his arms encircled my chest, fondling my breasts. The other kept pace between my legs. I bucked against him, forcing him into me faster, needing the roughness to satisfy me. The pain became sharper and so did the pleasure. He moaned.

"God, Elaine!"

I looked over my shoulder, pushing against him, feeling confident again. "I said yes, Ghalib. Ride me."

It was all of the encouragement he needed. He pumped hard into me and I met each thrust. He stroked and teased and rubbed as my hands gripped the restraining chains. His free hand stroked my arms sending shivering Drawing over my skin. He gripped my shoulder, using it as leverage to drive himself into me harder.

As I began to climax, I bit his hand which sent him over the edge, too. I bucked wildly, catching the perfect rhythm of thrust and stroke, feeling my anus clench around him as he strummed me like a musician.

His hand slid from my shoulder to my breast, clutching it. I hovered at the high point of my orgasm for seconds, tossing my hair back, crying out.

When Ghalib yelled, I smiled. We continued to move against each other until not one more ounce of pleasure could be derived. Then the shackles fell off of my wrists and I fell to the bed. Ghalib withdrew and fell next to me.

"Now, that was a fun side of you," Ghalib said, running a finger over the sweat on my chest.

"I didn't think I had sides," I said.

"I can hardly believe that you thought one night would satisfy either of us. Every time we finish, I can only think of our next time together."

The same was true for me. It was maddening. My climax gave me only a moment of relief before my heat built again. I didn't know if it was good or bad that Ghalib's passion matched mine. I might have been able to resist the Drawing if I hadn't had such an immediate tempter who was so willing.

The only real answer was to spend less time with my clothes off. I got off the bed and started to gather my things off of the floor.

He watched me pull on my pants. My shirt was in pieces. There was no saving it.

"I need a shirt," I told him.

He chuckled. "What for?"

"Dinner," I reminded him.

He stood lazily, completely unembarrassed by his nudity. And why should he be? His body was chiseled. I had to look away. He took the torn shirt out of my hands and ran it through his fingers. When he returned it to me, it was whole.

"I should put you back in chains and feed you dinner that way," he said. "Make you earn every bite."

I shot a look in his general direction and was surprised to see him dressed. "I've already earned every bite," I said darkly.

He laughed. "Touché."

I put on my shirt and jacket. He approached me, unbuttoning the top of my shirt again and straightening the collar on my jacket. "Are you sure dinner is what you want?" he asked, leaning so close that his lips nearly touched mine.

I lowered my eyelashes and let my breath play on his lips. "Absolutely certain," I whispered back.

He smirked. "Very well, Pet. Come."

We returned to the mansion, to one of the dining rooms. A small table was laid and waiting for us, a delicate feast clearly placed moments before our arrival. We both ate so enthusiastically that we didn't even speak. It wasn't until we were sipping our coffee that Matthew came in with a large stack of envelopes on a tray. He placed them before Ghalib, who sighed and rolled his eyes melodramatically.

"What are those?" I asked.

"Grateful acceptances to a musicale that you are going to give two nights from now," he said smoothly.

My coffee cup paused on the way to my lips. "That *I'm* going to give?" I asked.

"Trust me, Pet, it was the best option available. I've had literally hundreds of requests to meet you. A ball would have had you dancing all evening and barely meeting half the guests. Dinner would have been even worse. Everyone would have felt slighted to not have personal time with you."

"If I'm on a stage, singing, nobody gets personal time with me," I said lightly, slowly lowering my cup so he couldn't see it shaking in my hand.

"Quite the contrary," he said. "Everyone will feel as if they've had the chance to experience an Omnilight. You are a conduit. When you sing, the Drawing reacts."

I looked at him blankly.

"It's a very pleasurable sensation, listening to you sing. I noticed it that first night. It's almost a physical reaction to the sound of your voice," he said, opening envelopes and tossing the cards into a pile. "I imagine it's probably even stronger now, like the Drawing is stronger. To be honest with you, Elaine, I've never met a mortal with such gifts for manipulating my race."

I gave him a look. Surely he wasn't calling *me* manipulative. I decided to let it go. "And this musicale I'm giving in two nights? Do you plan to tell me anything about it, or are you just going to throw me out on the stage?"

He pushed the cards aside and lifted my hand. It was still shaking. "Nervous, Pet?"

"Alarmed would be a better description."

"Good," he replied. "About six hundred Architects and two hundred pets. I thought an hour of music should satisfy them, for now. No close contact with anyone, which satisfies me...."

"Where?" I asked. "Here?"

He cocked his head. "Come with me."

He led me out of the dining room, through the halls, to a set of double doors I'd never seen before. Inside was the most stunning auditorium that I'd ever seen. Gold gilded the walls and amber sculptures of lions snarled over the auditorium. Burgundy velvet covered the seats. The ceiling was painted with cherubs and adorned with a crystal chandelier. Ghalib pulled me up on to the lacquered stage where a piano stood.

I looked out at the huge room of empty seats. My stomach twisted uncomfortably. "I don't know if I can do this," I said, listening to the acoustics.

"Nonsense. You can and you will."

"What music?" I choked out. He led me to the piano. Sheet music was strewn all over it. There were a variety of songs, mostly pieces I'd sung before. Some music I'd only heard. Several were very primal. Very sexual. Something akin to a challenging thrill rose in me. "Can I go through these before I have to perform?"

"Where's the confident Elaine who locks her Master to a wall with reckless abandon?" he teased.

I raised my eyebrows. "She just learned that she has to sing for eight hundred people."

He laughed. "Come here when you wake tomorrow and the accompanist will be waiting for you. Practice all you like." He drew a finger down my neck. "Now, to bed. I want to make sure you're fully rested and recovered from the other night. You must be at your best."

I hurried to the back of the auditorium where the exit was. The seats were bathed in shadows. Still, I saw movement in the next to last row and paused, straining to see what caused it.

"Is something the matter, Elaine?" Ghalib asked from the stage.

I made out a shape. A person. He crept closer until he was in the faint light of the stage. Shaggy chestnut hair. Soulful brown eyes. Matthew. He must have snuck in to watch us. He looked fearful and shook his head frantically, silently begging me not to reveal him.

"No," I lied. "I just stopped to listen to the acoustics." I looked up at him. He seemed small from this far back. "Good night, Ghalib," I said, not looking at Matthew and heading straight out of the auditorium.

I used my intuition to get back to my suite, though I suspected it took me twice as long as it should have in the winding, confusing halls, hoping that I had covered for Matthew well enough. I couldn't worry about that now. I had a whole other host of things to worry about, starting with singing publically for the first time since college. I asked Lisa to wake me early, dressed for bed, and fell asleep almost immediately, shutting everything else out of my head.

Chapter 20

Differences of Opinion

I woke up because I heard a sound. The room was still dark. I flipped on the lamp beside my bed and looked around. Nothing. I pushed back my covers and crept to the bedroom door. "Lisa?" I called softly.

"No, it's not Lisa," someone said softly back.

A male voice. Not Jason. Certainly not Ghalib. I padded back to my bed and grabbed my robe off of the bed post. Before I turned around, there was a person standing in my bedroom doorway.

Matthew.

"Matthew, what are you doing here?" I asked. His presence here was confusing. I couldn't imagine why Ghalib would send him to me instead of Lisa or Jason.

"I... I heard this was your suite," he said, running a hand through his hair. The chestnut waves fell back into his eyes. "The door was unlocked."

A cold chill gripped me. "Does Ghalib know you're here?"

"No." He looked frightened but determined. "I needed to see you."

"Have you lost your mind?" I asked him, trying to turn him and steer him back to the exit. "You absolutely have to go." Where my hand met his arm, the Drawing tingled with a rich sweetness. If the Drawing had a taste, Matthew's would have been milk chocolate.

He wouldn't let me move him. Instead, he captured my hand and looked at me pleadingly. "Elaine," he said in a low voice. "I think I'm in love with you."

"Stop it. You're not in love with me," I said, pulling my hand away. "It's just the Drawing. That's all."

"It isn't," he insisted. His brown eyes were as earnest as any I'd ever seen. His cheeks suffused with pink at the confession.

"Regardless of how you feel about me, you can't be in here," I managed. "This is dangerous. Ghalib keeps a very close eye on me."

"He treats you like a... a thing. *His* thing," Matthew said, his voice stronger, his words coming in a rush. "I would never be that way with you. He would hurt you just for fun. I want to protect you. That's why I followed you to the auditorium last night — to make sure you were all right."

How could someone live here and be as naive as he was? If Ghalib decided he wanted to hurt me, nothing short of Nyx would stop him. "I can take care of myself. At the moment, I'm worried about you," I said, pushing on him again. "If you go now, you can tell him you got lost and went into the wrong room."

"Come away with me," he said, his eyes pleading.

"No." My voice rose with my fear. "Don't ever let anyone hear you say something like that. I'm an Omnilight and a pet. Ghalib will never stop chasing me. And if not him, the other Architects. Or Nyx."

I watched his face, waiting for it to dawn on him how fruitless his plans were. All I saw was determination. "Then you don't care for me at all?" he asked.

"Of course I care," I said. "But, even if I care, I can't run a —"

He didn't wait for me to finish. He kissed me full on the lips. I saw images of us kissing on the edge of a bed, him stopping to look at me, whispering his love for me in my ear and me, smiling sweetly back at him. I broke off the kiss. These images were going to give me diabetes. And they were only making things worse.

"No, Matthew," I said firmly. "I want you to leave."

"You don't mean that."

"I swear that I do. Get out of my room."

Tears came into his eyes. I wanted to reassure him or apologize for hurting him. But I didn't. I held his gaze steadily. Finally, he lowered his head. "If it's what you want," he said.

"It is," I said, forcing myself to remain stern. "Go."

He stood there for a minute.

"Now, Matthew."

He turned and slunk to the door, letting himself out. The instant he was gone my eyes prickled. He was just the kind of guy I would have gone for before Ghalib. A lump rose in my throat. It was as if I had rejected all of my old life by rejecting Matthew. It was like a part of me had died.

I crawled back into bed, hiding my face in my pillow. I let myself cry.

In the morning, Lisa woke me early. If she saw that I had been crying in the night, she didn't mention it and neither did I. I just climbed out of bed and dug through the closet until I found a casual dress.

Lisa brought me a thermos of tea and I took it with me. Then I wandered the hallways, trying to focus on the auditorium. It seemed to work; I arrived there much faster than I expected. A young woman, the same accompanist from the night I performed for Ghalib, waited on the piano bench.

We practiced all morning, her playing growing more fluid and complementary to my voice the longer we continued. After I'd been through every song at least twice, I decided to stop. I was nervous and it would be very easy to just keep going but I had to rest my voice.

"You're going to take their breath away, Miss," the accompanist told me with a pleased expression.

I smiled at her. "What's your name?" I asked.

"Allison."

"Thank you, Allison."

I went back to my suite. When I got there, Lisa wasn't in my room. I sat down with a book, realizing it was the first leisure time I'd had in the past I didn't even know how many days.

Too soon, Lisa came in. And she was carrying an outfit.

I glanced up from my book and I did a double-take. "You're kidding me, right?" I said. "I'm not wearing a corset."

"The Master sent it specifically," Lisa said, sounding nervous. "He said it was for tonight."

"I'm not wearing a corset."

"I won't lace it too tightly. I've done this before."

I stood and went over to look at the garment. The corset was the brocade bodice of a floor-length gown in shades of amethyst, violet, and rose; the skirt was the deepest plum.

"The Master has guests coming tonight," Lisa added.

"I guess I'm wearing a corset," I said with a sigh.

I put my book aside and let Lisa help me dress. I knelt before my bed, clinging to the bed posts, my skin powdered and a little cotton shift under the corset to make wearing it more comfortable. As if it could ever be comfortable.

She eased the laces tighter and tighter. My tiny tummy flattened. My breasts lifted and bubbled above the corset. My waist waned. I could barely breathe. "I think that's good, Lisa," I gasped. I couldn't bend at the waist.

The effect was transforming. Not only did it exaggerate my curves, it corrected my posture. I looked at myself in the mirror, hating the caged feel but admiring the feminine affect. I looked like an upside-down flower, with the rippling skirt and my whittled waist.

Lisa swept my hair up on my head and I put on my make-up. She had to put my shoes on for me because I couldn't do it myself. The heels were taller than usual. I hadn't been so uncomfortable since the Festival of Pets and it made my nerves jump. It was as if Ghalib wanted to ensure that I couldn't move very fast.

Far too soon, I heard Ghalib's echoing voice in my head. *Elaine.*

I started to sigh but I couldn't draw enough breath. I just shook my head. His call led me through the hallways to a wide archway. I stopped outside, before I crossed the threshold, and looked inside.

It was as if Ghalib had built a bistro right inside his home. Small tables were placed around the room with mostly couples sitting at them. I found Anna and Julia, their heads together, talking. Victor sat in the front with a blonde woman I had never seen before. Markus and Tobias were in the back and particularly noticeable because of their size. Ghalib, his white, white hair shining in the low light, sat alone at the table next to Victor.

At the front of the room was a stage. The red, velvet curtain was drawn and still. I bit my lip.

"May I help you, Miss"?" a servant that I'd never seen before asked me. It was a very good question.

"I'm Ghalib's pet." The damn word stuck in my throat every time. "I see him there. May I just go in?"

"Of course."

I entered and the room hushed for a moment. It was eerie. I paused where I stood, looked around at the dozens of pairs of eyes watching me. The corset wouldn't let me hunch, so I made a general nod to the room, fixed my eyes on Ghalib, and headed for his table. I know my face was hot.

"Good evening, Elaine," he said, standing. His voice was pleasant but there was a hard quality to his expression. It didn't stop his eyes from tracing my corseted form. He pulled out my chair and helped me into my seat. "You look delicious," he added.

"Thank you," I replied. I couldn't put my finger on it, but something was just wrong. The energy in the room was ramped up.

"I may have to insist on having you corseted every night," he said, his eyes lingering where my breasts bubbled at the top of the bodice. "It's a very enticing look on you."

"I can barely breathe."

"Then Lisa laced you up properly," he replied.

Ghalib seemed odd, too. He hadn't touched me, yet. I narrowed my eyes at him. "I thought you didn't like to open your home to a lot of guests," I asked lightly.

"Yes, well... I thought we might have a little prologue to your musicale tomorrow night. I've arranged for some special entertainment after dinner."

The servants moved between the tables, placing plates. I wondered if I would be able to eat. The food smelled wonderful but the thought of making the corset any tighter on me was hardly appealing. When my plate arrived, I took a small bite. Maybe I could ask Lisa to bring me some food later.

The scarlet curtain rose on that stage and a four piece string orchestra played softly. Low conversations carried on at the tables. It was a polite din. Ghalib didn't seem interested in talking and I was happy to oblige. After a while, the servants came to collect the plates and the stage curtain dropped.

The other guests turned to us expectantly. I felt a jolt of adrenaline. "What's going on?" I asked.

"I have a gift for you," Ghalib said. He drew a long, slender box from under the table and laid it before me. "Open it."

I glanced around again. Every eye was on me. I broke the ribbon with shaking fingers and lifted the lid. My mouth went dry. It was a long riding crop, like an equestrian might use to urge a horse. The handle was wrapped with black leather; the rod was the length of my arm and very springy. At the end was a loop of leather.

My eyes met Ghalib's. His expression was an odd mix of eagerness, irritation, and firmness. Heat coursed through me all the way to my stomach. I had a few guesses as to why he would give me such a gift and none of them were good.

"What do you mean for me to do with this?" I asked haltingly.

He lifted his eyebrows and nodded to the stage. As I looked, the curtain rose again. I was too shocked to even gasp.

It was Matthew, completely naked. He stood, his ankles spread far apart and bound to metal poles that rose up out of the stage to the height of his thighs. His wrists were lashed together and bound to a chain that hung from the ceiling in front of him, forcing him to bend at the waist. The room became deadly silent. I glanced around and watched the hungry eyes drinking Matthew in: his well-formed, muscular legs, his flaccid penis, and his sweat-coated chest. The gag that made his full lips misshapen.

Suddenly the riding crop made much more sense.

"I hear you had a guest last night," Ghalib said to me, his voice dangerously low.

"Yes," I breathed, "but I made him leave."

"Before or after you let him profess his undying love for you? Before or after he kissed you without my permission?"

"'This isn't my fault."

"Is there a reason you didn't tell me about his transgressions? Either the one last night in your room or the one last night in the auditorium?"

"He didn't do anything wrong. He was just following us around."

"*I'm* the Master here. *I'm* the one who decides if he did something wrong." His voice was still low but the intensity made me shiver.

"Ghalib—"

"Don't make excuses for him. I'm already questioning your loyalty."

"My loyalty?" Anger started to flair in me. What earthly reason could I have for being loyal to Ghalib?

Ghalib continued as if he hadn't heard me. "To prove that I am your only Master, you must take your new gift and use it on Matthew."

We were both to be made a spectacle of. Just looking at Matthew gave me a throb that I wished would pass. "No. I can't."

"Of course you can," he said smoothly. He took my hand and I suddenly knew why he hadn't touched me. If he had, the whispering Drawing would have given away his plans. He intended to shock me and he had succeeded. He placed the riding crop into my hands. "Now go."

"I can't do this. I won't do this," I insisted.

"You will," he replied, a cruel smile crossing his face. It was the first time he had ever looked at me that way and it made me shiver. "You'll do it without being ordered or I will have Victor whip Matthew and tomorrow, you will find yourself tied to that stage, stripped and on display, instead of conducting a musicale. Don't think I wouldn't love it. I almost hope you will defy me. Everyone in this room wishes you would."

I hated myself for my arousal. The room swam around me, all eyes and faces and toothy smiles. I stood. I don't know how I made it to the stage; my knees were so weak. But up in front of everyone, with the hot lights in my face, a calm passed over me. I stepped closer to Matthew.

His eyes begged me not to do it. I couldn't explain to him that I didn't have a choice. I ran my fingers through the hair on his chest, feeling the tingling, coursing Drawing. I felt the muscles in his arms as far up as I could reach and heard the audience rustle and sigh. "They want a show," I whispered. "Help me give them one."

I went behind him. I had never used a riding crop—not on a horse and certainly not on a human. I slapped it once into my hand and winced at the sting. I glanced up and noticed Ghalib looking impatient. I held my breath and snapped the springy riding crop across Matthew's backside. I didn't hit him very hard. He barely responded and Ghalib's jaw set. I could tell that his tolerance was waning.

I tried again, still feeling awkward. This time I snapped the crop and it made a satisfying sound as it bit into his skin. His whole body jumped and he let out a throaty moan. It seemed as if power flowed into me. I was aroused and in control. It was a crazy, unfamiliar feeling.

I touched the pink stripe I had caused. It wasn't even a welt—just a mark. I laid my hand on the small of his back, knowing that I could make this pleasurable for Matthew. It certainly wouldn't be his romantic, saccharine fantasy but it wouldn't be the torture he feared, either.

With my touch on his back, I watched his penis rise a bit. I knew that if I whipped him while he throbbed for me, it would be a different, more bearable type of pain. I ran my fingers over the curve of his buttocks until I felt him tremble. Then, I rested my hand on his inner thigh as I whipped him hard with the riding crop.

The response was as I had hoped. He didn't yell and fight. He gasped and moaned around the gag. His buttocks tensed even as they rose to meet each lash. His penis engorged to its full size, twitching every now and again.

The audience was affected, too. When I stole a glance into the bistro, ladies mopped their upper lips and gentlemen shifted in their seats. Even Ghalib leaned forward, his expression intense and hungry.

I continued to punish Matthew's buttocks, even as I stroked the inside of his thighs, letting my fingers stray dangerously close to his most tender areas. His penis never softened. I hit my stride with the crop, whipping him until his skin was bright and welts began to rise. I only stopped when Ghalib stood. "Enough," he said. "The boy is getting too much pleasure out of this punishment." Ghalib looked at me accusingly. "Take him back to his cell. Victor can come for him later tonight and complete his punishment."

Matthew's face turned panicked. I understood. Victor would be terrible, relentless. I carefully made my way off of the stage and back to the table where Ghalib stood. All of the Architects watched us.

"Don't send him to Victor," I whispered, hoping none of the other Architects could hear me. "Please."

"You are in *no* position to bargain with me," Ghalib said. "You should be concerned about your own future."

"I didn't do anything wrong," I said hotly. "And Matthew is just a foolish boy."

"I have made my decision about what is going to happen to him." I gritted my teeth and made an impatient sound. "I'm still trying to figure out what to do with you," he added.

I was grateful for my anger. It staved off the fear. "What to do with *me*?"

"For your punishment."

"You've got to be kidding me."

"I assure you that I am very, very serious."

I narrowed my eyes at him, gritting my teeth, not really trusting myself to talk. I half wished that I had done something with Matthew. At least Ghalib's outrage would make some sense.

He looked past me at the table where Victor was sitting with his blonde beauty. "Victor," he said, "join us. And bring your lovely companion."

Victor's face was in shadows like always. His head lifted towards us and he stood. I tried to suppress the fear that threatened to rise. If Victor was going to be involved with my punishment, I was in big trouble.

Chapter 21

Confrontation

Victor stood. "Christine," he said. He didn't say it loud but the blonde at his table still jumped. She looked like a doll: pink cheeks, blue eyes, golden hair. When she came over to the table, I saw bruises around her wrists.

"Please sit," Ghalib invited. They pulled chairs over and sat with us.

"How can I help you?" Victor asked. I couldn't see his expression because of the shadows that obscured his face, but his voice was smug.

"I gave you the opportunity to punish Mathew because I knew you would enjoy the experience. I wonder if you would do me a favor in return."

"If I can."

"I'm afraid I'm not stringent enough with Elaine. Would you like to spend an evening with her, teaching her the appropriate way for a pet to interact with her Master?"

I gasped and spoke before I considered my actions. "Ghalib—"

"Quiet, Elaine," Ghalib said to me. The command cut my voice off mid-thought. "See what I mean?"

Victor's voice was eager. "I would like that opportunity," he said.

"Excellent," Ghalib replied. When he turned to me, his expression was stern. "She told no one of Matthew's infraction. She's covered for him again and again. And she argued with me when I told her to use the crop on him." I shivered and could almost feel the blood draining from my face.

"Leave her alone with me for a couple of cycles and I will see to it that she never argues again."

"One evening," Ghalib replied, firmly. "And not alone. I will accompany her to ensure that my property is not damaged. Some day after the musicale."

I felt dizzy. Ghalib's intensity had turned to fierceness. They just sat there, discussing my future. Helplessness didn't begin to describe my feelings. I tried to calm my breathing; I knew they could see the rise and fall of my chest because of the corset.

"You're going to accompany her?" Victor asked salaciously. "Is that to say I won't have a free hand with her discipline?"

"I want to enjoy your Christine while you punish my Elaine," Ghalib said, looking at the blonde. She grew so red I was afraid she would have internal bleeding.

"How can I blame you?" Victor said softly, in an admiring tone. "However, I cannot deny that I've come out ahead. I've won an Omnilight for an evening with instructions to punish her." I could almost hear Victor's smile.

"Thank you, my friend," Ghalib said. "Elaine and I are going to retire now. I promise to contact you concerning her punishment. In the meantime, just tell Jason when you're ready to go. He will deliver Matthew to you." He turned to Christine. "I'll look forward to seeing you again soon, my dear."

Then, without a word, he took my hand and pulled me out of the room. The Drawing snapped between us. He walked too fast through the halls and I stumbled on my too-high heels. I gasped for breath that the corset wouldn't let me have. Ghalib didn't stop; he just pulled me on.

"This is bullshit," I huffed.

He stopped and glared at me. "You are insolent."

"You're childish."

He grabbed my arm and continued to pull me along. We reached a staircase that seemed to go down forever. I recognized it. The pathway to the prison. I couldn't resist or my teetering heels would have sent me sprawling down the steps. We practically ran to the bottom of the steps. The smell of human waste hit me at the same time as the cries of fear and moans of arousal became audible. Ghalib stopped in front of Carl and Joan who didn't even try to hide their delight. "Someone in trouble?" Carl asked.

"Someone needs to learn that punishments don't just happen to other people," Ghalib replied.

"I knew that," I said with venom. "I just didn't know that they happen for no good reason."

"Your *Master* thinks that there is a good reason."

"My *Master* is a jealous child with a bad temper!"

We glared at each other for longer than a few seconds. "Can I cut her hair?" Joan asked, playing with the curls that had escaped the up-swept 'do.

"No," Ghalib said. "No marks. No alterations."

"Can I fuck her?" Carl asked, licking his lips.

"Watch it," I told him in a snide voice. "You might make Ghalib jealous."

"I'm not jealous because Matthew wanted you," Ghalib said through gritted teeth. "It was because you wanted him."

I was so angry I could hardly form a sentence. "Are you *serious*?"

"I've had enough." He grabbed my upper arm and practically dragged me into the prison and down the endless hallway. One of the cell doors hung open and he headed straight for it. He didn't let go of my arm until he had shoved me roughly inside. Then, he closed the door with a loud clang.

"Nobody touches her," Ghalib told Carl and Joan, who had followed us. Ghalib wrapped his fingers around the bars and said, "You belong to me, Elaine. Don't forget that. Your comfort and your discomfort are at my whim." I glared at him. "I'm leaving you here to remind you of that," he continued. "When I come for you, I expect your gratitude for sparing you from the guards."

He turned and walked away and he didn't look back.

"Unbelievable," I said. And I hoped he heard me, too.

Joan and Carl waited until the door to the prison slammed shut to talk. "You should fuck her anyway," Joan told Carl. "Could be days before he comes back."

"She'll tell," Carl said.

The Drawing in this place was twisted and rotting, but it still whispered to me. I approached the bars. "I won't tell." They both looked at me surprised. "But you're still not going to touch me."

They both looked back at me and I knew I was right. They liked to pretend that they were separate entities from Ghalib but they knew the truth as much as I did: this was *his* house and *his* prison. I was *his* pet and they were *his* Dream Makers. It was infuriating.

"Come on," Joan said, taking Carl's arm. They exited the prison. I wished that I was going out, too.

I sat on the tiny prison cot and tried to ignore the festering flavor of Drawing that permeated the stones of this place. It was strong and it was soaked in indecency. If I stretched out my mind and listened, I could feel what was going on in cells throughout the prison. I knew the panicky cries were from a woman who dreamed she was being raped by her brother. The screams far in the distance were from a man who was reliving torture he'd experienced in a recent war. These people came here every night.

I sat on the edge of the cot and just tried to calm down. This was a black, negative place and the tainted Drawing seemed to seep into me. My stomach heaved and suddenly, I couldn't breathe. The corset was too tight; the cell was too small. I clawed at the catches of the corset until it popped open. Then I gasped for breath and sucked in the foul odors of the prison. It made my heaving stomach worse. I staggered to the corner where I vomited what little I was able to eat at dinner. When the retching subsided, I lay down on the cot and closed my eyes. I didn't sleep at all. The time was unending.

"What if he don't come back for you?"

I opened my eyes. Joan stood in front of my cell. "He will," I replied in a resigned tone.

"What if he don't?"

"Then at least I'll never have to see him again."

Her voice was scandalized. "You don't mean that."

"I swear I do. With all my heart." I rolled over and faced the wall.

For the first time since I accepted the collar, I couldn't sense Ghalib. He was probably in there, among the black whispers of Drawing. I wouldn't look for him. I hoped he couldn't feel me either.

I heard every sound, though. Moans of pleasure. Cries of pain. Weeping and begging. The lash of a whip. The crack of a paddle. The scrape of a heavy chain being dragged over the stone floor. I lay on my cot, my eyes wide open, wishing I was deaf.

At some point, one huge guard came to my cell. I sat up and tensed, ready to run if he tried to come in. But, he didn't open the door. Another guard joined him. Then a third. They just stood at the bars and stared at me, huge and hairy and lumpy, like ogres. Then, one unlaced his pants and released his grotesquely large penis. I couldn't imagine something that size entering me. He began stroking himself.

His masturbation turned my stomach again. Then another one unlaced his pants and started tugging at himself. The Drawing nudged me but the arousal was sickening. I sat on the edge of my bed with my eyes closed.

I couldn't shut out the sounds, though. Even after the three ogres finished and left, cries swelled all around me. Someone clanged something metal against the bars of my cell. I lay down and gritted my teeth. I couldn't have said how much time passed. It felt like days.

I felt Ghalib before I saw him but I didn't open my eyes.

"How did she do?" I heard him ask softly.

"She puked pretty quick but she didn't make a sound," Joan replied. "Not even when the triplets found her."

Their footsteps stopped in front of my cell. "Elaine?" Ghalib said.

I opened my eyes. My hair was a ratty mess from my tossing. I held the corset over my chest. I'm sure my make-up was smeared all over my face.

"Have you had enough of this place?" he asked me. I nodded, not trusting my voice.

I stood and Ghalib opened the door to my cell. I wanted to run for the exit but I forced myself to take slow steps. I reminded myself that I still hadn't eaten since I had been in here, that I was still on higher heels than I was used to, and that just being locked in the prison had left my legs weak and shaking. Ghalib stood in the threshold, so bright and beautiful in this place.

I stopped in front of him. "How long was I in here?"

"One cycle."

He put his fingers in my hair and fanned it over my shoulders. Then he tilted my face up and kissed me. The Drawing rose around us, giving me a little relief from the poisonous version of the energy. His lips slipped from my jaw, to my neck, and nibbled at my collarbone. Then he kissed his way back up to my ear. "Do not make me jealous again," he whispered.

"This is not my fault," I whispered back.

He pulled back and looked at me. "Do not make me jealous again," he repeated in a pointed tone. He glanced meaningfully at the cell behind me.

I gritted my teeth. "Yes, Ghalib."

"Who do you belong to?"

"I belong to you."

He pulled a lock of my hair between his fingers. "Wear your hair down tonight," he said.

I wished that I dared slap him.

He kissed my lips again, possessively, his hand cradling my head. The bloom of Drawing was like balm on my skin. He broke the kiss and brushed his lips softly against mine.

"I'll take you back to your suite," he said, a pleased quality in his voice.

Lisa met me as I came into the room. She was in full fuss mode. "Look at you, you poor thing. Let's get you into a bath and wash the stink of that dungeon off of you. I can't believe he sent you there with less than a day before your musicale. You'll have to have a nap and some food as soon as possible."

She pulled off the ridiculous shoes and there were sores on my feet. Lisa made little disapproving sounds.

She helped me into a hot bath that smelled of roses. I just closed my eyes while Lisa washed my hair and bathed me. I don't know if the Drawing made things difficult for her; if it did, she didn't make any complaints. She even helped me put salve on the sores.

After I was out of the bath and into nightclothes, Jason came in with a tray. "I'm so sorry, Miss," he said. "Drink the tea first. It will help your stomach." I had the passing thought that he must have spent a little time in the prison if he understood how ill it left you. I sipped at the tea. Honey. Mint. Something spicy, like cayenne. It warmed me all the way through.

He and Lisa stood by anxiously while I chewed on a couple of pieces of toast. Then, I looked at them. "Can I just sleep for a little bit?" I asked.

"Of course," Jason said, taking the tray away and tucking me in like a grandfather might. The bed was the softest place that I had ever been. I closed my eyes and fell asleep.

I could have slept for days. Lisa smoothed my hair off of my forehead and even though it was a gentle touch, I started awake.

"I'm sorry, Miss. We have to get you ready for your musicale," Lisa said.

It was the last thing I wanted to do.

I sat up. "Could you ask Jason to get me some tea, please?" I asked.

I had intended to practice today. Now, I was going to be lucky if I managed to properly warm up my voice. It was like Ghalib wanted me to fail. A hard, cold bolt of anger went through me.

We would see about that.

While Lisa sifted through my clothes, I sipped my tea and hummed scales. Then some of the more difficult music that I would be singing tonight. I couldn't relax. My stomach was doing flips. The stakes were so much higher now. If I displeased Ghalib, he could send me back to the prison. Another bolt of anger shot through me. Screw Ghalib; I didn't want to embarrass myself. And I wouldn't.

Lisa dressed me in a long, slim gown that was a glittering violet shade. I specifically requested low heels, both because of my sore feet and because I didn't want my shaking legs to make me fall.

"The hair has to be down tonight," I told Lisa. She didn't question it. She just set to work with her bush until my hair was sleek. "You're going to do well," Lisa said. "But it doesn't matter if you do or not. They all just want to see you."

"Will you be there?"

She flushed. "Not me. I'm just a servant."

Another shot of anger stirred me. Another servant at the whim of the Architects. I put on my make-up heavier than usual so that I wouldn't look pale on the stage.

Finally, Jason came for me. "How are you feeling, Miss?" he asked.

"I'll live," I said grimly.

"They're all seated. Are you ready?"

"Let's get this over with," I grumbled. He shot me a sideways look and then offered his arm. I took it, even though I was pretty sure I knew where the auditorium, and Ghalib, was located.

Chapter 22

The Musicale and Afterwards

"When I open the door, just walk up the aisle," Jason advised outside the auditorium door. "There won't be any introduction. Just nod to the accompanist when you're ready."

"Thank you," I replied.

He opened the double doors and a universe of eyes gazed on me. My breath came out of me like a rush and I froze. I had been prepared for the stage fright but not for the Drawing. It was almost palpable, pulsing in the air like heavy bass. I forced myself to breathe in and it was like I inhaled Drawing, it spread on my tongue, a savory taste, like umami.

It gave me courage. I stood up straighter, inhaled deeper, made a general smile and nod to the audience. I let my eyes run over the beautiful faces and the collared mortals. Then, I fixed my eyes forward and walked to the stage where Allison was already seated.

I set myself in the center of the stage and nodded to her. And as always, when the music started, I was transported. The first song was sad, tragic even. I let my voice play with the emotion and the Drawing flowed through me. The sadder I let myself become, the stronger the current. I watched the Architects respond and I focused, making the sadness more intense. I thought of home, of the places I would never go again and the people I would never see.

The piano music stopped as Allison began crying. I finished A cappella. When I was done, it was like all sound was swallowed. The room was silent except for throat clearing and sniffling. That was when I found Ghalib's face in the audience: three rows back, looking very satisfied. That's also when I saw a faint golden glow at the back of the auditorium. Nyx had slipped in and was standing behind the back row. She nodded her head at me.

I walked over to Allison and put a hand on her shoulder. "It's OK. Take a breath. The next one is fun."

The next piece was a driving, dancing, primal song. Allison started with lackluster energy but soon we were in concert again. The Architects slowly became more engaged, clapping the rhythm as I sang. Channeling the Drawing grew easier and easier. When I was done with the song, the applause was thunderous.

One song after another, each with a different flavor. The little gypsy ditty that spoke of dreams. Two arias about death. A fun little song about mangos. And another about a donkey. I paused when we got to the last five songs. All sensual. All sexual. Designed to make each Architect crave me and envy Ghalib.

I started singing without knowing what to focus on. But, by the end of the first song, the Drawing was delivering images to me. Ghalib's fingers in my hair. Victor's lips on my shoulder. The first two songs left the audience shifting in their seats. The third left them wiping sweat from their faces.

After the third song, Nyx slipped out the back, as quietly as she had coming in. She tossed one look over her shoulder as she went, as if the whole scene disgusted her. I wondered how this room must have felt to her, if the pulsing current was so strong for me.

The Drawing urged me to give them more. It was like there was a dam of sexuality behind me and I had but to step out of the way. When the fourth song started, I gave in. I saw images before my eyes instead of the eager audience. Their fantasies invaded my mind, making me pulse. Wild orgies and sensual coupling. Images of three, four, five of them taking me at a time. I swayed as the Drawing coursed through me. If I concentrated, I could see individual fantasies: Victor with a branding iron and a female brunette with a strap-on. I barely remember singing.

By the time I reached the last song, there was a general flush over everyone in the hall. Those with pets fondled them openly. Architects without pets reached for each other.

I narrowed my eyes at the thinly contained gentility. It was like a challenge to see if I could push them over the edge, urge them into utter wantonness. I took a deep breath for the last song and let my mind go purposely to Julia, to the altar, to my orgasm. I remembered Ghalib taking me on a dining room table in front of an appreciative audience. The Drawing vibrated over my skin, a pale reminder of the energy between us. I sang as I had never sang, feeling like my voice was touching each person. Ghalib's eyes flashed from his row but I looked past him, giving each of them what they craved. Somehow, I sensed that I was forcing the Drawing back on them, pushing it towards them, working them into a frenzy.

As my last note echoed through the hall, their heat reflected back on me. Those with free hands applauded me, yelling their approval. Most pets were already partially undone from their clothes; they were outnumbered by Architects and most had several tormentors teasing and stroking them. Women's moans; men's gruff outcries; pets on their knees before their Masters. Coupling in the seats, against the wall, on the floor.

I was a little shocked at what I had done.

Ghalib's eyes were unblinking on me. He was the only Architect that hadn't moved. He had a tiny smile on his lips.

Gracefully, he stood, a lithe unfolding of limbs. He picked his way through the throngs of passionate groups and joined me on the stage. "Why, Elaine, you've outdone yourself," he said with amusement.

His amusement didn't do anything to help my anger towards him. He enjoyed everything and paid for nothing. I couldn't look at him. "May I go back to my room?" I asked.

He scanned the lusty scene before us. "And remove the conduit? They'll riot. No, this must simply play out with you here."

There was no pretense in the room. It had become wild groups of sex. Clothes still dangled off of bodies, nobody taking the time to completely disrobe. Chains of lovers moaned around the room, one suckling another, even as they're taken from behind by someone fingering another and so on and so on. I saw Julia half hidden under Anna's gowns as Anna arched in pleasure. Then I watched a woman flip Julia's gown over her back and insert two long fingers into her.

Ghalib gave me a sly look. "If you want to be kind, you could help them."

"Help?"

"Continue singing. Urge them to fruition, as it were."

Drawing still pulsed around me. I glanced at the piano. "I seem to have lost my accompanist," I said with the slightest hint of humor. Allison had joined the fray and was bent over the seats of the front row being taken by a large male Architect.

"A cappella?" he suggested.

I nodded once and closed my eyes. It wasn't difficult to tap into the searing energy in the room. If anything, I was more aroused than before watching the display before me. The Drawing current was easy to channel. My voice was rich and true.

I channeled Drawing as forcefully as I could and I heard the cries rising all around me. It only encouraged me to drive them harder, to send them more energy. Trembling limbs were spread wide, held open; trembling lips, also wide, cried out as one. It felt like the whole room orgasmed together; the ground beneath me actually shifted. When I finished the song for the second time, a languid, breathless, half-dressed audience applauded me.

Ghalib looked smug. "Bow, Pet," he instructed.

When I did, they rose to their feet. The ovation felt like solid noise that would push me backwards. Ghalib's hand, hot, caressing, possessive, still rested on my shoulders, holding me in place. "Now, we can go," he said.

He led me down the aisle and out of the auditorium. Each audience member watched me but nobody tried to touch me. When we passed through the double door, my weak legs gave out. Ghalib' caught me before I collapsed on the floor. He eased me through the front door and sat me on the veranda steps. The air was fresh and salty.

"Better?" he asked with a smile.

He was acting like the prison had never happened. Because he had been satisfied by my punishment, I must be too. It was so frustrating. I struggled to my feet. "Yes. Much."

His eyes darkened. "You just made yourself very popular and me very coveted." I heard something behind us. Footsteps. "They're coming out," Ghalib said.

I wouldn't let him see my fear. I lifted my chin and waited for the first guests to leave. Ghalib's hand went to my back, playing with the skin there, making me flush with Drawing. Architects couldn't take their eyes from me; pets looked me up and down as well.

"Delightful, Ghalib."

"Fantastic acquisition."

Victor paused in front of us, Christine on one arm and Matthew on the other. Matthew was in a chest harness attached to a leash. He wouldn't meet my eyes. "Better than I hoped," Victor complemented Ghalib.

"Be gentle with your playthings tonight," Ghalib said with a smile.

"After that?" he replied, chuckling to himself. "We'll be lucky if we make it all the way home."

"I'll contact you tomorrow concerning our little arrangement," Ghalib promised. My anger flared again. It was hard to not pull away from Ghalib's hand.

Victor nodded. "I can hardly wait."

More people passed. More enthusiastic praise. Julia and Anna stopped briefly. "I'm never disappointed when you're around," Julia told me, kissing me. Ghalib's eyes were heavy on us; jealousy danced close to the surface. I didn't know whether to be pleased or frightened and the confusion made my anger surge again.

Markus and Tobias stopped in front of me; Markus hugged me like a bear and pressed a kiss on my cheek. "You are some lady," he said.

Finally, the line dwindled and all the guests were gone.

"That musicale exceeded even my expectations," Ghalib said softly. "Well done, Elaine."

"May I go to my room now?" I asked.

He looked at me hard for a moment. "No. I would like a nightcap with you." He offered me his arm and guided me towards his study.

I didn't know how to hide my anger from him. Even the Drawing didn't seem to mute it. Every jolt of fear made me angrier. Being alone with him was only going to make the whole situation harder. But I didn't have a choice.

Jason followed us into the study but Ghalib barely looked at him. "Cognac for me. Elaine? What would you like?"

"I'm not thirsty," I replied, glancing at Jason.

I read concern in the servant's expression. I knew why he was worried. I wasn't hiding my anger very well. "Perhaps some tea, Miss, to soothe your voice," Jason suggested.

"Very well. Thank you, Jason."

When Jason retreated I cast around for something to say before Ghalib could approach me. Instead of sitting, I went to his book cases and pretended to look at the titles. "You seem very calm," I commented lightly. "After all the frenzy in the music hall, I expected to see you enjoying yourself with Alexis in one of the aisles." I sounded odd, strained, and I knew it.

"I'm not calm," he said softly, "but the only person I wanted was occupied."

I didn't turn around. "That's so adorable."

Jason came in and laid the tea on a low table. He handed Ghalib his wide-mouthed glass of Cognac and beat a hasty retreat. I didn't blame him.

"Come here, Elaine," Ghalib commanded. My body responded and I gritted my teeth. I was really starting to hate my collar.

I stopped right in front of him but I turned my face away. "Look at me, Pet," he ordered. I had no choice. His eyes narrowed as he watched my expression. "Are you... angry with me?" he asked.

I lowered my eyes.

"Answer me," he instructed.

"Yes, I'm angry with you."

"Still?"

Finally, I looked directly at him. "I didn't deserve that punishment. And I don't deserve to be given to Victor."

Ghalib smiled. "Sometimes I forget how new you are here. Not all of your punishments will be fair from your perspective. It's the prerogative of a Master to do as he or she pleases with their pet."

"I'm still angry."

Ghalib chuckled which just served to make my temper boil even harder. "I shouldn't be surprised. Your passion is bound to express itself in more than one way."

He tilted my lips towards him and kissed me but my anger overwhelmed the Drawing for once. I didn't respond. I kept my eyes open. Ghalib opened his eyes, too, and broke the kiss.

"Elaine..." he said with warning.

"You can't have it both ways," I said. "You enjoy a mildly defiant pet one day, then punish me for the same behavior the next day."

Ghalib's voice took on a hard edge. "I can have anything I want. Which at the moment is you."

I took a step back. "No."

His expression turned determined. He leaned in to kiss me again and I turned my face away. His lips ended up on my cheek. "This is not a game you want to play, Elaine," he said in a low voice.

"We clearly want different things," I said quickly before his anger could rise again. "Perhaps we could reach a compromise," I suggested.

He drew back from me. His face was very serious. "You're my pet. I don't have to compromise."

"You do if you want a responsive pet," I said smoothly. "One that doesn't just lay there."

His eyebrows drew together. We both knew I had a point. "What are you suggesting?" he asked slowly.

I cast my eyes to one side and tried to think fast. An idea popped into my head. It would be a gamble but I couldn't think of anything else. "Do you play poker?" I asked, remembering how Lisa had been "won" from Victor. Lisa said Ghalib and Victor had a weakness for betting; I hoped she hadn't been exaggerating.

"I do."

"Five card draw? If I win, I return to my room and you don't complain. If you win, we return to your room and I don't complain." I held my breath and waited.

He cocked his head and was quiet for a moment. Then, a small smile started to form. "*Strip* poker. If you win, I'll grant you one favor, no strings attached. And, I'll let you return to your room. If I win, not only do you come back to my room naked, but you have to stay all night. Complain all you like."

"We have a deal," I said.

He offered his hand and I took it. The instant we touched, a bright flash of light blinded me. When I could see again, a table with a deck of cards had appeared in the center of the room. Also my shoes and stocking disappeared from my body and sat neatly next to the wall. "We each have four garments on," he explained.

I took my seat and the deck dealt itself. I picked up my five cards. A pair of sixes. I laid three cards on the table but with my new cards, I still only had a pair of sixes.

We showed our hands. He had a pair of kings. I took a deep breath and stood. "Wait," he said, standing. He reached for my zipper and I let him. Anything to distract his concentration. He was slow with the zipper, his fingers brushing my skin. His breath was warm on my ear. "Why are we playing this game when I know you want me?" he asked. My gown fell away and all I had covering me was my bra, panties, and half-slip.

"Because there are things I want more than you," I replied, taking my seat.

He raised his eyebrows. "Wine, Elaine?"

"Please."

He didn't call Jason; two glasses just appeared on the table.

My second hand was horrible and I was beginning to get nervous. Junk. Queen high. We showed our hands and he easily beat me with two pair. Quietly, he watched me as I stepped out of my slip and laid it with my gown on the floor.

"We can stop now," he offered. "Come back to my room with me. I'll even give you a robe. What do you think, Elaine?"

"I think you should let the deck deal," I said, sipping at my wine.

I won the next hand. A pair of jacks to his pair of fives. He took off his jacket. Then, I won the next. Two pairs to ten high in his hand. He literally lost his shirt. When I won the third hand in a row, his jaw clenched.

"We can stop now," I mimicked him, smiling at his underwear-clad figure. Boxer-briefs. I should have guessed. "Let me go back to my room and I'll ask for no further favors."

"I'm afraid not," he said tightly. I was beginning to understand how rarely he lost and how much he hated the sensation.

I shrugged. "As you wish."

For the next hand, I was dealt a straight flush. Six through ten, all hearts. "No cards for me," I said, leaning back. He gave me a long look, his jaw still clenched, and took two cards. When he showed his hand he had two pair.

I flipped my hand over and watched the flash of frustration before he brought his expression under control. I stood, walked over to where my shoes were, and slipped them on. I didn't bother with my slip or gown. I felt his eyes on me and I enjoyed it. How often did he look without touching? Nowhere near often enough.

I knew I wasn't quite done with him.

I came back over to the table and sat down on it in front of him. I was glad my bra and panties were lacy and see-through. All the better.

"You owe me something," I told him.

"What favor do you want?" he asked with a moody tone.

"No," I said with gentle emphasis. "We'll get to my favor in a moment. Right now, you owe me a garment." He blinked at me once. Understanding dawned on his face. "Go on," I told him, crossing my legs.

I watched him as he always watched me and I swear a light flush colored his cheeks. He stood and removed his last article of clothing, revealing what I already had guessed—that he was fully erect. I winked at him.

"Are you playing with me, Elaine?" he asked in a low voice.

"I'm surprised that you recognize the sensation," I told him. I slid off the table and walked close as I passed him, running a finger over his chest.

I reached the door and turned back. "As for my favor... I want for you to arrange for me to spend an evening alone with Julia and Anna. And you must be conspicuously absent. Ladies only. Drop me off in the evening, retrieve me in the morning. No questions and no punishments. Agreed?"

"I'm sure they would be pleased to host you tomorrow night," he said in a gruff voice.

"And you'll take me yourself?" I asked in a sweet tone of voice.

"Of course."

"Jealous?"

"Very."

"Good," I replied. "'Night, Ghalib. Thank you for a lovely evening." I exited without looking back.

I knew exactly what would happen. I would have sex with Julia and Anna and he would feel it through our connection. It would drive him insane. Satisfaction crowded out all guilt.

I wasn't lying to myself, though. I knew that treating Ghalib's jealousy so lightly was dangerous—foolish, even. I also knew that he wouldn't have spared me one iota if I had lost. Lisa waited in my suite when I returned to it but I was too tired to bathe or explain why I was only half dressed. I just crawled into bed and fell asleep.

Chapter 23
Equilibrium

I woke up because there was an insistent, frustrated, angry sensation invading my mind. I opened my eyes and tried to figure out if the feeling was a result of a dream, but, ironically, I still couldn't remember having any dreams since I had been brought to the In-Between. No, this was the same breath of intuition I felt when Ghalib called me. Even though he wasn't calling me, I knew that anger and frustration at the back of my mind was his.

I refused to feel bad. He had left me in that prison because of his own insecurity.

Lisa came into the room and fluttered around nervously. "Good morning," I greeted her. She didn't seem to hear me. "Lisa?"

She glanced at me, looking pale. "You're up."

"What's the matter?"

She sat on the edge of my bed. "The Master's in a horrible temper. We haven't seen him like this since before you arrived. Jason told me that he spent the night down in the prison. The guards said they could hear the moans until dawn. Then he locked himself in his suite."

This had everything to do with our little game of strip poker from the night before. I almost wanted to laugh. When I called him childish, I had no idea how right I was. "I won a wager with him last night," I said. "I'm spending the night with Anna and Julia tonight."

Lisa's lips fell open.

"He's going to be even worse while I'm gone, isn't he?" Lisa didn't answer. It was like she couldn't stop staring at me.

I sensed Ghalib's feelings shifting. Behind the swell of anger and frustration, there was more jealousy. The response to my evening with Anna and Julia surpassed anything that I thought he would feel. He wanted to be there; he wanted to prevent it. All he could feel was helpless.

"Could you give me a few minutes to myself?" I asked Lisa. "Close the door behind you?" She nodded and left.

I lay back on my pillows, closed my eyes, and for the first time tried to open myself up to Ghalib's thoughts. Usually, he was the one to use our connection. His commands invaded my mind. His emotions bled into me. But, this time, I was the one who took a deep breath and actively tried to use the bond between us.

He was frustrated and angry. Those were the simplest emotions to find. And oh, so aroused. He was still heated from the musicale, heightened from the poker, and aching. If I was honest, so was I.

Beneath that was the intense jealousy. Anna and Julia would get a full night with his pet. His thoughts flashed with images of him taking me which he tried to shove away. He wanted to call me. He knew he would force himself on me if he saw me, so he restrained himself. Still, his night in the prison had done nothing to sate him.

And that was the underlying cause for all of his frustration. His desire for me bubbled up through the anger, through the jealousy. No fantasies of Alexis. No memories of Victor. No flashes of other mortals. Only me. It was flattering in a scary sort of way.

It was a powerful feeling, too, knowing that I was the only partner he wanted. Knowing that I had the unique ability to satisfy him, where others couldn't. Knowing that at least a perfunctory morality prevented him from forcing himself on me. He didn't want me traumatized. It meant that I had some power over him. I had the ability to calm him before I left for the evening. I held the power to calm us both.

I wanted this power-play between us to smooth. The Drawing encouraged it too, as if my destiny relied on me finding my equilibrium with Ghalib.

I jumped out of bed before I could change my mind and tied my robe over my night shirt. I splashed some water on my face, took care of my teeth, and dragged a brush through my hair. Then I went out through the study and the sitting room.

"What are you doing?" Lisa asked me.

"Either making a very good or very bad decision," I told her. "I'll let you know."

I exited into the hallway and nearly ran into Jason who was hurrying past with a tray of coffee. I stopped him with a hand on his arm. "Is that for Ghalib?" I asked.

"Yes," he replied, looking nervous.

"You don't want to go to his rooms, do you"?" I asked. His eyes darted around but he didn't answer. "Give it to me," I commanded.

His eyes widened. "No, Miss. He's not himself. You shouldn't be around him when—"

"Give me his coffee, Jason. Stay away from his rooms for a while, if you can."

He heard the note of determination in my voice and handed me the tray. I didn't exactly remember the way to Ghalib's rooms but I just needed to follow my intuition. I ended up at a heavy, ornate wooden door. I knocked.

The door flew open. "About ti—" Ghalib stopped with surprise when he saw me carrying the tray. I walked past him, my heart thundering, my body aching. He seemed to be in one of his fierce moods. His eyes were wildly bright and he was shirtless, wearing only slacks. I felt his desire rise and his struggle to suppress it. Now that I had opened myself up to his feelings, I couldn't miss his flickers of emotion. I had never known that he worked so hard to stay so polite around me.

"Coffee?" I offered, pouring two cups.

He closed the door. "I didn't call you."

He was a throbbing contradiction. I knew he wanted me; he just didn't trust himself to keep his zeal in check. He held himself in tight control.

"Maybe not," I said in a low voice, "but I could feel you from my room. It's very distracting."

"If I wanted you, I would have called you," he repeated. "You really don't want to be around me right now."

I had never in my life tried to manipulate someone on purpose. Ghalib was feeling weak and powerless, even after his night in the prison. He was a conqueror without a battle to fight. He didn't want to turn me against him more, but his desire was nearly painful. I lowered my eyes to imitate a shyness I wasn't really feeling. "If that's your command, Ghalib," I said standing. I should have called him 'Master' but the word still caught in my throat. It didn't seem to matter to him; his arousal surged and with it, his hope.

He touched my arm as I walked past. "Wait," he said.

I stopped.

"Maybe I was hasty." His voice had that seductive purr to it. "Have coffee with me."

My heart jumped with anticipation. I resumed my seat and lifted my cup without looking at him. I could feel him watching me. He didn't take his seat; he paced around me like a caged panther. I let my voice shake a little when I said, "You were active last night."

"I was in the prison," he confirmed. "It isn't all dreamers down there. A few of my servants stay there as punishment." He paused. "And they stay much longer than you did," he added defensively. It was faint, but I felt the guilt at what he had done to me.

"Were you punishing them?" I asked in a voice ready to be scandalized.

His energy was much less haphazard than it had been just a few moments before. He was focused on me, trying to figure out what I was doing. But he still couldn't sit still. "Yes," he said slowly. "Some of them. Others I merely hurt."

I remembered him from our first night together. When he administered a punishment, you didn't enjoy it. When he caused pain, there was a chance you would. I let myself shiver. I knew he saw it.

"You still seem tense," I observed.

"I am," he said, his eyes heated and on me. He leaned over my chair, one hand on either arm, trapping me in my seat. "Why did you come here, Elaine?" he asked.

"I already told—"

"Why did you *really* come here?" He lifted my face with a finger and scrutinized my features. He narrowed his eyes, like he was concentrating. "You seem..." He paused for a moment, thinking for a word, "deceitful."

"Well, you already knew that."

"Dammit, Elaine!" he said, standing and pacing again. He wanted to play but he was much too worked up for that. There could be no delicate chase. There was having or nothing. "Are you just here to torment me?" he asked.

His frustration was, admittedly, a little frightening. But I also sensed that he kept shoving away images of me naked. He loved seeing me in my robe; it reminded him of the night of the ritual.

I lowered my eyes, only a little worried that I was too obvious in my manipulation. "I'm not trying to torment you," I said in a low voice.

Either he couldn't tell that I was acting or he didn't care.

The muscles in his chest were tense. His hands were balled into fists."Leave," he growled. "I'm not going to tell you again." But he didn't make it a command, just as none of his other demands that I leave had been commands.

I made my choice.

Since he hadn't commanded me, I imagined he wanted my defiance. I kept my voice low and serious. "No, Ghalib. I want to stay."

The instant I said no, he was on me. His teeth scraped the skin of my cheek and his hands roughly stripped my robe away. I struggled because I knew he wanted me to, pushing against his chest. He knocked my hands away, grabbing fistfuls of my nightshirt, shoving me backwards until I hit the wall. Then his lips were on mine. Hot, punishing lips. Harder than Victor's and more possessive. I bit his lip and lifted my chin, daring him to do more.

He scratched my legs with his fingernails, reaching under my nightshirt, and, with one deft pull, ripped my panties from me. I met his eyes, knowing that he was waiting for me to protest. When I didn't, it was as if he didn't know what to do first.

He clutched my backside, his fingers biting into my skin. Then, with a frustrated noise, he ripped away my nightshirt, pressing his skin against mine. Again, I struggled with him, pushing him away, wrenching my mouth away from his. My passion rose when he overpowered me, pinning my hands to the wall, pinning my head to the wall with his lips. The Drawing current between us boiled. I wouldn't have been surprised if our lips had come away blistered.

He stopped to look at me, naked, held against the wall. He was still fierce but I wasn't afraid; I was fierce, too.

"You should have gone," he said with a hint of warning.

I laughed at him. "Don't say things you don't mean."

He bit my shoulder making a sound that closely resembled a growl. He released my wrists and his hands went between my thighs, lifting me, sliding me up the wall with shocking strength. My hands went to his shoulders to steady myself.

"The second night you were here, you asked if I was going to hurt you," he reminded me. "I intend to hurt you, now."

I met his eyes. I couldn't keep the challenging smile from my face. "You intend to try," I taunted.

He lowered me quickly and I was impaled on him. I gasped and he moaned; the sensation was so overpowering. Current raced through us, shot out of us. He froze for a moment, swollen inside of me, and I understood why. His exploits in the prison, his temperamental punishment of his servants — it was nothing compared to this.

He thrust into me hard and I tightened my muscles around him until his hands gripped my legs. "You're going to have to work harder than that if you want to hurt me," I told him.

His thrusts were punishing and slow, pounding my hips into the wall. I rode him up and down, using his shoulders for leverage, using my pelvis to make him moan. Finally, with a low sound, he wrapped his arms around me and swung me to the floor without exiting me. From this position, he could ride me as hard as he wanted. I clutched at him with my knees and grabbed two handfuls of his rich, thick hair.

He untangled my fingers from his hair, pinned them to the floor, and rode me harder. He stiffened and I tightened my muscles around him again until he cried out and shuddered. He kept moving against me in jerky thrusts until finally, breathlessly, he withdrew.

I struggled to catch my breath. Silently, Ghalib sat up and looked at me. Some of the wildness was gone from his face. Then, without a word, he stripped off the slacks that had never made it below his knees and lifted me off of the floor. He carried me through two rooms to his bed and he laid me down gently, gracefully easing himself beside me.

He kissed me much more carefully, long and passionately, sending shivers all over me. Then, as gracefully as an acrobat, he moved on top of me, still kissing, softly tasting me. His hands roamed over me, teasing my nipples to taut, hard stiffness.

He worked his body between my legs, still muting me with his kiss. This was a whole different manner of passion; the anger had been easy to deflect and absorb but this rose us to a new level of Drawing. It was as if the energy vibrated at a different frequency. Something more intense, more vigorous, and more intimate.

His hands were artistic, touching this spot and that, waiting to test my body's response, repeating whatever I seemed to like the most. He found places on my body that I didn't even know could thrill. He finally broke the kiss and his mouth went to my breasts, his tongue teasing my nipples.

Without thinking, I put my hands in his hair again. It was soft, rich and long; it tickled my ribs. I thought he would force my hands away from him again but no. His fingers slipped up my arms and he used my shoulders to pull himself even with my face again.

He kissed me as his hands traveled, stroking my breasts again, going lower, urging my legs wider, daring one slow stroke through my wetness. I gasped and broke our kiss.

There wasn't a trace of amusement on his face. His lips returned to mine and he thrust forward, penetrating me again. I moaned. Suddenly, I knew what he was doing. The angry sex in his sitting room had been about his pleasure, his driving need. This sex was about mine. He thrust into me with long strokes, not bringing himself to climax but leaving me moaning and clinging to him. Again and again. Faster then slower.

"More, Pet?" he asked as he thrust.

"Yes," I gasped in his ear, kissing his neck.

Without stopping, he drove me again and again to my peak until we were both sweating and flushed. I rolled my hips against him, my wetness making his penetration smooth. His lips never stopped moving over my skin; it was as if he couldn't get enough of me just by having me. I felt him stiffen and fight it.

I broke our kiss. "You deserve an orgasm," I whispered.

"Elaine..." he protested, his voice shaky.

I met his eyes, feeling his hardness grow harder. I let my hands slide down his back to his buttocks and pulled him into me firmly. It was all he needed. In moments, he cried out and thrust hard into me.

I wrapped my legs around him and moved with him. When he was done, he just lay there on top of me a few moments and looked at my face. "You surprise me every day," he said, lifting himself off of me and lying beside me.

"Good."

"Do you still intend to go to Anna's and Julia's tonight?" he asked me.

I smiled at him. "Oh, yes. And you're still going to take me. I won a wager and I want my prize. Besides, I still haven't forgiven you for sending me to the prison. My night with Anna and Julia is my revenge."

"It's going to be agonizing for me," he admitted, not seeming altogether unhappy at the prospect of that sort of agony.

"Do you think you can behave yourself now?" I asked.

"Is that why you came here?"

"Yes," I answered. But I hesitated. The whole truth was a scary thing but the Drawing urged me to share with him. "That and because I could feel your frustration. I didn't like being the cause of it." I flushed and looked away.

"Why, Elaine. I'm touched."

"Shut up."

"I might be able to muster up a little more frustration, if you're up to it."

I smiled. "No thank you. I need to get ready for my evening out." I climbed over him, out of the bed, and stole his robe from his closet door. "I'll see you later tonight, Ghalib."

I could feel his surprise. I was a little shocked at myself, too. But I couldn't bring myself to be sorry. Something shifted between us, a level of understanding that I couldn't help but enjoy. And I had changed. A month ago, I blushed if someone complemented my figure. I wasn't sorry about that change either.

Maybe, once my evening with Julia and Anna concluded, Ghalib would return to his petty torments but I doubted it. There was something new between us and I knew that he was as eager to explore it as I was.

Chapter 24

Anna and Julia

Ghalib's jaw literally dropped when he saw me that night. My gown was pale pink and floor length with a low front and even lower back. The satin material didn't hide my hardened nipples.

"Promise me you'll dress exactly like this for me someday soon," he said.

"I promise," I agreed, tasting his mood. While he didn't love the idea of taking me to Anna and Julia for the evening, he was no longer angry. His jealousy was at least muted.

He ran his fingers along the inside of my spaghetti straps on my dress. "I will drop you off when the sun sets and pick you up when the sun rises," he told me. "Then I will consider my wager paid."

"As will I," I agreed.

"Come, Elaine, before I change my mind about honoring my debts."

He offered his arm and I took it. The room spun around me but I only had a few moments of disorientation before we stood on a rough path leading to a picturesque little house. Roses climbed the side of the stone building and flowering trees surrounded it. The air smelled like blossoms.

Julia rushed out in a pink dress. "Elaine!" she said, kissing me. "How wonderful! I thought it couldn't be true, that I'd see you so soon. And Ghalib, won't you come in?"

"I can't," he said gravely. "But send my regards to your mistress."

"Nonsense," Julia pushed sweetly. "She'll think you're mad at her if you don't say hello personally."

"Ghalib promised me that I'm to have the whole night alone with you and Anna," I interjected, smiling at Ghalib. "Don't make it hard for him to keep his promise."

"Indeed," Ghalib said, nodding politely. "Another night." Then he was gone.

"What was that all about?" Julia whispered to me, pulling me up on to the porch.

Anna came to the door and greeted me with a warm kiss that shot me through with electricity. "That was about Ghalib being a notoriously sore loser," Anna said. "He told me about your wager. Well done, my dear."

"You won a wager with Ghalib?" Julia asked, her eyes shining.

I bit my lip. "Strip poker. He wanted sex and I wanted sleep. The betting escalated from there." Julia giggled and clapped, leading me inside the house. The inside of the house was as delicate as the outside. Flowers decorated everything: in crystal vases, in sconces on the walls, potted and growing inside the house. Cut crystals hung in the windows.

"What I want to know," Anna asked, "is did you choose to come here because you enjoyed our company or because you knew it would upset your Master?"

I flushed. "Both."

Anna gave me a knowing smile and brushed my hair back over my shoulder. "Well, we're delighted. It might have taken months for Ghalib to share if left to his own discretion. And certainly we never hoped to have a private visit." She gave me a knowing look. "I hope Ghalib hasn't worn you out. I felt the two of you this morning."

I flushed.

"Oh dear," Julia said with a pout. "Will we have to be sedate tonight?"

I made a quick decision. "Not at all. What a waste of three lovely women if we spend the whole evening in conversation."

"I couldn't agree more," Anna said.

"Nor I," Julia agreed.

"Come along," Anna said, taking one arm. Julia took the other. "Let's forget Ghalib for tonight. Dinner first, then fun. And how lovely you look."

We dined reclining on cushions in an arboretum. "It's the Roman cus- tom—or at least it used to be," Anna informed me. Dates and olives. Light, soft bread. We laughed over the musicale the previous evening and they gossiped with me about other Architects and their pets.

"Wait until you meet Alexander and Paul," Julia said with glee.

I bit into a date. "Why?"

"Paul completely owns Alexander," Anna said with contempt. "Alexander should be the one in the collar. Mind you, this little vixen likes to be in charge from time to time." Anna glanced at Julia fond- ly.

"That's just for play," Julia smiled, looking at me. "Like the way you are with Ghalib, making wagers with him. He enjoys the game and you play it well." Julia was right.

Anna nodded. "Paul will flirt with women just to annoy Alexan- der and Alexander has no spine to punish him."

"Paul, himself, tried to bargain with Anna to see me alone. Can you imagine the audacity? Without his Master?" Julia said.

"Of course I corrected him, which he didn't seem to care for," Anna said.

I smiled a little to myself. I wondered how hard it would be to get Ghalib to have them over for dinner. He would probably enjoy the sport. I was starting to discover that I would, too.

"He was at the concert," Anna said slyly, as if she could read my mind. "Ghalib knows him."

"Oh, and tell her about Lady Stefania," Julia urged.

"Ah, Stefania," Anna said with delicate thoughtfulness. "She doesn't know how to just seduce a mortal, have them, and return them. Each one is made a pet; then, she has to go through the break- ing ceremony. It's so tedious."

"There's a breaking ceremony?" I asked.

"Not for Omnilights, my dear," Anna said gently.

"How many ceremonies have you been through with Stefania?" Julia asked. "Twelve? She should just take a page out of Ghalib's or Victor's book."

"Perhaps Ghalib's," Anna said. "Not Victor's."

"We used to visit Ghalib every couple of weeks," Julia said confidingly. "Mortal men, mortal women, sometimes one of each."

"And don't forget Alexis," Anna said with a smile. "When he was between mortals she was the victim of choice. I kept asking him what he was looking for."

I couldn't help but ask. "Were you and he..."

"Oh goodness, no. That would be a disaster. We're just good friends."

"Not Julia either?" I asked.

"No," Julia confirmed. "I'm not at all his type."

I snorted. "I was starting to think that he'd had every person, male and female, in this world and mine." Anna and Julia laughed.

"And you, my dear," Anna asked. "How do you deal with such a forceful personality?"

I flushed. "I'm finding I have a forceful personality of my own," I said. "I'm also finding that Ghalib enjoys a challenge. I don't know what it is about him that makes me act in ways that dare him to do his worst."

They both smiled knowingly and Julia lifted herself from her cushions and crawled over to me. She nuzzled my breasts through the thin fabric of my gown and kissed my collarbone. "I would take that dare," she said suggestively. I put my hands in her hair and drew her face towards mine, kissing her without reservation. I saw Anna recline and sigh, watching us.

"Shall we show her our special room?" Anna asked when our kiss broke.

Julia broke into a dimpled smile. "We haven't been there in weeks, Anna. How delightful! And with an Omnilight!"

"Your special room?" I asked, intrigued.

Anna stood. "Come along, Pet. Elaine."

She led us through the hallways until we came to a white door. Anna pulled a chain with a key from around her neck and unlocked the door. When she opened it, I gasped. It was a room padded in silk-covered cushions and filled with beautiful female Architects. They lounged around the room in lacy bits of nothing and looked up with a smile at Anna and Julia. And me.

"I just get so many requests from servant Architects that want to work here," Anna explained. "Honestly, I can only use so many maids, cooks and attendants. But lovers... those I can never get enough of." We all took off our shoes and stepped inside as Anna closed the door behind us.

"My lovelies," Anna greeted them. They gathered around her and Julia with welcoming kisses and sighs. "This is Elaine," Anna told them. "You must greet her, too."

They converged on me, wrapping slim arms around me. "Oh," the first one to touch me gasped.

I felt it too. Since each one was an Architect, they evoked the Drawing as Anna did. They touched me everywhere, their fingers sliding under my loose gown, their hands seeking more contact with my skin. It was beautiful, like being caressed with warm water. I moaned.

"She's an Omnilight," Anna said. "And she's here for the evening."

They peeled off Julia's and Anna's gowns, then Julia and Anna lifted mine over my head. Julia kissed my back and Anna chafed my nipples between her fingers. "Close your eyes, my dear. Everyone here wants to see to your pleasure."

I did and the women drew me down to the cushioned floor. Caressing fingers stroked everywhere: behind my knees, my collared throat, and down my arms. Soft lips kissed my stomach and legs. Soft tongues tasted my skin. The Drawing leapt in me; I couldn't lie still and I couldn't keep my eyes closed.

I was surrounded by sighing, ardent women. Julia, too, had been drawn down to the floor and was gasping in pleasure. "Anna," I called breathlessly. She came to me like a nude work of art.

"Yes, my dear?" she smiled. The women parted my legs and kissed my thighs.

"I want to taste you," I whispered. "Please."

The tongues parted me and I stretched to meet them. Anna drew a manicured finger over my lips. "How can I say no?" she replied. Carefully, she eased herself over me; I wrapped my arms around her legs and pulled her down further. She smelled like sweet musk.

Tentatively at first, then with undeniable enthusiasm, I stroked and licked. My tongue matched the battling tongue at my own sex and the Drawing in the room was thick, like fog. Anna's voice grew husky and low. "Yes," she urged me. "Yes."

My hips had been lifted and my back supported by several pillows so that tongues could explore me everywhere, even as I continued to pleasure Anna. At least four determined mouths stroked and licked and kissed at me. I moaned loudly against Anna as I trapped her legs with my arms, not stopping my strokes for a moment, giving her no option but to submit to my work. I followed the sway of her hips, forcing myself to concentrate on her. "Oh, God. Yes!" She finally cried in a rough voice, her skin pulsating against my tongue. Her wild moans heightened me and as she fell forward, crawling off of me, the battling tongues found my core. Teasing and licking mingled with waves of Drawing, until I exploded into orgasm and heard Julia's cries at the same time.

Anna, Julia, and the women kissed me. Once we all caught our breath, we lounged back against the soft cushions. One brunette stayed near me, playing with my hair. "Wow," I breathed. They all laughed.

Anna opened a cupboard in the wall and withdrew a small, delicate pipe. "What is that?" I asked.

"An aphrodisiac," she answered. "The evening will be wasted if we sleep now. Everyone here understands the draining power of a woman's orgasm."

She packed a glittery powder into the pipe. "I'm not sure I need that," I commented, knowing how quickly the Drawing renewed my arousal. Anna lit it and drew on it, passing it to Julia who did the same.

She handed it to me. "If you don't need it, it will just make the experience more pleasurable," she told me. "I want to have you next."

I smiled, dragging on the pipe, pulling the sweet, spicy smoke into my lungs. Immediately, I felt the effect. The room sharpened and color brightened. The throbbing increased within me. I drew on it one more time and passed the pipe to another girl.

Suddenly, everything seemed to sharpen a step further. It was like I could see the air. No, not the air. The Drawing. It swirled with the pipe smoke, a shimmering white, ghostly vapor. There was a halo around Julia where the Drawing couldn't touch her. Layers of the energy surrounded me, drawn to me like iron shavings to a magnet.

"Oh my goodness," I commented.

Anna smiled. "What, my Love?"

"I can see the Drawing," I said. I didn't feel tipsy or in any other way affected. Yet, I could see the energy around me as plain as light.

"You can see the Drawing?" Anna repeated, looking concerned.

I smiled and looked at it. I wondered if I could make smoke rings if I breathed it in. Immediately, in front of me, the energy formed a ring. I giggled. "I see it and I think I can control it."

Julia's brow furrowed. "Maybe the aphrodisiac is making her hallucinate."

A girl across the room smiled at me. Her skin was as dark as ripe plums. I smiled back at her. "I can prove it," I said, still looking at the beautiful Architect. "Will you be my guinea pig?"

She looked curious. "All right."

I watched the Drawing swirl around her and concentrated on bringing it closer to her skin. "Oh," the woman gasped, running her hands over her breasts. I concentrated harder. I could make the Drawing do anything I wished. It had been waiting for me to understand how to use it. I concentrated on bringing more Drawing around the woman, of swirling it around her waist, her hips, her groin. "My goodness," the woman gasped, opening her knees and clutching the arm of the woman next to her. I could see my object and urged the Drawing into her. She shuddered and cried out, tossing her head back and orgasming without even touching herself. Her hips undulated and I saw the moisture beading in her dark hair. When she was done, her breaths came in huge gasps. "Thank you," she said to me, taking the pipe from the girl next to her.

I could do more. I looked at Julia. "Would you still like to feel the Drawing?" I asked her.

Anna looked at me curiously. "Mortals that don't inspire Drawing can't feel it."

"May I try?" I asked her.

"Oh, please, Mistress," Julia added. Anna nodded slowly. I concentrated on the halo that surrounded Julia and watched it dissipate. The Drawing swirled around her like it did everyone else in the room.

"Good God," Julia said, practically panting. "How can you stand this without constantly orgasming?"

"It is intense," I agreed.

Anna sat forward. "Show me, Elaine."

I concentrated on gathering the vapor around her body. My control got better the more I practiced. I could swirl it around her nipples like a huge tongue. I could concentrate it between her legs without immediately bringing her to fruition. Anna's body rose in gooseflesh; her nipples hardened, and her breathing quickened. "Enough," she gasped. The other girls giggled.

"This is unprecedented," Anna said.

"This isn't just something Omnilights can do?" I asked.

Anna looked at me completely seriously. "Only Nyx completely controls the Drawing. Does Ghalib know of this?"

"I didn't know of this until five minutes ago," I told her.

"We must tell him. He's your Master."

A general outcry sounded from around the room.

"Right now?"

"Mistress, surely this can wait for morning."

"I barely got to touch her."

Anna and I looked around and our eyes met. A little, secretive smile formed on her lips, a smile I'm sure I mimicked. "I think Ghalib would be very upset if my wager wasn't fulfilled and I insisted on another night here," I suggested. "Perhaps we should wait until morning to tell him."

"I think you may be right," she replied in a voice like honey. "Now, shall we see what else you can do with your new gift?"

The night was filled with delights. We smoked the aphrodisiac, which I learned was called Amorite, and pleasured one another. At one point Julia shooed away the girls around me and crawled on top of me. "I've waited long enough for you," she said.

"You've had me," I replied, thinking of the altar. "I want you."

"We can both be satisfied," Julia replied, inverting her body over me. I let the Drawing flow between us as her mouth worked between my legs. I groaned and pulled her hips down to me, letting my tongue slide into her. The other women watched, idly stroking one another as they watched us squirming to get a better angle, moaning and stretching, our fingernails digging into each other's thighs.

She orgasmed first, with the help of the Drawing current. It was the only thing that could pause her working tongue. Then she redoubled her own efforts, teasing and playing with me until I clutched at the silken pillow and whimpered her name. My pounding orgasm left my muscles shaking.

More Amorite and more coupling. I manipulated the Drawing so that each woman had an orgasm without stimulation. They playfully argued over who would have me next and I basked in their attention. Finally, as dawn approached, we kissed the harem girls good-bye and Anna led Julia and I to her room.

"I know you've seen my fantasies when we kiss," Anna said to me.

"I have," I said smiling. She kissed me again and showed me the image of me tied to the bed while she and Julia had their way with me.

"Lie down," Anna said. I obeyed and straps wrapped themselves around my wrists and ankles. It was crazy. I had been brought to fruition again and again, and yet I throbbed for more. I drew the Drawing, like a dome around us. Anna and Julia reacted to it, kissing each other, touching one another in front of me. Soon, I was nothing but a captive spectator as Julia bent Anna over the edge of the bed, fingering and licking her, using her long, slim fingers to penetrate her. Anna gasped, grasping my leg and arm while Julia determinedly brought her to her peak. Anna cried out, thrusting her hips against Julia.

Then, they crawled to the bed and worked at me, teasing and taunting again until I broke out in a sweat. When there was gray light in the window, Anna crouched over me, her small, round backside hovering over my chest. Julia settled over my lips just as Anna's tongue started to play.

Anna moaned against me and I knew that Julia must have started fingering her again. We undulated against one another for some time, each of us so spent from the night of sex that we could take our time reaching our climax, enjoying every thrill, every stroke. I believe that Anna orgasmed first, then me, then Julia, but I wasn't sure. I knew only that my bonds loosened and I was sandwiched between Anna's and Julia's naked bodies, feeling each of their heartbeats.

A knock sounded at the door. "Come in," Anna called lazily, not bothering to lift her head.

A maid entered. To her credit, she didn't even look surprised. "My lady, Master Ghalib is here."

I sat up. The sun had just broken the horizon.

"Well, I suppose it is technically morning, now," Anna said dryly. "Show him into the breakfast room and ask him if we might have a word before he leaves."

"Yes, Mistress."

We all stood, worn and flushed. My clothes were gone, still probably in with the harem. I didn't even have shoes. "Here, my dear," Anna said, handing me pale blue cotton dress.

"Your hair is all tousled," Julia giggled. "It's sexy."

Anna and Julia simply put on robes and we headed to the breakfast room. I knew we had to tell Ghalib about my new-found talent. I couldn't begin to guess how he would react. But I wasn't going to have to wait long to find out.

Chapter 25
Julia's Transgression

I suppose Julia started out on the wrong foot with Ghalib when she came into the breakfast room with her arm slung around my shoulders, smiling broadly, looking like she'd had a beautiful night of great sex.

I had been trying to taste Ghalib's mood all the way from Anna's room to the breakfast room because I didn't know what to expect from him. Anger? Frustration? Lust? As we got closer, his moods became clearer to me. There wasn't much in the way of anger and his frustration was well under control. I also sensed that he felt something that resembled amusement. And while he was aroused, it wasn't entirely out of control.

But when we entered the breakfast room, with Julia and me acting so chummy, I felt his jealousy flash. He stood there looking as well-manicured as ever. Charcoal pants, casual shirt, his white hair shining in the early morning light, and his eyes greener than I remembered. His emotion didn't show on his face, but I still felt a chill of danger wash through me.

"Good morning, Anna, Julia," he greeted. Julia released me and went to stand with Anna, which made me a little more comfortable. "Elaine," Ghalib said, holding out his hand. I crossed the room and took it, even as Anna kissed him hello.

When our skin touched, the Drawing ripped through me. Not that I hadn't been feeling Drawing all night, but his energy was different. Just the perfect balance of smooth and harsh. Suddenly, with his touch, I knew why he wasn't crazy with sexual drive. I kissed his cheek and whispered in his ear. "Really? Alexis?"

His mouth quirked in amusement. "How do you know these things?" he asked me.

I shrugged. "Was it satisfying?" I teased.

"No. But it was adequate. It was enough to keep me from acting like a brute when I saw you."

"I hope you didn't tell Alexis that," Anna joked, pouring four cups of coffee. "We're likely to find our new Omnilight strangled in the night, a murder motivated by homicidal jealousy."

Ghalib chuckled. "Alexis has the rage but not the will." He looked at the coffee cups. "Anna, Elaine is tired and I'm eager to have her home. I'm sure you'll understand if we don't stay for coffee."

"But we have a lovely surprise to share with you," Anna said. "Please, Ghalib," she said in her most winning voice. "I know you won't be sorry."

He looked at me and sighed. "How can I refuse three beautiful women?" He led me to the table but didn't let go of my hand. I ended up having to drink my coffee left-handed. "What's my lovely surprise?" he asked.

"We discovered last night that Elaine can control the Drawing," Anna said. Her statement hung in the air.

Finally Ghalib spoke slowly. "Well, of course, when she sings — "

"She wasn't singing."

Ghalib looked at me and I flushed. "Anna gave me some Amorite," I said. "I could see the Drawing energy in the room. Whatever I willed it to do, it obeyed," I explained.

"Only Nyx can control the Drawing," Ghalib said.

"That used to be correct," Anna replied. "But now, both Nyx and Elaine can."

"It's true," Julia piped up. "Elaine made it so I could feel the Drawing, too. What an overpowering sensation."

Ghalib ignored Julia and turned to me again. "Do you still feel the effects of the Amorite?" he asked.

"No."

"And can you still see the Drawing?"

I concentrated on the air around me but it wasn't until I looked at where Ghalib and I touched hands that I could see the ghostly energy. "Just barely," I said.

Ghalib looked at Anna. "Do you still have some Amorite left?"

She nodded. "I'll get it." She swept out of the room.

Ghalib narrowed his eyes at me. "I don't think I've ever seen you look so vibrant and healthy," he said. "I expected you to be ragged. But no."

"I hardly feel tired," I admitted. "I'm sure I'll crash soon."

"I hope not too soon," he said with delicate suggestion. I flushed and he smiled at me. After everything I'd done, it was ridiculous that he could still make me flush.

"Shall I leave you two alone"?" Julia teased. Again, I felt Ghalib flash with irritation.

"No need," Ghalib replied without looking at her. "I had completely forgotten that you were there."

I gave him my best disapproving expression. "Be nice. I hadn't."

Anna came back into the room with her pipe filled. Finally Ghalib released my hand so that I could light the match and touch it to the Amorite in the pipe. I breathed in that same sweet taste and felt the same affect: colors brightened, my vision sharpened, and a throbbing started deep within me. I took another breath of Amorite and the air swirled in front of me. "There it is," I whispered.

"Do you see it?" Ghalib asked.

"Yes."

"Prove it," he challenged.

There was nothing I wanted more. I focused on the swirling mist. It seemed to like him; it swirled around him more thickly than any of the women from the night before. Only I attracted the Drawing more strongly.

I brought the Drawing to him, dropping it over him like a sheet: first watching his cheeks flush and his eyes widen, then seeing his breathing pick up, then seeing his hands constrict around nothing, and finally, most satisfyingly, a bulge rise in his pants.

"Enough," he said. But it wasn't an order, so I let myself push his patience a little. I intensified the energy, focusing on his groin. His hand found my arm and gripped it so tightly I was sure it left a bruise. Julia giggled and Anna gave her a stern look that she completely missed.

"Elaine, stop," Ghalib ordered breathlessly.

I had no choice. Julia smothered her giggles behind her hand and Ghalib shot her a sharp look, too.

He recovered quickly and turned to me. "I'm speechless," he finally purred. "How many people know of this?" he asked Anna.

"Me and Julia and my girls," she answered.

"Your girls?"

"The harem," Julia offered. "It's twelve Architects now, isn't it?"

"Will they talk?" Ghalib asked.

"Not if I swear them to secrecy," Anna said. Her expression turned sly. "Of course, it would help if I could offer them some incentive. An occasional visit from the Omnilight, perhaps?"

"With her Master?" Ghalib said pointedly.

"Of course."

"Then you may make them that promise, as long as they tell no one about Elaine," he said. His eyes turned to Julia who was still grinning broadly. The atmosphere in the room turned cold. Julia's smile faltered "May I borrow your pet for a few moments?" he asked Anna.

Anna cocked her head. A look of understanding passed between them that chilled me. "You may," she replied.

Julia's eyes widened and her smile dissolved. Maybe she knew that she hadn't been respectful enough with Ghalib. Maybe she realized that he didn't see her as an equal to Architects, or even to me. I remembered the first time I met her and realized how frightened she was of Ghalib. I shook my head just the slightest little bit and she seemed to get the message: don't show him you're afraid. Julia squared her shoulders.

Ghalib looked at me. "You claim that you can make Julia feel the Drawing?" he asked.

"Yes."

"Let me see you do it."

Julia twisted to look at her mistress. "Anna?"

"Listen to Ghalib. Obey what he tells you," Anna said, leaning back in her chair.

Julia wasn't comfortable and I could feel it. And the Drawing told me why: she didn't like performing for men. It was OK if men were around when she was satisfying another woman but she didn't like them watching her as she became aroused. She didn't like them touching her, either. Something from her past....

"Elaine," Ghalib said with warning. "Don't make me order you."

I brought the Drawing to her skin as delicately as I could. She still sucked in her breath. Any Drawing must have felt like torrent of sensation to her.

Ghalib stood and walked over to her. He separated her legs and knelt between them. He was so tall that he was eye to eye with her. "I do not like being laughed at, particularly not by a mortal and a pet." He slid his hands to the insides of her thighs. She tried to push her thighs together but he held them open then forced them wider. "Not even by the pet of a dear friend, like Anna." He moved his hands further under her robes and her face contorted, like she was fighting emotion. "You don't like it when men touch you, do you?" he asked.

"No," Julia whispered.

"But I'm going to touch you now. And you're going to enjoy it despite yourself, aren't you?"

Julia didn't answer.

"Aren't you?" he pushed.

"Yes," she whispered.

"Do you believe that I can make you climax?" he asked.

"Yes."

"Good," he said. He moved his hand further up under her robes and she whimpered. "None of that, little Pet," he said. "Tell me you like it."

"I... I..."

"Say it."

"I like it." I could barely hear Julia's voice. I knew she didn't like what was happening to her at all. The Drawing around her was all jagged and wrong.

I watched Ghalib's hands begin to work under her robes and saw Julia's body tense. Beads of sweat stood out on her face. Anna's expression was cold but amused; I was getting very uncomfortable. Julia's eyes filled with tears.

Ghalib leaned in to Julia, who tensed even more. "You aren't very damp," Ghalib said. He glanced at me. "More Drawing, Elaine."

"Anna?" Julia said, distressed.

Anna was completely cold. I had never seen her that way. "You know better than to laugh at an Architect, Pet. Ghalib is my friend and you have embarrassed me. This is your punishment."

Julia shuddered and closed her eyes. "No," Ghalib said gently. "I want you to look at me. I don't want you to imagine that anyone else is touching you." Julia opened her eyes and her lower lip trembled. "Elaine," Ghalib prompted.

I couldn't. I wouldn't do this. I wasn't cruel and I wouldn't help Ghalib hurt Julia like this. I pulled back on the Drawing and Julia opened her eyes to look at me. The fear that was still on her face decided me.

"No," I told him.

He looked over his shoulder, his hands still deep between Julia's legs. He narrowed his eyes at me. "Use the Drawing to stimulate Julia," he ordered.

For a split second, I involuntarily complied. Then, my anger surged. It overcame the order and I pulled back on the Drawing again. "No, Ghalib," I repeated. The collar, an adornment I had hardly noticed since it shrunk into my skin, loosened. Just for a moment, I noticed it there, slack and warm. Then it tightened and joined with my skin again.

Ghalib removed his hands from Julia and stood. "Are you defying me?" he asked. His voice was hard but shaken. I knew it was because I had resisted a direct order; I wish I knew how I did it.

I lifted my chin. "Yes."

He strode across the room, grabbed my upper arm, and lifted me out of the chair. My heart started to race, though anger definitely trumped fear this time. "I am the Master, Elaine," he growled. "You need to internalize that idea."

"You're cruel and a bully," I snarled back, pulling my arm out of his grasp. "You should experience helplessness sometime. It would be an eye-opening experience for you."

I glared at him. Ghalib had told me about some of his brutality but I hadn't really let myself imagine how he "played" with aggressive women, how he had used Lisa, how he wanted to use me. Julia still had tears in her eyes.

He looked at me for a moment like he didn't know what to do

with me. "Get on your knees," he finally ordered. My legs buckled and I fell to the floor. I saw Anna and Julia, Anna amused and Julia horrified.

Ghalib fumbled with his pants. My anger surged again. "Are you sure you want to do that?" I challenged. "Anything you put in my mouth isn't likely to come out whole."

He stared down at me, stunned. "You wouldn't dare."

"Try me," I snapped. "Otherwise, you'd better *order* me not to bite you. Or you could always rape me some other way."

When I said the word "rape" he backed away a step like he'd been slapped. I was on my feet as quick as I could be, glaring at him. He looked confused. "I'm not..."

"You're not what?" I snapped.

He looked at Anna and Julia, then back at me.

Then, he crossed the room to Julia. "My apologies, Julia. I'm afraid I got carried away."

"You were on a rampage," Anna said. "It was magnificent. No need to apologize."

"I feel that there is," Ghalib said, not looking at her. "I am sorry," he said again, his voice low. Then returned to me, stood behind me, and put his hands on my arms. "Elaine, we should go."

Julia finally looked up at us and offered a watery smile. She mouthed 'thank you' as the room began to spin and the walls melted. Before I could really feel the disorientation, we stood in the foyer to Ghalib's mansion.

I took a step forward, breaking our contact, just wanting to get to my suite. He stepped around me and blocked my way. "I owe you an apology, too. I shouldn't have used you that way."

"You're better than that, Ghalib," I told him, looking directly in his eyes.

For the first time, he was the one who looked away. "It's very sweet that you think so."

My anger started to ebb. "Apology accepted."

He looked back at me. "While you were gone, I made an alteration to our living arrangements. I considered it one condition to bringing Matthew back to my home. If it's not to your liking, I can change things back. We'll come to some other agreement."

"What's the change?" He offered his arm and I took it. I could feel that his emotions were a muddle. He led me through the halls and stopped in front of the door to my suite. Next to it was the ornate wooden door to his. "We're neighbors now?"

"Yes. Lisa has a room inside your suite, since I believe I can trust her to behave with you. Unfortunately, I don't have such confidence in some of my other servants." His lips twitched into a mischievous smile. "There's a door adjoining our rooms from the inside."

"You're completely indecent," I told him.

"I promise to knock if I want entry."

"Before or after you break down the door?"

He chuckled, some of the glow returning to his face. "So, shall I leave the rooms this way?"

"Might as well," I replied. "You said that it was one of the conditions for bringing Matthew back. How many conditions are we talking about?"

"There's one more," he replied smoothly.

"And that is?"

"I'll tell you tonight after dinner," he replied. He leaned down and kissed my cheek. "Get some rest, Elaine."

He turned and went into his room. I watched him go, wondering what he had in mind. Whatever it was, I would need to be fresher to deal with it so I took his advice. First I would take a nap, then I would deal with whatever he had planned.

I hardly slept. It was like the night had been more invigorating than exhausting. I kept my eyes closed and let my mind wander; I hadn't really had much time to just think.

I didn't even know myself, anymore. I couldn't gauge how long I had been in the In-Between. In the time before I accepted the collar, I kept account of the days according to when I slept. But now, I had no idea.

I throbbed constantly. Even now, with no stimulation at all, there was an ache deep within me. It was a fire I didn't know how to extinguish. I was left wondering if it had always been there, even when I was working in a boring office. Could I have always been this creature? One that teased and played and delighted in the pleasures of my own body?

I looked forward to seeing Ghalib again. It was shocking to me, knowing that I felt that way. He was my captor, my Master, my kidnapper, and all of my being revolted against rewarding him for what he had done to me. Nonetheless, punishing him was like punishing myself. Denying him pleasure was denying my own.

I might have drifted off for an hour or two but I awoke long before Lisa came for me. When she arrived, I was digging through my closet.

"This for tonight," I said, holding up a dress. It looked like something a Greek goddess would wear: white, one shouldered, draping to the floor, a gold rope criss-crossing over my torso. "What do you think?"

"It'll be perfect," she said, heading for the closet. "I know there are some shoes I saw in here that would match exactly."

I let her hunt and went to bathe. It didn't take long to get dressed after that and Lisa made short work of my hair, which she swept out of my face but kept the back long. She slid a gold armband over my bicep and gave me sandals with glittering straps that went around my ankles.

"Beautiful," Lisa sighed.

"And comfortable," I added.

I was restless. I didn't know how long it would be until dinner. "I'm going to take a walk," I said. "I'll hear if Ghalib calls me."

I imagined the foyer, willing the house to take me directly there. Nonetheless, it still took far too long to reach the front door. For some reason, Ghalib's house just loved to run me around in circles. Once I was outside, though, it was just a short walk to the rocky beach. The altar where Julia and I performed for the Architects was still there. The wind tugged on my hair and dress; I tasted the salt.

I left my sandals on a bluff and waded into the surf. I had only been to the ocean once in the physical realm. The beach was packed with browning bodies and scampering children. Still, I loved it. Now, the water was warm on my toes. I closed my eyes.

"Venus rising from the sea."

I turned and Ghalib stood on the beach behind me. He was in navy pants and a white and navy shirt; it looked like he just stepped off of a yacht. "Are you following me?" I said over the surf.

"You know me better than that," he replied. "I'm stalking you, not following you." He closed the distance between us and put his arms around me, which was odd. His hands usually played over my skin but he almost never held me. The Drawing leapt in me, like it had just been waiting for his presence to really ignite. "Did you sleep at all?" he asked.

"I couldn't."

"Then would you care to start our evening a little early? I can tell you my second condition for retrieving Matthew. When you go to Victor tomorrow night, we can bring him home with us."

"Tomorrow night is the night with Victor?" My voice shook.

He released me, brushed my hair to one side, and kissed the back of my neck, sending my heart into a crazy rhythm. "I promised him," he said in a low voice. "But, now I'm promising you that I won't let him get too enthusiastic." Somehow that didn't comfort me much. "Enough about that. Rright now, I'd like to talk about us."

He came around to the front of me; my feet were covered by the lapping waves. He was even taller with me buried up to my ankles in sand. He lifted my chin and looked at me with a contemplative, sober expression. "Why is it that I never feel in command when I'm with you?" he asked so softly that I almost missed the question.

I looked back at him, equally serious, "Because you aren't."

He considered me for a moment. "No, I'm not, am I? But tonight, I would like to be. That's my second condition for Matthew," I lifted my eyebrows and he drew his thumb across one. "Remember the room you inspired?" he asked.

"The one where I handcuffed you?" I said with a teasing lilt.

He wouldn't let me make the mood lighter. "Yes. That one. I would like to return there with you tonight."

A coldness shivered through me. Even now, that room was intimidating. The chains and shackles, the toys and whips and blindfolds, the heavy iron apparatus that let you be bound this way and that. The statues that could animate. I know he heard my shuddery breath.

Why was I so scared? Was there any point when I would get used

222

to his intensity? "If that's what you want," I managed.

"Are you sure?" he asked. "There must be no tricks this time."

"You're no fun." He didn't answer. His eyes searched my face, his expression serious, almost stern. My breath stopped for a moment. I didn't hear the surf. "Very well," I agreed, "No tricks."

The amusement never returned to his face and that just heightened my nervousness. "The things you do for Matthew," he said. "I'm not sure my jealousy wasn't well-founded."

I flushed and tried to look away but he wouldn't let me. Finally, I met his eyes. "And the people on the bus, and Lisa... one might think I'm looking for excuses to stop resisting you."

That thought hung there for a moment. Then, he slid his hand down my arm and gripped my wrist. "Come, Elaine," he said, leading me away from the sea.

Chapter 26

Mastered

The room was just as I remembered it: an odd mix of decadence and hard, metal edges. I imagined myself bound to the apparatus in the middle of the room, bent over and spread, tied so tightly that I couldn't even wiggle. A shiver shook me.

"You agreed to this," Ghalib reminded me.

"I did."

"Take off your dress." It wasn't an order, but authority still rang in his voice.

I felt like he'd never seen me naked before. My cheeks and ears were scorching. I think it was the first time that he didn't insist on undressing me. He just stood back, his arms clasped behind his back, and watched. I loosened the gold ropes around my torso, slipped the zipper down, and stepped out of the gown.

"Your bra and panties, too," he said softly. I had left my sandals at the beach so when I complied I was completely naked except for the armband.

I didn't try to cover myself; I met his eyes and waited.

"Turn," he said.

I turned slowly on the spot. Knowing that he was watching me, knowing that he was slowly taking his time to assess me, made my skin feel raw. I hadn't been self-conscious about my body since I'd come here. Mostly because when I was naked, the Drawing had been such a distracting force. But with Ghalib several paces away, the Drawing wasn't strong enough to really sidetrack me. He'd done this with hundreds of women, probably. Perhaps models and athletes. Were my curves too deep? My thighs and hips too generous? My breasts too small?

When I faced him again, I kept my eyes lowered. He finally stepped close to me. He didn't force me to look up and he didn't touch me. He just circled me from closer and let his eyes linger wherever he liked.

He glanced up and nodded once. I turned to look; one of the statues was moving in exaggerated slowness towards me. Real fear coursed through me. Ghalib did nothing to help my confidence.

I recognized the statue: it was the angel that had taken my hand on the night that Ghalib explained to me what he was. The muscled, beautiful, carving with the distracting phallus. My heart stuttered nervously when the stone hands gathered my wrists and held them behind my back. The statue was a little bit rough and I winced.

Ghalib just stood there for a moment and watched my nervousness. "I could have him take you," Ghalib threatened. "I've done it to others."

I didn't say anything. I sensed even that would spark his jealousy, but I stayed quiet.

"You sandwiched between me and stone?" he pushed. The statue's penis brushed my hip.

I didn't know how a woman wasn't damaged by such a thing. But then I remembered Alexis from one of those first evenings here and her desire to 'play' with Ghalib's latest creation. I lifted my chin and waited.

He stepped closer; the statue just restrained my wrists. He drew his fingers over my skin as I waited powerlessly. He pinched my breasts and my backside. "Take her over there," Ghalib said, indicating the location with a jerk of his chin.

The statue practically carried me and when I saw where it was leading me I grew a little dizzy. Two boots, spaced at least shoulder-length were placed in an open section of the floor. They covered as high as the knee and resembled the boots I wore last time I was in this room. Except these had heels so high that one would practically have to be proficient in ballet to walk in them. Not that walking would be an issue — they were fixed to the floor. There was a chain looped from the ceiling over the boots. My stomach flipped. Surely he didn't mean to....

The statue lifted me and placed my feet directly into the boots. Then, it wrenched my arms together and chained them in place. It lifted me a little to get my chained arms over the chain from the ceiling, pulling on my shoulder, taking the pressure off of my feet.

Ghalib watched all of this from across the room, his eyes aglow. I didn't know where to look; I was scared, awkward, and aroused. A shiver went through me that rattled the chains. It only seemed to make him more pleased. He stepped up close to me again, loosened all of my hair and pulled it over my shoulders until it draped both of my breasts. He stroked my breasts through the silkiness. Heat rose in my chest; my nipples hardened.

His other hand went between my legs and he stroked me quickly, as if he was testing me. His finger came away slick and I shuddered again. He pressed it to my lips and I let myself look at him as I drew it slowly into my mouth, tasting his skin and my musk as one intoxicating flavor.

"How do you feel?" he asked me, extracting his finger.

"Helpless."

"Anything else?"

"Frightened."

He drew his finger back through my wetness. My breath came faster. "Anything else?" he asked again.

"Aroused."

"Yes," he said, nodding in approval. He circled me again, talking as he strolled. "Usually, when I take a mortal, this is what I do first. Bind them and evaluate them." I wanted to ask a question but I kept still. Somehow, he seemed to know. "Go ahead, Elaine. I'll gag you if I want you to stay silent."

My mouth went a little dry. "Why didn't you do this to *me* when I first arrived?"

"I was concerned it would traumatize you," he replied. His eyes flickered to my hardened nipples. "Overly concerned, it would seem," he said.

He walked to the other side of the room and took a blue scarf off of the wall. He returned to me, looking heightened, bright, wild. I tried to strangle it, but I made a little frightened sound. He cocked his head. "What's this, Elaine? Have I finally broken through your composure?"

I had to struggle to keep myself from hyperventilating. I didn't trust myself to talk.

He came up very close to me, so close I could feel his breath against my lips. "Who do you belong to?" he asked.

"You."

From this close, his eyes glittered like a faceted emerald. "I don't think that's really true," he whispered. I pinched my lips together. He was right.

He backed away a little and tied the blue scarf over my eyes. The thick, rich fabric covered from my forehead to the bridge of my nose. I couldn't see a thing.

"I want something from you. Tell me that whatever it is, I can have it," he said.

I hesitated. I probably would have agreed but I didn't agree fast enough. A stinging slap struck the back of my legs. It didn't hurt much but it surprised me and I yelped. I wasn't sure if it was Ghalib or the statue striking me.

"Tell me I can have whatever I want," he repeated.

"What is it you want?" I choked.

Another slap, higher and harder. "Tell me I can have whatever I want," he said a third time.

"You can have whatever you want," I said quickly.

His hand caressed the spot he had just struck. Drawing rushed through me; the throbbing intensified. "Anything?" he asked, daring me to defy him.

"Anything," I agreed.

"I want you to relive your best memory. I want you to tell it to me now, in as vivid detail as you can recall. Don't stop talking until I tell you to."

I didn't have to think hard. My life in the mortal realm had been difficult. Full of responsibility and worry. Only a few events stood out over the rest of my life.

He slapped me again, much harder across my buttocks so that it really hurt. I gasped but I didn't cry out. "Start talking now, Elaine."

"I won a vacation to Florida once," I said. When he didn't slap me again, I kept talking. "It was a fluke thing. I never win anything. There was a lottery at the company where I worked and I won six days in Panama City Beach."

His hands stroked my buttocks. "Go on," he said.

"My parents died in a car accident when I was nineteen. My sister, Rachel, had just gotten married two months before and I wasn't hearing from her as much as usual. I decided to just go to Florida alone. They put me in a beach-front condo. One whole wall was a window, looking out over the beach. That first night, I slept on the couch instead of the bed so that I could leave the door to the balcony open and hear the ocean."

I felt Ghalib's lips at my neck and the Drawing buzzed over my skin. He licked my neck up to my earlobe. "Don't stop," he warned, pressing a flat, leather strap against the skin of my backside.

"I spent every day on the beach," I said in a rush. "I'd never been anywhere like that before. People walked the streets in their bathing suits. I could hear parties with loud music from up and down the beach."

I thought I heard Ghalib drop the strap. He ran both of his hands over my buttocks and pinched me hard once. I gasped but kept talking. "On my second day there, I went out on a chartered boat. Everyone else was deep-sea fishing but I just wanted to be out on the water. It was so vast and strong. I felt tiny. One of the boatmen took me all over our boat. Miguel was his name."

"That was very kind of Miguel," Ghalib said. I felt his lips travel to my breast. He brushed my draping hair out of the way and licked my nipple. My breath became ragged.

"He *was* very kind to me," I said, forcing my shaky voice to continue. "He took me to a seafood place that night. He said that tourists didn't go there but it had the best food in the city. He was so different from anyone I'd ever met: bronze and easy-going and happy."

A sharp pinch on my nipple. "What!" I cried out.

"That was for making me jealous," Ghalib said.

"He was never my lover," I protested. "And I only saw him that one night."

"He wanted more though," Ghalib said with assurance, his breath warm against my nipple.

"Yes," I admitted. "But that just wasn't me. I never had a fling or a one-night-stand. I was all alone; I had to be careful. He took me home that night, asked to come up to the condo, and when I refused, kissed me good-bye, and left."

"I'm shocked you let him get away," Ghalib said, moving to my other breast, letting his hand continue his work on nipple he had bitten.

"It's more shocking to me, how I've acted since I've been here."

"Really?" Ghalib said. I could tell he had stood straight because his voice was above me now. His one hand still played with my breast and the other rested on my hip. "You seem like a natural." His fingers traced a trail from my hip to my inner thigh and I bit my lip. I think I heard him chuckle. "What was your favorite part of the vacation?" he asked.

"The beach," I said without thinking.

Ghalib's fingers dipped into my wetness and he started to stoke me gently. Much too gently to bring me to climax but with enough friction to make my legs shake and my voice tremble. "Make me see it," he said.

"The sand was powdery. And white." I forced myself to try to concentrate on the beach. It wasn't possible to ignore the stroking between my legs, though. "The water was a blue I've never seen before or since."

He pushed a finger into me and I gasped. "Don't stop talking unless you want me to stop," Ghalib instructed.

"One evening," I continued with a trembling voice, feeling my hips sway against his hand, "there weren't a lot of people on the beach at sunset." I allowed myself a couple of panting breaths and continued. "I found a sand bar and walked out on it. I can't tell you how wonderful it was. It was as if I was miles away from the beach, surrounded by the bluest water anyone had ever seen. Yet, it was only up to my calves."

Two fingers went into me and I moaned. My head fell back and his lips were on my neck. His fingers picked up speed.

"That last night," I continued without being prompted, "I went down to the water to watch the last sunset." Ghalib withdrew his fingers and I had to control myself not to go limp. I heard him doing something. "I'll never forget it," I said. "The sky was on fire. It was so beautiful I cried."

Something thick nudged me between my legs. "I sat on the beach and watched the crescent moon go across the sky most of that night," I continued. "There weren't as many stars as I had hoped, but it was enough."

Ghalib entered me in a quick thrust. I cried out, feeling him throb inside me. I bit my lip, not going on with the story.

"Do you want me to stop?" he asked.

"No," I said.

"Then you need to keep talking," he said gently.

I didn't say anything. I felt his penis twitch within me.

"Elaine..." he prompted.

"I don't want you to stop. I want you to sweat."

"Excuse me."

"If I don't finish with my story, you don't move, right?" I said with just a hint of teasing. "Your rules, not mine."

He pulled off my blindfold and I blinked against the light. He didn't give me a chance to adjust; he just crushed his lips against mine. Then, he thrust into me so hard, he lifted me. "Fuck my rules," he said.

No, I thought, fighting a smile. *Fuck me.*

He did and I didn't object to anything that night. I wanted to know if he could slake this fire in me, if the throbbing could possibly be satisfied. I wanted to know if my drive truly matched his.

He sent the statue back to its corner and took me from behind, pulling on my hair like reins. He sat in a chair and pulled me on to his lap, holding my wrists behind me and burying his face in my breasts. He left bites on my back and I left scratches on his. Nothing could make the throbbing ebb. After all that, I only wanted Ghalib more.

At the end of the night, when he finally pulled me to the bed to lay there, rather than have sex, I still wanted him. I could feel that he still wanted me. It was maddening.

"You don't even look tired," he told me.

"I'm not," I said, propped up on one arm.

"We missed dinner," he said. "Are you hungry?"

I thought about it. "No, not really."

He narrowed his eyes at me. "Are you still mortal?"

I laughed. "As far as I know."

He put his hand in my hair and pulled me down for another kiss. My lips would probably be bruised later today. Bruised and swollen, like before. But I didn't draw back. He pulled me down on top of him and felt his hardness against me. I reached down and ran my hands over his erection. He smiled. "Don't you ever get worn out?" I asked.

He stroked the wetness between my legs. "I'm just trying to keep up with my pet," he said.

"There's a more important issue to discuss," I said, rolling off of him and sitting up. "Did you feel in command?"

"Mostly."

"You're pleased?"

"Very."

"So, what about Matthew?"

"He can come back tonight."

"Then I think I'm done here," I said with a teasing tone.

I stood and started towards my gown, which was in a heap on the floor, but Ghalib grabbed my hand and pulled me back. He had an odd expression. I tried to taste his mood but I couldn't decipher it. "What is it?" I asked, sitting beside him on the bed.

"Once more?" he asked. "Just because you want to. Not because I'm blackmailing you."

I looked at him a moment. Then I straddled his lap and pushed him down playfully. "All right," I agreed. "But this time, I get to be on top."

I returned to my suite more than an hour later, and tried to sleep. It didn't come easy. I was energized. It was like I had taken a stimulant. I didn't even want to close my eyes. But I forced myself to try. After a while I must have drifted off because I sensed that time had passed. I didn't feel any more rested, though.

I left my bed. I wandered through my suite. That's when I saw the tray in the sitting room. Fruit and bread. A tureen of a rich, creamy soup kept warm with a small flame underneath. A note in a thick envelope and a wooden box.

I opened the note:

> *If you are still mortal, you must eat. Don't forget that tonight you must endure Victor. You'll need your strength. Also, I've left you a present. I'm sure you'll be able to find a use for it.*
>
> *P.S. I haven't told Victor of your newest gift. I thought you might like to surprise him.*

I looked at the wooden box and opened the lid. Inside was a clear, glass pipe loaded with Amorite and a box of matches. I smiled. Then I served myself soup. Ghalib was right. I needed my strength.

Chapter 27

On Top

I spent the rest of the day on the beach. It was starting to be my favorite place. The wind calmed me and the sound of the waves was like music. It was so different than Panama City beach. This place was rocky and the water gray. I imagined that this was how Maine would look.

I was also trying to think of how best to handle Victor. Just because I could control the Drawing didn't mean that I could control him. This was going to be a delicate operation. What if he enjoyed hurting people more than sexual gratification? I was reluctant and a little bit nervous when I returned to my room.

I planned to dress that night like a virgin sacrifice, exactly to Victor's tastes, but at the last minute I changed my mind. I chose a long, shimmering dress in midnight blue. The way it shone reminded me of the observatory. The night I lost control. It was off the shoulder and showed my collar perfectly, lest Victor forget that I belong to someone else. I wore my hair down and straight. It fell like a sheet of silk.

"You look beautiful," Lisa told me. "But maybe I should give you an up-do. Victor likes to pull hair."

"He'll just take it down," I replied darkly.

Lisa just shook her head. "I'm just glad the Master will be there, too. I can't imagine why he agreed to this."

A tremor of fear went over me. What if the Amorite didn't work like it had before? What if Victor didn't care as much about the Drawing as hurting me? What if I didn't really have any gift to influence him at all? In that case, Victor was going to have the evening of his life and I, most certainly, was not.

I took a breath and went to the sitting room while Lisa straightened my room. The Amorite pipe waited for me. My gift from Ghalib. I lit a match and touched it to the aphrodisiac. Sweet, spicy smoke rolled into my lungs. Everything sharpened around me; I could see the threads in the fine upholstery. I drew another breath of Amorite. The throbbing started within me and the air took on a smoky look. For good measure, I pulled on the pipe one more time and I could see the currents running through the room. The heat in me grew.

A knock sounded at the door that adjoined Ghalib's room and mine. Before Lisa could make it out of the bedroom, I answered it. Ghalib stood there, wearing slacks and a shirt open at the collar. "I felt you smoking the Amorite and I couldn't help myself," he confessed.

"Come in," I invited. He looked pleased.

His eyes rested on me. "I'm starting to begin to wonder why you wear your most alluring clothes on nights when I'm not your focus."

"Really? You think so? Well, tomorrow night, if you like, you can choose my outfit."

"I would like that." His face took on a puzzled expression and he narrowed his eyes. "You're not nervous, are you?" his eyes got a faraway look and I recognized what he was doing: tasting my mood. "You are," he said. "Why?"

"It's Victor," I said, as if his name alone could explain it. "He's a sadist. Not to you, he wasn't. To you he must seem like a creampuff but mere mortals like me—"

"You're not a mere mortal," Ghalib interrupted me. "Do you see the Drawing?"

"Yes."

"Can you control it?"

I played with the currents, bending them and shaping them. "Yes," I finally said.

"Then you have more tools than I had when I mastered Victor." I looked away but he turned my face back to him. "I couldn't have done what I did to him if he hadn't wanted it," he said. "I didn't overpower him. At any point he could have called for his servants and he would have been released. He *wanted* what I did to him."

"I just have to figure out how to make him want it again?" I asked.

"Smart girl."

"I want a little more Amorite," I said, picking up the pipe. "You?" I offered.

A small smile played on his lips. "Perhaps it would be better if I abstained. I'm going to have a difficult enough time being a gentleman with Christine."

Wildly unexpected jealousy twisted in the pit of my stomach. Ghalib cocked his head at me. "I felt that," he said in a low purr.

I flushed. I couldn't help it. "I'm just nervous," I covered.

"That's not what I felt," he teased. It was probably just anxiety and high emotion but his teasing made me mad. I reflexively forced the Drawing away from him. He was like a mortal, with a halo around his body.

"Now, now, Elaine. No need to be vindictive," he said smoothly.

I turned away from him, lit the pipe, and ignored his teasing. And I kept the Drawing away from him for good measure. The more Amorite I took, the easier it became.

I felt him approach me from behind so I wasn't shocked when he ran his hands over my hair. He kissed the edge of my ear. "Why are you jealous?" he whispered.

I turned to face him and brought the Drawing back around him. He shivered. "I have absolutely no idea," I confessed.

He gave me the lightest kiss on my lips. "You can use that with Victor, you know," he said. "No Architect likes to be cut off from the Drawing. It's very uncomfortable."

I gave him the lightest kiss back. "Thank you. And thank you for my gift, too," I said. Again, a tremor went through him. "Shall we go?" I asked.

Ghalib chuckled. "Victor doesn't stand a chance."

We arrived outside of Victor's stone mansion. It was still snowing, as it had been the night of the Festival of Pets. The wind still cut through me but Ghalib hurried me to the door, a protective arm around me. A butler let us inside and I warmed myself in front of the fireplace.

Victor approached us from a hallway and Christine trotted behind him. She was exactly how I remembered her: golden hair, blue eyes, and a face like a doll. Her dress was blue and edged in islet. "Ghalib. Elaine. Welcome to my home again," Victor said.

"Hello," Christine echoed in a tremulous voice. I smiled at her and she smiled back.

Ghalib stepped up to her and seemed to tower over her. She swayed back, away from him. "Hello, Christine," he said. She flushed and he tilted her head up. "Are you going to entertain me while Victor is with Elaine?"

"Yes?" she said.

"Is that an answer?" he pushed gently.

She flushed even brighter. "Yes, Sir."

"We're going to have such fun," he purred at her. Again I felt a twist of jealousy and Ghalib shot a sideways glance in my direction.

Christine didn't notice any of that. "Yes, Sir," she said again in a low, frightened voice, her cheeks looking almost sun burnt.

"See, Elaine?" Victor said, sliding next to me. "That is how a mortal should respond to an Architect."

I looked through my eyelashes at Victor. "I seem to not share Christine's fear of your kind."

"A deficiency, I'm afraid," Victor commented. "But, no matter. I'm here to rectify your deficiencies."

Victor circled around me, not unlike how Ghalib did. His fingers were more adventurous than Ghalib's usually were, though. He stroked my backside with his fingers and pinched them until I gasped. He did the same to my breasts, through the thin dress and bra, making tears come to my eyes. Victor saw the tears. "How lovely," he said. Ghalib's jealousy tingled over me. "Shall we?" he asked, offering his hand. I took it.

"Excuse me," Ghalib said, "Did you have a room for us, or would you like me to enjoy Christine here in the hall?" He wore an expression somewhere between wry humor and irritation.

Victor blinked at Ghalib. "Of course. Follow me."

He led us down a long hallway lit only with torches. The walls and floor and ceiling were all stone. Each door was a heavy, wooden one. Where the dining hall and ballroom had been elegant during the Festival of Pets, this part of the castle was coarse.

"Here, Ghalib," Victor said, opening a door on a masculine, utilitarian bed chamber. Victor was almost rude to Ghalib. I could sense that he was eager to have me alone. Over-eager.

Ghalib put his hand on Christine's back. "Remember, don't leave any marks on Elaine. No bruises; no cuts."

"As you wish," Victor said.

Ghalib smiled down at Christine. Her eyes were as wide as pie-plates. "Come along, Christine," he said. The door closed behind them.

Victor led me down the hall, not speaking to me. He opened a door down the hall from the one he opened for Ghalib. "Go inside," he ordered. I complied.

He slammed the door and I jumped. I calmed myself, looking at the swirling Drawing around us. It hadn't abandoned me. I still had power.

Ghalib would have teased me for my nervousness. Victor didn't waste his time with such things. He came around to the front of me and yanked my dress below my breasts. He pulled my bra down too. The dress straps that looped my arms restricted my movement.

"Not even one mark on these breasts," he commented. When I didn't answer he grabbed me by the neck, quick as lightning and pushed me against the wall. I stumbled, my long gown too long now, and tangling around my ankles. Victor didn't care. He was strong enough to right me with just his hand on my neck. He held me against the wall with force. "Did you hear me?" he said.

My anger started to rise. And so did the bulge in Victor's pants. "Of course I heard you," I said.

"Louder."

"Of course I heard you."

"I wish I was free to mark your breasts. I would brand you as I did Christine. She has a "'V'" on her hip now. I intend to put another on her breasts." He pinched my nipple sharply and I yelped. Victor's breathing picked up. "Not all pain leaves marks though," Victor said, releasing my neck. He reached into the inside pocket of his suit jacket and pulled out a silver chain with two clamps attached to it.

Though I'd never seen them before, I was sure they were nipple clamps and I was sure they would hurt. The Drawing whispered to me, urging me to wait, to endure as much as I could, to let myself feel fear. Victor's arousal would only work to my benefit in the end.

He clipped one of the clamps on to my hardened nipple. Oh, it hurt. The Drawing rose within me to make pleasure and pain cousins. He clipped on the other and, once again, tears sprung to my eyes.

"It's all right, Elaine. You can cry." I blinked and a tear fell. He pressed his chest against mine, making my nipples ache, and licked the tear off of my cheek. "Oh, how I wish you were mine," he whispered. I brought the Drawing around him just a little and let another tear fall. I could feel his hardness against my hip.

He kissed my lips, grinding his chest into mine. I whimpered with pain and he kissed me harder, biting my lips, his tongue invading my mouth. I increased the Drawing around him bit by bit. Not so much that he would notice anything but his pounding desire. He pulled on the chain between my breasts; I cried out. The sounds were muffled against his lips and he drew back just the slightest bit. "Beautiful," he murmured. "I can't wait any longer."

He swung me from the wall and shoved me to the bed. It was an enormous, four-poster thing with a hook on the ceiling directly over it. Before I could really do anything, he bent me over it, sliding my gown up, yanking my panties down to my thighs. He clasped my wrists, snapping something metal around them, and forced them up until my shoulders wrenched and I squealed. His hardness pressed against my anus.

The Drawing told me that now was the time.

I sucked all of the Drawing in the room to me. There was none around Victor. The power sizzled over my skin like electricity. I concentrated to force it towards certain parts of my body: my breasts, to ease the aching pain, my legs, anywhere Victor wasn't touching. His hardness became substantially softer.

He froze. I could tell he wasn't hard enough to force himself into me anymore. And I could tell he was confused.

"What's wrong?" I asked innocently.

"Shut up," he growled, forcing my arms up again, hurting me, making me cry out again. He had a momentary jolt of arousal. I sucked that sexual energy to me as well and he softened again.

He lowered my arms. I looked over my shoulder at him. "Are you

OK?" I asked, careful to hide my smile.

"I'm fine," he snapped. But the metal cuffs around my wrists clicked and opened. He released my arms.

I rolled over and sat on the bed, pulling off the metal handcuffs and setting them on the bed next to me. His penis was utterly flaccid. I looked at it pointedly and for the first time, saw Victor flush. "Am I doing something wrong?" I asked innocently.

He didn't answer me. I saw my chance.

"Could it be that you're tired of being a big bully?" I asked seductively.

"No," he said. But he looked completely uncertain. I almost felt bad for him. Almost.

I reached down, concentrating the Drawing into my hands, and ran his penis through my fingers. He groaned and swayed towards me. "I can help you out Victor," I whispered, stroking him gently.

"I've never...."

"Lost an erection before?" I finished for him. I got a little rougher with his penis and he grabbed my shoulder. "Take off the nipple clamps," I instructed him.

He hesitated and I let go of his penis. Without the Drawing from my hands, it started to shrivel. Immediately, his hands went to my breasts, carefully taking off the clamps. It didn't matter how careful he was, the pain was terrible. I gritted my teeth but I couldn't contain the sharp intake of breath.

"Take off your shirt," I instructed him. He wasn't used to taking direction; he didn't know what to do. "You don't have to," I said with a shrug. "I could just leave."

He stripped his shirt away. It was so easy, I wanted to laugh.

"Might as well take everything off," I added. He quickly complied.

"Now," I said, letting the words wait on my tongue, letting my eyes slide over him. I imagined him taking me roughly and the Drawing almost got away from me. "Put the nipple clamps on," I told him. He reached for me again. "On you," I clarified. He looked at them. "Now," I said. He pinched the clamps on to his nipples and winced. "Good," I praised. I grabbed the handcuffs and snapped them around his wrists. "Stand on the bed and string the handcuffs over the hook."

He couldn't get the handcuff chain over the hook without standing on a low pile of bedding. Even then, he struggled to suspend himself. When he was good and secured, I pulled the bedding away from his feet, leaving him standing on tip-toe to relieve the strain on his arms. Then, I let the Drawing go. The room was thick with it; it was as if it had multiplied while I restrained it. Victor's erection rose.

"You?" He gasped. "Can you control the Drawing?"

"I can," I said. His face was purple and the flush went down to his chest.

"Release me!" he ordered. I kicked off my shoes, pulled my dress and bra up over my breasts, and climbed on to the bed. "Release me or I'll—"

"You'll what?" I challenged. I went behind him and reached around to finger his penis lightly, letting the Drawing pass from me to him. I cupped his scrotum, stroking it until his breath became ragged. "Are you going to call for help?" I asked, gripping his penis more firmly, finding his rhythm, scraping my teeth against his shoulder as I jerked. He moaned and hardened even more in my hand. Abruptly, I stopped.

"No," he whispered.

"No, what?" I asked.

"No, I'm not going to call for help. Just keep going." It was like music, hearing him say that.

I felt the tension in his muscles. I jumped down from the bed, quickly rummaging through his nightstand drawers. I found a whip with a thick handle, a pot of heavy lotion, and a hairbrush. I found much, much more, actually, but those were the items that I took out and laid on the bed in front of Victor.

His eagerness turned to fear. "Elaine, take me down. All I wanted was sex with you. We can still do that."

I stood and slapped him hard across the face. His penis didn't soften in the slightest. "You're lying to me, Victor. You didn't just want sex."

I knelt, his penis an inch from my face. I could smell his dark muskiness. He thrust his hips forward and lost his balance. I licked the tip of his penis and he whimpered. "Do you like that?" I asked.

"I could like it more."

I blew on his penis. "The fact is, you've upset me, the way you like to hurt people," I said, licking his penis again on the word 'like.' I reached for the pot of lotion and rubbed a dollop between my hands. Then, I went around behind him and lubricated his anus.

"Elaine...."

"Shh," I hushed. Then, I lubricated his whip handle. It might be just a tad too large, but I remembered what Ghalib had told me. The more Ghalib hurt him, the more Victor liked it. I grabbed the brush and cracked it against his buttocks. Victor yelped.

"More?" I asked.

Victor didn't answer so I reached for his penis again, letting it slide through my lubricated finger. "More," he said hoarsely.

I cracked his buttocks again. Then I hit him with the side with the bristles. Back and forth, again and again. His hips swayed to meet the brush. I kept going until I saw bruises blooming on his skin. "I think you're ready," I said.

I held the whip handle against his anus. It was actually perfect for this purpose because it was tapered. The thin end would slide into him easily but the thick end would really stretch him. I teased the first inch or so inside and heard him gasp.

"Elaine, pet, don't do this...."

I slid the whip handle in a little further and reached around to his penis again. It was so hard and I stroked it. "Tell me to stop," I said, taking a page out of Ghalib's book. I moved my hand in a rhythm even as I worked the whip handle deeper and faster.

"I... I..."

"Just one little word, Victor." I turned the handle as I thrust and jerked him harder. "Say it and you'll get your wish. I'll just walk away and not violate you anymore."

I thrust the handle to the hilt and he cried out, but he didn't say anything.

I pulled at him, keeping the strokes just a little off, wanting to thrust into him longer, harder. I wished that I had a penis, so I could bend him over and drive him with my body. "Tell me what you want, Victor."

He didn't say anything. I let his penis rest on my hand as I worked him with the whip.

"No, please, Elaine," he gasped. I could hardly believe how he begged. It scared me a little, what I had done to him.

"No, what?" I asked, moving the whip handle slower. "No, you've had enough?"

"No! Keep going. Please!"

It was enough. I pounded him with the whip handle and I stroked his erection. I didn't tease him any longer. Both of my arms found the same rhythm and I prayed he was close. My arms couldn't take much more. The muscles burnt.

He tried to thrust in both directions but in the end, he had to let me finish him. Which I did. He screamed — literally screamed — when he orgasmed. I milked him a bit longer until I saw his legs tremble. Then, maliciously, I yanked the whip out of him in one smooth movement. He cried out and hung loose from the ceiling.

I came around to the front of him and Victor looked utterly drained. I lifted his chin and kissed his lips softly once. "Thank you for a wonderful time, Victor. I think I'll be leaving now."

I hopped down, put on my shoes, and set off to Ghalib's and Christine's room.

Chapter 28

What Comes Naturally

I didn't have the slightest qualm about leaving Victor chained to the ceiling. Someone would find him eventually. I considered myself kind for taking the whip handle out of him before I left.

I crept down the hallway and tried to feel Ghalib's mood. It was amused and... bored. Bored? That couldn't be right. I pressed my ear against his door but didn't hear a thing. Did I dare go in?

What the hell. It was a night of firsts.

I knocked softly and pushed on the door; it swung open noiselessly. Ghalib sat on the bed and Christine knelt before him, her head bobbing over his crotch. I would have believed that she was performing oral sex if he had looked even remotely aroused.

"I'm sorry," I said. "I'll wait outside."

"No," Ghalib said. "Come in."

I edged towards a chair and perched on it. I couldn't help but watch the passionless, perfunctory movement. It was like she understood the mechanics of what she was doing but took no pleasure in it.

"How did it go?" Ghalib asked. His voice was even and steady.

"Good. Just as you planned, actually."

He grinned at me. "Is he still...."

"Hanging from the ceiling."

"Good girl."

I looked at Christine. Up. Down. Up. Down. "Christine?" I asked. She took Ghalib's penis out of her mouth and looked at me with those wide, blue eyes. "What are you trying to do?"

"What he asked me to," she said, distress in her voice. "I've been at it for ever so long and nothing's happening."

Where did Victor find this girl? "It doesn't look like you enjoy it very much," I commented.

"I don't." She looked like a little girl pouting, though I guessed she was in her early twenties. "It hurts my jaw and makes my throat sore."

She was unbelievably cute. The Drawing swirled around us. I thought of my success with Victor and smirked. Ghalib had helped me with him; maybe I could help him with Christine.

"It doesn't have to hurt," I told her. "Would you like a little lesson?"

She smiled. "Yes, please."

"First of all, you're not the slightest bit aroused. I can tell. It's so much more pleasant to be aroused yourself when you want to bring pleasure to someone." Ghalib watched us, his eyes glowing, his pants still around his knees. "I'm going to tell you a secret."

Her eyes lit up like a child's.

"I'm something called an Omnilight. I can help you enjoy sex. Would you like that?"

"Oh yes."

"I'm going to kiss you," I told her. She closed her eyes and puckered. It was the cutest thing I had seen in a long time. I puckered and pressed my lips to hers. Then I dissolved the halo around her and brought the Drawing to her skin. Her pucker melted and her lips parted. I kissed her gently, letting the Drawing swirl around her. She kissed me back, her arms going around me. When I broke the kiss, she moaned. "Wasn't that lovely?" I asked.

"Can we kiss again?" she asked. Ghalib chuckled.

I kissed her again. She was so soft. I nibbled on her upper lip and her lower lip, letting my tongue touch hers gently, bringing up the intensity of the Drawing until I saw her hands brush over her own breasts. Then I broke the kiss again.

"How do you feel?" I asked.

"Like I want something," she replied, flushing. I couldn't help but pity her here with Victor, never feeling anything. It must have been terrible.

"Good," I said. "Ghalib wants exactly what you do." I looked at

Ghalib. "Care to help with this experiment?"

I had never seen him look so amused. "I wouldn't miss it."

"Could you give us a little more room to move around?" I said, nodding at his pants.

"Only if you join me," Ghalib said, his tone pointed.

I looked at Christine. "He's such a man. Always so visual. Take off your dress."

She removed her dress and I removed mine. Ghalib took off his pants and sat back down on the edge of the bed as he watched us. Christine wasn't wearing a bra so I took mine off, too. "Better?" I asked Ghalib.

"Better than better," he replied.

Christine ran her fingers over my breasts and flushed even brighter. "Mmm," I encouraged, touching her back. I heard her gasp at my gentle fingers and saw the bruises near her nipples. I kissed her again and this time she kissed me back with so much enthusiasm, I wasn't worried about bringing the Drawing to her.

"Ladies," Ghalib said with amusement, "I'm waiting."

Christine jumped back but I pulled her in for another kiss. "He can wait," I whispered. She giggled.

We turned to Ghalib and I moved between his legs, kneeling in front of him. Christine mirrored me. "Ok, Christine. Tell me. Have you ever touched yourself?" I flicked my eyes towards her panties.

Her face went scarlet. "Yes," she said in a low voice.

"Think about how you do it." If possible, her face went a brighter red. I decided to just push ahead before she passed out with embarrassment. "Ghalib isn't unlike you are. You wouldn't just start rubbing yourself as hard as you could, would you?"

"No," she said, dropping her eyes. "I like to... to...."

"Tease?" I asked. "Stop and start"?"

"Yes."

"Just like him." I leaned forward and let my mouth hover over the head of his penis. I licked it and listened to his breath shudder. "You try it."

Christine imitated what I did and I brought the Drawing to her tongue. Ghalib moaned. "Did I do that?" she asked.

"Yes," I said. "Your mouth has all sorts of textures." I brought my

245

lips just over the head of his penis and slid it halfway down the shaft and back up, repeating it a couple of times. "You try," I said. "Make sure your lips are wet and don't use your teeth."

I let the Drawing gather around her lips and watched Ghalib shift restlessly as she went up and down slowly on his shaft.

"And don't forget to use your tongue," I advised. "Especially on the underside where it's sensitive. He may like it if you lick his scrotum, too." I licked with broad, generous strokes over the soft skin and up the underside of the penis with the hard tip of my tongue. Ghalib's hands went into my hair and he tried to urge me to take him in. I pulled back.

"Now you try it, Christine," I said. Ghalib groaned. I grinned at him. "You agreed to this."

"You two are driving me insane," he said.

Christine looked at me. "That's a good thing, right?"

"A very good thing."

She imitated what I had done. I made sure that the Drawing went with her, heightening the experience. When Ghalib put his hands into her hair to guide her to take his penis, she didn't pull away. She took him in. She used her hands to stroke him as her head went down slowly and back up.

"Much better," Ghalib praised, his voice husky.

"We're going to play a game, Christine," I said. "Don't stop what you're doing."

I went around behind her. Ghalib watched me. He was slightly flushed but nowhere near enough. I slid my hand around Christine, to her stomach, lower, into her panties, and stroked her hair there. Slowly, I slid my finger into her folds and ran it through her wetness.

"Do you like that?" I asked. I already knew the answer; her legs spread so far in response that I could get both hands into her panties. The fabric slipped down a little and I could see the raw 'V' branded on her hip.

She hummed an "mm-hmmm" in response, with Ghalib's penis in her mouth, making his eyes close with pleasure.

"I'll keep doing this as long as you keep pleasuring Ghalib. He'll tell me if you get sloppy," I teased.

"She's doing wonderfully," Ghalib praised, his voice getting a little shaky.

She kept going, moaning, her legs trembling. She went faster then slower, stopping to concentrate on the tip, then taking the whole thing again. I was so proud of her; she was such a fast learner.

"If you make Ghalib orgasm, I'll make you orgasm," I promised. My hand got wetter.

My breath came faster, just to see Ghalib and Christine enjoying themselves so much. Ghalib watched me and I maintained my eye contact with him, even as I kissed Christine's back and brought the Drawing to her lips and genitals. She bucked against my hand, sucking at Ghalib enthusiastically. He put his hands in her golden hair to guide her into a rhythm.

I could feel she was close and I slowed down. It worked like a charm. She gave a strangled moan that pushed Ghalib over the edge. He shuddered and thrust, making a sound like a growl. When I was sure he was finished, I resumed my rhythm with Christine. Soon she cried out, her legs spreading even further.

"Easy," Ghalib said, pulling her mouth from his sensitive penis. I smiled and Christine completed her orgasm. When she was done, she got up and threw her arms around me.

"Thank you," she whispered.

"Trust me when I say it was my pleasure," I told her.

She wouldn't release her arms from around me so we sat on the floor together and looked up at Ghalib. "So what's next"?" I asked. "Are we done here or would you like for me to leave you and Christine alone for a little longer?"

Ghalib chuckled. "I think you're forgetting something, Pet."

I tried to think but nothing occurred to me. "Remind me?" I asked.

"Matthew?"

"Oh crap. You're right. I completely forgot."

He smiled and I could feel his satisfaction. Clearly Ghalib's jealousy was wasted on my feelings for Matthew if he could slip my mind so easily. "We're going to have to go and talk to Victor about bringing him home," Ghalib said.

"That's going to be a fun conversation," I said darkly.

Christine and I pulled our dresses back on. Ghalib arranged himself until he was again a perfectly groomed gentleman. Then, he led us out of the room and down the hall to where I had left Victor.

He pushed open the door and chuckled. "I never thought I'd see you like that again. I'm ashamed of myself that I didn't think of the nipple clamps."

Christine gasped to see Victor hanging from his handcuffs, trying to get the chain back over the hook and failing miserably without the extra bedding to give him height. The nipple clamps were still firmly attached to him and the bruises on his backside had darkened.

"Would you please get me down?" he asked Ghalib.

"I like you up there," Ghalib teased. "I've half a mind to send Elaine home and spend some time on you myself." Victor's penis rose and Ghalib chuckled again. "But, I've actually come back to talk business. Elaine satisfied me that Matthew was no threat so I've come to ask for him back."

"A pity," Victor said. "We were having such fun, he and I."

"Be that as it may...." Ghalib said, his voice stern.

"Matthew," Victor called softly to the empty room.

The boy appeared before us. The same Matthew. Shaggy brown hair. Eyes like a puppy. He looked at Victor and his eyes widened. "Master!" he gasped, jumping on the bed and lifting Victor off of the hook. He helped Victor sit on the edge of the bed which I was sure was completely unnecessary; I couldn't have hurt him that badly.

"Ghalib and Elaine have come to take you home," Victor told him.

"No!" Matthew exclaimed.

I blinked.

"Excuse me?" Ghalib said.

Matthew flushed and lowered his eyes. "Forgive me, Master."

I stepped forward. "You don't want to come back to Ghalib's home?"

He flushed even brighter. I saw pink marks across his back where Victor must have strapped him. I wondered if he bore a brand, too. "I... I...."

"For Christ's sake, just say it," I demanded.

"I love him."

"You love Victor?"

He nodded.

I leveled a look at him. "You've got to be kidding me." He lowered his eyes.

Ghalib laughed. "He falls in love more often than Casanova."

Victor took off the nipple clamps and cringed. Then he pulled Matthew's face to his chest. Without a word, Matthew licked at his sore nipples. "I will admit to affection for the boy. He's a very satisfactory submissive."

I narrowed my eyes at Matthew, feeling a little miffed. "You should let Victor keep him. They deserve each other."

Ghalib was quiet for a moment. He watched Matthew licking at Victor's chest with an almost disgusted look. Ghalib cast a sideways look at me and a small smile started played on his lips.

"I very rarely just give away my possessions," Ghalib told me. "However, I might be willing to consider a trade."

Victor's face sparked with interest. "Go on."

"You may keep Matthew if you would allow me to take Christine."

Christine's hand slipped into mine. She gripped me so hard, it almost hurt. I didn't need to be an Omnilight to know that Christine wanted out of this house more than she wanted anything else.

"Christine?" Victor asked. "Why, she has no skills at all. What do you want her for?"

"I see potential," Ghalib said with a shrug. "And Elaine likes her."

Victor looked at Christine. "Step forward, girl," he ordered. She complied, letting go of my hand. He looked her up and down, as if he was looking for something he hadn't seen before. "She's a squealer, if you hurt her," he said thoughtfully. "But the sex is dreadful."

Ghalib shrugged. "Decide which you want: Matthew or Christine."

"I'll take Matthew," Victor said. Matthew flushed and laid his head in Victor's naked lap. Victor idly played with his hair.

I gave a disgusted sigh and feigned intense displeasure. Honestly, if he wanted to stay with Victor it was fine with me. But it did hurt my pride that he fell for someone else so easily.

"You should have seen what I endured for you, Matthew," I said to him. "I hope you're happy."

Matthew wouldn't look at me.

I turned my attention to Victor, who also seemed amused. "Whip him a few times for me," I said.

"I will."

"I think we'll go now," Ghalib said. I tasted his mood and felt him holding back laughter. "Thank you, Victor. Come along, Christine."

Ghalib didn't talk to either of us until we were outside in the snow again. Then Ghalib made us stand in the sharp wind while he looked at me. "Matthew should have seen what you endured?" he echoed, amusement coloring his words.

"What?" I replied. "It's not like I could *really* punish him for being a weak fool. That guilt trip was the only weapon I had."

"I wouldn't like to think that you just *endured* that night," Ghalib pushed, his green eyes cutting through me more than the wind.

"I hope you know better than to believe every word I say," I replied. "I've already told you, I'm deceitful."

"So...."

I stepped up close to him. The effects of the Amorite were starting to fade but I still had some control. I brought my lips to his, letting the energy flow between us. I stood on tip-toe to whisper in his ear. "Any time you need me to show you how much I liked it, say the word."

His arms went around me and he kissed me possessively. He bent my body back and it yielded to him. When he finally released me, his eyes were hot and glowing.

"Christine is freezing," Ghalib said, noting her shiver. "Let's get her home."

Ghalib put Christine in the room next to mine and I sent Lisa to see to her. She was so grateful. She couldn't stop thanking Ghalib or squeezing my hand. It was downright cute.

We left Lisa and Christine in Christine's room and Ghalib walked the few paces with me to my door.

"I get to choose your outfit tomorrow?" he asked.

I considered his impish expression. "Should I be sorry that I made you that offer?"

"Tell me about what you did to Victor."

I narrowed my eyes, trying to decide if he was just being eva-sive or if there was deeper meaning to his question. "You saw what I did."

"Tell me about the part I couldn't see."

I nodded slowly. "I let him get aroused. I let him hurt me a little and bully me, then I separated him from the Drawing. He couldn't perform."

"Devious," Ghalib said, smiling.

"The rest was easy. He was so shaken by impotence."

He narrowed his eyes. "He was completely lifeless without the Drawing?"

"Absolutely flaccid. Is that strange?"

"When you withdrew the Drawing from me I still wanted you."

I flushed.

"Did you enjoy mastering Victor?" Ghalib asked.

My face grew hotter. "I did."

"You are the most intriguing mortal I've ever met," he said softly. "I *must* have you to myself again soon." He just looked at me and I saw the same emotion I did when I first came to this world: like he wanted to devour me. Except I was feeling something akin to that myself.

"Now, to answer your question, I suspect you'll be pleased at what I select for you to wear. I'm going to ask you to indulge me to-morrow night. I have something planned."

"So secretive," I said.

"I want your reaction to be spontaneous." He gave me another one of those predatory looks. "Now kiss me."

It was an order. He hadn't given me an order in ages, not even when he took me in the bondage room. When we kissed I jolted with his particular flavor of Drawing: the rawness, the passion, the long-ing, and the need. He pushed me back against my door and kissed me slow and hard, his tongue forcing my mouth open before I could do it willingly. I flashed with images again; I felt what he wanted. Days, uninterrupted.

My hands went into his hair; the lush, thick texture was becoming my favorite part of him. His hands went into my loose hair, too. He kissed me as if it was the first time, until my breath was ragged. I wasn't the only one feeling the effects; he gripped handfuls of my hair.

I broke the kiss. "Good-night, Ghalib," I whispered.

His lips traced my jaw. "Don't tease me," he said. "Invite me in."

I hesitated. It was strange, but it was like my room was the one place that I had just for myself. He had been inside only once and never for sex. For some reason, I wanted to keep it that way.

"Why not *your* room?" I asked.

"Not ready to let me in, yet?" he whispered, kissing the side of my neck.

He dropped another soft kiss on my lips. He gave me his slow, seductive smile and backed away. I watched as he walked to his room and let himself inside.

"Who's teasing who?" I said with an unsteady voice. He chuckled as his door closed.

Then I went into my own room. Lisa wasn't there so I drew my own bath, soaking in it until the water was tepid trying to clear my mind of everything: the arousal, the fear at what I was becoming, and the tingling thrill of my own power. I just wanted to relax. Just forget everything but the luscious scent of my bath and untangling of my muscles.

When Lisa came in, I sent her to her room, asking for a little more time alone. It was actually nice to drain my own bath, pick my own nightshirt, and turn back my own covers. I felt a little like the woman I once was.

Just as I was getting ready to get into bed, there was a soft tap at the door. It wasn't Ghalib; I would have been able to feel him. I opened the door carefully, just cracking it.

It was Christine, standing there in a long cotton nightgown, flushed pink. "Are you OK?" I asked. "Do you need something?"

"I couldn't sleep," she confessed, flushing brighter. "I couldn't stop thinking about you and Ghalib."

I smiled at her. "Victor was pretty mean to you, wasn't he?"

"It isn't just that," she said. "I never..."

"Never what?"

"Nobody ever touched me the way you did."

My jaw dropped a little. "You never orgasmed with another person?" I asked.

She shook her head. "And I was thinking, I mean, I was wondering if you would give me another lesson."

Oh, boy.

Chapter 29

Empowered

I wasn't about to let Christine go the same route as Matthew. She may not be completely sure of the rules around here, but I was. I stepped out of my room and closed the door behind me.

"We can't do anything at all without Ghalib's permission," I told her. "That's how Matthew ended up with Victor—by breaking that rule."

Christine got this look of sweet determination. "Then could we ask him? I mean, if you want to."

I thought about it a moment. Ask him? He probably wouldn't get upset about that. "I do want to, so let's give it a try."

We walked down to his door and I knocked lightly. I could hear him moving around inside. When he opened the door, I just looked at him for a moment. He wore a pair of pants that looked like yoga pants and no shirt. It was as casual as I'd ever seen him and it stunned me. He was chiseled, beautiful. I flushed and looked away.

"Elaine? Christine? Is everything all right?"

I forced myself to talk because I knew Christine wouldn't. "Christine was left unsettled by her experience with us. She wondered if she might have another lesson. She didn't understand that you must give your permission."

I sounded stiff and formal. I could only glance at him for a moment at a time. It was as if I was looking at the sun. I don't know why I was acting like such a fool, unless it was because he seemed so much more human dressed and looking like this. An insanely beautiful human. Like a high-paid male model. I wished that I had sent Christine back to her room and just gone to sleep.

He looked at me curiously. Then he smiled that predatory grin. "Of course you may, Christine. I'm pleased that Elaine brought you to me. I would have hated to have to punish you so soon. Come in."

Christine went in first and I moved to follow her but Ghalib stepped in my way. "I think Christine and I should have a private lesson just now."

Then I *did* look at him. My lips fell open a little. Was he really telling me not to come in his room?

"Private?"

"Good-night, Elaine," he said, shutting the door. Again, that wildly unexpected jealousy flared. I wasn't sure who I was jealous of: Ghalib or Christine. All I knew was that I was left out and it was an awful feeling. I stood there for a moment, wondering if he would reconsider. He didn't. Slowly, I went back to my room, casting looks at his door as I went.

Thankfully, I couldn't hear them. Unfortunately, though, I still had the connection with Ghalib. I tried to shut it out but I couldn't. He was aroused. The newness of Christine and her willingness to please appealed to him. The more I tried to ignore it, the more it invaded my mind. He was kissing her; the sensation was so vivid I could almost sense the pressure of her lips. I could imagine her soft sighs. I climbed into bed, pulled the covers over my head, and sandwiched the pillows over my ears.

It didn't help.

I knew the exact moment when her lips went around him. I could feel her sucking on him, teasing him the way I taught her. It was maddening. I could also feel his pleasure, his euphoria, at the sensation.

It was poetic justice I supposed, after my night with Julia and Anna. No wonder he hadn't spent that night alone. I didn't even try masturbating; I knew it wouldn't be satisfying. Then I felt his roguish, mischievous side flair and knew that he was aware of what I must be feeling. That he was enjoying Christine even more knowing he had teased me before he left me at my door and continued to drive me to distraction now.

I laid there until he entered Christine. Then I couldn't take it anymore. I pulled on some comfortable jeans and a t-shirt and left my room. I wandered the hallways, heading wherever the sensation of

Ghalib and Christine coupling grew fainter. I passed Ghalib's studio; sculptures and carvings were crammed into every inch of workspace. I walked in. The angel that had moved was gone and a huge soldier with an erect phallus had taken his place. Ghalib must have been working like a madman while I slept.

I exited back to the hallway and wandered for ages, getting no further from the maddening sensation of Ghalib and Christine. I felt more detail than was comfortable. They had finished one session of sex and she was shyly trying to leave. Ghalib enjoyed toying with her gently, not letting her leave, not letting her dress, and hearing her stuttering replies to him. He was deeply satisfied, both at his acquisition of Christine and of his prolonged torture of me.

When he started kissing her again, the claustrophobia, like what I experienced in the prison, hit me again. I wanted fresh air; I needed to be outside. My pace quickened. I wished for a way out and the halls led me to the foyer. Without a second thought, I exited the house through the front door and headed for the beach. I set myself on a rock and watched the moon-trail on the water. I listened to the waves pounding against the beach and breathed mouthfuls of the salty air.

Distance helped. Or maybe it was just the increased distraction: the ocean waves, the wind, and my motion making everything more bearable. The details seemed muted. I got the general sensation of the love-making but not the intricate details. It was far more manageable out here.

I was so tired and the sounds of the waves so soothing. I wished that the nagging arousal would leave me. How long could they keep at it? All night, probably and into the day if Ghalib had his way. I sighed and looked around. There was a grassy knoll down the beach a ways. It didn't look too rocky.

I strolled down there, laid down, and stared up at the stars. Eventually the moon set and even more stars became visible. A million of them with a milky streak across the sky. It could have been my sky from home.

Eventually, calm rose in me. I was too exhausted to move. I just closed my eyes and drifted away.

I awoke first because there was a panicky sound at the back of my mind. And when I opened my eyes I blinked against the rising sun. It was beautiful on the water. I could never figure out if the water faced east or west; I swore the sun both rose and set there.

Elaine! Come here!

I sat straight up. My body was in instant motion in response to Ghalib's order. I jumped to my feet and took off at a sprint to the house. I got the feeling he had been calling me a while. I'd been so tired I slept through his summons. Or maybe it was the distance. Or the waves. I didn't know; I just knew he sounded anxious, frightened, and angry.

By the time I was inside, I could hardly catch my breath. Still, his mental voice was practically screaming for me. I had no control over my body as it propelled me towards his study. I could hardly breathe; I ran clutching at my side. I didn't even knock before I threw the study door open. I dashed inside, gasping for breath.

He looked up, his jaw clenched, his hands clenched, his glare so intense it felt like he wanted to hit me. "Where have you been?" he demanded. His voice was harsh.

"On the beach," I panted. "I fell asleep. Couldn't you feel me?"

"No. Not while you were unconscious. I thought you were gone somehow or someone had taken you." He strode across the room to me and grabbed me by the shoulders. "How dare you frighten me like that?"

"I didn't mean—"

"I want to hear two words from you. I. Apologize."

"I apologize."

"Tell me you're mine." His hands tightened on my shoulders like clamps. I felt my bones grind against his.

I gasped. "Ghalib—"

"Say it."

"I'm yours."

"Show me."

I was starting to get frightened. He looked wild and his fingers hadn't relaxed at all. "I don't know what you want from me." My voice caught on a sob.

"I don't know, either!" He released me and paced to the other side of the room and faced away from me. "More than you are prepared to give, I suspect."

I closed my eyes and felt his mood. He had been scared. Really scared. He thought I was gone and he felt empty. There had been no connection between us while I slept. He came looking for me and couldn't find me. Lisa didn't know where I was either and for the first time since I arrived, he felt lonely. His emotions hurt me.

"I went outside because it was driving me crazy, feeling you and Christine," I told him. "I wasn't trying to leave."

"Because you don't want to leave me or because you know you can't?" he asked, still facing away from me.

I thought about lying. I decided on the truth. "Because I know I can't."

He turned around. "Why don't you ever invite me into your room?"

The question took me off guard. "I don't know."

"I do. You're still holding back from me."

He was right; I was.

"Why?" he asked.

The words were out of my mouth before I even knew what I was going to say. "Because you're going to hurt me."

He looked completely confused. "I was just teasing you last night with Christine."

"I know."

"Then, I don't understand what you're afraid of."

"I know that, too."

"Explain it to me," he said, frustration tingeing his voice.

I lifted my chin and looked him in the eyes. "Tell me you belong to *me*," I said.

"I don't," he replied. "I'm the Master; you're the pet. You're mine; I'm not yours."

I just looked at him.

"Elaine, surely you can't be asking me for equality."

"I'm not asking for anything. I'm just trying to tell you why you feel me holding back. You have all the power. You want me to give everything freely, yet you could discard me at any moment and I wouldn't have even my life to go back to. The other Architects would use me. I would become a thing no more prized than a unique sex toy." The idea made me nauseous.

I was holding back because I didn't want him to obliterate me.

He seemed stunned. "But, I wouldn't…"

"Promise me," I said in that same low voice.

He made a frustrated sound. "I don't owe you any promises."

"OK, then," I replied. "But understand that I just can't give myself the way you want me to. Physically, though, I am yours. I can't seem to resist it. You'll need to be satisfied with that."

He looked like he wanted to argue. He put his hands under my arms and lifted me on to his desk, eliciting a little squawk from me. Then he kissed me as he had the night before, demanding that I part my lips, tasting the inside of my mouth with hot strokes of his tongue. The images that flashed in my mind were a kaleidoscope of things we had done and things he still wanted to do. Bondage. Romance. Whippings. I was growing dizzy.

I broke the kiss. "Ghalib," I protested breathlessly.

"No," he told me. "I want you."

I gulped deep breaths. "I don't want to pass out."

"You won't," he said. "I forbid it."

He kissed me again, urging me to lie back on the desk and I did. He fumbled with my t-shirt and jeans. My clothes were usually easier access. I pulled my t-shirt off myself; I hadn't bothered with a bra last night when I fled my room. His lips went to my nipples. He kissed them, bit at them, kneaded them with his hands and teased them with his fingers. I pulled his head towards me, urging him on.

A knock sounded at the door.

Ghalib ignored it and unbuttoned my jeans, kissing my stomach. I couldn't think. His lips were doing amazing things to my skin. The night before had been about everyone but me. I was tense and wanted him, too.

The knock sounded again, louder.

"Nyx is here, Sir." I recognized Jason's voice. "She's asking for Miss Elaine."

"Nyx, herself?" Ghalib asked through the door.

"Yes, Sir."

Ghalib head snapped up. He narrowed his eyes at the door, then at me. "Tell me the truth," he ordered. "Do you know anything about this?"

"No."

"You didn't see her last night when you were outside of the castle?"

"I swear I didn't. I haven't seen her since the night of the musicale."

"The musicale?"

"You didn't know she was there?"

The knocking sounded again. "Sir? What would you like me to do?" Jason sounded scared.

"Take her to the library," Ghalib called. "Tell her that we'll be with her shortly." He cursed softly under his breath. Then, he looked at me, topless, still lying across his desk. "I would really like to just let her wait while I have you. But, since it's Nyx...."

He offered his hand and helped me off of the desk. I grabbed my shirt and pulled it back on. When I had fastened my jeans, Ghalib offered me his arm.

He paused at the door. "Elaine, I don't know any other way than this," he gestured towards the disorderly desk top, "to show you that I don't intend to discard you. That you have no reason to be jealous of Christine."

I flushed.

Nyx was just as I remembered her: golden, wild, her hair blowing in a breeze I couldn't feel, her face so delicate and beautiful, it nearly broke my heart. She was standing, or perhaps floating, in front of a bookcase.

She turned her eyes coldly on Ghalib. "I didn't ask for you."

"I am Elaine's Master. You will not see her without my permission. No matter who you are."

"You Architects and your tedious protocol," she replied. "May I have your permission to speak to the Omnilight alone?"

He glanced at me. "Do not harm her."

"I assure you, Ghalib. I mean her no harm."

"Very well." He glanced at me, then exited the room, closing the door behind him.

Nyx and I looked at each other for a moment. "Your name is Elaine?" she asked.

"Yes."

"My name is Dionysia."

I had a moment of shock. "You're a mortal?"

"I was. I don't know what I am now, besides Nyx. I've been here a very long time."

"How long?" I asked, sitting down across from her.

"What was the year when you were brought here?"

"2012."

She looked shocked. "More than two millennia." I opened my mouth and closed it again. Two thousand years here as Nyx. A mortal that didn't die. It was mind numbing. "I am tired of this place," she said matter-of-factly.

"I can imagine."

"Can you?" she asked. "You seem to be doing well here. The Drawing clings to you. The Architects covet you."

"I can be a different person here. I was very unhappy and very lonely in the mortal world. I don't even think I knew how much until I came here."

Nyx looked sad. "I was a vestal virgin, a powerful woman in a time when women had no power. But I was also an Omnilight. I was brought here, forced to submit, forced into acts I had sworn never to do."

"Oh my God. I'm so sorry." A virgin—here—with these creatures.

She looked at me and her eyes glimmered, like her tears were molten gold. "The Nyx who ruled then was tired of her position, as I am now. She told me that if I agreed to take her place, I would never again be forced to do anything I didn't want to. But I would be fixed here until another could take my place. It was not an honor. It was a responsibility. In life, I was mistress of the sacred fire that must never go out; here I'm mistress of the Drawing which must never ebb. Without it mortals couldn't dream. Architects could not build dreams. Both worlds would fall into disarray."

"You hate this life. You've given up everything to do this," I realized.

She nodded. "And now I want to be selfish. I want my duty to end. I want for you to replace me as Nyx."

I gasped. My heart thundered.

She continued talking as if I had no reaction at all. "I tested you by giving you more Drawing. You consumed it like wine. You shouldn't be able to control the energy yet, but with Amorite, you can. And the way you interact with the Architects — it's as if you were born for this life."

My mind wouldn't accept what she was saying. I didn't know how to even contemplate it. How could I accept such a responsibility? What would it do to Ghalib? I drew a breath and tried to form a thought. "I don't know what to say."

"Say nothing. And tell no one of what I've offered you. In three days, come to my home if you accept."

"You know that I can't do anything without Ghalib's permission."

"Come here, child."

I stood and crossed the room to her. I remembered how her touch had rendered me unconscious, so I was nervous. She cocked her head at me. "Be calm. You are strong enough for this."

She leaned in and I thought she was going to kiss me. But she didn't. She pressed her lips to mine and she breathed into me, like she was giving me CPR. It was as if she infused my muscles with strength, my mind with understanding, my body with power. I wanted more. The longer she breathed into me, the better I felt. I wondered if I would ever need to sleep again. If I would ever need to eat. If I would ever need anything.

She drew back and looked tired. "No one can command you now," she said. I was distracted. I could see the Drawing without the Amorite and clearer than I ever had before. Her hair seemed to be floating on a breeze because it was caught in the Drawing current. Her body was almost lifted by the energy. She moved on it, like a butterfly on a draft.

I touched my neck. "The collar?"

"Remains as a decoration only."

I thought about what she was saying. "How much freedom do I have? Could I go back to the mortal world?"

"You can go anywhere."

"I could see my sister?"

"This very instant. No one could stop you—not even me."

"If I didn't want to come back, I wouldn't have to, would I?"

She looked tired. "No. And I will understand if you choose that life over the one I'm offering to you."

My imprisonment was over. Just like that, I had the power to return home. To start my life over again. If no one could command me, I was safe from the other Architects, too. I didn't know whether to laugh or cry. Nyx had just freed me.

"Thank you," I said. "I'll consider your offer."

"Come to me in three days with your decision."

"I will," I promised. And I watched her go.

Chapter 30
Just Because I Want To

After Nyx left, I sat there stunned. Literally stunned. I watched the patterns of Drawing in the room and rolled them into donuts and fig-ure-eights. It was so easy. I barely even needed to think about it.

I was free. I had options. I could return home to the mortal realm. Taking what I had learned here, I could reshape my life. I didn't have to be a lonely boring secretary. I could be aunt to my nephew. I imag-ined myself at home, in my apartment but the image left me oddly empty.

Or, alternately, I could replace Nyx. The idea was so immense, it scared me. Never to die. To be mistress of a force as vital as the Draw-ing. Where would I live? Would I have to cloister myself like Diony-sia? What would be my relationship with Ghalib? The questions were endless.

Or, I could ignore everything that Dionysia had said and just pre-tend that nothing had changed. Or better yet, go back to her in three days and demand that she remove this power. Demand that she re-turn me to the way I was before. Being an Omnilight had been respon-sibility enough.

I closed my eyes and put my head in my hands. I was still in that position when Ghalib came into the room. I could feel him so sharply, it was almost like telepathy.

"Elaine? Pet? Are you harmed?" he asked.

I looked at him. Even my vision had sharpened. He was brighter and more alive than he had ever seemed. I had grown used to the constant throbbing when I was around him but this time his presence stirred something deeper. It was an aura of heat, a demanding need.

"Can you still feel my mood?" I asked.

His eyebrows furrowed. "You're very aroused."

I felt something like relief. Maybe he couldn't order me any longer, but our connection wasn't completely severed. I don't know why it comforted me, but it did. "I'm on fire," I responded.

"Nyx funneled more Drawing into you, didn't she?" he asked.

"Yes," I replied, standing. Everything else fell away: Nyx's amazing offer, her tragic past, my new conundrum. There was only Ghalib.

"How do you feel?" he asked, looking at me with a worried expression.

"I want you."

"Pardon me?"

"You heard me." My voice was strange to me—demanding, husky, dark and sultry.

He crossed the room to me, watching me carefully. His hand moved towards my forehead like he was testing for a fever. "Are you sure you're al—" As soon as his hand touched my face, his words cut off with a sharp hiss of breath. I could feel it, too. What had once been a current was now a rip tide. I jolted with the sensation.

I took his hand off of my forehead and licked each of his fingers, from the pad to the tip, watching his eyes widen. "Give me an order," I whispered to him.

"Elaine, you're worrying me."

"Please, Ghalib. Order me to do something."

"Kiss me," he commanded, his eyes bright.

It wasn't like before. I felt the pull, the compulsion to obey but I didn't have to comply. It was like being tempted with good food when you're on a diet. It's hard to say no, but completely possible. Again, I felt something like relief. Nyx hadn't obliterated everything, just loosened the ties that bound me.

I went up on tip-toe to kiss him and the moment we touched, I realized that I could now control the images I sent him. I could send him what I wanted—just what I wanted. I kissed him deeper, pushing him into the arm-less desk chair, climbing on to his lap, straddling his hips. I kissed him from above rather than below, which felt different and right, somehow.

Then, I showed him images of us coupling in his bed, in the hall, on the floor. I put my hands in his hair and tilted his face back. His hands went behind my back and under my shirt, scraping at my skin.

The Drawing was unbelievable. It made my desire like napalm. Kissing just made it worse. Touching made it unbearable. I ground my pelvis against him and he moaned.

I pulled open his shirt and fell in front of him on my knees, kissing from his nipples to his belt and back up again, licking at the ripples of his stomach.

"What did she do to you?" he gasped. But he didn't try to stop me; he let me do what I liked.

I opened his pants and he didn't need any encouragement. I only took him into my mouth because I knew he would like it. I didn't imagine how much, though. He took his hands from my hair and balled them into fists on his lap. I put my hands over his and continued to work him with my mouth. I forgot my desire and concentrated on his.

"No... no," he said, pulling me off of him. I was surprised, but only for a moment.

He pulled my shirt off and yanked at my jeans. I slapped his hands away and took them off myself. "Do yours," I told him. In moments, we were both naked.

He sat back in the chair and I mounted him. He was erect; I was wet. The Drawing shot through us like lightning and I stiffened for a moment trying to catch my breath.

"Move," he ordered. I didn't try to resist. Without arms, the chair was perfect. I could plant my feet on the floor and control every thrust. I took him in all the way and rubbed against him, catching the perfect friction.

He gripped my backside with both hands. I gripped his shoulders knowing that he had the ideal view of my breasts as I rose and fell on him, knowing he couldn't help but see the jiggle as I rubbed.

I threw my head back and reveled in sensation. I rode him, grinding myself into him. He pulled me against his chest so that the Drawing tripled. "God, Ghalib," I cried.

"Say that again," he gasped.

I leaned in closer to his ear. "Ghalib," I moaned softly. Then I knew what would please him even more. My lips brushed his ear as I whimpered, "Please. Don't stop."

He thrust into me hard and his whole body shuddered with an unexpectedly sudden climax. The orgasm that ripped through him, ripped through me, too. I continued to ride him, reaching for my own peak. Suddenly I was there. He moaned appreciatively in my ear, thrusting into me harder, even though the peak of his own pleasure was past. He clutched me to his body, moving against me until neither of us could breathe.

"Whatever Nyx did to you, I approve," he panted.

I lifted myself off of him and flopped on to the rich wool rug. "I think I really needed that." The throbbing was by no means sated but I wasn't completely out of control any longer. The Drawing was like ribbons around us. I saw that it ran between us, too, even though we were physically separated.

At least we were physically separated for a moment. Ghalib lowered himself to the rug next to me and traced patterns on my skin. "Is there anything else you need?" he asked suggestively.

The Drawing between us seemed thicker when we were closer. I rolled so I faced him. "I should be asking you that, Master."

I sensed his arousal and watched as Drawing gathered to his skin. It was fascinating. I didn't try to manipulate the Drawing; I only watched it.

"You like that, don't you?" I asked him, my voice that same seductive purr he liked to use. "When I call you 'Master'?"

"I like it better when you call my name."

Usually that would have made me flush, but at the moment, I was beyond embarrassment. I stroked his chest with my fingertips and watched the Drawing, like smoke trails, flowing from them. I rolled a nipple between my fingers, listening for his breath to grow ragged.

He captured my wrist and rolled on top of me grabbing my other wrist and pinning both over my head. "Are you trying to drive me insane?" he asked.

I grinned. "Maybe."

I pushed on him with all my strength and was surprised when he moved. It seemed like Nyx gave me physical strength, but now I knew for certain. I used my momentum, my hips and the element of surprise to pin him with his arms over his head, just as he had me a moment before.

"More revelations," he said, twisting under me until he toppled me. We rolled around on the floor, wrestling, kissing, and fondling each other's body any moment either of us had a free hand. Chairs crashed around us. I heard a lamp break. The Drawing in the room grew thick; I couldn't see the ribbons anymore the room was so filled with thick fog.

He pinned me to the ground and with one quick move, he wedged his thighs between my legs and thrust. My back arched, lifting him. "I win," he announced.

"Hardly," I replied, using my hips to turn us so that I was on top. He slipped a little and I pushed him back into me, making him moan deep in his throat.

He tried to mimic my movement but I countered him. I pinned his hands over his head again. "Why don't you just lay back and relax," I suggested, riding him up and down in a slow, fluid movement.

He shuddered.

I continued my slow ride, rocking my hips against him, keeping his hands pinned, letting my breasts dangle over him. He started bucking into me faster but I slowed his pace, slamming hard and slow. I was strong. I could satisfy him.

I watched the Drawing swirling in the room and I suddenly realized something. It wasn't just attracted to us; we were creating it. It flowed out of us when we were joined. Poured out of us. If this was the building material for dreams, our coupling produced a lot of it.

His gasps became increasingly like whimpers. I didn't alter my pace or intensity. I didn't release his wrists, though he struggled. I just rode him. Before long, he cried out again, thrusting his orgasm into me. I let him finish and fell on the floor beside him.

"Should I be concerned about you?" he finally asked. "Physical strength, a sex drive like an Architect, and near perfect instinct of what I want."

"Near?"

"I wanted to be on top."

"Oh, I knew that," I said, grinning. "I just didn't care."

He lifted himself up on one arm. His hair was like a silver sheet. "Seriously, Elaine. Are you all right?"

I checked myself. Except for the persistent throbbing, I felt great. "I think so."

"What did Nyx want with you?"

"She keeps giving me power," I said, evading the truth. "I think she likes to see what I do with it."

His mouth became a troubled frown. His usually smooth face creased with worry lines. "I don't like her visiting you like this."

I sat up. "Why not?"

"I don't trust it."

I wanted to push for information but I didn't want him to become suspicious. "I would think it would be normal for Nyx to be interested in an Omnilight," I said.

"The last one, the boy that wasn't very strong, didn't pique her interest at all."

"Oh."

"It's been *ages* since she came out to see any of us," he added. "It's very odd, the way she's acting."

"I wonder why she's so solitary. Is it, like, a rule, or something?"

"No. As far as I know, she makes her own rules."

"So she can do whatever she likes?"

He narrowed his eyes. "What's your interest in her?"

"I was just curious."

"Did she say anything about you coming to work for her again? If so, you should remind her who you belong to."

I shook my head. "She doesn't want me to work for her."

"Are you telling me the truth, Elaine?" The question was an order, too.

"I am," I promised.

"She'd better not have," he said darkly.

My heart went a little faster. "Why are you trying to put yourself in a bad mood?" I asked with a light, teasing tone. "If this is how you behave when I satisfy you, I'm going to stop being so compliant."

He chuckled. "Oh, no you don't. I have a big night planned for us."

"Really?" I asked.

"And I expect you to be very compliant."

"Oh, do you?"

"Yes," he said, standing. I stayed on the floor, watching his body unfold from below. It was stunning. He offered me a hand and helped me to my feet. "You should try to get some rest in your bed before this evening. I want you fresh."

I pulled on my panties. "Whatever pleases you, Ghalib."

"Mmm, now that's what I like to hear."

Chapter 31

Addiction and Revenge

I returned to my room, less anxious but no less confused. What was I going to do? Sparing Nyx would hurt Ghalib. Leaving the In-Between would hurt them both. I didn't even know if I was fit to live in the waking world any longer. But opting to stay here would be like betraying Rachel. Abandoning her. Now. When she had a child on the way. The thoughts tumbled in my head like laundry. I brushed my hair and finally decided to try to lose myself in sleep.

Before I did sleep, I crept down the hall and knocked on Christine's door. She answered it herself, looking frightened. When she saw me, her blue eyes filled with tears. "Oh, Elaine! Are you angry with me?"

I smoothed her golden hair back and she leaned into my hand. "What for, Sweetheart?" I asked.

"I didn't mean to spend the night with Ghalib," she said in a rush. "I meant to spend it with you."

"That's not your fault," I told her. "Of course I'm not angry with you. I just wanted to make sure that you were OK. Was he gentle with you?"

"Very," she said flushing. "Much better than Victor."

"I should hope so."

She giggled. "But it still wasn't what I was hoping for," she said in a shy, little, frightened whisper.

"We'll get our chance," I said. I wasn't sure how I was going to make that happen, but I promised myself that I would. Especially now that I had command of the Drawing, I could make it wonderful for her.

"What are you doing now?" she asked me. "I'm a little lonely."

I glanced behind her into her room. Just one room — not a suite. A bedroom with a vanity. And a chamber pot in the corner. I might have to talk to Ghalib about her accommodations.

"I need a nap, but why don't you come into my room while I sleep. I have a library. As long as we don't pleasure each other, I can't imagine why Ghalib would care."

Her eyes lit up. "You really wouldn't mind?"

"No. Use my sitting room and read my books."

She followed me back to my suite and I showed her the library. The excitement in her voice as she read the titles was so sweet. I recommended a few, went to my bedroom, and fell into the bed. I was just barely drifting off when I felt the mattress move.

"Christine," I murmured, "we can't."

"I just want to nap with you." She pulled my arm over her and her back pressed into the curve of my chest.

I didn't argue with her. I just let unconsciousness take me.

Lisa woke me. I was alone in the bed and the room was dim.

"I sent Christine back to her room before the Master found her," Lisa said. "You really shouldn't take such chances, Miss."

"We didn't do anything. She was lonely." I sat up and stretched. I could still see the Drawing as sharply as I had before my nap. Its ribbons spiraled around Lisa as if she was a gift. That's when I saw the outfit hanging on the closet behind her. "Holy crap, Lisa. Is that what Ghalib sent me to wear?"

"Yes," Lisa replied. "Don't you like it?"

It was a dress, but not like the delicate evening gowns I was used to. The full skirt was cream and the bodice looked like little more than a slip. A black, leather underbust fastened over it. The leather work was amazing and the lacing severe; leaving the breasts pushed up and covered only by the thin material of the creamy bodice. The skirt hem rose in the front to what I guessed would be just above my calf, which would just perfectly show off the black, leather knee boots with high heels and buckles that sat waiting on the floor underneath. Matching black, leather, fingerless gloves that laced like gauntlets hung next to the dress. It was somewhere between high fashion and a costume. I could barely wait to try it on.

I cocked my head and considered the clothes. "I think that I may love it."

I bathed quickly and Lisa helped me dress. I put on makeup and left my hair down, trying to imagine what 'big plans' Ghalib could possibly have for us tonight. I was hoping that it would be enough of a distraction that I wouldn't have to think about Nyx. Eventually I was going to have to, though; tomorrow morning, I would only have two days left to make up my mind.

I laughed when I looked at myself in the mirror. The outfit gave me the look of a bad-ass pirate with a dominatrix streak. "I think it suits you," Lisa said.

"I think so, too," I replied. "That's why I'm laughing."

Elaine.

Ghalib called. His voice echoed in my mind and relief echoed with it. It was one more way that things between us hadn't changed. My legs poised to move, but I knew I could choose to ignore the summons if I wanted to. I stood. "I have to go," I said, exiting my room.

"Have fun!" Lisa called after me. Her voice rang with mirth and I wondered if she didn't already know what Ghalib had planned for me tonight.

I followed the hallways, distracted by the swirling mist, and finally came upon him waiting in a corridor. I saw him before he saw me, dressed in black slacks and a white shirt open to the waist.

Before I could speak, he turned. His eyes sparkled. I didn't even have the chance to greet him; he had crossed the hall to me like he hadn't seen me in weeks. His fingers tilted up my face and he kissed me, his lips soft and searching — even a bit tentative. He flashed with images of us in my room, in my bed. I sent back images of he and I kissing on the beach.

He broke the kiss with a little moan. "I can't stop thinking about you," he said, brushing my hair over my shoulder and kissing my neck. "Ever since this morning, I just want more. You're like a drug, Elaine."

I lurched with longing and guilt. How could I become the next

Nyx when I had done this to him? How could I leave him when I craved him, too?

"You want me here in the hallway?" I teased. "Jason could come by at any moment."

"He's seen worse," he said, his kisses dipping to where my cleavage peeked out from the cream material of the bodice. "And we've done worse."

"Don't remind me," I said, hiding my grimace and trying not to think of Markus' dining hall.

He ignored me, kissing lower on my breast, easing the material down, until his lips and tongue found my nipple. He didn't bite; he just used the softest parts of his mouth to tease my nipple to hardness. He eased the material down on my other breast and started his slow work there.

A whimper escaped me and it only encouraged him. He kissed down the corset, over my clothes, leaving my breasts exposed. He went on his knees and ran his hands up my legs above the boots, over my backside. "No undergarments at all?" he questioned impishly. "That's not like you, Elaine."

"You didn't send any," I replied smoothly. "I was trying to be docile."

He slid his hands up the inside of my thighs. "Open your legs," he ordered. I had no desire to fight him. "You should be rewarded for your obedience," he said. His fingers opened me and his head disappeared under my skirt.

With Ghalib's brand of Drawing and my new sensitivity to it, the first stroke of his tongue nearly undid me. I very nearly just crumpled into a heap. He lapped at me a few times and I seemed to want to rise into orgasm almost immediately. The only thing that kept me from it was sheer will. I wanted to prolong the sensation. I wanted it to last for hours. I actually only held out a minute or two before the searing orgasm had me clutching at my own breasts.

Ghalib stood, grinning at me, and pushed me back against the wall. I reached forward, undid his pants, and pulled him by his erection towards me. It only took him a moment to get into position and thrust up into me. I wrapped my legs around him.

He didn't start slow or easy. The roughness was wonderful. He put all of his force behind every thrust and I tightened my muscles around him. "Why can't I get enough of you?" he breathed. I don't think I was meant to hear him but I did.

I put my hands behind his neck under his hair and watched his eyes. His fixed on mine. There was no sound in the hall but his grunts, my whimpers, and muffled rhythm of my hips bumping against the wall. I just enjoyed the friction, my arousal, the lush feel of his skin under my fingers and his hair over my arms and hands.

I pulled myself closer to him and brushed my lips over his. With it, I gave him a flash of vision. Me naked and tied to his bed. Another light kiss and another vision. Me whispering, 'no'. I kissed him again, my kisses matching the rhythm of his thrusts. The flashes I sent him growing more graphic. Me trying to twist away from his lips. His mouth traveling over my reluctant body. The moment I relax. The moment I whisper, "Please, Ghalib."

He groaned and thrust with a shuddering intensity. My pleasure rose again. In seconds he was pumping his orgasm into me, even as I cried out with my own. When we were finished, he held me there looking at me for a moment. Then, he lowered me gently to the floor, taking a seat beside me.

"Better?" I asked.

"For the moment," he replied.

He didn't look as happy as he usually did after sex. I bit my lip. "Something's wrong," I said, tasting his mood. "You're upset."

"I've been thinking about you all day," he confessed. "I nearly called you from your nap. If you had tried to deny me now, I think I would have become rather ruthless."

"I didn't deny you, though."

He stared at the floor. "I'm not used to such little self-control."

I felt his mood again. There was something more there, too. I waited for him to look up at me. "What else?" I asked, my heart speeding up.

"I've felt this way only once before," he replied. "When I was just a Dream Maker. She was a member of the Gentry class—just a servant—but I wanted her and I pursued her. Finally, she agreed to one night."

"Did she hurt you?" I whispered.

He smiled. "No. Not at all. We shared a hint of Drawing. Nothing compared to the intensity of this, but for the longest time after that experience I couldn't stop thinking about her. I wanted another night. She flatly refused. It was an obsession for a while and it became my motivation for rising to the Gentry class. In time, my desire for her ebbed, thank goodness. But, during the affair it was passion without limits. I've always wished to experience it again."

I nodded knowingly. "That's why you like aggressive women. You've been looking for one more powerful than you."

"That's probably accurate."

"Have you seen that Architect again?"

"Oh, yes. She was my first conquest when I became a lord. Of course the experience wasn't as satisfying for me. She was no longer the powerful one."

I caught his eyes and held them. "But, I am, aren't I?"

"Yes, you are."

"Are you saying that you're addicted to me?" I said with light teasing.

"I'm saying that the danger is definitely there. I could take you again this moment."

I chewed on my lip. "What would happen if you did form an addiction? Would you need to give me up?"

He chuckled. "No. The only danger would be if I were to somehow lose you. Which, Elaine, eventually I will do. You're mortal. I'm not. The withdrawal from my one experience was very difficult. Withdrawal from a lifetime of experience with you would be maddening."

I looked down at the floor. "So what do you do?"

"I don't know."

"Perhaps Nyx would remove some of the power she's given me."

He snorted. "Have you ever attempted to talk to Nyx? She is completely immovable."

"We could try, at least."

He lifted my chin and made me look at him. "Are you concerned about me, Pet?" His voice was light but his eyes were serious. I could feel that my answer mattered to him.

I flushed. "I shouldn't be, but I am."

He chuckled. "Well, I seem to be able to control myself for the moment. Perhaps we should move on to my plans for the evening. That is, unless you're hungry."

"No," I replied. It seemed like I hadn't been hungry in days.

He offered his hand and I took it. He led me to steps that seemed to spiral down forever. A shudder went through me. "The prison?" I asked in a shaky voice.

"Shh," he hushed. "You won't be alone this time."

"This place makes me sick. The Drawing is very wrong down there."

He stopped at the top step and turned to me, brushing his thumb over my lips. "I shouldn't have left you here as punishment," he said. "It will never happen again."

I kissed his thumb. "Thank you."

"I'll come up with something better," he continued with a twinkle, leading me down.

"Jackass."

He laughed and it echoed off of the walls. Immediately, the temperature dropped. I tried to distract myself from the dread I felt. "So, will you tell me what we're doing tonight?" I asked.

"You're going to help me with a punishment," he said. "I think you may enjoy this assignment."

"I don't know about that. I'm not much into punishing," I said.

"You seemed to enjoy disciplining Victor," he pointed out.

I felt my face grow hot. "I dominated him; there's a difference. He actually enjoyed himself."

"Well, this time I'm hoping that *you* enjoy *yourself*."

We walked down a little longer. I needed more conversation if I was going to keep control of my nerves. "This Architect who sparked your addiction. Have I met her?"

He smiled at me. "In fact, you have."

"Who was she?" I asked.

We came to the door where Carl and Joan waited. "Has someone been bad again?" Carl asked hopefully.

"Only Ghalib," I answered pertly.

Joan smirked at me and I winked at her. Carl opened the door for us. It was so different down here from how it was up in the main part of the house. The Drawing wasn't white wisps of smoke that wreathed everything like ribbons; it was more like a sickly, yellow miasma. I shuddered. I didn't want to walk through it.

Ghalib looked at me when I stopped walking. "The Drawing is tainted down here," I said as a weak attempt at an explanation.

"This is where people can go to explore their darkest, most depraved dreams. The Drawing isn't tainted here; it's flavored," he explained.

I closed my eyes and tried to think of it in those terms. I couldn't understand it. It was like taking the most delicious white cake and adding mud to the mix.

He started leading me down the hall and I concentrated on the vibrating energy where our hands touched. It gave me a little bit of respite from the nauseating negativity. When we passed into the corridor with cells on one side and stone wall on the other, Ghalib smiled at me. "You were wondering about the Architect who first sparked my addiction," he reminded me. "You're about to see her."

I must have made a confused face because he laughed. Was he telling me that there was an Architect down here in the prison? He drew me on and I followed. Finally, he stopped me in front of an empty cell. "Stay here," he whispered in my ear. He dropped a light kiss on my lips, producing a breath of Drawing, and continued down the corridor alone.

A few cells away, he stopped. He crossed his arms and grinned at whoever was inside. They didn't seem to appreciate his smirk.

"Damn it, Ghalib, you sonofabitch! How dare you leave me here like this!"

I struggled to place the voice. It was familiar. Female.

"I grew busy," Ghalib said with his careless air.

"I could feel your busyness," she said. "Do you never stop screwing your Omnilight?"

My face grew hot.

"Not if I can help it," Ghalib replied, nonplussed. "She's an amazing creature. Besides, I told you not to come back here. You should heed what I say."

"I knew you didn't mean it," she said more softly. "The novelty of your pet will wear off eventually."

He snorted. "You have no idea what you're talking about. However, I'm about to educate you."

Ghalib faced me and held out a hand. I walked to him and took it, finally facing the cell.

Alexis. Stripped and bound and hanging from the ceiling by chains. Her legs were long and slim. Her dark curls fell to her waist and her breasts were larger than mine. She looked down on me with contempt.

"Don't you dare, Ghalib," Alexis spat. "You will not let your cunt whore touch me."

Anger rose in me and with it, the power that Nyx had given me. I narrowed my eyes at her. "I am *not* a cunt whore," I bit back at her. "I am an Omnilight. I deserve respect and you *will* give it to me.

Chapter 32
Broken

Ghalib chuckled. "I think I like you even better when you're heated," he said.

My face was burning with anger instead of embarrassment, for once. Alexis was bound and hung and completely powerless. She chose this position, throwing herself at Ghalib, and she had the audacity to call me a whore.

I touched the prison door and it sprung open. Ghalib shot me a look of surprise but I ignored him. It seemed like the most natural thing in the world, now, that the prison should respond to my will. I walked over to Alexis. I ran my hand down her back, feeling her emotion. She loathed me. She felt like I was the reason that Ghalib no longer wanted her.

"Don't touch me, you piece of filth," she snarled.

"It isn't because of me that he doesn't want you," I told her.

"Shut up."

"It's true," I said. I came around to the front of her. So beautiful. Powerful in her own right and willing to give it all away. She, too, wanted what she had with Ghalib all those centuries ago. She wanted him to beg for her and she hadn't accepted that things had changed. "Is this really better than not having him at all?" I asked, gesturing to the chains.

She spat on me. It landed on my shoulder. Rage flashed. I slapped her as hard as I could, then I backhanded her other cheek. My palm hurt and I watched as a mist of Drawing rolled off of her.

"You like abuse," I said. It wasn't a question.

"Lying bitch," Alexis hissed.

I stepped up to her quickly and covered her mouth with my hand. "You can't fib to me, Alexis. I can see your arousal." My eyes met hers and I saw fear.

Ghalib stepped into the cell and wiped the spittle off my shoulder with his sleeve. "Then it's Victor you want," he said. "Not me. I don't know why you're so hostile towards him."

I felt her thoughts and gave a dry laugh. Alexis protested behind my hand but I ignored her. "She was enjoying the pain when he hurt her. He doesn't like it when people aren't shivering and frightened of him. He refused to practice his sadism on her. She refused to go back."

She bit the hand I held over her mouth, making me bleed. "Fuck you," she growled at me, struggling against the chains. "If you touch me again, I'll fucking kill you."

I wiped my bloody palm on her chest, calling her empty threat. I lifted my eyebrows while she made the chains rattle, trying to get at me. "I don't actually need to touch you, Alexis."

I gathered the Drawing—the yellowed, oily prison Drawing mixed with the pearly, white Drawing that drifted off of Alexis. My mind wove it into a long lash. I snapped against her backside. She squealed and jumped. "What the fuck was that?" she demanded.

"That was me," I told her, "and I'm just getting started." A breath of Drawing rolled off of her and I wove it into my ribbon. Again, I whipped her backside, harder this time. She actually yelled. Drawing seeped out of her but I didn't let it linger around her. I gathered it into my lash and continued to thrash her with it.

I flogged the back of her legs, raising welts on her creamy skin, collecting her pleasure to create more pain, to mix it with the negative, twisted Drawing of the prison. Ghalib watched first me then her, his cheeks tinged with pink. He seemed to struggle with himself, swaying towards me and pulling himself back as Alexis broke out in a sweat, yelling curses at me. Finally, he walked behind me and ran his fingers up the back of my neck and onto my scalp. "Don't stop," he said in a low voice. "I want to see what you're doing to her." He pressed his fingers against my head.

I brought the ribbon around to the front of Alexis and snapped it on her breast. She shrieked. Her nipple came to a tawny point. I repeated it on her other breast. Ghalib gave a shuddery sigh behind me. "That is very creative," he said.

He stepped up even closer to me. His need pressed against my backside. His one hand stayed pressed against my scalp but the other played restlessly with my skirt, pulling up the hem. The Drawing in the cell increased, vapor pouring off of me and Ghalib, and with it the length and breadth of my whip increased, too.

I snapped the lash again, moving lower, striking her stomach, her hip, coming dangerously close to her pubis. "Alright, dammit! Call off your bitch," Alexis cried, her voice still angry, but also husky. I stopped the whipping, and looked at Ghalib.

His fingers touched my bare thigh. I gave a shuddery gasp. "She's not my bitch, Alexis. She's my pet. *You're* my bitch. I would like to sever that relationship, but you seem determined to demean yourself."

"Once upon a time, you were begging me," she reminded him.

"Once upon a time, you were interesting," he retorted.

She froze and her lips parted. After what I had done to her, Ghalib's comment was the thing that had really hurt her. "How can you say that?" she asked.

"Because it's true, Alexis. I'm so very bored with you."

"Not long ago I entertained you for the whole night while your pet was away," Alexis said, her voice quavering. "Was I so boring then?"

Ghalib's voice was cold. "If you hadn't visited that night, I would have taken a servant. You're nothing more to me than an orifice."

Her eyes filled with tears. I was torn into two pieces. On the one hand, she was a vile, hateful creature and deserved anything she got. On the other hand, she groveled for him to use her and absorbed every sort of abuse. It was a little bit pathetic.

"I think we're done here, Elaine," Ghalib said, pressing on me to move.

"Could I...."

He came around to the front of me. "What is it?" he asked.

"Could I have a moment alone with Alexis?"

He cocked his head at me. "Are you sure about that?" he asked. I nodded. "All right. I'll meet you by the guard."

After Ghalib left the cell I noticed a tear streaking Alexis' cheek. "What?" she snapped.

I walked over to her and touched her shackles. They sprung open. She stumbled a little and I caught her. "You deserve better than this," I said, lowering her to the ground.

"Fuck you," she replied, but I could tell that her heart wasn't really in it.

"Go home. Stop doing this to yourself." I smoothed her hair out of her face. I didn't have to fear her, so I could just feel badly for her.

I left her there on the cell floor and made my way out to Ghalib.

Ghalib didn't ask me what went on in the cell after he left and I didn't offer the information. Instead, he took me upstairs to a dining room and asked for some food. I still wasn't hungry but when they carried in the dishes, the smell was too good to resist.

"So," Ghalib said after I had nearly finished my soup, "I hear you didn't nap alone this afternoon."

I laid down my spoon. "Is there nothing you don't know?" I asked.

"My spies are everywhere."

I looked at him directly. "Am I in trouble?"

He tented his fingers and rested his chin on them. "My spies tell me all you did was sleep in the bed together."

"She was lonely. Her room is so Spartan. I offered her my library and sitting room but she just wanted to cuddle."

"And I find myself jealous."

I couldn't help but smile, even though I knew how dangerous his jealousy could be. "Are you telling me that you need a snuggle, Ghalib?" I teased.

He flushed lightly.

I tilted my head, suddenly taking him a bit more seriously. "Really?" I had never seen him look so uncomfortable. I looked at him a moment longer and made a sudden decision. "Push your chair back," I told him.

I didn't expect him to agree but he obeyed almost immediately.

I came around the table and sat on his lap. I pulled his head down to my chest and held it there. His arms went around me. I wasn't prepared for my reaction.

"Your heart is like a rabbit's," he said softly.

I stroked his hair and didn't answer. I knew why I hadn't touched him this way sooner; it was so personal. His cheek was against my breast but, for once, it wasn't sexual. I hardly knew how to react.

Around us, the Drawing began to gather. The mist that had been dissipated throughout the room crawled slowly towards us. It enveloped us and I got the warm, comfortable sensation of being wrapped in a blanket fresh out of the drier. It wasn't the wild shivering Drawing I was used to. If this Drawing had been an animal, it would have purred.

My heart pounded harder. This wasn't erotic but it was very intimate. Fear gripped me for no reason I could define. I tried to stand but Ghalib's arms tightened around me. "Please don't run from me," he said.

My breathing picked up. I felt trapped but I forced myself to relax back into his arms. He sighed. "I'm doing my very best," I replied. "Every time I get used to how things are between us, it feels like you change it."

He chuckled. His hands started to wander and the Drawing started to vibrate. He kissed my breasts through the material of my bodice.

"Much better," I said in a throaty voice. "Thank you."

"Anytime."

I stood and went back to my soup. "How about you?" I asked. "Better?"

"Yes. My jealousy seems to have completely abated."

We made it through the rest of the meal with just light conversation. I couldn't help but remember how uncomfortable I used to be eating with him. Spending time with him. How his admiring eyes drove me to tremble. It was like I had been another person entirely.

Just as I was beginning to wonder if our evening was over, Ghalib turned a serious face towards me. "We have an invitation this evening and I'm afraid that we cannot decline."

"Where are we going?" I asked.

"A breaking ceremony. It's when—"

"I know. When the link between an Architect and a pet is severed," I said, remembering the stories of Stephania and her collection of Pets. "So, who is severing their link?"

He gave a sad smile. "Anna and Julia."

My lips fell open. They had seemed so good together. Affectionate and sweet. It was like hearing your favorite couple was getting a divorce. "No," I breathed.

"I can't help but feel a little responsible."

"This isn't your fault," I said, cold hardness entering my tone. "This is entirely on Anna. She should have protected her pet."

"That isn't how Anna tends to be," Ghalib replied.

"And that's why she's been through so many girls."

Ghalib shook his head. "I'll admit that I wasn't sure of Julia when she was introduced to me. She is much more head-strong than Anna's usual choices. But, after a while, I saw how well they worked. I had hoped it would last through Julia's life."

I sighed. "Do we do anything as part of this ceremony?" I asked.

"You'll witness. I'll help collect her memories so she doesn't remember us. Hopefully, it won't last long."

He stood up from the table and offered me an arm. I stood and took his arm. The disorientation I usually felt when he transported me didn't bother me this time. I just felt a blast of wind in my face and when I opened my eyes, I was standing around a circular reflecting pool with a dozen other architects. There were no other pets. Anna and Julia stood off to one side; they weren't talking.

I turned to Ghalib. "May I go and talk to Julia or would that be bad etiquette?"

"Go ahead," Ghalib said.

I walked away from the Architects, feeling their eyes follow me. When Julia saw me she smiled a sad, small smile. "I'm glad you came," she said.

I hugged her. "I'm so sorry. What happened?"

"Anna is cruel and I'm tired of overlooking it."

Anna's blue eyes snapped towards us. "That is the role of a pet," she said coldly. It seemed to me like they'd had this conversation before. "You serve my needs and I make sure you want for nothing."

"Well then, you didn't do your part because I wanted for kindness."

Anna turned away.

"Are you sure about this?" I asked.

Julia nodded. "I can't trust her. If I can't trust her, being forced to obey her just becomes torture. I'll go back to being a waitress. At least I'll have my self-respect."

Another Architect appeared next to the reflecting pool. "They're all here," Anna said.

Julia squeezed my hand. "I think I'll miss you most of all, Omni-light," she said lightly.

I kissed her lips and smoothed her ruddy curls. "Good luck."

Julia walked to the reflecting pool without Anna. I turned to follow but Anna put a hand on my shoulder. "Elaine, the breaking ceremony is painful for the pet. I brought some Amorite. Do you think you could help her through it?"

"I will," I said. "I don't need the Amorite anymore." I bit my lip. "Why don't you just apologize? This is silly."

Anna shook her head. "That isn't how I work."

"You're being very foolish," I told her.

Anna lowered her eyes and walked away. Fourteen Architects stood around the reflecting pool. Anna and Julia stood in the middle of the ankle-deep water. I stayed back, watching the ribbons of Drawing float around.

Anna spoke in a clear, cool voice. "We're here to sever the ties between Julia and I, Pet and Master, mortal and Architect." She turned to Julia. "This will end your connection to the In-Between. Do you understand?"

"Yes," Julia said.

"This will end our joining, my obligation to you, and your obedience to me. Do you understand?"

"I do."

"Say that you do this of your own free will."

Julia took a breath. "I do this of my own free will."

"You no longer belong to me," Anna said, her voice quavering for the first time. "You no longer serve at the pleasure of your mistress."

Julia yelped in pain and I got a little closer. Her collar, the triple layer of pearls she had worn since I met her at the Festival of Pets, peeled up at the back of her neck, taking a layer of skin with it. Blood ran down Julia's back, spotting the low neckline of her white dress.

Anna didn't need to look at me. I brought the ribbons of Drawing down around Julia. I wrapped them around her neck and circled her body with them. I didn't even have to concentrate on melting her halo. I knew the Drawing couldn't take the pain away, but it would at least make it more tolerable.

Julia looked over at me and mouthed, 'thank you'. I concentrated to keep her tightly wrapped in Drawing while Anna peeled the collar away. Blood flowed freely, soaking her dress, dripping into the reflecting pool. Julia moaned, sweat standing out on her skin, but she didn't yell again. It took far too long to strip the collar away, but I could tell that Anna was trying to be gentle. When she finally had the bloody collar free, Julia was pale.

"Quickly," Anna said, steadying Julia.

Balls of light flew out of Julia and each of the surrounding Architects did their part in catching the balls. I remembered what Ghalib had said, that he would be collecting memories at the ceremony so that Julia wouldn't remember us. As each Architect caught the memories, they crushed them, letting the dust crumble to the ground. The balls of light flew out slower and slower, until they stopped altogether.

Then, Anna released Julia's arm and stepped away from her. Julia fell like someone had dropped a trap-door under her. One minute she was there and the next, her head disappeared under the water. Julia was gone.

For a moment, there was nothing but silence. Then, Anna lifted her eyes from the pool, looked around at the other Architects, and said, "Thank you for your witness and help. I wish to be alone now."

As quickly as the Architects arrived, they left. Silent, without a word, they just disappeared. It was as if everyone there could feel Anna's pain. Ghalib looked over his shoulder at me, then walked over to Anna.

"I saved this one for you," Ghalib said, handing Anna one of the balls of light.

Anna put her hand over it. For a moment I wondered if she would crush it, but she didn't. She took it and cradled it in two hands, like a baby bird. "Thank you, Ghalib."

He walked over to me. "Ready, Pet?"

I nodded. He took my arm and, again, I felt the blast of air in my face. I didn't close my eyes against it this time and I could actually watch the dining room forming around me. It was the exact room we had just left, except now there was dessert laid out on the table. It was a slice of carrot cake. My favorite. And I really didn't want it.

I was shaken. I took a breath. "Would you mind if I—"

"Please stay, Elaine," Ghalib said. "If you can't eat, just sit with me."

I sat at the table and started playing with the cake with my fork. He sat down, too, but didn't touch the food at all. "There isn't a breaking ceremony for Omnilights," he volunteered.

"I know. Anna told me."

"But, if it were possible for you to break with me, would you want to?" he asked.

I hesitated. I *did* have the chance to break with him. Right now, I could go back to the mortal world if I wanted to. I wasn't entirely sure why I hadn't done it yet.

I tasted Ghalib's emotions. He was insecure.

"And do what?" I finally asked. "Go back to my life as a secretary? I don't know if I could."

"So you would stay here because it is more interesting than your mortal life?" he replied.

I dropped my fork with a clatter. "Why don't you ask me what you really want to know?"

He looked up at me, his eyes intense. His gaze burnt my skin. "What is that?"

"If I'm fond enough of you to stay with you voluntarily."

He didn't blink or look away. I couldn't either. "Well?" he finally said.

"Order me to do something."

"Elaine—"

"Order me to do something," I repeated.

"Come here," he ordered. "Sit on my lap."

I was tempted but it was very easy to shake off the temptation. I stood and walked to the door of the dining room. I opened it and looked back, feeling the collar loosen on my neck and tighten again. Ghalib's eyes were wide.

"I *am* here voluntarily, Ghalib. And every time I obey you, *that's* voluntary, too." I walked through the door and shut it behind me. Then I went back to my room, dismissed Lisa, changed my clothes, and sat alone thinking about the situation I was trapped in.

Chapter 33
Unfinished Business

After a few hours of staring at my wall, I stopped denying what I needed to do: see my sister. It was selfish of me to have waited this long since Nyx gave me the power to leave. It took hours of painfully honest thinking to realize that I didn't really want to go back to the physical world to live; seeing my sister may compel me otherwise and it was the reason why I hadn't made the trip so far.

I had to admit, being a pet in the In-Between was easier than being a responsible adult in the physical world. There were no choices required of me. There wasn't any responsibility. As much as I loved my sister, I was tired of responsibility. I had given up everything to raise her: college, relationships, even a better career. And now, it seemed that fate had asked me to make that choice again. Would I choose to be a loving, supportive sister or would I choose this pleasure-drenched existence? It didn't seem fair that I had to choose.

Besides, how would I explain my absence to Rachel? I couldn't tell the truth. She would think that I was insane. Literally insane. Even if I didn't tell her about the In-Between, the Dream Architects and the Drawing, she would be mystified at how I could stay with my kidnapper. And if I were her, I would feel the same way.

There was one way around the shirking responsibility without returning to the physical world: I could accept Dionysia's offer and replace her as the Nyx. As Nyx, I could finally have all of it: freedom, means, and power. However, it would be a double betrayal: both Ghalib and Rachel would be hurt by that choice. Only Dionysia would be pleased. But, after two thousand years, didn't she deserve that?

Abandon Ghalib and Dionysia for Rachel? Abandon Rachel and

Dionysia for Ghalib? Abandon Rachel and Ghalib for Dionysia? My mind circled endlessly, unable to come up with an outcome that I could live with.

I couldn't get around the idea that leaving Rachel felt like an abandonment of her. It was stupid. She was a woman, now. She had a husband. But responsibility for her wouldn't just slip off of my shoulders. I was the only person who knew all of her fears. I knew why she woke screaming in the middle of the night when she was fourteen. I knew that she loved peanut butter on her waffles. I knew how to make her laugh, even when she was in a dark, depressed mood.

Even if I felt responsibility to my sister, didn't I have a greater responsibility to the in-Between? They *needed* a Nyx. Dionysia didn't want to play that part any longer. All of the In-Between and the physical world relied on the flow of the Drawing.

It was all true, but it wasn't the reason why I wanted to stay.

My sad, selfish, painful truth was that I enjoyed the strangeness of the In-Between. After thirty years of dull work and painful struggle, Ghalib's world was more vibrant and interesting than anything I had ever experienced. Even without being an Omnilight, I think I would have enjoyed the endless possibility that the In-Between represented. Shame settled over me for being so weak. My brain spun like this for hours.

Finally, I decided that I simply had to see Rachel. I couldn't be a coward about this. No matter what my final choice was, I had to see my only family again. Quickly, before I could talk myself out of it, I thought of Rachel's home. Her sweet little house with her husband, Jackson. I imagined the yard and visualized myself there. I closed my eyes and concentrated. I waited, afraid that Nyx had been wrong about my ability and equally afraid that she had been right. Finally, I heard the sound: that strange cracking that was like being on the inside of an egg peeling open.

I opened my eyes and I was there. I was in Rachel's front yard, standing inside of her gate. For the first time in I didn't even know how long, I was in the physical realm alone. The night sky was hazy and starless. The colors were duller than I remembered; the solidness more unyielding. The air was humid. I was struck by a strong sense of freedom. I could call the police. I could announce that I was safe. I could go to my apartment. I could hug my sister.

I hadn't expected for there to be Drawing in the physical world but it was there. Wisps, only. Probably snatches of the energy that came back with dreamers. It didn't matter, because no human could feel it. No human but me. I played with the smoky vapor, rolling it into cork-screws. It was good to know that at least that much of the In-Between had come with me and that I still had control over it.

I crept up to the open window of Rachel's' and Jackson's living room and looked inside. I could only see the back of Rachel's head but I knew it was her. Jackson sat on the couch with her, watching television. Oscar, their cat, slept on the back of the couch. I could tell Rachel and Jackson were holding hands. Relief flooded me at the sight of my sister.

"I'm thinking that if it's a girl, I want to call the baby Elaine," Rachel was saying.

"What if it's a boy?" Jackson asked.

"I was thinking maybe Bart, for the man who tried to save her on the bus."

"I didn't know that you liked the name Bart," he said.

She shrugged. A little sound, like a sob, escaped her. I cringed.

Jackson put his arm around her and held her close. "The police don't know if she's dead, Rach. They could still find her."

"They could," she said doubtfully, sniffling. "But they have no idea who took her. There's no sign of where they went."

"If it's really a sicko with an obsession for her, like the police said, he might not kill her. He might just keep her. We could still get her back."

Jackson had a tired sound to his voice, like this was a ritual they went through every night. I had always liked my brother-in-law. And I liked him twice as much now. It took a bit of energy to stay ahead of Rachel's negativity. I was grateful that she had him.

"I don't know if that's any better," she muttered. "If we don't find her, he could torture her for years."

"Don't think like that."

"She took care of me. I let her do it too long. She gave up stuff for me even when I was old enough to take more responsibility."

"Rach—"

"I just wish that I could show her that I can be selfless, too."

Jackson turned on the couch. "Stop doing this to yourself." His voice was almost harsh. "She knows what a great person you are."

"I know," she said quietly. "I just don't know if she knows what a great person I think *she* is."

They quietly watched the television a little longer and I spied on them from the window. He kissed the top of her head every once in a while and she shifted, as if she was uncomfortable.

As I stood there watching them, I knew that I couldn't go inside and talk to Rachel. It would be the ultimate in cruelty to show up like that and disappear without any explanation. That would be what I had to do if I didn't want to stay in the physical world. The longer I stood here, feeling the weight and dullness, the density of matter and the lack of Drawing, the more I knew that my future lie in the In-Between. Whether as Nyx or as Ghalib's pet, I wasn't sure. But I just couldn't stay here.

I suddenly accepted that my responsibility for Rachel was past. Distance had given me perspective. She wasn't my grieving thirteen year old sister who needed me; she was a strong woman with a life of her own. She would be fine. She didn't need me to take care of her any longer.

There was only one thing to be done before I could leave. I needed to find a way to ease her worry. I wanted to lure Jackson outside so that I could talk to him alone. Even as I considered how to do it, I knew that it was a bad idea. He loved Rachel; he would never accept me leaving without seeing her. And how could I blame him? Besides, what could I say? I couldn't tell them the truth. There wasn't a lie that would fit and let me return to the In-Between tonight. A note would be equally as useless. My mind raced for a solution.

I couldn't show up, but I might be able to talk to her if I could get my hands on a cell phone. I peeked through the window one more time and backed out of their yard. I wanted to cry and laugh at the same time. It was like how I felt at High School graduation, knowing that one life was behind me now and a relative unknown was before me. That some things had to be given up so that other things can be gained.

I knew that I probably could have transported myself to some public place to find a person with a cell phone but I decided to walk. It cleared my head and calmed me down. I didn't want to be crying on the phone with her. It didn't take long for me to find a twenty-four hour convenience store with several people milling around inside. One young man stood outside, smoking a cigarette.

This was just the sort of man that I avoided in the past, for fear of what they might say or do to me. Now, I had no fear. I brought the Drawing with me when I approached him. I melted the halo around him when he looked up at me and watched the color flood his pale face.

"Hello," I said.

"What's up?" he replied, looking me up and down. It was almost laughable how little effect it had on me after Ghalib's heated looks.

"I was wondering. You wouldn't happen to have a cell phone I could borrow, do you?"

"I might," he replied. "You using it to call your boyfriend?"

"No," I said, neither denying of admitting the presence of a boyfriend. "My sister."

He made a low, approving sound. "Yeah, you can use my phone."

He handed it to me and I let the Drawing tickle him. "Thanks," I said. "It won't take a minute."

I dialed my sister's number. My heart actually pounded. It was Jackson who answered. I lowered my voice and tried to make it sound gruff. "May I speak to Rachel?"

"Hold on."

In a moment, I heard my sister's voice. "Hello."

I swallowed twice before I responded. "Hey, Rach. It's Elaine."

"Oh my God! Are you OK? Where are you?" She pulled the mouthpiece away from her face. "It's Elaine!"

"I'm fine. I'm not hurt." My mind flashed to what Ghalib would think of that comment.

"Did you escape? What happened? I've been freaking out here for three months!"

Three months. Longer than I thought. "I wish I could tell you what happened to me," I said slowly. "But I can't. I just wanted you to know that I'm well and I'm not going to be home for..." *Ever?* "A very long time."

"What?"

"I love you, Rachel. You're the best sister anyone could have asked for. If I had it to do over again, I would do everything exactly the same."

"No, Elaine. Where are you? Let us come and get you."

"I'll keep an eye on you when I can. Jackson is a great husband and your baby is going to be a beautiful boy. Stop buying pink things for your kid."

"Wait. Please. Don't just disappear again."

"I have to. It sucks, but I do. I miss you so much and I love you all the time."

"I love you, too Elaine." Her voice hitched into a sob. I couldn't take hearing her cry. So even though I could have told her a million other things, I ended the call. Quickly, before the guy with the cigarette could say anything to me, I erased her number from his phone.

"Thanks," I said, handing it back to him. "I really appreciate it."

"Enough to go have a drink with me? Talk about our future together?"

It was just the lightness I needed to melt the lump in my throat. "No," I said, smirking at him. "Not quite that much." I gathered the Drawing to him and waited until his breath grew ragged again. Then I stepped close to him, the way that Ghalib did with me during our early days together. Slowly, and for longer than was casual, I kissed him on the lips. Then I broke the kiss, grinned at him, and said, "Thanks again."

I went behind the convenience store. There was a little alley with a dumpster. I closed my eyes and imagined my bedroom in Ghalib's mansion. I thought of the draping plants that covered the window and scented the air. I thought of the comfortable bed and the pale rugs on the floor. I visualized it as clearly as I could. In a moment, I heard the sounds of the splintering between the physical world and the In-Between. And, much to my relief, when I opened my eyes, I was back in my suite in Ghalib's home. I was alone. If I was lucky, nobody even knew that I had gone.

I laid on the bed but I couldn't close my eyes. I couldn't cry, either, even though the ache in my chest hurt. I was still thinking about the life I had abandoned and the duty I had left behind while the light in my window went from black to gray.

Chapter 34
Reward for Good Behavior

Lisa came in early and urged me to try to sleep. I didn't think I was tired but when I closed my eyes, unconsciousness took me. And when I woke the whole next day was gone. Lisa was sifting through my closet for a gown. I had this evening, another day, and another evening before I had to make my choice before Nyx.

"What do you think, Miss?" Lisa asked, holding up a glittering red gown. It was cheerful and beautiful and just the dress I needed.

"Yes. Perfect," I said. I let her dress me and sweep my hair up on my head. I didn't even have to think about how I looked, I had such confidence in Lisa's skill.

"Thank you," I said. "You always do such a good job." She colored at the compliment.

I could tell Ghalib was in the hallway, so I didn't wait for him to knock on the door. I went out to him. I expected some sort of confrontation because of my display the night before. I thought he might insist on knowing how I resisted him or demand another demonstration of my power but that didn't turn out to be the case.

He held himself with a confident mien that was reminiscent of my first days here. He wore a tuxedo. His eyes swept over me twice before they lit with approval on my face. "Come here, Elaine," he commanded.

I obeyed and felt his unrestrained delight. Delight that I obeyed when I wasn't forced to. When I reached him, he kissed me with heat. The Drawing roiled around us. He held my arms at my side, then restrained both wrists with one hand so that he could caress down one side of my neck as he kissed down the other. I was amazed at how much his touch affected me. Confusion and frustration slipped away.

"Needing a fix?" I asked breathlessly when his lips nipped at my neck.

"I decided not to worry about the future and enjoy the present," he murmured against my skin. "I've hunted this feeling for so long, I won't ruin it by worrying about it."

He kissed my ear, biting my earring. "That's the spirit," I gasped.

He chuckled and released my arms. I tried to bring my breathing back to a normal rhythm. "You were so tense last night," he said. "I could feel you fretting."

"I was just bothered by Anna and Julia," I lied. I held my breath, hoping he hadn't sensed my excursion out of the In-Between.

"I used you terribly with Alexis and caused you stress, so tonight will be about your relaxation," he said. "Christine and I have a whole programme planned for you."

I lifted my eyebrows. "Christine and you...."

Christine came out of her room in a glittering white dress, her gold hair piled on her head and her cheeks pink with excitement. "Did you tell her?" she asked excitedly.

"Not yet," Ghalib said, his voice indulgent. "I thought we would show her."

She giggled and clapped her hands like a child. I was happy to see her happy. I gave her a quick squeeze. "You look lovely," I told her.

"And you're just dazzling," she replied.

"Come along, ladies," Ghalib said, leading us through the house. Christine took my hand, twining her fingers through mine. When we reached the main hallway, Jason and Lisa joined us. Christine smiled a conspirator's smile but didn't say anything.

We walked outside of the mansion and though I thought we might go down to the beach, Ghalib led us in another direction. Inland. Before long, we reached a ridge. A trail led steeply down.

"You may want to give me your shoes and clothes, Miss," Lisa said, grinning.

I looked towards Ghalib and Christine, who were already stripping. "Are we doing naked hiking?" I asked.

"No questions, Elaine," Ghalib said with mock sternness.

I pulled my shoes off and handed them to Lisa. Then my sparkling red dress. Finally, my lacy, red undergarments. Ghalib watched me; he was already naked, looking like something Michelangelo might have carved. Christine was equally stunning, everything about her pert. I stood up straight. "All right," I said. "Now what?"

Ghalib took my hand and led me down the steep trail. There was foliage all around but it was soft and flowery. The air smelled like nectar. And the ground was soft dirt without a single rock. After a few moments, the steepness leveled off and we came into a clearing.

A wide, deep pool of mud, the size of a tiny lake lay before us. It was a gray-green color and I felt warm humidity rising from it. A mist lay over the surface. "Get in," Ghalib said. "You'll love it."

"A mud bath?" I asked.

Ghalib came up behind me, his nudity pressed casually to mine. "It's not just any mud," he said, his mouth and nose buried in the softest part of my hair. "Try it."

I stepped forward and as soon as my foot touched the mud, I knew he was right. It was soft and warm and infused with Drawing—the calm Drawing I had experienced the night before. The kind that swirled around Markus. I sighed and stepped in deeper. Ghalib followed behind me. He helped me ease my body into the velvety, warm semi-liquid until I was shoulder deep.

I don't know how he got into a sitting position, but he pulled me onto his lap, letting the buoyancy of the mud suspend me there. I stretched my legs out and flexed my ankles. The Drawing felt like fingers over me, hands soothing me. "Oh, my God," I sighed. "How marvelous."

Christine waded into the pool until she was next to my legs and she started massaging my calves. I glanced back at Ghalib. "She got a lesson in massage today while you were sleeping," he said.

"She's a fast learner," I said, feeling the tension drain out of me. Ghalib's hands slipped around me and he stroked my body. My heart beat faster but not in an insistent way. My body tingled.

"I can feel your pleasure," Ghalib said in a low voice. "You're flavoring the Drawing. I feel like I'm sitting in a pool of contentment."

Christine looked up. "Would you like to feel it?" I asked her.

She flushed. "Yes, please."

"You must tell me if it's too intense," I said. I melted the halo around her and her eyes closed.

She drew in a long, slow breath but her fingers never stopped working on my legs. "It's wonderful," she said, taking deep breaths. "It's perfect."

Ghalib stroked me. His fingers ran over my breasts, over my thighs. He didn't touch me to bring me to climax but to please my skin. I started to feel like a very satisfied cat.

Christine's fingers worked on the tension in my legs, moving from my right to my left. She rubbed a particularly stubborn knot. "Mmmm," I breathed, my eyes closed.

"You can't make noises like that," Ghalib whispered in my ear. "I can barely contain myself as it is."

"I can't help it," I murmured. "This is heavenly. I'm going to have to insist that you stress me out more often if this is my reward."

He kissed behind my ear. "We're not done."

"Mmm," I moaned again, teasing him.

Ghalib's hands didn't stop and he nuzzled my hair. "We have bushels of invitations but I am desperate for a night alone with you. Tomorrow? Just the two of us without even Christine?"

"I'm your pet. You don't have to ask me."

He turned me so I faced him, pulling my legs out of Christine's grasp. "I *am* asking you," he said.

His emerald eyes searched me. Heat came into my face and I felt a shyness I hadn't felt since I first arrived here in the in-between. "Yes," I said softly.

A little smile played on his lips. We just looked at each other. It felt like time stopped.

"Are we getting out?" Christine asked, wading over.

"We are," Ghalib said without looking away from me.

After another beat, he helped me to my feet. We were covered in gray-green mud, so much so that I didn't even feel naked. Ghalib took my right hand and Christine took my left. He led us along the edge of the mud pool and down another soft trail, like three golems.

The blossoming foliage parted again and there was a pool of crystal clear water. Steam rose off the water and in places, the surface bubbled. "Mineral springs," Christine said happily.

"The only way to clean off after a mud bath," Ghalib added.

They led me into the water. It was warm, like a bathtub, almost. The bottom of the pool was covered in smooth stones and in places, jets of warm water shot up from the ground. We swam around, even though in most places the water didn't come higher than my chest. We left trails of mud as we moved and helped each other clear mud from the places we couldn't reach.

Ghalib swam up behind me, wrapping his arms around me and pulling me backwards. "Ghalib!" I shrieked, laughing, trying to get my footing under me. He kept my head above water but I had no control over where he was pulling me.

Christine bounced after us, looking playful. We ended up in a shallow place, where the water was just up to my hips. "Get on your knees," Ghalib ordered. "Spread your legs."

I obeyed, only my neck and head above water. His elation jumped again at my obedience. Christine knelt in front of me, so we were eye-to-eye, and she pulled me forward by my hips.

A jet of warm water hit me between my legs. "Oh, God," I gasped. Ghalib knelt behind me, his hands cupping my inner thighs, opening me, moving my hips in slow circles over the jet. Tentatively, Christine drew her fingers over my breasts and leaned in to kiss me. I moaned against her lips.

The jet of water was relentless. Ghalib's hands moved me masterfully; I didn't fight him, even though my body wanted to find its own rhythm. He pressed himself against my back and we rolled our hips together like we were dancing. Ghalib's erection pressed against my backside; it was almost as if I could feel it throbbing.

The Drawing rolled off of me; reflexively, I gathered it to us. Christine's fingers grew bolder on my breasts, kneading them as she kissed me. Ghalib's rhythm grew faster. His lips were on my neck; Christine's were on my cheeks.

The slow build to orgasm was delicious and teasing. I rose and hovered. When the climax finally crashed over me the cries ripped from my throat. Ghalib didn't change the rhythm, even when I peaked and it stretched the orgasm even longer. When I was done, I slumped back against him and he pulled me away from the jet.

"Are you feeling more relaxed?" Ghalib asked.

"I'm not even sure I still have muscles," I replied.

Ghalib led us out of the pool on a pebbly path. At the end, Jason and Lisa waited with our clothes and towels. We dried off quickly, slipped back into our evening clothes, and headed back to the mansion.

"Oh, that was too much fun," Christine said, giving a little skip.

"Are you hungry, now?" Ghalib asked.

"I am," Christine said. "Are you, Elaine?"

Hunger was starting to be less and less of an issue for me. Still, I had to remind myself that I was mortal. And that at least Christine still needed to eat. "Food sounds good," I replied.

We went up to the mansion and Ghalib led us to a room with glass walls. Greenery decorated the room. I felt Lisa's hand in this. The blooming tree in the corner looked like one in my room. In the evening light, with candles on the table, it was simply breathtaking.

We ate finger-food and chatted. I discovered that Christine had lived in a tiny rural community. She'd never flown in an airplane or stayed the night in a hotel. Her most adventurous experience was the night she lost her virginity with her boyfriend, who lost his virginity that night, too.

"I thought I was going to marry him," she said, pink coloring her cheeks. "I don't see how I possibly could now."

"Do you like it here?" I asked.

"I didn't like it at Victor's." Her face flamed even brighter. "But, I really like it here with you two. I wouldn't choose to go home."

"Nor will you have to," Ghalib said affectionately. "Elaine and I have been enjoying you very much." Christine's smile was the sweetest and most delighted I had ever seen.

Christine took a deep breath. "I was wondering... I mean...." She lowered her eyes, as if she was sure she would be denied.

Ghalib lifted her chin. "What is it, little one?"

"Would you mind if I explore when you don't need me?" she asked. "It gets dull just looking at my room."

"Good luck with that," I grumbled. "These hallways just meander for miles."

"The house just likes to toy with you," Ghalib said affectionately. "As I do." He looked at Christine. "Of course you should explore," he told her. "My Pet hasn't seen half of what my home has to offer." I rolled my eyes.

"What?" he challenged, smirking. "I'll bet you didn't even know that I have a casino on the first floor, did you? Or a bowling alley in the basement? The skating rink on the roof?"

"No, I didn't," I admitted. "My room seems to be on a loop of hallway. I never get very far."

"Perhaps my house dreads your absence as much as I do," Ghalib said. Heat came into my face.

"My father used to talk about the evils of casinos," Christine said. "I always thought they must be such interesting places."

Ghalib and I laughed. "I've never been in one either," I admitted.

"Would you like to see?" he asked.

"Oh, yes!"

Ghalib led us down and opened a wide double door. The room glittered like a fair. The carpet was bright hues of red and orange in a paisley design. Gaming tables sat around the room, craps tables against the wall, and a roulette wheel in the middle of the room. Three shimmering chandeliers lit the room.

Christine looked as if she was seeing her first Christmas tree. "It's so pretty," she said. "It doesn't look evil at all."

"It is what you make of it," Ghalib said.

"Like most things," I added.

Ghalib looked at me with a curious expression "We should play cards again," Ghalib finally suggested, slyness creeping into his voice.

"No thank you," I replied. "I intend to keep my perfect poker record. One game. One win."

He chuckled.

Christine touched the roulette wheel and Ghalib moved closer to her. "Careful, Christine. If you spin the wheel, you have to abide by its rules."

Instead of numbers, this roulette wheel was marked with words. SLAVE FOR A NIGHT. WHIPPING WITH A RIDING CROP. RECEIVE PLEASURE OF YOUR CHOICE. PUBLIC ORGASM. AAA.

"What's AAA?" I asked.

Ghalib looked at me and didn't smile. "Anything, anytime, any-where."

My throat closed and my breath stopped. But Christine gave us both an impish, little smile and before either of us could stop her, she spun the wheel. Ghalib turned to me. "She's adventurous."

"More so than I am," I replied.

"Nonsense," Ghalib whispered in my ear. "Has she allowed herself to be taken on an altar? On a dinner table with an audience? Has she given me a night of unrestrained control over her? I think you're very adventurous, Pet."

The wheel clicked slower and slower as it rolled past PUBLICAL-LY BOUND NAKED and GAGGED FOR SEVEN CYCLES. Christine bit her lip as she watched the wheel turn. It slowed to a crawl and finally settled on, PLEASURE LOVER OF THE SAME SEX.

Christine's eyes glittered when they lit on me, but it was Ghalib who reached for me. "Just what I was hoping for."

"Tonight, you want to watch," I teased.

"I'll be supervising," he told me, in a low gruff voice. "It's time Christine had her next lesson," he said, kissing me between each word. "Care to help me?"

"I wouldn't miss it," I breathed.

Christine really didn't need a lesson. She was superb operating on instinct alone. Her lips and tongue brought me to orgasm again and again, with only a little help from the Drawing. Ghalib melted into the background, watching. Every once in a while he interrupted to kiss me or to stroke Christine. For the most part, he urged her to please me and stayed out of her way.

I didn't know how she could learn so much so fast. From the perfunctory oral sex with Ghalib to a creature whose tongue never tired. I helped her feel the Drawing watching her arch and squirm with pleasure.

Whenever we tried to bring Ghalib into our fun, he resisted. I couldn't understand it. He had been erect virtually all night without a break. Surely he craved release. Still, he provided Christine with a strap-on and instructed her to take me with it. I guided her hips until she was comfortable with the movement; before long, she had me whimpering. It only encouraged her to go faster, harder. I clung to her and she moaned my name as she penetrated me.

I wanted to taste Christine and it took the better part of the night to convince her. Finally, she gave in. I kissed and sucked, making it slow. Her legs, which had only been open a little wider than my head, spread like a flower as I teased my way between her folds. Her mouth was a surprised O.

Ghalib noticed her shock, too. "Have you never been taken this way, Christine?" he asked.

"No. I, I haven't." She gasped, rolling her hips. "My boyfriend thought I smelled funny."

He knelt beside the bed and kissed her lips, stroking her breasts as I slowly licked and kissed and nuzzled her. I heard Ghalib whispering in her ear. "Your boyfriend was a fool," he said. "He doesn't know what an experience he's missed. Elaine is enjoying your taste. Show her you enjoy it, too or she may not let you reach a climax. She may just tease you all night...."

Christine responded to his whispers, gasping our names alternately. I would have gone on for hours, even with the ache in my jaw. I didn't need to though. She grabbed the pillow behind her head and ripped the pillowcase when she strained against it. Her voice was throaty and loud when she cried out. Her hips bucked again my lips but I wouldn't let her get away. She pulsed against my mouth and I matched her rhythm. When she was done, she collapsed in a heap.

"Thank you, 'Laine," she said softly, rolling over on Ghalib's bed and holding his pillow against her chest. I sat up and grinned. Barely thirty seconds after her orgasm and she was already asleep.

"I think I fell asleep right after my first time, too," I whispered to Ghalib. He came over and helped me out of bed.

"You must be tired, too," he said.

"I think I am," I replied. "I'm at least very relaxed. Thank you for tonight, Ghalib."

"There will be many more," he said, his eyes skimming over my naked body. My heart sped up even as dread and guilt washed over me. There would be *one* more night, at least. Then I would need to choose. I didn't know if I could choose to be without him. "I'm going to plan for just the two of us tomorrow night," he said. "Is that still acceptable?"

I flushed and looked away. "Of course."

He lifted my chin and made me look at him. "Are you certain? If you would rather have company —" he asked.

"No," I interrupted, meeting his eyes. "Just us tomorrow. I'm absolutely sure." His eyes glowed with pleasure. Then I slipped out of his room without even tying a robe around me. I needed to get away before he could ask me why.

Chapter 35
Making Things Harder

I slept. I don't know how I slept, but I did. And when I woke up, I still didn't know what I wanted to do. I wanted to be the Nyx; I didn't want to be the Nyx. I wanted the power I had to defy Ghalib; I didn't want the responsibility it brought with it. Lack of choice was easier; lack of freedom was frustrating. Every possible decision felt like it would leave me regretting something.

There were moments when I wanted to strangle Nyx for confusing me like this.

I climbed out of bed and stretched. "How long do I have?" I asked Lisa.

"Hours, Miss," she said. "The Master asked me to let you choose your own clothes tonight."

I nodded and looked in my closet. I found what I wanted right away. It was the gold dress I had refused the first night that I was here. The one I had never worn. It hung at the back of my closet, the full, shimmering skirt rich and floor-length; the bodice slim and glittering with gems. I had thought that it was so fussy my first night and now, after all of the corsets and evening gowns, it hardly seemed fussy at all.

It didn't take long for me to bathe, put on my make-up, and slip into the gown. Lisa carefully curled my hair into a loose tumble down my back. I looked in the mirror and nodded once. I imagined Ghalib would like it.

I didn't want to stay in my room; I was just too restless. The halls seemed willing to oblige me, this time, taking me to the front door with only a little extra walking. Ghalib would be able to find me down

at the beach so I left the mansion. But not even the beach was soothing this night. The water was gray, the wind rough, and it seemed to
mirror my mood.

What was I going to do?

I don't know how long I stood there, looking off into the vast-
ness of the ocean. But I knew the exact moment the winds calmed. It
was the same moment the gray water shimmered with color and the
waves stopped pounding and started to flow. As I watched, the shallow water glistened into a clear, true aquamarine. In the distance, the
water deepened to sapphire. And under my feet, the rocks melted into
pure, white, powdery sand.

I took a step forward. I knew this place. My beach, my perfect
beach in Panama City. I never thought I would see it again and its
sheer beauty made my throat tight.

And, of course, I knew who had done this all for me.

I turned and Ghalib crested the bluffs. He surveyed the beach and
indulged in a pleased smile; then he saw me and his smile froze. It
was such an odd expression, I thought something was really wrong.

He came up beside me, appearing stunned. "You're breathtaking,
Elaine." He took both of my hands and held them out, looking at me
in a way that made me bashful. "It's exactly what I would have chosen for you to wear tonight. I believe it's better now that when I first
wanted to see you in it."

He wasn't even looking at the panorama. My face felt fevered. I
turned back to the ocean. "I can't believe you did this," I said, making a wide gesture that took in the entire beach. "I don't know how to
thank you."

He didn't touch me; it was a little surprising. "I consider myself
already thanked," he said, his voice husky.

I looked back at him. "Is my sand bar here, too?"

"Go see," he said.

"Come with me," I invited, taking his hand. The spark of Drawing
that shot between us was unimaginably sweet. And strong. It jolted
me enough that I had to pause to catch my breath.

We went into the water together, leaving our shoes on the hard,
white sand. His pants got wet. My hem did too. I didn't care. We
walked out on the sand bar and stood in what felt like the middle of

the ocean, in the heart of an aquamarine gem, and just looked.

"Isn't it wonderful?" I asked.

"That is just the word I would have used." I looked back at him and his face glowed in the golden sunlight. "Are you hungry?" he asked. "I have something planned."

"Famished," I lied.

He led us back to the beach. A tent was set up in the soft, dry sand a little further from the water. There was a table underneath set with wine glasses and a lantern. We didn't even bother with our shoes.

Two chairs sat next to each other so we could both watch the ocean. We sat down and Jason poured the wine. "Shall we have a toast?" Ghalib asked.

I grinned, remembering the second night I spent here and the toast he made when I still couldn't speak. "To the pleasure submission brings?" I teased.

He lifted his glass and touched it to mine. "To you, Elaine."

How did he do that? My breath caught again and it was like I hadn't been here in the In-Between for ages. Like he hadn't taken me every way imaginable. Like we were just meeting for the first time.

Jason served us seafood and we ate, watching the sun go down over the water. The sky blazed in reds and oranges and pinks. I had trouble swallowing. It felt like another ending, just as it had in Panama City Beach. The beauty hurt.

"Can I ask you something?" I said, trying to distract myself.

"Of course," Ghalib replied.

"How did this start, this thing between me and you? How did you find me in the first place?"

Ghalib chuckled. "You came to my prison. I noticed you one night when I was hunting for a new romantic partner. Usually, I search erotic dreams until I find someone I like, then show up in the mortal realm to bring them back."

"Like you did me? Off their bus on the way to work?" I asked, only half kidding.

"Actually, you would be my first official abduction," he said.

"I don't know whether to be flattered or horrified," I joked.

"I usually don't have to be so forceful. Most women — and men, for that matter — are willing enough to come with me when I ask," he said. "I assumed that you would be the same. I remember how you were in that dream, your hair all down and long, your voice very throaty and erotic," he continued as I flushed. "You were so sensual. You had created this room with restraints and whips, not unlike the bondage room that I created for you. Also, you kept saying, 'please'. Whatever it is you yearned for, you weren't getting it."

"So you came for me?" I asked.

"I did. I was waiting outside your apartment the next morning and I couldn't believe what I saw. This mousy little thing in a dark, ill-fitting business suit. Your hair was twisted up so tightly, not a single strand escaped. I thought there must be some sort of mistake. Surely you weren't the same woman having the erotic dream the night before."

I lowered my eyes. I felt so different from that woman. But I knew he was right. I hadn't ever wanted anyone to notice me. It seemed that women who got noticed, got hurt. "I'm surprised you didn't run in the other direction," I said.

He laughed. "Are you kidding? It was too intriguing. You started coming to my prison every night. It was like you were taunting me." The heat seemed to radiate off of my face. He stroked my cheek, looking amused and tender. "I was addicted to your dreams. I should have known then that I was in trouble."

I laughed a little. It sounded nervous. "How long do you think you watched me?" I asked.

"Months," he replied. "I went into your apartment when you were at work. I followed you to work a couple of times, so I'd know how you got there." He said these things like they were just normal things to do when you take an interest in someone.

"I didn't know I was under such scrutiny," I said, trying to lighten his intensity.

He wouldn't have it. "I started to form a plan," he said. "I added your suite of rooms to my house. I knew from watching you that you were very quiet. I wasn't going to be able to engineer a meeting and if I did, I certainly wasn't going to be able to convince you to go anywhere with me."

"I've had to be very careful, to keep me and Rachel safe," I said.

"And I had to be very careful not to scare you too badly. I think

I liked the challenge," he admitted. "My other problem was that you can't just bring a mortal forcibly into the In-Between without damaging them. I needed you to agree to come with me."

"So you hijacked my bus? Made a bunch of threats and caused a big ruckus?" I asked.

"Essentially," he agreed. "I figured if I had to make a scene, it might as well be big and dramatic. It was a bit of fun for Markus and me. Those were some of Markus' servants who came with me to kidnap you. He thought it was amusing I was going to such lengths for a mortal." He looked at me for a very long minute. The heat that had barely ebbed from my face flooded back. "I knew from the moment I touched you that I wanted you as my pet."

"The Drawing," I said, remembering the electric charge and his surprised expression.

"Yes," Ghalib said. "But not *just* the Drawing. It was shocking when you shook my hand on the bus. I was sure you would refuse to touch me. I couldn't believe that you were so polite that you accepted a handshake from a hijacker. I was entranced. Then, when you touched me, I felt the Drawing and I knew I had found my match."

Jason came to clear away the plates and I stared out at the darkening ocean. "You put a lot of effort into this," I said softly, almost to myself.

"Every moment worth it," he replied. "It looks like our ride is here."

I looked at him. "Our ride?"

He offered his hand and I took it. He led me back down to the water. There were two small sheds. He had a tiny smile that told me he was keeping secrets. "As much as I love your gown, I'm going to ask you to change into something more comfortable." He motioned for me to go inside the shed and there was a loose, white skirt and a navy and white shirt to go with it. I changed into it quickly and slipped on the comfortable shoes, as well. Ghalib emerged in a matching outfit.

He led me to the water's edge. In the darkness, I hadn't seen the little long-boat that was beached there. We both climbed in, facing each other. "Where are we going?" I asked, as the boat started to row itself out to sea.

"I will admit that I have been distractingly jealous of Miguel since you told me the story of Panama City Beach," he said.

"The boatman who took me out to dinner?" I asked. "Why?"

"Because he shared experiences with you. I would like to share a similar one." We were approaching something. A very large ship. I could see the lights over Ghalib's shoulder. "Have you ever been on the ocean at night?" he asked.

"No."

"Good."

The boat drifted alongside the ship and we climbed a ladder to the deck. I don't know the first things about anything nautical but I had to ask. "Is this a yacht?"

"A small one," he said shrugging.

"I didn't know you had a yacht."

"You didn't know I had a bowling alley, either."

I laughed and he pulled me to the front of the ship. There was one huge reclining lounge there. It could have held ten people. Ghalib urged me to lie down. All of the lights on the ship turned off. "Look up," he said.

There were a million stars. No, a billion. A milky streak stained the sky. There wasn't any moon and with the boat lights off, it seemed like I was in the middle of the cosmos. "Oh, my God," I breathed. "That's too beautiful."

Ghalib lay down beside me and clasped my hand in his. "I thought you would like it." He sounded pleased.

"Did you know that Victor doesn't care for the stars?" I asked. "I've never met anyone who isn't awed by them."

"What makes you say that Victor doesn't like them?" Ghalib asked me.

"When we were in your observatory, he told me that he prefers his pleasures to be more in reach."

Ghalib chuckled. He kissed my hand. "That's the difference between he and I," Ghalib said. "I believe the stars *are* in reach."

We stayed on the yacht far too long, feeling the roll of the water, watching the stars. He didn't point out constellations or ruin the silence. I counted four shooting stars.

Finally, he stood. "You must be tired," he said, regret in his voice. "Even if you don't know it, the motion of the water can do that to you. I don't think you've been sleeping properly and I don't want to see your health suffer."

I let him lead me back down to the long-boat that sped us to shore. He took my hand and led me back up to the mansion. We meandered and stopped to look at the sky. Still, it felt like no time before I was standing in front of the door to my own suite.

"Good-night, Elaine," Ghalib said. "I must arrange for more nights like this." My panic leaped and I had the sudden urge to cry. More nights? I had until sunrise.

He bent and kissed me once softly on the lips, then turned for his own room. I watched him, my heart thundering in my chest. If he went into his room, I might never see him as my Master again. I didn't know why that bothered me. Not that long ago, I would have been skipping for joy at the thought of freedom.

His hand reached for the knob.

"Ghalib?" I said.

He turned to me. I must have looked distressed because his brow wrinkled. "What is it, Pet?"

"Would you...."

He stopped and cocked his head. "What?"

I thought of all the missed opportunities in my life. All of the times I had decided to be safe. I didn't want to be safe anymore.

I bit my lip and took a deep breath. "Would you like to come in?"

He closed the distance between us in three long strides. He looked shocked. Stunned.

"Please come in," I said. "I don't want the evening to end yet."

I didn't even wait for him to say yes. I took his hand and pulled him after me into my suite. I closed the door behind him and led him through the sitting room and through the library, into my bedroom. Lisa was there, hanging up the gold gown.

"Would you please excuse us, Lisa?" I asked. She looked around at the two of us and jumped to obey.

Ghalib stripped off his shirt and I stripped off mine. We couldn't get any further than that without kissing. And once we started we couldn't stop. The Drawing was so strong and so sweet, it pulled us together like magnets. Vapor poured off of us. I didn't even try to manipulate it. I didn't need to; it roiled around us doubling and doubling and doubling again.

We kissed as he stripped away my bra and skirt. I helped him off with his pants. Within moments we were naked. I pushed him down on the bed and straddled his legs. He was fully erect. Neither of us needed anything else to stimulate us.

I looked into his eyes. He cocked his head, looking more serious than I'd ever seen him. He didn't urge me to take him. I drew my fingers over his lips and he kissed them.

I wasn't playing it safe and I wasn't going to worry about who was going to hurt who. I took a deep breath. "I'm yours, Ghalib," I said.

His lips parted. His green eyes widened. The Drawing moved towards him even as more of the vapor poured out of him. "Say that again," he breathed.

"I'm yours."

Then I moved forward and impaled myself on him. I stopped once he was fully buried in me to catch my breath; Ghalib seemed to need the same moment. The Drawing was shattering. There was no other word to describe it. I felt like I was shivering into a million pleasure-drenched pieces.

He was the one who finally moved, thrusting into me in long, hard strokes. I caressed his body; he reached up to touch my breasts. We met to kiss and it was as if we couldn't stop; we couldn't pull our lips from one another. He sat up, never breaking the kiss, pulling me to him, pressing my chest to his, never stopping the thrusts that left me ragged and gasping.

I slid his hands up my back and into my hair, pulling my lips from his. I pressed his fingers to my head. "Can you see it?" I gasped.

I wanted him to see what we did to the Drawing. He looked around, thrusting harder. His eyes focused. "Is this all us?" he panted.

"It's all us," I said. The room was so thick with Drawing, I could barely see him, though he was only inches from my face.

The muscles in his legs tensed and his thrusts seemed restrained. "Don't hold back," I whispered in his ear. I could tell he was still fighting it. I didn't want him to battle his own pleasure. "Please, Ghalib," I moaned, knowing how he loved to hear me beg. "Please."

He shuddered and thrust, clutching at me, his whole body shaking. His orgasm felt like an explosion. He ground himself into me. When he stopped moving, I kissed him and he stood, lifting me. Then he turned, laid me gently on the bed and started his slow work on my body.

He knew my tastes by now and expertly went to the places that left me arching and moaning. Then, slowly, gently, he eased himself next to me, stroking between my legs with his fingers. While he stroked, he kissed my face and whispered into my ear. "You've ruined me for anyone else. I don't know if I even can be satisfied by another."

I laughed a breathy, gasping laugh. "Alexis, Christine, and Victor will be so heartbroken. Have I left anyone out?"

"You've left hundreds of people out. Not that any of them matter." His fingers quickened and I writhed against him. He continued to whisper. "I could take you again this minute."

"Do it," I urged even as my hips followed his stroking hand.

"Not yet," he said. "You're glorious to watch, too."

His fingers slipped over me, increasing their pressure, increasing their speed. I exploded into climax, pulling my legs back, unable to control my movement. I finished but still felt the warmth, the tingling deep within.

"Don't stop," I begged.

"No?" he asked his fingers growing lighter, staying just a little off from the perfect spot.

"Please, Ghalib," I begged, feeling myself rising again.

"I'm not sure I'm quite convinced," he teased.

"Oh, God. Ghalib, Please."

He picked up his pace and I rose to my second orgasm. Before I was even done gasping, he was between my legs. "Say yes," he told me.

"Yes," I gasped. He slid into me and took advantage of my wetness.

We did this all night. First me teasing him, them him teasing me.

My lips around him, eager to taste his climax, then his tongue fluttering over me. Him entering me from every position and me discovering all of the new delights that came with each new friction. Finally, I could sense the morning was breaking. He fell on the bed next to me.

"And I intended to let you just rest tonight," he said.

I rolled on my side and played my fingers along the ridges of his chest. "Blame me," I said. "I didn't want to rest."

"You need your sleep," he said. "You barely doze. You hardly eat. I don't want you to shorten your life."

I looked at him. As a mortal, my life must seem very short to him. How would he deal with that?

"Elaine?" he asked.

"You're right, of course," I said.

"I would like to make some arrangements for this evening. I'm afraid that I may have to accept an invitation or two. The other Architects will start to complain if I don't at least let them see you."

I smiled at him. "Do what you must, Ghalib."

He got up, looked down at me, sweeping his gaze over the length of my body. "Rest. I'll see you tonight."

I smiled but didn't say anything. I couldn't bring myself to lie to him. He leaned over me and kissed my lips. Then he turned to go. I fought the urge to call him back.

When he was in the bedroom doorway, he turned back. "Elaine?"

I sat up. "Yes?"

"I'm yours, too."

He hurried out of my suite and I looked after him. His words spun in my head. I fell back on my pillows.

Elaine.

A voice summoned me. But it wasn't Ghalib's. I recognized it immediately. Nyx was calling. My time was up.

Chapter 36
Good-bye and Hello

I tried to sense where Ghalib was headed before I climbed out of bed. When I left to see Nyx, I hoped that he would just think I was asleep. Ghalib went to his room. Then he headed downstairs to his study. He was a warm ball of contented feelings.

I riffled through my closet, grabbed the first thing I found and put it on. I took a deep breath, tried to calm my nerves, and went to my sitting room.

Elaine?

Nyx sounded impatient and it was starting to irritate me. After all, she had been Nyx for two thousand years; she could wait five minutes until I was ready. I stood in the middle of the room, taking one last look around.

Nyx had told me that all I needed to do was will myself to the mortal realm to get there. I hoped the same was true when it came to finding her. I closed my eyes, pictured her delicate, beautiful face, and whispered a mantra aloud.

"I need to see Nyx. When I open my eyes, I'll be there with her. I need to see Nyx. When I open my eyes, I'll be there with her...."

The air became hot around me. I felt the sun beating on my face and saw it glowing through my eyelids. When I opened my eyes, I stood in an oasis surrounded by a vast desert. Palm trees and a scrub of grass sprung up out of the sand. I could hear water trickling. There was a moderate sized tent, like something a fortune-teller might have, set on the edge of the oasis. It was the only bit of color in sight; bright red and blue fabric formed the walls of the tent and glittering gold ropes edged it.

The female envoy stood outside the tent like a guard. She nodded to me. "Elaine," she greeted me.

Nyx stepped out of the tent. Her golden glow seemed dim in the bright sun. And she looked tired. But her long hair still caught on the streams of Drawing. She still walked with an aura of power.

"I wondered if you might not come," she said.

"I wondered, myself," I replied.

She looked at me hard for a moment. I felt like she knew everything about me. There wasn't anything I could hide. "You have misgivings about replacing me."

"Yes."

"Tell me. Perhaps I can calm your fears."

I paused, trying to remember everything on my list of concerns. "You're two thousand years old," I said. "Is it terrible? Does your body hurt?"

"The Drawing keeps me healthy," she said. "I barely feel the passage of time any longer."

That was good, at least. "What does the Nyx do?" I asked. "Ghalib said that nobody had seen you in ages."

"The Nyx is keeper of the Drawing. We oversee the Architect gentry who make it. You can use it to encourage them to produce more. You can also step in if they are unfairly treating a mortal." Her face turned bitter. "The gentry are so lusty, I've never known there to be a shortage of Drawing. This world has run well without interference from me."

"Interference?" I challenged. "You mean involvement?"

The envoy made a disapproving noise and Nyx looked down her nose at me. "Semantics," she said. "Do you have any other concerns?"

I hesitated.

"Something else?" she asked.

"I wouldn't be able to be Ghalib's pet anymore, would I?"

She gave me a stern look. "No. The Nyx is no Architect's pet."

I looked away. It was the problem that I knew it would be. Ghalib would be so hurt. I didn't know if I could do that to him.

"If you enjoy that demeaning status, then you have no business even considering being the Nyx," she scolded.

"How dare you," I snapped back. "You made this offer. Rescind it if you don't think I'm equal to the task."

We glared at each other for more than a couple of seconds. I wasn't afraid of her and I think she knew it. She needed me more than I needed her. She was the one who eventually looked away. "The Nyx cannot be a pet," she said in a gentler tone.

"I don't know if I can accept your offer, then. I think I would miss Ghalib too much."

She narrowed her eyes at me. "Why?"

"I like him."

"You mean, you like fornicating with him," she said disdainfully.

I bristled. "Yes, as a matter of fact, I do." I liked his company, too, but I wasn't going to share that with Nyx.

She snorted in another sound of distain.

My temper flared again. "We don't all hate sex like you do, Dionysia. If a celibate, lonely existence is what is required to be Nyx, no wonder you've been stuck with the job for so long."

She looked at me for a long moment. "I do not understand why you would want to deal with these vile creatures," Nyx said softly. "To me, they're nothing more than animals in heat. Every one of them. Especially your precious Ghalib."

"I don't think they're vile; I think they're passionate," I said.

Nyx finally spoke. "You may have as much contact with the Architects as you like," she said. "You could still enjoy a relationship with Ghalib, just not as his submissive. It would only be a question of whether or not he would enjoy that relationship with you."

"Can he accept that his priorities must change if he wants to be with the Nyx?" the envoy asked me.

I had no idea how to answer that question. If I wanted to stop living life safe, this was the ultimate test of that. Freedom like I'd never known. Power beyond bounds. If Ghalib couldn't accept me this way, last night was meaningless. His caring was conditional. For the first time, becoming the Nyx sounded like something I wanted to do.

"You've chosen," Dionysia said. I realized I had. Her smile was heartbreaking. She took my hand; the Drawing made me warm all over. "Thank you. I crave an end to this existence."

"What happens to you when you're not Nyx any longer," I asked.

She drew me towards her tent. "I die."

"Wait! What?"

"I die, Elaine. The Drawing sustains me. No human body lives for two thousand years without supernatural help."

"Do you have to?" I asked.

She smiled sadly at me. "I want this end. I want this rest. If I could have had my will, my replacement would have come centuries ago."

She pulled me into her tent. It was so exotic on the inside: lined with pillows, draped in satin, glittering with ornaments. Incense burnt on one side of the room. The smoke mingled with the Drawing. The envoy stepped inside and stood just inside the tent flaps.

"The Drawing will help you," Dionysia told me, leading me to a bank of pillows. "Likely, it will come more naturally to you than it did to me. You already have such mastery of the power."

She pulled me down onto the pillows. We sat facing each other and I took a deep breath. "OK, how do we do this?"

"You must kiss me. And you must accept what I give you."

I leaned forward and she did too. Her lips were soft when they touched mine—full, rich, and lush. She took both of my hands. I wondered if she had been kissed by anyone else in two thousand years. Then, she breathed the air out of her lungs into mine. I didn't think I could take all of her breath but my lungs kept expanding, accepting. Finally, I felt a surge of energy, a kernel, a core of her being transferring from her to me. It was the heart of Nyx. Her life force. The thing that kept her alive.

I accepted it.

She drew back and smiled at me; it was beautiful. We both glowed golden. Heat infused me. The ever-present throbbing leapt again pulling me to a new level of arousal.

"What do you feel?" she asked, her voice weak.

"Euphoric," I replied. My voice was stronger; it seemed to echo.

"Curious," she replied. "I felt burdened and I have ever since."

"I don't," I said. "This is heavenly. I could fly."

"Pull the Drawing to you," she instructed. I did. It was as if I was draining her. Her glow diminished and her skin paled. I hesitated.

"No," she whispered. "Finish." I did as she asked and it didn't take long; I had already absorbed most of her power.

The collar around my neck loosened. The clasp opened and it tumbled to my lap. The beautiful work of filigree and gems would never tighten around my neck again. I would never again be a pet.

"Thank you," Dionysia said; her voice breathy and faint.

"You have nothing to thank me for," I replied, mine echoing with strength.

She smiled. "Thank you anyway." Her hands loosened on mine and I let her go. As soon as we lost contact, her body slumped. She fell onto her pillows, her eyes staring lifelessly. She was gone.

I'm not sure why I cried for her. Nor why I buried her at her oasis with the help of the envoy. I didn't know if that would have been the custom two thousand years ago or what she wanted done with her body. But, I wouldn't leave her there in her tent, slumped on the pillows.

It was only when I was outside, working a hole in the damp sand with one of her ornate bowls, that I noticed the pull on my hair. The Drawing tugged at me, seeming purposely catching on me. It was tangible, to me. I could have walked on one of the ribbons. It would lift me if I wanted it. It would dig this hole if I asked.

The Drawing enjoyed me as much as I enjoyed it.

"What do I do now?" the envoy asked me when we were done with the grave.

"What did you do before you did this?" I asked.

She laughed a little. "I was a servant in the Gentry class."

"You could return to that. I doubt things have changed much." She looked horrified at the thought. "Wherever I end up, you can come with me," I told her. "Would you wait for me outside?"

She nodded and let herself out.

I lay down across her cushions, trying to gather myself. I wasn't the least bit tired, but I needed to calm myself. The collar was on one of the cushions and I slid it on to my arm. I fastened the clasp so I wouldn't lose it; it meant too much to me.

There was so much in my mind. I closed my eyes and could sense every member of the Architect gentry. Every Dream-Maker. Thousands of them, each one's mind open to me. Victor getting ready to play with a new mortal, toying with Matthew, enjoying the sameness of his existence.

Matthew, sweetly confused. He would never be a lord. It was right that he remain a servant; he would play his part as beautifully as everyone else.

Anna, in pain she would never admit. So prideful. So broken-hearted. Trying to go on with her existence but the Drawing avoided her. It couldn't ease her pain.

I hesitated, but then I searched for Ghalib. Immediately, my heart sank. He knew I was gone. He felt the broken connection; he couldn't sense me any longer and he felt betrayed. He had no idea where I could be.

I stood. I couldn't let him wallow in uncertainty. Being Nyx hadn't eased my nervousness at dealing with Ghalib in the least. I had expected to feel like a whole other person, but I didn't. I was still just Elaine — with benefits.

I left the envoy — I didn't even know her name — with Jason and hurried into the hall. Ghalib was in his study and the hallways yielded to my wishes to get there quickly. I hesitated at the door. Usually, he knew where I was but we didn't share that connection any longer. I could feel him but he wouldn't be expecting me. I knocked gently.

"Not now," he barked.

I bit my lip. "I'll wait for you in my sitting room," I called softly.

I backed away from the door but I heard him moving swiftly across the study. He ripped open the door. His face was wild: worried, angry, panicked, hopeful. He saw me, blinked, looked at me again, and shook his head like he was trying to clear his vision. "Elaine?" he said, sounding more uncertain than I had ever heard him.

"It's me," I assured him. "Can I come in?"

He opened the door wider and closed it behind me. Then, he touched my face and drew back with a shiver. He eyed my neck. "Your collar. It's gone." He scanned my glowing skin and my fluttering hair. "Nyx," he said with a dead tone in his voice. "She recruited you."

"Yes," I replied.

"How could you?" he asked. "I thought... I mean, you said..." He let out his breath in a frustrated sound. "There's no way for me to stop sounding like a smitten mortal. I'm disgusted with myself."

A chill went over me. Was it possible that he would reject me? I stood up straighter. "I'm not sure I understand."

"Weren't you happy?" he asked. "Hadn't I given you everything you wanted?"

"I wanted freedom, Ghalib."

He snorted. "Well, if you think you'll have that with Nyx, you're very naïve. I'm shocked she let you come here to say good-bye."

"What?"

"You're just another possession to her. Nyx is cold, Elaine."

It took me a moment to understand. Then, I wanted to laugh.

"Very cold," I agreed with dark humor. "She's dead. She died when she made me her successor."

He stared at me for a moment. His jaw dropped. "I thought she overruled me and recruited you to become her pet."

"No, she didn't want a pet. She wanted an heir. I'm the new Nyx."

His face was a frozen mask of confusion. Then, it was as if the realization hit him. Before I knew what he was doing, he fell down on one knee and bowed his head. "Nyx..."

I knelt down in front of him. "Don't do that." I tried to pull him to his feet but he wouldn't budge. "I'm just Elaine," I told him, taking his hands. "I'm still yours."

The Drawing that flashed between us was like a bolt of lightning. Every time I experienced Drawing with him, I thought it couldn't grow any more. But I knew, now, that the power liked him too; it liked how he used the Drawing. It liked us together. It would always grow.

He looked up at me and I recognized the heat in his eyes. I couldn't have been happier to see any expression. Then he looked away like he had done something amoral.

I put my fingers under his chin, as he had done to me a hundred times, and tilted his face towards me. Then, without asking permission or waiting for a sign, I kissed him. The Drawing hummed around us and he moaned against my lips.

I broke the kiss and smiled at him. "I thought you liked powerful women," I teased.

"I do," he said in a husky voice.

I leaned in and kissed him again. I showed him images of us twined in my bed. Memories from the past and plans for the future. He deepened the kiss, pushing me backwards.

I let him. In a moment he was on top of me, kissing me, his hands in my hair, then sliding under my skirt. I grabbed a handful of his hair, pulling his head back so I could taste the skin of his neck. "God, Elaine!" he gasped.

We stripped our own clothes away because it was faster. I wrapped his naked body in Drawing. He moaned, his breath coming fast. "May I take us to a bed?" he asked breathlessly.

"You may," I agreed.

There was no disorientation. Nothing odd accompanied the feeling of transport. No blasts of air or dizziness. It was as if I was fully part of this world now. The study was gone and his bedroom sprung around us. I barely even had the time to find the bed before he was on me, biting at my nipples and pushing me on my back.

No preamble. No teasing me. He entered me as soon as we were in a position where he could. We cried out in unison. I brought the Drawing around us, wrapping us together, knowing it, as much as I, was his addiction.

"More Drawing?" I offered.

"No," he said, surprising me. "I won't be able to concentrate on you."

He rode me hard. It was the only thing that could satisfy me. He pulled my hair and bit my shoulder. I urged more. When his hardness grew even harder and I knew he was near his peak, I reached for his backside and spread his cheeks. I could barely reach his anus, but it was enough. I slid a finger into him as far as I could reach.

It was just the thing he needed. His back arched and he slammed into me two more times before he was calling my name. When he was finished, he rolled off of me. We both just lay there gasping for a moment. I had to clear the Drawing a little to be able to see him clearly.

He sat up on one arm, looking at me. "I can't believe it. You're

Nyx now."

"Yes."

"So, you can't be my pet," he said matter-of-factly.

"No."

His eyes stroked the length of my body. "Are you going to leave? Get a place of your own?"

"I'd like to stay, if you would be agreeable. Me and my envoy."

His face blazed with joy. "I am very agreeable," he said in a low voice, kissing me once. "We could be companions," he suggested. "It would be like it was when you first got here. No collar. No orders."

An idea occurred to me. I bit my lip. "That would be fine for me but...."

"What?" Ghalib asked, sounding concerned.

"There won't be a mental connection. At least for you," I added.

"You can still feel me?" he asked.

"I can feel every Architect, Gentry and Dream-Maker," I said closing my eyes.

"Well, that hardly seems fair," Ghalib said. "You can sense me but I can't sense you."

"I know," I said with mock regret. "I don't like it either."

"Isn't there anything we could do about that, my Nyx?"

I looked at him from under my eyelashes. "There is, but I don't know if you would say yes."

"Ask," he urged.

I slipped the lifeless filigree collar off of my arm, where it had remained through all of our love-making. In my hand, at my will, the filigree tightened until it was a solid band. The gems coalesced into one large emerald, exactly the color of Ghalib's eyes.

"Tell me that you belong to me," I purred.

A small smile played on his lips. "Are you asking me to become your pet?" he questioned.

I ran my finger over his lips. "I am. Of course you can always refuse—"

"I belong to you," he said, leaning in to kiss me.

"Tell me you do this of your own free will," I said, as he traced his kisses down my neck to my breast.

"I do this of my own free will," he said, continuing downward, licking a path over my stomach.

"Tell me you serve at the pleasure of your mistress," I managed in a shaky voice as he kissed the inside of my thighs.

He pushed my legs apart. "I serve..." He kissed between my legs. "At the pleasure..." He divided me with his tongue. "Of my mistress."

I struggled to sit up so that I could snap his collar around his neck. It made him look more masculine, somehow. He grinned at me, licking me in one long stroke. "Don't you want to give me an order?" he purred.

I fell back, stretching luxuriously, opening my legs as far as they would go. "Yes, I do. Don't stop."

I heard his chuckle. "Yes, my mistress."

Chapter 37
Epilogue: One Year Later

Lisa stood back admiringly. "You were right Miss. The black gown makes you look more golden."

"Is that a good thing?" I asked.

"Definitely."

She stood behind me, looking at the elaborate outfit I had chosen for the evening. Midnight black and glittering with gems like stars. Opera gloves, so that I wouldn't harm any of the mortals I came in contact with. Nothing around my neck, not even a necklace.

My envoy, Kawalli, stood in the corner, looking painfully uncomfortable. "I should be coming with you. I attend you when I'm not carrying your messages to Architects."

Ours had been a difficult adjustment. She believed that the Nyx should be above all of the sex and debauchery of the Gentry class. I, on the other hand, believed that the Nyx should be right in the middle of everything. How else can you really keep track of all of the little intrigues?

"You don't want to come to the Festival of Pets," I told her. "It's nothing but flirting and claiming."

"Being an envoy isn't about my desires. It's about attending to—"

"I don't need you to attend me," I interrupted. "Now, go do something you enjoy." She blinked at me like I had just told her to kill a Jabberwocky. I sighed. "Would you please go and check on my sister?" I asked. "And while you are at Lillian's home, have a cup of tea with her and find out as much as she can tell you about Rachel."

My sister dreamed in a lovely home with a Mistress named Lillian. As soon as I had settled myself as the Nyx, I went to see her. She was delighted to have me visit to see my sister. I watched Rachel, dreaming of me, dreaming of her ten-month-old son, and dreaming of Jackson.

Kawalli seemed relieved at receiving a specific task. Before I could even thank her, she was gone. Our relationship was definitely a work in progress.

"Maybe you should choose a different envoy," Lisa suggested, sitting me in a chair.

"I would if it didn't mean she would have to go back to the servant class," I said. Lisa brushed out my hair until it was one silken sheet. The Drawing would catch it and it would look windblown before long but Ghalib always begged me to wear it down. I liked to reward him when he begged so beautifully.

"I think I'm ready," I said.

"Oh, don't forget." Lisa handed me a leash.

"Thank you, Lisa. I almost forgot." She flushed with pleasure. When she first found out that I had been elevated to Nyx, she jumped around me like a mouse and refused to touch me. I think she thought I might strike her down with a bolt of lightning. Thank goodness I managed to calm her down.

I let my senses range out. Ghalib waited in the hallway. I was pretty sure Christine was with him. "I'll see you tonight," I told Lisa.

"Have a good time."

I went into the hallway. Christine and Ghalib grinned at me. Christine wore a stunning gown in robin's egg blue and a collar with a large, round opal. Ghalib looked dapper as ever in his tuxedo. Instead of a tie, he wore his shirt open at the neck and let his collar show.

"You look delicious, Christine," I said, cupping her face with my gloved hand. She shivered. We were working our way towards being able to touch one another again. The first time I contacted her skin as Nyx, she passed out.

"So do you," she said earnestly. "The other Architects are going to go crazy."

"No leash, yet?" I commented, teasing. She only wore the collar.

"He won't ask me," Christine pouted.

Ghalib grinned. "If I was her Master, I would have to put an end to her dalliance with one of the stable girls." Christine flushed pink. "See, now," he said. "You're not ready to serve just one Architect."

"You have a stable?" I asked him.

Ghalib rolled his eyes. "Someday you'll let me give you a proper tour of this house."

"I seem to recall getting through three rooms during your last 'tour,'" I reminded him. "Something about the tapestries on the ground floor gets him very aroused." I winked at Christine and she giggled.

"Touché," he replied.

"I guess we will be the only leashed pair from this house," I said holding up the chain.

Ghalib's smile was pure delight. The glittering chain was long enough that he could move fairly freely. It snapped to his collar and my end locked around my wrist, like a shackle. No other pet would be bound to their Master; I had made it specifically for him and me.

"That is very generous, Mistress," he said teasingly.

"I took a page out of your book," I replied. "It opens when I orgasm. You can remind me of how generous I am later."

He kissed me as I snapped the leash in place. His lips started to nip at my jaw and the Drawing flowed from his skin.

"Behave," I told him, swatting him playfully.

Jason came into the hallway. "Mistress? Sir? It's time."

I smiled at Jason and he flushed. Now that I was Mistress of the house, I had a say in how the servants were treated. I gave Ghalib full control over anyone in the prison, but Lisa, Jason, and the rest of the house workers were under my jurisdiction. Things ran much smoother without the constant fear of punishment.

Ghalib, Christine, and I walked together down to the entrance hall. "Shall I transport us, or will you?" Ghalib asked me.

"Why don't you?" I said.

Ghalib took us to the swirling snow outside of Victor's mansion. I couldn't feel the cold but I saw Christine shiver. Ghalib protected her with his arms and we all hurried inside.

I had barely shaken the snow from my hair when Victor knelt before me. "Nyx, I'm honored that you made it to The Festival of Pets."

I rolled my eyes. "How many times must I tell you, Victor? Call me Elaine."

He rose off of the ground, at least. "I just can't seem to remember to address you so informally. Perhaps you would like to come back after our little affair and school me." He shot a sideways glance at Ghalib and I felt Ghalib's annoyance. I also sensed Christine shiver behind me.

I had an idea and smiled. "My pet is my surrogate disciplinarian," I said. "What do you think, Ghalib? Could you remind him of my name for me?"

"It would be my pleasure," Ghalib said, his smirk black velvet.

Victor's face went white but I also could feel his arousal. "I'm sure that won't be necessary, Elaine. I can—"

"Nonsense," I cut him off. "When does this affair end? After moon-set?"

"Yes," he replied, if possible growing paler.

"Ghalib will be here promptly." I turned to Ghalib. "Make sure you teach him so he won't forget."

"I already have something in mind."

"Very good," I said. "If you'll excuse us, Victor."

We meandered a few steps away, looking around at the other Architects who hadn't gone into the dining hall yet. "You're very devious," Ghalib told me.

"I did it for our Christine," I said.

Her face flushed. "Thank you, Elaine."

I touched her cheek with my gloved hand again.

"Markus is here," Ghalib said, nodding over my shoulder. Markus had quickly become one of my favorite Architects in the In-Between. The Drawing around him was so calming that I spent many afternoons in his dining hall.

I turned and smiled. He wrapped his huge arms around me until it was as if I was being hugged by a bear. I put my arms around him and my hands couldn't touch.

"Nyx! How good to see you!" he teased.

"Ugh, stop. I can take it from everyone else, but not from you."

He let me go and I greeted Tobias. I offered my hand and he flushed in pleasure at the pulse of energy that I sent to him through the glove. He was wearing the same heavy iron collar and heavy chain leash that he had been wearing the last time. Markus grinned at Ghalib and Christine. "You two look well."

"I will admit that I am immensely content," Ghalib said.

"I'm glad to hear that, my friend." He looked from me to Ghalib. "Will I be entertaining the two of you soon, or is there some sort of waiting list that I should get on?"

"I could spend every moment of every day visiting and I still couldn't satisfy all of the requests," I said.

"But, for you, there is always an invitation," Ghalib added.

"My Tobias has asked about your Christine," Markus said. Christine flushed.

"Christine is only my guest," Ghalib said. "She may choose her lovers as she pleases with my full support."

Christine gave Tobias a sultry smile. "I would be delighted."

I saw the heat in Tobias's expression and decided they made an excellent match, even if they were both mortals. I caught Ghalib's eye and said to Christine, "If you perform publically, I'll make sure the Drawing is part of the experience." Her cheeks turned cherry but both hers and Tobias's eyes shone with delight.

"I think it's settled," Markus said. "I'll contact Ghalib to set up the details."

I spied Anna over Markus' shoulder. "Anna is here with her new girl," I said. "We should go talk to her."

I kissed Markus' cheek and we crossed the hall to Anna, who stood in front of the fireplace with a beautiful dark-eyed, dark-skinned girl. The girl wore a golden collar, but no leash.

"Anna," Ghalib greeted her, kissing her. "I haven't met your companion."

"Leila, this is an old friend of mine, Ghalib," Anna introduced. Ghalib put his hand under Leila's chin; her eyes lowered while he admired her. "You must kiss him to please me," Anna said. Leila offered her plum-colored lips to him and he kissed her far too long.

"This is my mistress, Nyx," Ghalib said.

"My name is Elaine," I corrected, putting my gloved hand on the girl's arm. First she jumped a little, then she seemed to melt under my touch. "It's a pleasure to meet you," I added warmly.

"And this is my companion, Christine," Ghalib said.

Christine looked at Leila in interest, but the girl couldn't look away from me. Not even Ghalib could catch her eye. I smiled a little to myself.

"I think nearly everyone is already in the dining hall," Anna told us."

"We should go, too," Ghalib said.

"Yes," I agreed. I looked at Anna; I could still sense her pain. I forced the Drawing closer to her. "I asked Ghalib to check on Julia when he went to the mortal world to get me some things," I told her. I was almost sure that Anna stopped breathing. "She's doing well," I continued. "She's attending college. Business school."

Anna's lower lip trembled. "Thank you, Elaine."

"One other thing," I said. "She draws sketches of you. She doesn't know why, and she doesn't remember who you are, but she's done dozens of portraits."

Anna nodded. I moved towards her and she accepted my kiss. It wouldn't heal her broken heart but it would glow within her for a while. She would at least feel some relief.

"Shall we?" I asked Ghalib and Christine. They nodded.

We walked down the hallway to a huge set of double doors. "Ready?" Ghalib asked, looked first to me, then Christine. We both nodded and he rapped twice.

The doors opened and the same sight met my eyes that had the previous year. Hundreds of Architects, all attached to mortals mingling around the room. But, unlike last year, when we entered all but unnoticed, all of the Architects turned to look at us.

I heard the whispers of "Nyx!" as we entered. A hush went over the room.

I felt like a bit of fun, so I stopped walking. I looked around at the beautiful faces, the majestic costumes, the well-manicured pets. Ghalib stood a little behind me and Christine stood, hidden behind us both. The room was silent.

I let the Drawing swirl closer to the crowd and felt them shifting with arousal.

As one, the whole room sunk to their knees around me. Only Ghalib and Christine remained standing. It was a heady feeling.

I looked over the room of kneeling Architects and mortals. Ghalib put his arms around my waist and whispered in my ear. "You are utterly magnificent."

"Aren't they lovely, Ghalib?" I asked, letting the crowd hear my praise. "I must reward them."

Even on their knees, they shifted in anticipation. Some of them had met me before. Those that had knew what was coming next. I dropped a blanket of Drawing over them and watched as the coupling began.

If you enjoyed this story, you can sign up for a free membership at
ForbiddenFiction.com and discuss it with other readers and the author
at the _Held in Dreams_ story page
at http://forbiddenfiction.com/library/story/AB1-1.000093.

We do our best to proof all our work, but if you spot a text error we missed,
please let us know via our website Contact Form
at http://forbiddenfiction.com/contact.

Author's Notes

Held in Dreams is a story that has taken so many different forms, it's hard to believe that this is the final version. I've tried to make it a young adult novel. I tried to write it just for my own enjoyment. But, I found that form fits function. This story is best as an erotic tale teased out to readers a little bit at a time.

I enjoy writing fiction with a fantasy element. I believe that's probably twice as true when writing erotica. With the fantasy element, sex really can be that good every time. Held in Dreams has a strong and flexible fantasy setting that isn't part of a previously described mythos. On the one hand, developing the rules of a new fantasy world offers amazing freedom as a writer. On the other hand, it's a minefield of potential plot-holes and inconsistencies. Thank heavens for good editors!

Held in Dreams is rich with seduction and sex; nonetheless, I hope it's Elaine's story of empowerment and self-discovery that draws the reader through the novel. I hope that, despite the supernatural nature of the characters, that readers can identify with the relationships between them. And if all else fails, I hope the sex stimulates the reader in all the right places!

—Ava Burquette, March 2012

About the Author

Ava Burquette has published short stories in the fantasy, sci-fi, and horror genres under the name of her respectable alter-ego, who wishes to remain anonymous. When she isn't writing, she plays repetitive but addictive games on her phone, argues politics on-line with strangers, and analyzes the effectiveness of television commercials. Ava lives with in Pennsylvania with her very patient partner of fourteen years.

About the Publisher

ForbiddenFiction.com is a publisher devoted to writing that breaks the boundaries of original erotic fiction. Our stories combine intense sexuality with quality writing. Stories at Forbidden Fiction.com not only arouse readers through sensations, but also engage them emotionally and mentally through storytelling as well-crafted as the sex is hot.

ForbiddenFiction.com is also designed to be a social reading environment. You'll have fun even if just reading the latest post each day, yet you will have the chance for so much more. Readers and authors can be part of ongoing discussions of specific works and individual authors as well as more general topics.

Sign up for a FREE Membership today at ForbiddenFiction.com